BLOOD DEVOTION

THE BLOOD SAGA: BOOK 4

By

MAQUEL A. JACOB

MAJart Works ©2023

MAJart Works

2001 NE Aloclek Dr #211

Hillsboro, OR 7124

www.majartworks.com

Cover Design by Dar Albert

www.wickeddesigns.com

Illustration by Nelli Valova

https://www.dreamstime.com/blackmoon979_info

Blood Devotion/ Maquel A. Jacob -1st ed.

ISBN 978-1-950438-32-7

CHAPTER ONE

The Enemy Within

A combined stronghold.

Yutel Dakien rubbed his chin at the thought, a smile creeping. His burly six-foot eight frame paced the length of the royal chamber in the East palace. A massive room spanning a thousand square feet with elaborate carvings on the walls. They reminded him of German chapel decors. His immaculately tailored suit jacket, a half size too small, seemed ready to rip open with each heave of his massive chest. Smooth tanned skin combined with a strong jawline graced his beautiful features and full lips.

The pure definition of manly.

His stride covered one end to the other in ten steps. The thick, dark grey carpet muffled the strike of his boots. Rays of early sunlight fanned out across the room, giving it an eerie glow. Shadows moved up the pale-colored walls. Fresh fruits and cured meats piled on a long table set against the side wall scented the room.

He halted his steps to run a hand through his short cropped, dark blond hair that went closer to a deep caramel brown.

Emperor Tavelo's suggestion, via his proxy, Pridric Strana, who sat nearby, to blend the covens sounded feasible. When the merchant covens operating on Earth returned to their home world, they received mixed feelings from their family leaders who Still saw them as children.

The Dakien clan offered to bring his people into the fold as apprentices not ready for galactic trade. A business he'd done for the last two centuries on Earth with the other clan offspring. Not as long as the merchant families, obviously, though seasoned, nonetheless.

"You are correct that even if our three covens, Endaga, De Luce, and Greiger merge, we will still be a third the size of the main family hordes." His voice boomed. "There are already signs of strife due to our presence."

Pridric glanced up at him from the plush seat in the corner of the room. His stark blond hair hung down his back in a single braid, the tip curled behind his waist. Yutel noticed the dark patches under his eyes. The usually angelic Pridric looked exhausted.

"All Earth merchants will operate out of the second harbor to keep things separate. Combining your coven with Endaga and De Luce will give your businesses a decent armed force to handle security."

"True." Yutel crossed his arms. "And you? Will your coven find a home elsewhere or be absorbed by the Strana clan?"

Terrified. That was the only way to describe what came over Pridric's face. He sat silent, his mouth parting slightly as if about to speak, then shut.

"Never mind. You don't need to answer."

"So, what do you think?" A woman blurted.

Yutel turned his head toward the voice, startled as he realized he forgot there were others in the room. Eterenia Jaubro, head of the De Luce coven and mother to his niece, Princess Adelia, gave him a stern stare. Another one with bright blonde hair that cascaded down to her waist. Yutel shook his head. Both were anomalies like their family clans.

"It depends on the territory we acquire. I would prefer enough land to create a fort. Or a compound."

"Understandable. I wouldn't want it any other way." Tavelo Endaga, now emperor of the East, stood near the floor to ceiling window overlooking the harbor. He wore a silver robe with a sleeveless blue cassock over it, secured by a wide sash of the same color. "On Earth, I would have shrugged it off." His jet black hair hung loose, nearly touching his thighs.

Emperor Tavelo.

He still couldn't say or think it without a smirk. That brooding, bloodlust driven youngster now ruled over Cellaxa, along with Emperor Manel of the West, his deranged counterpart. It would be comical if the circumstances weren't so tragic.

And why has everyone grown their hair out to such extremes?

It seems they had regressed to some odd timeline in their lives. The last time he had long hair, he was not yet a century old. He shook the thought from his mind and focused on the conversation at hand.

"Are you sure you don't want the Endaga coven to remain in the palace?" Yutel averted his gaze from Eterenia to Tavelo. "I'm sure you could use more royal guards on your side."

"According to Tervan, he has no confidence in the palace guards to begin with," Eterenia scoffed.

Yutel pinched the bridge of his nose along with the others in the room. Tavelo and Eterenia's eldest son exasperated him. Though a brilliant strategist and fighter, he could be a bit much most days.

That the arrogant shit wasn't attending the meeting surprised him. To verify his absence, he scanned the corners of the room.

"How about this?" Yutel leaned against one of two gaudy statues gracing the inner part of the chamber. "We build an abode big enough to accommodate our three houses with separate entrances to differentiate us. That way, it doesn't appear we have merged."

"Deceive our own clans?" Eterenia raised her

brow in amusement. "My family is not treating my coven like the enemy."

"Good for you," Yutel glared at her. "House Dakien and most of the others do." He glanced over at Pridric clenching his fists. "I worry for Chalayl. The Boresso clan are heartless."

Tavelo turned around to meet Yutel's gaze. "I agree. The more divided we appear, the better off. We have to wait for things to get better. For our families to accept the fact that we are no longer saplings lacking knowledge of trade."

"And how long will that take?" Eterenia walked over to the other plush seat opposite Pridric.

"According to my uncle, the other clans seem to struggle with our profits, not including theirs. And that we have our own insignias and contracts." Tavelo clasped his hands behind his back. "We may surpass them soon and they are not ready to be second tier."

"Then what?" Pridric leaned forward. "We just pretend to submit to their will?" His face went pale. "I won't do it!"

Yutel let out a sigh. "No one is expecting you to."

"I would never let you, either." The way Tavelo delivered those words made Yutel side glance at Eterenia who reared back in her seat confused. Tavelo reached into his sleeve and pulled out a small device the size of a credit card. "It's getting close to morning meal. Let's schedule another time to go over the logistics."

The sound of boots against marbled floors and the idle chatter of servants moving through the halls grew louder. Sunlight intensified, brightening the room tenfold. Daybreak had arrived.

As Yutel left the room, two royal guards appeared at his sides to escort him. He turned back to stare at Tavelo, Eterenia, and Pridric. *Will they be alright?*

❁ ❁ ❁

Master Boresso stood out of range of the blood splatter when one of her nephews struck Chalayl with too much force. That won't do. She couldn't have the other clans get wind to reprimand her. A group of clansmen held back Chalayl's children who came to see her. The Bryhel twins, Olette and Olivier, her eldest of the Dakien bloodline, Chiron, and Caden, the abomination she spawned with a Kataling leader.

They tried to stop the assault, Caden ready to morph, when Master Boresso ordered them restrained. She would never murder her own blood. But she did not tolerate incompetence. It warranted punishment, though not this extreme.

Whimpering on the floor, her niece seemed smaller than her large build. Chalayl had regressed to a childlike demeanor since returning involuntarily to the clan. Only Chalayl stayed at the family homestead. Her coven house refused to merge with them, citing their treatment of their … Queen? Master Boresso snorted, a grin forming. How narcissistic.

"You dare to complain when you can't even get our formulas right?" Her nephew screamed into Chalayl's face. "You're nothing but a giant dumb beast who should never have been in trade to start with!" He raised his fist for another blow.

Master Boresso held up her palm. Two other clansmen stepped forward and pulled him away.

"Enough." She went to kneel beside Chalayl. "Those narcotics your coven house created has caused many problems for the Boresso name despite them being under your own umbrella. It's because you are not at the skilled level of our clan."

Chalayl wiped blood from her mouth with shaky hands. Her eyes glazed over as if blocking off her soul. That won't do either. Master Boresso rose to address Chalayl's offspring.

"There's no reason for such violent reaction. This won't harm her. She'll recover by the end of the day."

Olivier leaned forward; his arm muscles taut against the men restraining him.

"That you think it doesn't harm her shows how evil you are."

Master Boresso's eyes narrowed.

"And you wonder why her house refuses to do business with monsters like you." Chiron glared at her as he wrenched free of his captors and went to his mother's side.

"How dare you say that to me?" She bent over, her hand ready to grab hold of his hair to yank him back. "This is between our clan…"

A high-pitched shriek stopped everyone where they stood. The clansmen moved away. Caden stood poised to strike, his black curved talons glistening in the sunlight coming from the open foundry doors. Master Boresso retracted her hand and straightened her posture.

"You are to report to the third wing for instruction with the head chemist after midday meal." She ordered Chalayl. "Get cleaned up. I don't want you strolling our corridors like some weakened beast."

Master Boresso left the workshop with her clansmen in tow, the children released to comfort their mother. That not one came from the betrothed clan selected for her smacked of disrespect in her eyes. All that negotiating with the Stranas resulted in nothing. Even in the face of doom, fleeing their homeworld for survival, those ungrateful offspring couldn't honor their family's wishes.

"Are you alright?" Olette caressed her mother's thick, chocolate brown hair. "Please, speak to us."

"… " Chalayl's voice was barely a whisper.

"What was that?" Chiron asked while wiping more blood from her face.

"You shouldn't be here."

Their mother's voice finally reached them.

"Screw that!" Olivier snapped.

"You may not be the greatest mother, but that doesn't mean I want to see you being abused." Caden knelt with the others to surround her.

She hiccupped; her cries hitched as tears streamed down her face. They all remained together on the floor waiting for her to finish letting out her anger and sorrow. After what seemed like almost thirty minutes, their mother straightened herself into a kneeling position. She wiped her face, interfering with her children, trying to do the same.

"It's fine," she sniffed. "I'm okay. This is nothing."

"The hell it isn't!" Chiron cried out. "You have to leave this place."

"No. I need to learn the Boresso formulas. They are my birthright, even if I was never meant to learn them."

"What does that supposed to mean?"

Olette stood, towering over her.

Their mother simply gave a pitiful smile, with eyes devoid of emotion.

"I'm just a dumb animal," she whispered, her gaze lowering.

Caden loomed over her, his expression full of rage. They locked eyes. His mother flinched.

"Don't you ever say that again." His tone dripped with malice.

"Exactly." Chiron crossed his arms.

Chalayl got off the floor, her children followed.

"I promise," she ran her hand across the top of Olivier's head. "I won't let them break me. Once I learn what I can, our house's labs will be able to create better products." Her shoulders slumped. "I just need to endure a little longer." She smiled again. "Wait for me."

"If we think for one moment your life is in any danger, we'll raze this stronghold to the ground."

Chiron glanced at the others. They nodded in agreement.

"So hurry up and get back to us."

Her lips quivered as she tried to hold back more tears. *I'm a terrible mother.* She acknowledged that. *I'll do better.*

Reconstruction of the East harbor moved ahead of schedule. Coven workers gladly participated in its build, knowing it would house their wares apart from the main clan families. A space port of their own with official registry from the trade commissioner.

The sound of planks being laid, and individual docking stations installed, echoed along the shoreline. Tools banged and roared in a steady beat.

Katalings pulled loads down the makeshift ramps to the docks. Their bulky frames taking up the width, forcing the workers to either get ahead or behind them. Well-toned muscles strained under their smooth, black, leathery skin. Their red eyes glowed in the rolling mist covering the lower decks.

Despite the muted midday sunlight, the workers broke into a sweat. A mild heatwave made the air muggy. The only reprieve came from the cool breeze swept in by the ocean. It curved around the giant communication tower blocking the south.

Holnar Bryhel crossed his arms while surveying the progress. Standing next to Yutel, he held his own in size. A half foot shorter and equally stocky, he commanded respect. He too wore his dirty blonde hair cropped above the ears, tapered in the back. The dark grey trench coat matching his tailored suit lay open, its hem flapping in the wind.

"Think we can speed it up?" He asked Yutel.

"In a hurry?" Yutel snorted.

Holnar shook his head at Yutel's navy blue suit jacket straining against his chest, ready to burst.

Will someone please remedy this man's tailoring issues?

Tavelo had volunteered, yet Yutel refused.

Stating it being more of a trademark at this point.

"If it gets us to break away from the main clans sooner than later, yes."

"I heard a rumor." Yutel's brow scrunched.

"Regarding the Boresso clan?" Holnar nodded. "I hope it's not true."

"Yet, we both know it probably is. I'm worried about Chalayl." He glanced over at Holnar. "And Pridric."

Holnar stiffened. Chalayl's strength would get her through the hard times. For Pridric, his fear of his own clan would psychologically cripple him into submission.

"The last thing we need is the Stranas trying to get their hands on Pridric." He uncrossed his arms. "Though I'm sure Tavelo won't stand for it."

They turned to each other. An unspoken secret passing between them.

The bang of metal on metal drew their attention to where it came from. A floating crane operator was maneuvering the remote controls on his tablet to correct its position. Attached to the lift bars, the signage for House Sapienti swung gently. Its family crest displayed prominently in the center separated the name and dock number.

An Earth owl with brown and golden feathers peered out, the eyes made of a jewel that reflected like mirrors.

"Looks good," Holnar commented. "Can't wait to see what ours will look like when it goes up."

"Which is why I requested a dock on the other side of the main ramps away from you." Yutel ran a hand across his head. "Our crests are similar, and I don't want anyone confusing my company with your mediocre fare."

"Oh!" Holnar sneered. "We calling each other names again? You second rate inventor."

"Hmph. I believe Earth has more things with the Grieger name on them than your Marchand."

"Yet, I don't see much of your technology in the hands of the masses, like ours."

Footsteps came towards them from behind. They turned around.

"Are you two done sizing up each other's manhood?" Darean Callesi, head of house Sapienti walked up, the tip of his cane striking the wooden planks. "And you wonder why our elders still view us as children."

His aesthetics, once the ideal for the other covens, had shifted in uncertainty. The previously coifed dark brown hair kept above the neck now flowed freely in waves past his shoulders. Instead of an impeccable over the top ensemble, Darean wore a muted rust shaded suit with a black coat. He looked nothing like his old self.

A Renaissance pimp popped into Holnar's head.

"What in all Cellaxa are you wearing?" Holnar asked in disbelief.

Darean raised his arms, spreading them wide. His cane dangled between his fingertips.

"Does it not suit me? I decided to tone down the Gothic vampire attire and go with something less jarring." He lowered his arms. "We would stand out too much on this planet."

"Who cares about that?" Yutel snapped. "And no. You look ridiculous."

"Like a man ready to give up on his style and identity." Holnar's eyes widened in jest.

Darean frowned at them, his lips pursed thin.

"It's about branding. Wear your suits and represent House Sapienti proudly." Holnar smirked. "We were merely giving each other friendly jabs."

"Between Tavelo, Pridric, Eterenia, and you two, I wonder which group is the youngest sometimes."

"Stuff it, old man." Holnar turned away from him as he stood beside him.

"You look older than all of us," Darean scoffed. "Earth must have aged you tenfold."

It was true.

Darean and he were the oldest and attended most of the meetings to represent the covens as a whole. Tavelo and Eterenia looked, and were, too young. Chalayl's sensuality was an issue, and Pridric too deceptive, and Yutel tilted far on the brash side.

Darean caught sight of his sign being welded to the top section of his assigned dock.

"I like it." His lower lip protruded as he nodded in approval. "Can't wait to open it for trade. We no longer need to use our family clan docks on the West." He turned to Yutel. "Can we speed this up?"

Yutel sighed with exasperation and stared at him. Holnar snorted.

They were all chomping at the bit.

Emperor Manel watched the progression of the East dock from the window wall behind his throne. His narrowed eyes scanned the area, his irises a golden glow in the light. He averted his gaze to the land outstretched before it. The building of homes and transport routes scattered the landscape.

The tight leather battle suit under his imperial red and black robes made low ripping sounds as his crossed arms rubbed together. His jet-black hair, left to go wild atop his head, blended with the upper part of the suit.

His personal guard and mate, Gallic, came to stand next to him, his hand on the hilt of his sword as always, ready to strike any enemy who dared to harm Manel.

"I know you want to bring Cellaxa back from the brink of disastrous trade." Gallic stared down at the docks. "Don't you think this is too ambitious? Too soon?"

"Apparently, you and everyone else does." Manel let his arms drop to his sides. "We must move forward. Delaying it makes no sense."

"I get that, I do." Gallic brushed a hand down his arm. "I worry the backlash is getting worse."

"What for? Do you plan to not do your duty to protect me?"

Manel held back a snicker as he saw the horrified look on Gallic's face. Then anger replaced it.

"Don't." Gallic's eyes narrowed. "I will always protect you with my life. Don't ever doubt me."

"Yes, yes. Of course. "Manel waved a dismissive hand.

Gallic caught it mid swing. "I mean it."

Manel sighed, clasping his hand with his. "Stop being dramatic. I know that. You cite it every day."

"Just so you know," Gallic mumbled.

"As for the increased resistance to change, they will adapt soon enough."

"You believe that?"

"It's not a belief. Those greedy merchants will cease their protests when revenue flows."

He resumed his observation of the docks and construction of the land.

Yes. The booming trade will shut them up.

Class Divides

Master Strana's forearms lay flat on the round table console. His peridot-colored eyes peered into the hologram of the Strana holdings with financial tags floating beside them. The sleeves of his off-white tunic lazily caressed the surface from being pushed by the circulated air blowing above.

Tall, at six foot eight, with striking blond hair past his shoulders, he exuded dominance and fear. Every merchant on Cellaxa knew not to cross the Strana clan. Vindictive, backstabbing, and powerful. Their motto explained them to a tee. Be callous. Demand loyalty. And emerge victorious. They came in second behind the Jaubro clan who currently ruled Cellaxa's trade industry.

He stood, sliding his arms back until only his hands remained on the console. On a separate screen in the right-hand corner of the hologram, the stolen data of the Ambrook coven financials displayed. The fact that his youngest sibling created a new trade company with their clan motto angered him.

Pridric's lack of knowledge and incompetence did not sit well. He still saw him as a scared brat who refused to go down the depths of deception required when it came to fulfilling contracts.

Weak.

Master Strana lightly drummed his fingers.

"What do I do with you, Pridric?"

The rebuild of the second harbor neared completion. Only a few years left before it would be operational. A handful of small shipments already went through.

And then there was the other issue. Tavelo Endaga. The Stana clan despised the Endagas for centuries, making sure their spawned didn't mingle together. Yet, somehow, Tavelo and Pridric became friends. Though Master Strana suspected they were much more than that.

Pridric's newfound hatred of him after their father performed a mindset recalibration made him think the procedure possibly failed. That Pridric feigned hostility for show.

The door opened, causing the hologram to fade as light from the hall hit it. His cousin, head of acquisitions, walked up and stared at the displayed data. The hologram brightened as the door swung shut.

"I find it quite remarkable how it made such profits despite its inefficiency." He pointed to a few lines above. Tapping the virtual console, it pulled up more data. "Even the wording of the agreement isn't ambiguous enough. The client came come back and litigate the issue."

Master Strana frowned.

Thinking about it enraged him. Their clan didn't do refunds. Ever.

"And Trade Commissioner Polp won't entertain the idea of a merger to make Ambrook a part of us."

"He won't be swayed." He closed the document. "I understand his hesitance. Two streams of revenue looks better for Cellaxa. That trumps any deals to combine companies."

"It would if Pridric came back like he's supposed to." Master Strana said through gritted teeth. He turned to his cousin. "Any updates from our spy?"

"Pridric remains in the palace acting as that Endaga's adviser." His cousin spat the words out like venom. "He has yet to set foot outside its walls."

"He's hiding from me." The cruelty in his eyes made his cousin flinch.

Ahh. Yes, I should rein that in.

Many pointed out how outwardly he conveyed his feelings.

"Is there a way to lure him out? Once we get hold of him, the deal is sealed."

"We're looking into it." His cousin glanced over at him. "What if…"

Master Strana's eyes glowed, a faint silver.

"If he refuses to leave that Endaga's side, then we have no choice."

"A shame, really. That said, your father should have remedied that situation long ago."

"My father tried to mold that defect into something useful, knowing it would be a lost cause." Master Strana crossed his arms. "It's not like he needed more offspring. He should have killed it right after his mother expired on the birthing slab."

"Indeed."

"I want an inspection done on the next Ambrook shipment that comes through the Strana port."

"Trade Commissioner Polp will demand having a monitor since we do not own the goods."

"That's fine. If Pridric won't come himself, we'll just have to bully his proxy."

Master Strana removed the data chip from the console and both holograms disappeared, along with the virtual controls. He placed it in a small compartment under the edge of the console.

"Come, we have much work to do." He turned and walked to the door. His cousin followed him out as he opened it. "Send another spy. I want to know everything Pridric does."

Giant dirigibles moved in slow motion above the main docks, awaiting their turn to unload the cargo they carried. Falson lounged around the Callesi transport ramp, checking the manifest of the next shipment on a ten-inch tablet. His father had finally relented to allow him access and take lead over distribution.

He had his own company, of course, which he had to negotiate with his father to make a subsidiary of the Sapienti brand. They needed to work together, not rivals of themselves. He smirked. *Our motto says it too.*

He stared a the sign attached to the bay.

Together we can achieve anything. As long as we stay focused on our path.

His guardian and mate, Demetri, observed the foot traffic, wary of anyone who came too close to them. *Such paranoia!* Granted, there appeared to be some clans moving against the Earth Coven companies. He understood that his parents and the other leaders were basically young adults when they left Cellaxa.

It's been over two hundred years! How much older must we be to have their clans recognize them as full adults?

Falson let out a small laugh. They could say the same of the coven leaders' offspring.

Guess it's part of our DNA.

The sky above darkened as the nearest ship cruised over to the first available Callesi dock. Technicians monitored the tethers that shot out to grab hold and keep it steady while its bottom opened. Three platforms filled to capacity lowered onto the pad below. Callesi workers swarmed them, removing each container with swift efficiency. Better and faster than the dock workers on Earth.

A green and yellow skinned creature with long matching tentacles cascading from its head down to its back walked towards him. The hem of the rusty red leather coat brushed along the calves covered in the same material. As it got closer, Falson noticed feminine features and the three breasts bouncing in the low-neck tunic.

Her mouth moved. No sound. The translator's output had a delay.

"Greetings, Callesi." She tapped the earpiece, making the tiny red-light flicker. When it spoke again, the issue sounded fixed. "Have you reviewed the manifest?"

"I did. Were there any complications?"

"None at all. The pirates seem to be taking a rest." He saw a tail swish from behind. "I have not seen you before? Are you a new study?"

"Oh. I am Darean Callesi's son, Falson."

"Darean?" The creature's eyes narrowed in thought. Then they widened. "Ahh! The young master's offspring!" Her face went slack. "Please, send my condolences."

Falson suddenly felt awkward. The reason his father and the others fled also came after the brutal murders of their parents. He scratched the side of his face nervously.

"Yes, uhh, I will do that."

"I am Xelan from Astbar."

"It is a pleasure to meet you."

"Hmm?" She struck a pose, one hand on her hip. "Do you need a mate? I am a female of my race. We could have fun." A sword appeared right below her chin. Demetri glared, ready to slit her throat. "Oh? He's a bit possessive."

"Demetri," Falson sighed. "Put it away." His love reluctantly sheathed his weapon. Falson stared at the flirty creature. "Did you try to seduce my father too in his younger days?"

"Of course." Her green lips curved into a mischievous smile.

He didn't want to take the conversation any further. Rumors about his father circulated for centuries. The number of children he spawned had yet to be confirmed at present. Falson knew the six he grew up with. For all he knew, there could be six more.

He cleared his throat, holding the tablet so she could see its screen. "If you can confirm the payment amount, I will authorize the transfer of goods."

Xelan retrieved a data stick from her left cleavage and tapped it on the screen where the cursor blinked. It changed to green, and a congratulatory message displayed.

"Let's get your shipment processed." She turned away, her hips swaying. "Maybe we could get a drink later." She winked at Demetri as she said it.

"She's..." Falson smirked.

"A menace," Demetri blurted out angrily.

"I was going to say cheeky. Maybe even a bit sexy." Falson could feel the glare coming from him. He laughed. "Are you seriously worried about me getting seduced by her?"

Demetri looked away, embarrassed. "Of course not," he mumbled.

"Good. We should take her up on it." Demetri raised his brow. Falson sighed. "To get more information on Cellaxa trade. I feel like we're being left out of the loop. My father included."

The merchant clans had an iron grip on the trade and didn't want 'children' in the way of profit. At nearly a hundred years old in Earth terms, he had considered himself an adult.

I will not be treated like an infant!

Fear and loathing.

That's what the Volshins and Katalings received whenever they ventured out of their community into nearby towns. As a protected ancient species, both emperors bequeathed them a large swath of territory to reside on. Where their kind had lived before the battle that nearly destroyed Cellaxa over a thousand years ago.

The families who employed them continued to demand their services. This time it depended on if they wanted to continue. Volshins were especially wary of their employers, seeing no reason to case the skies for anything other than watching the docks. Even then, the imperial soldiers already did so.

The Volshin Luamis, and the Kataling Omeron were their species' leaders on Earth. Upon returning to Cellaxa they found themselves in the same situation as the covens. Regarded as untrained children, the two moved their own clans to a separate part of the designated territories far away from the elders. To have their trust in protecting the clan children turned to disrespect made them hostile. They now didn't trust themselves to keep their anger in check.

Walking side by side down the walkway on a busy street, the two appeared intimidating. Those coming towards them either crossed to the other side or made a wide berth. The people behind kept their distance, whispering insults.

Luamis glanced at the heavy clouds. His blond hair moved with the breeze, at times coming across his face. The Deep red overcoat draped over his shoulders shielded him from the cold. Under it, he wore a cream-colored tunic with ruffles down the front and along the cuffs. Black calf boots accented brown leather pants. With grey eyes piercing the heavens, he resembled a benevolent god.

In contrast, Omeron's muscular frame exuded respect. The tight-fitting tunic left no questions to what lay beneath. His leather pants, though the same as Luamis' hugged differently. A scowl on his face made his golden eyes more sinister behind dark, wavy hair cascading past his ears.

Unapproachable. Both of them.

And they preferred it that way.

"There's probably nothing up there but bad current," Omeron addressed the skies.

"Still. It wouldn't hurt to check. Get a little bit of exercise in." Luamis dropped his gaze and watched a family of four move away from them, the woman clutching her youngest child to protect him. From what? He glared at them. "You'd think we were prowling the streets eating children."

"At least that would give them a reason to treat us this way."

"They've had us under their thumbs as slaves for too long. The current generation and the ones before them know no different. Having the emperors restore our status makes them look bad."

"As it should," Omeron replied with gritted teeth. He locked eyes with a man walking with his mate. The hatred in that stare spoke volumes. In the last seconds, the man veered off to go around them, his mate gripping his arm in terror. "Though some are a bit bold when challenging us."

The business center where the clan leaders met for their financial meetings loomed ahead. Figures carrying plates and carafes moved within the windows. Two empty transports sat in the driveway.

At the entrance, Luamis and Omeron peered through the open doors to see what the situation looked like before entering. Only the coven leaders were present. With a sigh of relief, they walked in.

Holnar caught sight of them and broke off his conversation with one of his assistants.

"Ah, good! You made it." He approached them. "I'm glad you decided to hear us out once more. I know we're still not on the same page these days."

"It's not that," Luamis answered in a forlorn tone.

"Well, we can discuss it soon. Please," Holnar gestured to the conference table lined with twelve seats. "Get comfortable. The servants will bring more drinks."

Those not in attendance were a glaring absence. Tavelo had to remain in the palace for a while, with Pridric opting to stay by his side. The Boresso clan barred Chalayl from interacting with the other coven leaders. Eterenia gave no excuse for backing out of the meeting, sending her proxy, Armon, instead.

The vampire made them uneasy.

When the invitations came to the cavernous abode the Earth Volshins and Katalings found to claim as a home, Omeron refused it outright. His eyes glowed red as if ready to morph, scaring the young page into fleeing. Luamis managed to persuade the messenger to come back, and accepted the request.

Volshins and Katalings only cared about the clans' financial status as it pertained to their treatment. The more wealth, the better off. When there was a downturn, food and other necessities got rationed. The coven leaders did the same thing on Earth, causing the split from them.

That was no longer the case. Luamis and Omeron barely heard a word of the conversation. They drank in silence while waiting to hear whatever request the coven leaders posed.

"I take it neither of you agree?" Darean Callesi asked, loud enough to break them from their reverie.

The two glanced around the table as everyone stared at them in anticipation.

"I'm sorry." Luamis set his cup down. "Could you repeat that?"

"They weren't even listening," Chancellor Rayne scoffed.

"It's fine." Darean raised a hand, signaling a stop for any further criticism. "The West emperor has allotted the maximum number of royal soldiers to guard the Main docks and its skies. That leaves zero to maybe a handful for the East docks. Would your clans be willing to lend a few with compensation?"

"What kind of compensation?" Omeron finally set his cup aside, crossing his massive arms.

"As citizens, you are entitled to payment for services rendered." Holnar lowered his head. "I know you feel wary of us after all we've done. Looking back, our actions mirrored our parents. We should have found a new solution, not repeat the same atrocities."

Luamis glanced over at Omeron. Their leaders had remained on Cellaxa and prioritized the main docks. They saw no reason to assist in the rebuilt East dock, depleting their own resources. Volshins and Katalings were never paid for their work. This sounded like a good start.

"What kind of coverage are you requiring?" Omeron asked.

Tension lifted from the room, replaced by a more relaxed atmosphere. Armon leaned forward, one hand covering the other as he spoke.

"Three shifts to minimize fatigue. We don't want to push you to the edge of exhaustion. If that is too much, please tell us know what works best for you."

Luamis and Omeron frowned, contemplating the idea.

"Cellaxa has thirty-two hours in a day." Yutel propped one arm across the back of his chair while the other's hand lay on the table. "If we calculate like Earth to eight-hour shifts, that should sweeten the deal."

That did sound better. It also meant needing a smaller workforce.

"Then you only need eight Volshins and eight Katalings for each rotation." Luamis nodded while speaking. "What say you?" He turned to Omeron.

"That will do. How much is the pay?"

Yutel tapped on his tablet then slid it towards

them. Luamis caught it as it came before him. Omeron and he glanced at the proposed salary. More than enough for the job. Considering the small amount of resources they consumed, it would stretch far.

As if reading their body language, Darean Callesi addressed them.

"Maybe you can try living a little and purchase amenities for your homes. Visit the Endaga workshops for new casual or event wear."

The clothes they wore came from hand-me-downs and leftovers from previous battles. Cellaxa Volshins and Katalings dressed decently because their previous masters demanded and supplied them. On Earth they had to fend for themselves, scraping by with resources they stumbled upon.

Luamis slid the tablet back to Yutel.

"We can accept this. I hope it is in good faith." He eyed Armon. The vampire winked at him. "If we see one instant of misuse, the deal is off."

"Agreed," the leaders replied in unison.

"When do you want to start the rotation?"

Omeron uncrossed his arms to pick up his drink.

"There've been a few skirmishes during construction. We can hold off for a week if that's alright." Holnar's brow furrowed. "I'm thinking it may be a sabotage attempt."

"That's obvious." Armon smirked. "And I can give you two clans who would be the culprits."

"Strana and Boresso," Holnar blurted.

The room went silent.

Luamis and Omeron watched the anxiety creep on all their faces. Infighting never ended well. Especially elders against their younger generation of kin.

"I believe it is time to assert ourselves." Armon gave a sinister grin. "Show the elders of this world you are more than capable of holding your own, not in their shadows." He stared at Luamis and Omeron. "That goes for your kind as well. Despite being on

Earth for so long, you're not inferior to your elders."

"But we are." Luamis bowed his head. "We don't have the same experience or strife compared to them."

"No!" Yutel slapped the table with one hand, making it tremble. Luamis flinched. Omeron gripped his cup tighter. "You were simply unable to show your true might on Earth. They were under imperial control, forced into slavery, working days on end in their true forms. If anything, they are weaker."

Luamis perked up. He had never thought of it that way. Omeron's lips pulled back to reveal gritted teeth. Anger. They felt it collectively in their soul. One thing the masses didn't understand about their species. The two could sense each other across vast distances. A bond that could not be severed.

The two returned to the ancient territories in one of the transports designated to take them to and from their homes. It reminded them of the shuttle systems on Earth. They didn't mind having their own. That way, only those who lived there or were invited to the sector were allowed in.

The scenery changed from older multilevel houses to empty land before reaching the newly constructed homes on the outskirts of the Eastern border. It spanned towards the West where the Katalings could have freer range.

Luamis had a compound built near the center of the territory. His family had grown, taking in some of the younger Volshins who the elders hid from the emperor. Omeron's stood the next housing over. For some reason the two leaders found it better to stay close to each other.

Omeron's home could accommodate over one hundred members. It currently had forty which meant more than enough room for growth. He didn't know if accepting more would benefit him. He didn't see himself as some great leader.

Nothing like his father.

His father, the Kataling leader on Cellaxa. When he returned home, they had a tense reunion. He didn't like that he spawn a child with Chalayl. Omeron's brother didn't even bother to approach them. What would make him avoid their father?

Caden spent more time at the main house than the palace. Omeron didn't blame him. Too much drama going on. Luamis nudged him.

"What are you thinking?"

"That my home feels empty."

"Hmm. Well, most Katalings are of royal blood. Not a lot have freedom outside the palace."

"True. I just wish it wasn't the case."

The transport stopped at the pick up location for the Volshin provence. Luamis got out and stood at the door.

"Things are changing. Keep that in mind." He moved out of the transport's way. "Don't forget the monthly community meal in three days."

The doors shut and the transport made its way to the Kataling district. Omeron leaned on the window, pressing the side of his face against the cold glass. He may be huge and menacing but he hoped one day people could see his gentle soul.

Ancient Ties

Manel, Tavelo, and their inner circle pulled scrolls and tablets from the shelves locked away down in the archives. A small room recently cleared of dust barely contained the group, forcing them to squeeze past each other along the walls. The single window set high near the ceiling let in a shimmer of the setting sun, casting the room in a golden haze. Clear crystallized information slides fed into the machine accessed footage from long ago. The more they consumed, Manel and Tavelo grew angrier.

Eterenia watched a feed projected from the machine. Her face scrunched in concentration as her eyes tracked every movement in the image. Tavelo looked over at Pridric reading a scroll left by Eterenia's mother before being mated to the Jaubro clan. So many secrets.

"If all of this is true," Eterenia said, pointing to the hologram, "then every clan is related by blood one way or the other."

"Hmm." Manel pursed his lips. "Except for my bloodline. Why keep it yet, let the Volshins spread through different clans, diluting their lines?"

"Maybe it wasn't the old emperor's idea," Tervan replied. He rose halfway off the table on his forearms and stared at Pridric before addressing his father. "From what I'm seeing, it appears to be purposely done by one clan." He nodded towards Pridric.

He looked up at the same time. The gesture not lost on him. Pridric frowned. Tavelo saw the fear and sorrow in his eyes. The Strana clan. From the information so far, that is where the Volshin bloodline began. More than half the species thousands of years ago came from there.

"What made them change course and start to delete Volshins from their lineage? They didn't target any other clans." Manel's youngest brother, Lendor, flipped through a tablet displaying birth records. "What was the catalyst? It seems extreme."

"And our father let it happen, not caring about the plight of Volshins." Manel tossed a heavy scroll onto the nearby table. Its weight caused a thud on impact. "He had no intention of stopping the genocide."

Tavelo plopped into one of the clear hardback chairs. A design created from a single mold to eliminate joints. The seat curved slightly for easier sitting. Still uncomfortable. He wiggled a bit to find a better position. They had been inside the archives for over three hours. He started to tire.

"I think we should stop for now. I don't want to dive into Strana data without the proper frame of mind." His head fall back over the top of the chair.

"It will no doubt be ugly," Lendor added.

Pridric appeared to stiffen. Tervan raised his brow. Manel glanced over his shoulder at him. Eterenia removed the crystal slide from the machine and walked over to place it back on the shelf with the others. She gave Pridric a worried look.

He knows something about the Strana clan's agenda regarding Volshins.

Tavelo sat up. And it terrified him.

Master Strana watched the progress of his workers on the docks. With arms crossed, his black trench coat flapping behind him in the cold wind, he resembled a dominating aristocrat. His bolo hat remained on his head, no budging. Under the open coat, he wore a plain white tunic and black leggings that showed off his physique.

Volshins patrolling the area shrieked in the grey sky. He looked up and saw one with a beautiful multicolored mane tail. His stoic expression turned to disgust. A Strana Volshin. Only a handful existed. Less than twenty if he remembered the records.

Too many in his clan's eyes.

Movement on the docks caught his attention. His assistant, Roren, came up the ramp towards him.

"What are you doing down here?" Master Strana let his arms drop. "How is this part of your information gathering?"

"Before you cry foul." Roren stopped a few feet from him. "Dock workers hear lots of things. I just recently found out the Endagas are considered to be of imperial lineage since they have the most Volshins at the moment."

"How sickening."

"It should be us." Roren barely got his words out when Master Strana grabbed him by the throat, lifting him inches off the ground.

"No, it shouldn't. I will not allow recognition for that hideous title." Realizing he had overreacted, Master Strana released his assistant. "My apologies. I didn't mean to take my anger out on you." While his assistant straightened his jacket, he asked. "Any word from our spy?"

"Pridric is hard to locate most days. He not only refuses to leave the palace, he hides from everyone, including Tavelo, when not performing his duties as his advisor."

Master Strana's eyes narrowed.

"I don't buy it. Pridric can be sneaky. But, he

won't avoid being seen for long."

Come, brother. Show me how daring you are.

Servants milled past Adelia, tugging her youngest child behind her with the other two in tow. House Grieger appeared overcrowded. The merger between De Luce and Bryhel had begun months ago. They had plenty of room, so she didn't understand why she needed to maneuver through the abode like a New York street walker.

"Momma, stop!" The little one cried out of breath. Adelia halted in a panic. She turned around and looked down at her poor child, red-faced with sweat on his brow. "You're too fast," he coughed.

"Please slow down, mother." Her oldest, Sully, gave her an angry stare, also out of breath from protecting his younger brother, Addy, who stood in front of him. "What's the hurry?"

"I just..." Adelia exhaled slowly, calming herself. "I wanted to get through all these people quickly."

"He's five." Sully pointed at the little one. "His tiny legs are not that fast. You're literally dragging him across the floor."

Adelia flinched. Shamed by his words, she bent down and picked her son up. She held him close, as she resumed to thread her way through the crowds. Her older sons kept close. At the end of the long walkway, they came to a foyer. She turned to the left, heading for the main quarters.

At the communal dining room, she spotted her father talking with one of the cooks. He happened to catch sight of her and gave a confused smile. Finishing his conversation, he waved her in.

"What brings you here unannounced?" He took a second look. "And why are you all so winded?" He took the youngest from her and let him bury his face in his chest.

He could feel the rapid beating inside the child's chest. "It's okay. You can relax, sweetheart." Patting the boy's back.

"I wanted to see you. It's been a long time." Adelia pointed to her young one. "Since he was born, actually."

"It's been that long, huh?" Her father kissed the top of the boy's head. "He's grown a lot."

"Well, he's gonna get bigger than me, so."

"Still, you should have let us know. We could have had an escort waiting for you."

"See?" Sully cried out.

"Come. Let's get to the family wing." He led the way, cuddling the boy as he walked.

The family wing held Yutel's immediate relatives, which included her father's. Adelia followed him into a sitting room furnished with two chaise lounges, small side tables, and various artworks high on the walls for an unobstructed view.

In seconds, Yutel Dakien came into the room, bringing a gust of air, along with his commanding aura permeated it.

"Adelia!" His booming voice always made her cringe. "What did you think you were doing, coming through the main halls like that?"

"I asked the same thing," her father said, giving her an admonishing stare.

"Can we let it go?" Adelia gestured to her sons. "My children are parched from all the excitement."

"And whose fault is that?" Sully stared coldly.

"Don't test me, child." Adelia looked over at him with glowing red eyes. He rolled his and fell onto a nearby loveseat.

Yutel caught her off guard in a bear hug, lifting her off the ground.

"It's good to see you!" He let out a hardy laugh.

"Ugh! Put me down, uncle!" She squirmed. "I'm not a child!"

"Hmm? Aren't you though?"

Yutel set her down and smirked.

"Don't tease her and make her mad," her father told him.

"Fine."

Uncle Yutel dropped into one of the plush chairs. Even that action seemed over the top. Everything he did demanded attention. Chiron, his son with Chalayl, was no better. He arrived in a suit with a flare of arrogance, sneering at Adelia before giving her children a smile.

"I heard you snuck in and got caught up in the rush." He sat on a chaise. "Serves you right."

At half his father's size, people regarded him as a mini Yutel. Stocky, full of muscle and strong. Unlike his father, he inherited Kataling blood that lay dormant for now. Everyone in the Dakien clan personified the Greiger motto they took homage to.

A good fortune may only be built through the brute force of creativity.

They got the brute force down pat in action and appearance.

Adelia envied their fierceness. She could never pull it off with her soft features and pretty blonde hair. A contradiction when it came to fighting. Her enemy always underestimated her skills. Her sons, on the other hand, had no such issue. Half werewolf, they took after their father's stature.

"I heard there's going to be more merges of clans soon. Is it really necessary?" Adelia reached for a slice of bread from the basket set in the center of the table by the servant. She talked while chewing. "It defeats the whole purpose of establishing ourselves apart from the main families."

Chiron snorted. "It's exactly for that reason." He leaned back in his chair. "The Dakien house may not look down on us, but the others do."

"Not Jaubro or Endaga," Adelia huffed.

She saw her uncle's face scrunch. His stare locked with hers.

No! That can't be true.

Then again, she hadn't looked too deep in the merchant accounts or the family transactions. For all she knew, the Jaubro merchants were undercutting the De Luce shipments.

"You're too naïve," Chiron said. "The merchant families have done trade for millennia or more. While we've only established ours in the past couple of centuries."

More servants came with drinks, small portions of assorted meats, and fruit. Her boys dug in like ravenous hounds. Even the smallest one climbed onto the table to grab a fruit the size of his hands.

"Stop being greedy!" She tried to swat their hands.

"They're fine," her father waved a hand. "We have plenty."

"What brings you here, anyway?" Chiron asked.

Adelia shrunk back in her chair, frowning. She glanced over at her sons, then her uncle.

"I feel," she shrugged. "Like I don't have much to offer here."

"That's an understatement," Chiron laughed. He instantly regretted it.

"Don't ever say that again." Yutel's glowing red eyes bore into him. Her father gave him a dirty look. "You will not disrespect her. She has more than earned her title."

Adelia's expression slumped. Her body seemed to feel gelatinous, as if she would slide right out of her seat onto the floor in despair. She only showed her vulnerability to one other person. Tesul.

"Listen to me." Yutel leaned forward. "Take time to familiarize yourself with this world. You will find your calling in due time. There's no reason for you to take the reins in De Luce trade. That was never your role to begin with."

"It just feels like I'm doing nothing." Adelia ran both hands across the top of her head then rested them around her neck. "And everyone is acting weird inside the palace."

"Hmm?" Yutel grinned with intrigue. "How so?"

"My mother seems to be conflicted on whether she wants to remain by Tavelo's side. Tavelo doesn't go anywhere without Pridric at his. Tervan creeps around them all suspicious. To top it all off, Tamar's mother resurfaced."

That made Yutel and her father rear back in shock.

"Suggestion," her father raised a finger. "Stay clear of that creature. Nothing good would come from engaging her."

"As for the other issue." Yutel tilted his head to one side. "Tavelo has a type."

Adelia gave him a questioning stare. She ran the images of Tavelo's mates in her mind. A type? Seeing them all together, she hissed in recognition of his words. But, what did that have to do with Pridric?

❀ ❀ ❀

Released from her prison within the Durante walls when the entire coven boarded the ship back to Cellaxa, Tamar's mother, Maritze, stayed out of sight in the palace. After a few years, she decided to make her presence known.

Tamar visited on occasion to check in. Tavelo had yet to confront her, not even acknowledging her existence.

So be it.

Per the royal decree, the palace advisors relayed her status as consort for birthing the emperor's off-spring. She smirked. How droll. A princess or royal anything was the last thing she wanted to be.

She rounded the corner of the long, marbled hallway and caught sight of Eterenia in royal robes looking dejected. Maritze followed her gaze and fell on Tavelo speaking with Pridric in a tight huddle.

Ahh! She grinned.

A quick glance around found Tervan hiding in

the shadows, also looking on. She walked over to Eterenia.

"Not liking their bond?" She gave an evil smile at her startled expression as she turned to her.

"What?" Eterenia stepped back. "Where did you come from?"

"Really? Is that what you want to say to me?"

Standing next to Eterenia, she appeared common. Wearing loose fitted dungarees and a flowy pleated gold shirt, she resembled a dock worker. The brown hooded robe's hem dragging on the floor added to the look.

Her blonde hair, full like a lion's mane, framed her face in chaos. She had no reason to tame it down into a slick, pristine style.

Hearing her voice, Tavelo and Pridric averted their stares from each other and locked onto her. Tavelo's expression went slack before his eyes narrowed.

"I'm surprised you didn't demand I be put in the dungeon for eternity. You hating me so much."

Tavelo didn't appreciate her snark. His eyes glowed silver.

"I have never hated you. That's your own interpretation of my actions. You tried to have me overthrown as coven leader. You made yourself my enemy."

"Ha!" She raised a finger to her lower lip in mock surprise. "Because you were an awful leader." She dropped her hand. "You still are. Emperor." Pridric turned from her. "I see old habits die hard."

Eterenia looked at her, confused. Pridric tensed.

"What are you talking about?" Eterenia's hands balled up at her sides.

"Oh, didn't you know?" She gave her a crooked smile. "Tavelo always had a type."

With that, she resumed her stroll through the palace halls to get a lay of the land. Looking back over her shoulder, she saw Tavelo staring angrily.

❀ ❀ ❀

Pridric slammed his chamber door shut and slid down in front of it. He drew his knees in to rest his head on them. He felt like a child running away from his parents after doing something wrong.

But, I didn't do anything wrong!

According to his family, he had. Frolicking with a dirty Endaga in their eyes deserved death. The Stranas tolerated the Endagas during trade, yet still devised ways to steal their clients or sabotage shipments.

In their youth, it didn't matter much. His family never publicly admonished him for being friends with Tavelo. All the clan children within similar age groups were allowed to mingle. After the first time Tavelo and he spent time alone, his family saw a shift in their connection.

Every child between the ages of one hundred and one hundred and five years old was required to undergo a hunting test. The elders paired them up and sent them into the treacherous forest, where large animals roamed. They had four weeks to find, track, and kill one to present to the elders at the end.

Pridric drifted off as his memory of that time took over.

Cellaxa two hundred and fifty years ago

Grey sky, stiff wind, and the scent of fresh rain marked the start of the hunting trials. Now past their mid-years, bordering on adulthood, the group of young carnivores stood in a huddle awaiting their assignments from the elders. The dominating twelve clans each presented a child.

"You must only use your bare strength to take down your prey," the elder of the Jaubro clan yelled out. "Those of you with Kataling or Volshin abilities are forbidden from using them. We will inspect the carcasses for any signs of the rules' violation."

A few feet shuffled in the thick grass, cut short to create a clearing. The rest of the grass stood six feet tall, obscuring the scenery. Mist hovered along the trees, far out in the dense forest. The elder called out the pairs for the hunt.

Pridric tried to hide his nervousness. In a plain white tunic and leather leggings, his demeanor seemed docile. His blond hair barely grazed his shoulders, and the black boots hadn't seen any action yet, the tops gleaming. A serrated knife for removing any fur and deboning lay inside a sheath attached to his hip.

A few feet beside him, with Holnar blocking his view, stood Tavelo Endaga. Silent, his posture erect, and a serious expression etched on his face. The jet-black hair, also laying right at the shoulders, accented his blue eyes. When Holnar's pairing was called, he moved out of the way, giving Pridric a clear line of sight for Tavelo. Beautiful as always.

Every participant had been given the hideous haircuts the night before the trial. While it seemed unflattering to most, Tavelo managed to pull it off.

"Tavelo Endaga goes with Pridric Strana."

Pridric's head shot up and he saw his father's and brother's faces fill with disdain. They kept their ire in check and simply nodded. Tavelo didn't respond at all. He stayed unmoving, his expression blank. He finally turned to meet Pridric's gaze and simply nodded. Since they were already close to each other, they remained in position.

"If anyone is not out by the deadline, you will be marked a failure and held back for two years before granted permission to retake the trial. If any of you die during the trial, your clan will be marked with a failure and contracts restricted."

The atmosphere grew tense with anxiety. Reputation meant everything in the merchant clans. For one of their children to fail basic hunting skills meant that clan had not raised them properly.

In the past two hundred years, no child had failed. The children at present vowed to continue that streak.

Chalayl, looked glum. Her large frame, made bigger with her ample breasts and round buttocks, screamed battle maiden. Pridric had a feeling she would outpace her partner and take down a beast herself. He thanked the stars he didn't get paired with her.

"The trial begins now."

The elders walked off, leaving the children on their own to venture into the trial grounds.

Tavelo moved forward. A neat loop of wire rope sat attached behind him near his lower back. Pridric felt embarrassed that he hadn't thought to bring some. His partner seemed more prepared.

"I didn't bring any," Pridric blurted out.

Tavelo kept moving, heading to the deepest part of the forest.

"That's fine. We only need this much anyway."

He never looked back.

The further in they got, the darker it became. Giant trees got closer together, blocking the dim daylight from reaching the forest floor. It took nearly two days before they found a monster to slay and another day of tracking.

Pridric hid in the thicket next to Tavelo, watching their prey snort the air for their scent. Tavelo didn't find some medium-sized beast for them to take down. No. What he went after turned out to be one of the few giant creatures that would normally take four hunters to kill.

The beast loomed nearly ten feet tall. Its thick elongated neck accounting for three of them. A solid body rippled with muscles atop two trunk like legs with sharp claws. The arms set right below the end of the neck had six-inch-long talons.

Perfect for skewering its enemy.

The tracking had turned into a game of cat and

mouse. Instead of them hunting it, they were on the run. Or so Pridric thought. Tavelo had something up his sleeve.

"It's going to come at us. What's the plan?" Pridric whispered in Tavelo's ear.

Tavelo's unwavering stare frightened Pridric. A sinister wildness crept into his eyes.

"Just follow my lead." Tavelo unhooked the rope from his waist. "Here." He held it out, not looking at Pridric. "Make sure you get the timing right."

Pridric stared at the rope in terror. He reluctantly took it. The monster's head swiveled towards them.

Oh no! His fear of what Tavelo's plan entailed became clear as he leapt from the thickets. Pridric closed his eyes, building up the courage to follow. In the few days he had with Tavelo, one word came to mind.

Reckless.

Tavelo's body adjusted midair into an attack stance, his fingernails now sharp black talons. His eyes glowed silver and fangs protruded from his pulled back lips. He looked more monstrous than their prey. Coming down right on the creature's back, he tried to pierce its hide. His talons only went in an inch before the creature threw him off with a hard shift to the right.

It howled in rage, throwing its head back. Thin rivers of blood seeped from the tiny puncture wounds. Tavelo scrambled from where he landed a few yards from the beast and charged it. The beast turned to face him, and they collided. Tavelo caught its arms, stopping it from slicing him into thirds.

Pridric unraveled the rope. With precision, he whipped it out towards its legs. The end of the rope lassoed around the first leg, then curved onto the other. When it went taut, he pulled, only to be swept off his feet. He went sailing forward in the air, right into a tree. He relaxed his body before impact. The one thing that saved him from broken bones.

Not to be deterred, seeing Tavelo fight with the creature, Pridric dropped to the ground and tugged hard. Tavelo stood bloody from the claw swipes when the creature head butted him, forcing him to let go. It didn't fare any better as Tavelo returned the favor. Pridric stared in awe at Tavelo going head-to-head with something three times his size.

The creature let out an ear-piercing roar in protest of its legs being dragged backwards. Pridric's eyes turned blood red as he strained with every ounce of strength to bring the thing down. It made a sharp side movement, sending Pridric airborne once again. This time, it gave him the advantage. He didn't let go of the rope, so he ricocheted around by letting his feet hit the nearest tree to launch him.

Tavelo already jumped up, poised to strike. Pridric used the momentum of his swing to add strength to his pull. The creature roared again as it pitched forward, not able to stop itself. Before its neck hit the ground, Tavelo's talons sunk deep into its major artery near its shoulder blade.

It thrashed about, trying to get Tavelo off. Pridric came around to tie it down with the other end of the rope, and its claws grazed his back. He fell to his knees directly in front of its face. The malice in its eyes made Pridric flinch.

"Move!" Tavelo's voice startled him.

Right when he tightened his grip on the rope, the creature swung its other arm, swatting him to the side. Tavelo's features seemed to blur as he swooned from the hit. Together in one move, Tavelo wrenched himself to the side, rolling the creature on its side while Pridric grabbed hold of its head and twisted the opposite way.

Its last howl shook the trees, then died out. The creature's tongue flopped out. Tavelo, with eyes bulging and drool dripping from bared fangs, jumped down and ripped it from its mouth. He tossed it over his shoulders and turned to Pridric.

Both bloody and injured, they stared at each other for a split second, letting out small laughs. Tavelo's talons and fangs retracted. He suddenly grabbed Pridric by the face and kissed him deeply, fiercely. Pridric couldn't get a breath. The taste of the creature's blood mingled with their saliva. Tavelo's rush sent them to the ground, where he pulled at Pridric's clothes in a crazed desperation.

Despite the pain in his back from the claw wounds, Pridric shifted into female form without thinking.

Tavelo sat up to remove his blood-stained tunic, then Pridric's. He stripped them both naked in mere seconds and rammed his swollen cock into her. Pridric gasped at the new pain flooding her body.

"Ahh!" She tried to speak, but that sound was the only thing coming out. Tears filled her eyes and ran down the sides of her face. Tavelo placed his hands on the ground at her sides as he leaned over to kiss her once more. "Tavelo," she finally got out.

Their mating bordered on violence, fueled by the high of bringing down their prize. They knew, even in that state, their souls were intertwined. Pridric reached up and cupped Tavelo's face in her hands. Their eyes locked for a moment. A kaleidoscope of colors swirled in both. She couldn't' tell if it was a trick of the sparse sunlight that pierced a section of the clouds.

On the tenth day, Tavelo and Pridric dragged the giant creature to the clearing, where the elders waited to see who would pass the trial. The wire rope held, keeping the carcass bound. Pridric had re-wrapped it, so the beast appeared more compact.

They trudged forward in silence, purposely looking dejected to throw the elders off.

"The second pair to complete the trials. Tavelo Endaga and Pridric Strana!" Master Jaubro shouted the announcement.

"What madness is this?" The Bryhel master cried out. "First Chalayl Boresso, now these two? These beasts they are bringing out are far more than they should be capable of killing."

"That just shows who the real monsters are." Master Jaubro replied.

Pridric felt an ominous presence. He turned to his father and brother standing in the elder circle. Their blood-red eyes bore into him like hot iron rods. They can sense it!

He would never tell anyone that they had killed another beast and ate it down to the bone, mating every day while still on a murderous high.

Tavelo Has A Type

Another royal meeting in the duel imperial throne room designated for both emperors left Tavelo bored. He despised politics. Even on Earth, he tried to steer clear of it every chance he got. *That's what delegates are for!* Pridric kept notes as usual. His fingers tapped the tablet, inserting data.

He sat leaning to one side in his chair, the side of his head resting against his fist. A prickly tingle ran up his spine, signaling his groin tightening. He felt his eyes glow for a second as he watched Pridric engrossed in his duties.

"That concludes our reports for the day." The magistrate's voice broke him out of his daydreaming.

"If we may, emperor Tavelo," the royal advisor turned and addressed him. "A private meeting with the monarchs."

Pridric rose, tucking his tablet under one arm.

"I'll go ahead to consult with our palace teams."

"Meet me in the planning room before midday meal," Tavelo commanded.

Pridric and the other assistants left the room. Gallic again, felt reluctant to leave Manel's side. The royal advisor set himself on a chair near the far wall for a full view of the room. Manel, along with his siblings, Tavelo's uncle, and Master Jaubro awaited his words.

"As you know, the royal houses have neglected

the protocols for too l long. That said, Manel has now acquired a compatible mate, and the bloodline is secure. Which leaves you, Emperor Tavelo."

Manel let out a snort, giving Tavelo a side glance.

"Yes," he hissed. "When are you going to snag yourself an Empress?"

Tavelo sat upright, surprised by the nature of the conversation. An Empress? He hadn't thought about it at all.

"You have multiple mates who have birthed off-spring for you. Does any of them fit the role?"

"Those women are trash," Manel's older sister, Maxellia, exclaimed. "You'd do better to start over."

Tavelo turned red eyes towards her. "You will not insult the mothers of my children."

"Hmph!" She returned his stare in kind.

"I did offer," Manel said playfully.

Everyone turned to him in horror.

"I refuse to give in to your insane idea of a Volshin, Kataling hybrid. Stop asking." Tavelo sighed in exasperation at Manel's pouting.

Then he thought about his choices. Empress. A mate devoted to him alone and the empire. Willing to continue his bloodline with more offspring. Neither Eterenia nor Maritze fit that description. He loved Eterenia, except it only went so deep. Nothing on the level of soulmate or forever.

"I need time to think on the issue."

Tavelo rubbed his lower lip.

"Please do not dally too long." The royal advisor stood. "I am preparing the royal tree and would like it updated within five years."

Manel let out a loud burst of laughter. His eyes twinkled as he wiped his eyes.

"Better hurry, Tavelo. Your true mate may slip from your grasps if you wait too long."

A sense of fear gripped Tavelo. He waited until the rest of the room cleared before leaving. Empress. The title kept going through his head.

Its sounded enticing as he thought of who he cherished in that capacity. In the hallway, he saw Manel standing off to the side, staring at him.

He knows.

❀ ❀ ❀

Pridric walked out of the conference room after briefing the palace organizers with the daily reports. He had an hour before his meeting with Tavelo. Sunlight shining through the atrium wall windows assaulted him as he stepped into the main hallway.

Ugh! He was not a fan of sunny days, yet didn't enjoy the extremely gloomy ones either.

Royal house members strolled along in hushed conversation. Ire amongst the classes still lingered. The old ways needed to change. *Can't they see that?* He saw the same thing on Earth.

Was this some universal strife?

Defeated, not wanting to think of it anymore, he took a deep breath and continued down the corridor towards the strategy room. He could check on a few things while he waited for Tavelo.

To his surprise, he found Tavelo coming towards him as he approached the entrance. The look on his face told Pridric something dire crossed his mind. Tavelo's brow furrowed.

"What's wrong?" Pridric entered the room first, then glanced back. Tavelo still didn't look up. "Did Manel say something ridiculous again?"

Tavelo finally stared at him with steely resolve.

"The royal council suggested I find an Empress to rule with me."

Pridric halted placing a chip on the data platform. Sharp pain hit his chest, causing him to falter. He regained his composure and set the chip down. A multitude of holoscreens popped up in the air.

"Is that so?" Pridric tapped images on the console to rearrange the screens. "Well, you do have Eterenia as a candidate. I'm sure Tamar's mother is out of the question."

"Why do you say that?" Tavelo's terse tone shocked Pridric. Did I anger him? He dared not turn around to see his expression. "Answer me."

Pridric opened his mouth, then shut it to take a deep breath.

"She is the only one who knows what it means to be a Queen. Empress would be an easy role for her to assume."

"A coven Queen does not make a ruler of worlds."

The way Tavelo spoke it with such disdain, Pridric's mind spun with answers to the issue.

"If not the mother of your children, then who?" Pridric got angry. "You pursued her for decades, no centuries, not once looking at anyone else seriously. Even Maritze, you simply tolerated until she turned against you." He realized his voice had risen.

Heat flushed his body as he gave Tavelo a hostile stare. Why am I angry?

Tavelo's arms wrapped around his waist in an instant, turning him around so they stood face to face. He slammed Pridric against the nearest wall. They shared the same breath while Tavelo's irises turned blood red.

"I've only ever wanted one being in my entire existence." Tavelo's lips got within millimeters of Pridric's. "Be my Empress." He said it like a demand than asking. Pridric's eyes widened in shock.

"What?" Pridric felt panic strike, tensing his body. He tried to get out of Tavelo's clutches. "You don't mean that. Why would you say that to me?" He struggled, to no avail.

Tavelo would not let him budge.

Their lips met, exchanging heat. Pridric instinctively parted his to let Tavelo invade. Tears streamed down his face as he felt the familiar ferocity of Tavelo's passion. His body relented despite his mind desperately screaming to stop him.

The half second their lips disengaged, Pridric took advantage.

"Please, Tavelo." He placed his hands on his chest to push him off. "Someone may come."

When he looked into Tavelo's eyes, he flinched.

"I don't care."

He pushed himself closer and locked his lips on Pridric's once more. His hand slid inside the waist of his leggings and pulled at the bottom of his tunic. It traveled across his hips and grazed the side of his buttocks. Pridric gasped in surprise, letting Tavelo's kiss go deeper.

For the first time in over two and a half centuries, Pridric shifted to his female form. The transition brought pain, having not done it in so long.

Tavelo watched her face etch with her body's struggle. She tried to turn away, forcing their lips apart. In his own fashion, he chose to ignore her plight, yanking the leggings down. He used his foot to push them to the floor, making Pridric's only option to use hers to remove her boots. Tavelo undid his robes to expose his naked body beneath.

Without warning, he hefted Pridric up the wall and entered her. His robes concealed them their position that forced Pridric's legs around his waist. Pridric cried out, reliving Tavelo's brutal mating. His thrusts were relentless.

Pridric endured, not wanting him to stop yet knowing this couldn't end well. She took hold of his neck and braced herself for the worst to come.

Searing pain flooded her body as they climaxed together, her talons clawing his back under the robes. Her vision blurred as she fought to not lose consciousness. Tavelo held her up, not letting go.

"Pridric. Look at me." Her eyes fluttered. "Stay with me."

Pridric focused on him and finally caught his stare. Sadness consumed her. As if reading her mind, Tavelo placed a hand behind her head so she couldn't turn away. Their eyes locked.

"I won't let you go ever again." His lips brushed hers. "Say yes."

"Tavelo," Pridric whispered, caressing his face after retracting her talons.

Noise from the outer corridor broke their tender moment. They disengaged, realizing how sweaty and sticky they were. That couldn't be helped. Once again in a panic, Pridric forced her body back into male form, bending down to scoop up the discarded leggings and boots.

Getting dressed came not a moment too soon. Tervan and Tavelo's uncle entered the room to find them leaning over the data platform. Tervan gave them a dubious stare as he glanced at the frozen holoscreen that had not been accessed in quite a while.

Pridric averted his gaze with dread.

Tervan knew too much and too observant to not gain more knowledge. Tavelo glanced over at him. Unspoken dialogue occurred between father and son.

❀ ❀ ❀

"You didn't answer me." Tavelo removed his outer robe and tossed it on his bed.

Pridric paced Tavelo's chamber. He stopped in the center of the room.

"You can't just ask me that. I need to think."

"Why? What stops you from being mine?"

"There's Dania, Chase, the coven." Pridric's hands shook. "My family. The Strana clan."

Tavelo frowned. He knew the first list of reasons were easily remedied. The last item is what terrified Pridric. There had to be a way to find what happened so long ago when Pridric suddenly turned on him. Hated him more than any Strana. He went out of his way to see Tavelo suffer even on Earth.

"Then I'll give you a little time." Tavelo stood close behind him. "I won't take no for an answer."

49

Pridric turned around and their lips grazed each other. The kiss took Pridric off guard, letting Tavelo pull him close. He tasted and smelled every drop of Pridric's essence. Euphoria he had experienced once before with no one other than Pridric made him giddy. This time, Pridric got out of his hold.

"Stop. Please. I must bathe before midday meal."

"What for?" Tavelo's sinister smile as he cocked his head to one side appeared to frighten Pridric.

"I can't go eating with my family with…" Pridric struggled to say it.

"The scent of mating on you? My scent?" Pridric's face went flush. "I don't mind. We'll all be together, anyway." He sniffed at Pridric, inhaling deeply. "You smell delicious."

Pridric's brow scrunched in annoyance.

"Don't you even know how to restrain yourself?" He walked to the door. "I'm leaving."

Tavelo patiently watched Pridric enter the corridor and head towards his own chamber. No rush, really. He wanted to stir the pot. It had been a long time coming. Pridric's words from earlier hit him hard. He had indeed switched to finding a new mate after Pridric's hateful rejection centuries ago. It smacked of the Strana clan's hand in it.

Settling for what he could get while gaining better status for the Endaga clan seemed like the right course of action then. Everyone wanted a piece of Eterenia, and he vowed to take her as a trophy to flaunt to the other clans. He grew to love her, though not the same as he did Pridric. His investment went deep.

The spawning of offspring proved inevitable.

As for Tamar's mother, that rang true. A mere toy to play with until he could have Eterenia, resolving that Pridric would never belong to him as long as the Strana clan wished it so. His soulmate forfeited, he lived a life of regrets. He had treated Maritze badly and understood her desire to harm him.

She would never forgive him.

And she had every right.

No more.

Tavelo stripped off his robes. He entered his chamber's private bath connected to it. Reluctantly, he picked up the washing sponge on the edge of the basin before sliding into the prepared warm water. Oils and petals converged on him. Leaning his head back, he tapped the sponge against its surface. He raised his arms together to smell Pridric's scent one more time, then submerged the sponge.

He carefully wiped away the dried sweat that mingled with the smell of hard mating.

Am I really such a terrible being and patriarch?

He thought of his offspring, especially Tervan and Tamar. Neither saw any redeeming traits in him. They expressed it often.

Pridric. He wanted offspring with him. Maybe as many as he had now. The thought of what their children would be like sent elation through him. A blond-haired doppelgänger of himself or a dark-haired one of Pridric. He giggled despite himself.

"My beautiful Empress. Come back to me."

He slid further down in the basin until the water reached his chin. His eyes glowed red with lust.

There would be no sneaking into the personal chamber he shared with his mate, Dania. Pridric stepped over the threshold of the entrance and stood silent with his hands loose at his sides. He could see her moving around in the bedroom, straightening out the bedding. She sensed his presence and looked around to find him. Her smile faded.

Pridric walked towards her, his legs feeling like lead, and tried to avert her stare. She came closer to him, and he stepped back.

"Don't. Please."

Dania tilted her head.

"Sit, Pridric." Her tone commanded.

He sat on the edge of the bed, careful not to go full on to prevent his odor from seeping onto it.

"So it has finally come to this." Dania stood over him. "I knew one day your fake hatred of Tavelo would disappear." Pridric stared up at her, his eyes wide. "If you ever had the chance to get him back, you would take it."

"I, you are my mate," Pridric whispered. "The mother of my offspring."

Dania stroked his cheeks.

"Oh, Pridric. I know you love me. Just not as much as you love Tavelo."

Pridric shook his head, attempting to release her grip. "Don't make excuses for me!"

"I'm not." Dania let go. "We all knew this would happen at some point. Everyone except Eterenia and you."

"He," Pridric's breath shuddered, "asked me to be his empress."

"Oh? Of course he did. He only wants you."

"I can't…" Pridric clenched his fists tighter. "I'm not," he trailed off.

"Tavelo needs you!" Dania grabbed a fistful of hair at the top of his head. Her angry tone scared him. "We will be fine, as always." She let him go once more. "Go bathe. I can smell his scent all over you."

Pridric's face went pale as he rose to enter the bathroom. He undressed in a daze, leaving his clothes in a heap on the floor. Forgoing the large basin, he headed for the shower. He turned on the spout and let the hot water rain down on him from the spigot above.

For a long time he stood there, suddenly not wanting to wash himself off. He breathed in the last remnants of Tavelo's scent, then reached for the soap hose. The foamy suds covered his entire body with the aroma of fresh herbs and flowers.

❀ ❀ ❀

Tervan observed his father's circle for weeks, gathering intel on their traits, every mannerism, and status. He deduced his father's type based on them. Blonde, statuesque, an aggressive nature, yet easy to force into submission.

A walking contradiction. Complicated.

He let out an aggravated sigh as he watched the entourage of women enter the lounge area slash reading room. He stayed quiet, stealthily spying as they talked. Because he knew the topic coming ahead. The moment he heard the royal counselor advise his father to find an empress, Pridric became the first person in mind.

The strange back and forth of words when they met to strategize the crowning ceremony stayed with him. His father saying Pridric loved him and he, in turn, acknowledging it. Their bond ran deeper than he thought.

The quiet lounge room gave way to conversation when Dania, Eternia, Grasilda, and Maritze arrived to gossip. They sat at an equal distance from each other. The servants brought extra carafes of brew and a dried meat platter. Bloody servings would be too messy for a midday snack.

Eterenia sat in the chair at the head of the small table. Dania, on her left, settled into a chaise, with Maritze across from her on a loveseat. Grasilda took residence in the high-backed chair on the end next to her.

"What is going on in that silly mind of yours, Eterenia?" Maritze asked, smirking over the rim of her teacup.

Eterenia's head shot up, and she locked eyes with her. Grasilda shook her head in disappointment.

"Must you antagonize everyone? There's really no reason for it." Grasilda slowly raised her cup to her lips. "Is it envy?"

"Absolutely not!" Maritze laughed.

"I simply can't stand her entitled ass." The vulgar Earth slang made Dania and Grasilda wince. "She constantly lorded over us, shoving her queen status in our faces."

"I did no such thing!" Eterenia's shoulders tensed as she leaned forward. "I had no say in the matter in the beginning. As for on Earth, you could have gone out and took over a coven if you wanted to be Queen so badly."

Maritze grinned, laying one arm along the back of the loveseat with her legs wide apart.

"Don't assume I wanted to be like you. See? That's the issue right there." She tilted her head back, staring intensely at Eterenia. "At least you don't have that burden here."

"Things could change. The royal counselor wants Tavelo to pick an Empress. Now's your chance to get in his good graces." Eterenia smirked.

"Hmm? Why would I want to be his Empress? We barely tolerate each other. Speak for yourself."

Eterenia clenched her hands into fists on her lap while chewing on the corner of her bottom lip.

"I don't want to be selected. Even though I have spawned his children and am the likely candidate, I would have to decline."

Dania frowned at her in disgust.

She also detested Eterenia's sense of entitlement currently on display.

"I am certain Tavelo knows what he wants. And who is best suited to rule by his side."

"It is not something to choose lightly," Grasilda added. "His selection would already be on record since the decree."

"He has."

Dania reached over to set her teacup and saucer on the table. The room went silent. In a shadowy corner on the other side of a bookcase, Tervan strained his hearing.

"Tavelo has chosen Pridric."

Eternia gasped. Maritze burst out laughing. Grasilda nodded in approval.

"What! Why would he," Eterenia sputtered. "Pridric is not…" Her eyes widened at Dania's lack of concern. "How would they carry on the royal bloodline?"

Maritze stared at her incredulously. "Oh, did you not know?" She covered her lips with the tips of her fingers.

"Stop it." Dania gave her a warning look. "You know she doesn't."

"What don't I know?"

Dania let out a sigh.

"Tavelo and Pridric were always meant to be mated. The Strana clan refused to accept that and forbid Pridric from spending time with him."

"But that means," Eterenia struggled with the information. She saw Pridric anew, realizing he fit Tavelo's type to the letter. "In that case, why didn't Tavelo try to pursue you as well?"

Dania scoffed, waving her hand in front of her.

"I am not bold enough to catch his eye. I wouldn't tolerate his antics, which I deem worse than Pridric's."

Her personality lay on the quiet rage spectrum. Tavelo could never treat her the way he did Eterenia or Maritze. She'd slit his throat in his sleep. It's why Pridric mostly behaved, not straying too far to the edge to feel her wrath.

"I don't understand. The title of empress should go to at least someone who already has offspring."

"You stated you didn't want to be empress," Maritze chided her.

"Why would he start over and not, at the very least, ask me?" Eterenia's brow furrowed. "I was a coven Queen. My qualifications exceed the basics and I have spawned three of his bloodline."

Grasilda's eyes widened at her audacity.

They realized she didn't hear how she sounded. To admonish Tavelo for his choice when she had no intention of taking the role.

"You're forgetting one glaring obvious thing." Maritze gave a Cheshire grin, malice twinkling in her eyes. Eterenia stared at her, confused. "He didn't ask you." She pointed at Eterenia, emphasizing the word didn't.

Eterenia looked as if she had smacked in the face. The cold hard truth indeed glared at her. Tervan felt a slight amount of pity for his mother. Deep in her soul, she knew her love for Tavelo only touched the surface. A shallow adoration based on obligation.

"Is he going to announce it?"

The edge in Eterenia's tone did not go unnoticed.

"There's no rush." Grasilda replied. "He can wait until they have offspring." She eyed the other women. "Of course, there is the real reason to keep it secret for now."

Maritze snorted, lowering her arm, and sat up correctly. Dania remained silent while Eterenia again, looked confused.

The Strana clan.

Their reaction to Tavelo and Pridric mating would involve bloodshed and murder. Tervan agreed with Tamar's mother. His own lacked the same knowledge because her clan sheltered her. She learned combat and hunting skills like everyone else, but never showed interest in the other clans. And the Jaubros didn't feel a need to tell her either.

"And what would that be?" Eterenia asked, now angry at not being in the loop.

"You should ask them," Dania replied.

The way the other women glanced at Eterenia spoke volumes. They didn't trust her. Tervan tensed, as he too felt the same way. His mother may endanger Pridric if his presence became a threat.

Tavelo cornered Pridric against the wall between the dressing chest and the bathing room entrance inside his chamber. The overt lust and desperation oozed from him. Pridric stared at him wide eyed as his attempts to stop him failed.

Sunrise brought hazy pale light through the windows' sheer curtains. Morning meal had yet to be announced.

"Tavelo," Pridric got his arms under his to place both hands on his sides to push him off. He didn't budge an inch, closing in. "I have to get ready for…" Tavelo's lips sealed his.

"You still haven't answered me." Tavelo said when he pulled away. His hands roamed Pridric's body, removing pieces of clothing as he went.

Once again, Pridric shifted without thought, obeying Tavelo's silent commands. A dampness formed between her thighs, and she squeezed them to stop it. Her body heat rose as he kissed her more, his tongue running along the side of her neck.

"Ahh!" She shivered, not wanting to cave so soon.

"Tell me," Tavelo whispered in her ear. His robes dropped. Pinning her to the wall, he entered her roughly. A sharp Ngh! Escaped her lips. "Be my empress," he asked again.

Pridric felt every thrust in her soul. Her eyes glazed over in ecstasy as her mouth opened.

"Don't," she strangled out, "leave," her breath shortened. "Me." Her hands went up the sides of his back and clasped his shoulders.

Tavelo's fangs grazed the flesh behind her ear. "Never," he breathed. "Say yes."

"Yes." Her voice, barely audible, "I'll be your empress."

She gave in to his brutality, tears streaming down her face.

Tavelo pushed off the wall and turned, sending them onto the bed. There he ravaged her to his heart's content well past morning meal.

Pridric felt something strange when they both were on the verge of climax. Pain. Different from before, exploded inside her at the same time Tavelo released his seed.

She thrashed beneath him, forcing him to grab hold of her arms to keep her stable. Her back arched off the bed, and she screamed, a high-pitched tone converging with it.

Tavelo knew something didn't feel right as they came together. Pridric's skin seemed on the edge of burning, heating the room itself. When she fought to get up, then convulsed, he pinned her down.

"My love, look at me. Please, hear me." The screaming emitting from her made him stiffen. "Pridric! Open your eyes!"

Her eyelids fluttered, opening for a few seconds. Tavelo hissed in despair. Kaleidoscope irises stared back at him. Volshin eyes. Her lids closed once more, and another round of thrashing commenced. This time, her screams came out garbled as if she fought to breathe.

Not wanting to let go, he had to in order to find the pressure point to still her. The released hand slammed into Tavelo's chest, almost knocking him back. He looked down and saw her tear-filled eyes pleading with him to stop the pain.

"Bear with me. I'll help you. I promise."

He found the area and pushed hard. Her body slowly went limp, her legs sliding down from his waist to land on the bed. Relief and sadness exuded from her eyes as they closed. Her head fell to one side, smearing bloody tears on the sheet below.

Still inside her, Tavelo feared to move.

He caressed her cheek, frightened and angry. Then finally snapped out of it and gently rose from the bed. At the terminal on the other side of the dresser, he hit the commlink.

"Send the royal physician to my chamber now."

He tried to sound calm, but heard the anxiety in his tone. Looking back at Pridric, Tavelo covered his mouth with one hand.

"Please. Hang on a bit longer."

The royal physician entered Tavelo's chamber with two assistants. He immediately whipped out a body scanner and positioned it over Pridric. The needle thin strobes cascade down, taking images from head to toe. His first assistant handed him a sedative gun.

"She's already asleep," Tavelo protested. Wearing only an outer robe with a sleeveless duster, he paced for a moment, then stood out of the medical group's way. "That's unnecessary."

Tavelo commended the man for arriving within a half hour of his call, considering the royal medical wing's location from the Western Imperial palace.

"I assure you, it is." The royal physician injected the drug and returned it to his assistant. Then took the tablet his second assistant handed to him. "We don't want her to awaken anytime soon."

He went through the data uploaded from the scanner and hissed. Tavelo saw his expression change from horror to anger. Four tiers of imagery displayed on the screen. Exoskeletal, muscles groups , organs, and dermis. He tapped to zoom in and used his fingers to rotate each one for a 3D view.

"I'd like to congratulate you on impregnating your mate, but the condition of her body is not ideal for spawning."

"What did you say?"

Tavelo rushed forward, his eyes glowing red. The two assistants blocked him, forcing him to halt. He moved back to the middle of the room. Recognizing his irrational behavior, he calmed himself. Pridric's condition didn't stem from what the man had done.

"She can't be moved for a few days. We must get her into the medical wing the moment she is stable."

"What's wrong with her?"

The royal physician straightened his posture and glanced over at him.

"Her insides are a mess. I've never seen anything like it. I can say that it was done intentionally." His eyes narrowed. "Her anatomy resembles a Volshin."

Tavelo nodded. "Her eyes became multicolored before she went unconscious."

"Is that so?" The royal physician's shocked face seemed almost comical. "Then it's worse than I imagined." He waved at his assistants to move and walked towards Tavelo. "Keep her warm and don't disturb her. It would cause more harm."

"Why?" Tavelo seethed. "Why is this happening?"

"Don't fret about this. I said her body wasn't ideal as it is. I never said it couldn't be remedied."

"You can fix it?" Tavelo gave him a dubious stare.

"Once we see how much damage has occurred, I can map out a plan for repair."

The three walked past Tavelo to exit the chamber. Tavelo waited until they reached its threshold before speaking.

"I thank you for coming so quickly to attend to my empress."

"Of course. We can't deny an emperor's call." The royal physician glanced back over his shoulder. "Again, my lord, do not disturb her. I hope you have more restraint than rumored."

As they left, Tavelo turned to the bed. The pain etched on Pridric's face had disappeared, and she slept soundly. Every word the royal physician said fueled his rage.

How did her body get that way?

More importantly, did Pridric know of her Volshin abilities?

How many of us lay dormant?

Down To Business

Trade Commissioner Polp skimmed the decades old contract forms from each merchant house and shook his head. Each cited standard wording with variations to accommodate the unique business of the clans. Trade with a new planet and the distribution of its goods to others required updated clauses.

"This will not do," he tsked.

He set his tablet down before him on the dark lacquered wood table. Three giant ceiling fans turned above inside the top seven merchant clans' meeting place. Nothing much had changed over the centuries. Its furnishing remained barebone, with only the main table, the chairs, and a food station.

He couldn't understand them not giving it a makeover, considering the amount of revenue they each collected.

"I'm sure they only need slight revisions." Master Callesi balked at the man's creased brow. "The main points are sound."

"A few adjustments for freight transport should be fine." Master Strana flicked his fingernails, not bothering to look up. "The entire agenda is to make a profit. Am I wrong?"

"That may be the end result, sure." Commissioner Polp tapped the tablet with one finger. "But it must be done ethically," he stared at Master Strana, "and benefits not only Cellaxa but the clients as well."

"That is what's broken now," he added.

Master Strana's eyes flashed bright red. He didn't like being singled out, yet the trade commissioner had good reason to. The other leaders gave him a quick glance, except for Master Endaga, who refused to acknowledge him throughout the meeting.

Sour grapes.

Commissioner Polp researched ways to remedy the situation and found it fell solely on the Stranas to change their ways. He looked over at Master Jaubro sitting straight at the head of the table, exuding authority. His newly tailored light grey ensemble, courtesy of the Endagas, gave an air of leadership above all others.

"I agree with the Trade Commissioner." Master Jaubro finally spoke. "A new era of trade has arrived, and we are stuck in our ways. This meeting is also a farce." Clearly insulted, the others erupted into cries of protest.

He raised a hand to silence them. When they chose to settle down, he glared at them.

"Every merchant of trade from our clans should be in attendance. Are we going to continue cutting our children out of the deals? When it was them who brought this new trade agreement with Earth to us?"

"They are still just that!" Master Boresso spat. "Children! They are not seasoned enough to take on the bulk of our trade."

"And yet, here they are doing exactly that." Master Endaga turned his glowing jing red eyes towards them. "And they did it in under a century."

Silence blanketed the room as the clan leaders stewed. The hard truth hit them in the face. Those children they sent away had come back as established merchants having learned from their elders.

A feat the leaders wanted to deny yet couldn't.

The Trade Commissioner didn't like the darkening atmosphere. He rose from his seat.

"Please draw up new contracts and schedule a meeting with me at the main office. I'll relay the same to the Earth coven merchants. An inclusive coference will take place after those appointments are complete. We will go over each one together for a better view."

He slid his tablet off the table and headed for the door. As he stepped out into the midday gloom, he raised his head to the sky.

"I look forward to see what you all come up with."

Commissioner Polp had only been gone less than a minute before Master Bryhel slammed a fist on the table.

"That pompous bureaucrat!" Her lips curled back to expose clenched teeth. The edge of her mouth moistened with drool. "How dare he come here and condescend us like that?"

"Calm yourself!" Master Jaubro scanned the room at all their faces. "What part of his words were false? Enlighten me."

"He's assuming we don't know how to operate our businesses," Master Strana replied.

"No," Master Jaubro locked eyes with him. "He knows we are not on the same page. And that some of us cause harm with back handed deals violating said contracts."

"I propose we talk with our children before our appointments to get an idea of what they have in mind." Master Boresso said. "That way we can steer them towards our agenda."

"Absolutely not." Master Endaga planted his hands flat on the table and pushed himself up. "You didn't hear one thing being discussed. All of you missed the point entirely."

"Indeed." Master Callesi nodded in agreement.

"If you're going to speak with them, open your minds to learn something new," Master Endaga snapped.

He walked off, not bothering to say goodbye.

The rest of the clan leaders fidgeted around a few minutes more before Master Jaubro called the end of the meeting.

"Let's think on what's needed and adjourn for now. There's much to go over."

He too rose, followed by the rest. They walked out into the sun trying to pierce the clouds, giving off a harsh light grey that hurt their eyes. Another fine Cellaxa day ripe for commerce.

The offspring of the merchants' offspring.

Children running businesses with their own.

The Trade Commissioner shook his head again, fascinated by the situation at hand. He sipped from a fancy chalice filled halfway with a hard Earth liquor Holnar called bourbon. Though tasty, it burned his throat going down. His eyes stung from the assault.

Holnar laughed.

"Good, strong stuff, yes?"

"How do you get used to something like this?" Commissioner Polp smacked his lips. "Or is the pain the purpose?"

"Something like that." Holnar glanced over at the rest of the occupants in the room.

"Well, I guess we should get started then." He set his chalice on the small table between them and turned slightly sideways in his chair. "Good evening."

Scattered before him in the Marchand Company's meeting room, every coven leader and their offspring involved in trade waited for him to speak. He noticed Emperor Tavelo and Pridric Strana sent proxies. Understandable. Each leader had various Earth liquors in their glasses. He would ask later to try each one.

"As you may have heard, the revenue meeting with the top merchants concluded days ago. Your numbers were not a factor. I wish to remedy that, along with setting up both docks to accommodate every shipment."

"And how do you plan to separate the data?" Darean raised his hand, so he knew who spoke. "Or are you lumping us all together?"

"No, no!" Commissioner Polp waved a hand. "I want to keep yours, your children, and the current merchants as individual streams. The combined revenue will reflect the family clan status for trade purposes."

"So, we're still being pushed under the umbrella of our parents," Yutel huffed.

"It can't be helped. Whether you trade on Earth or on some other planet, you're still part of your clans."

"You want to create new regulations taken from our input on rewriting the contracts." Holnar said.

"Correct. I must warn you, your elders are not quite on board. Except for the Endagas and Jaubros." He could see frowns, and lips curl to reveal fangs. Such a touchy subject. "Regardless, we at the trade commission needs the data."

"We will contact you when we're ready to set up our meetings."

Holnar seemed a capable leader. Commissioner Polp approved.

"Good, good." He grimaced at the chalice and decided to toss the whole contents down his throat to avoid insulting his host. The burn intensified, leaving him gasping for air as he set the empty glass down. "Ergh!" He grabbed his chest, feeling the heat explode through him.

Chuckles erupted. Holnar reached over to pat him hard on the back.

"That's the spirit! Take it like a warrior."

I'll take a pass on trying them all for now.

A servant came to escort them out, and he took one last look at the newly minted Cellaxa merchants.

Children. Trade was about to get exciting.

Holnar waited a few minutes after the trade commissioner left to address the others. He stepped off the small platform, no longer needing to show dominance for the man.

"Now that, that's over," he plopped down at the table with his finance person and personal assistant. "Let's talk timelines."

"The East docks are almost complete. Coven crests should be done soon as well to attach to the bays." Darean's head of production scrolled on his tablet, reviewing data. "I think we should have had them made on Earth first and shipped here."

"That would be an insult to the craftsmen here." Eterenia leaned forward. "We must utilize Cellaxa in its entirety if we want to gain respect."

"So, the trade commission wants to see what kind of contracts we all come up with up and take the finer points to heart." Yutel's mouth downturned. "Hmm. I've got the feeling our parents have a few nefarious conditions in theirs."

"That's a given. It's also why new contracts must be created." Holnar exhaled loudly. He looked over at his own children. "We say it's not a competition. But I see otherwise. Just as we wish to gain our elders' respect, you should strive to gain ours."

"I won't tolerate excuses and weak dealings from my bloodline," Darean announced tersely.

"We wouldn't have it any other way, old man," Chase snickered, his eyes blood red.

Holnar saw Darean and the other leaders perk up at the dig. Old? Surely that brat jests!

"Careful," Eterenia chided them. She, too, took offense, letting her glowing red eyes lock with Chase's. "Our bite is much stronger than yours."

"Bring it on," Tamar replied, raising his chin in defiance.

Holnar burst out laughing, startling everyone. Within seconds, more followed. Wiping tears from his eyes as he calmed himself, he nodded.

"Let's see how business savvy you are then, brats."

Chase led the other offspring leaders out of the meeting room into the courtyard of the Marchand estate house. It overlooked a cliff where the city below came into view. He took a deep breath and turned to face them.

"And now we have to show some real chops."

He frowned.

"I didn't even think about Cellaxa trade contracts!" One of Chalayl's three daughters wailed. "We simply copied our parents to get the ball rolling."

"Yeah, we really need to go through all of it. I'm sure we're invisible to the head merchants." Tamar paced for a bit then stopped, tapping his lower lip. "We need to see the current regulations."

"The trade commissioner would gladly send us a copy when asked." Chase sighed. "Who wants to comb through it and share the main points?"

Four hands rose in the air. Good. Chase felt relief for not needing to volunteer someone. Baltise stood beside him with a concerned expression.

"What is it?" Chase probed her face for a hint.

"The Strana clan. I feel like they want to destroy us. But why?"

"I think you're over-analyzing this. I'm not sure that's their agenda."

Chase had met Pridric's older brother, Pravin, the new Master of the Strana clan. He seemed cordial at first, giving limited advice during the battle. Now the entire clan appeared hostile. Dangerous.

And gunning for Pridric.

"I hope so." Baltise turned away. "But I don't think so either."

Fair enough. Olivier eyed him from across the field of flowers. We got our work cut out.

The East docks activity doubled with the daily installation of the final structures. Unlike the main docks in the West with simple merchant markers, each company bay would have the coven crest of its owners above them. Directly beneath, lay a smaller emblem for the offspring companies replicated on the bay next to the parent one.

Workers barked orders at the machine operators to guide them. The promenade spanned the entire length of the pier, the last few feet left to finish. Newly built compartments gleamed in the sunlight peeking through the clouds.

All Cellaxa could see it.

Tavelo stared out his throne room's window, his arms crossed while he watched the progress of the docks. He received the report from the trade commissioner's meetings and agreed to the plan. Right now, he couldn't focus.

Pridric still lay unconscious, incubating with his spawn, her internal body a mess. The royal physicians opted to keep her sedated for now until they assessed all the damage they found. There were only two outcomes. Either the Stranas were truly monsters, or some injury caused it.

Both options possible.

Tavelo gripped his biceps, feeling his nails dig into the fabric of his robe sleeves. He didn't try to fool himself into thinking it the former. Dania checked on Pridric daily while he went about his emperor duties. He also ordered a trusted group of coven agents to search for the Strana spy, who he knew lurked within the palace. The way Pridric kept hidden most of the time clued him in on the reason.

He brought his focus back to the docks. The Durante crest hovered in the air, suspended from rungs on an industrial crane. In bold letters, the coven motto glinted clearly for all to read.

Stability that lasts and endures. To always help those in need.

The same applied to the Endaga clan.

Their convictions both helped and hindered them in trade. And in life. None of them regretted that path. Rejecting advice from greedy merchants to go the same route as the others.

"Marveling at the construction?" Manel entered his throne room with Gallic by his side.

Tavelo turned to look over his shoulder. Although Manels demeanor oozed the usual malice, his pale complexion and altered gait gave away his condition. The royal council appointed most of the imperial tasks to him instead of dividing them amongst the monarchs.

With Pridric out of commission for a while, he still had Innego, Eterenia, his uncle and Tamar on his side of the court. Manel had four siblings to aid him as well.

"It's not going fast enough for my taste. And the merchant clan leaders are making a fuss."

"Yes, they don't like competition." Manel stood next to him. "Especially when it's their own blood relations leveling the playing field. I must say, those crests are genius. A lot of the other merchant clans are envious."

"My family has no qualms about the Durante brand, nor that."

"Because the Endaga clan is too nice." Manel's brow scrunched as he squinted from a headache.

"You need to rest." Tavelo waited for him to turn his head, so they stared at each other. "I mean it." He pointed to Gallic. "Why are you not taking care of your emperor and mate?"

"Don't you dare accuse him of not doing his duty." Manel frowned angrily.

"I won't apologize because I'm right."

"You can say that since you don't have as many duties. I must attend two more meetings this day before evening meal."

Manel's heated tone angered Tavelo more.

"No."

Manel's head tilted back in surprise.

It took a moment for him to regain his composure. "What?"

Tavelo turned away from him to face Gallic.

"Take him back to his chamber. You are not to let him leave until evening meal."

"You don't…" Manel got out before Tavelo glared at him.

"Lendor and Tamar will take your place at the meetings. I'm sick of the unbalanced agendas from the royal council. We rule as one, not separate."

Gallic swept Manel in his arms and headed for the entrance. Manel struggled for a few seconds, not having the will to harm his mate, then relented. Tavelo sighed. Right as he went back to the window, Innego walked in. He glanced behind him at Gallic carrying Manel down the corridor, then raised his brow at Tavelo.

"Who's the emperor again?" Innego quipped, letting out a chuckle.

"We both are."

"True. You wouldn't know it though." Innego looked out at the docks. "Progress?"

"Hmm."

"I wanted to let you know. I'm going to have a look at the royal guards' training. It seems Tervan is interested in a merger."

"And you think it's a bad idea."

"Compared to the lower ranked soldiers, Tervan is an infant. The two of us are not much better."

Tavelo pinched the bridge of his nose. Trade, infrastructure, imperial duties. Politics. He hated all of it, yet he vowed to make Cellaxa better than it had been the past few centuries.

"How about you go see Pridric and get an update on our beloved new Empress?"

"I have a…" Tavelo took a breath as Innego gave him a terse stare.

"That's what I am here for. Go." Innego swung his arm out towards the entrance.

Not needing to be told twice, Tavelo exited his throne room in haste.

Inside the royal medical bay, the silence weighed heavily in the air. Tavelo's skin prickled, giving him anxiety. He reached the private area where two royal physicians catered to Pridric. Her frail body lay still, a small bump raised from her belly. The only sound came from the soft blips of the monitoring equipment.

A holoscreen displaying her anatomy in 3D tiers hovered above her head.

"Emperor Tavelo," the first physician greeted him as he finished administering another round of sedatives. "You're here early. Lady Dania just left moments ago."

"I decided my Empress was more important today."

"Of course."

"What have you found out?"

The two physicians eyed each other for a moment. Dania came into the room.

"My apologies. I forgot my cell." She stopped short, letting Tavelo's question linger. "Yes. I want to know the reason too." She turned to Tavelo. "Am I permitted to stay?"

Tavelo nodded.

The physicians stood on the other side of the bed. The first brought out his tablet and scrolled through data until he found his notes.

"Our findings are nothing short of horrific. It appears a procedure to sever her Volshin traits was performed not long after coming of age."

Tavelo's eyes turned red.

Dania cried out, clamping a hand over her mouth before removing it.

"Why? For what purpose?"

Then he stopped himself.

Dania and the physicians stared at him.

Of course, he knew the answer. The Stranas were trying to eradicate the gene from their bloodline.

"I'm afraid it gets worse." The second physician laid a hand palm up over Pridric's belly. "it followed another. The extraction of an unborn."

Tavelo's eyes dimmed as the color drained from his face. Dania turned to him in confusion.

"What did you say?" Tavelo whispered.

"The surgery can only be described as butchery. Whoever did it showed no regard for preserving the womb."

"Almost as if they wanted to make sure it would never function again.," the first physician added.

"So that's why." Tavelo faltered, stumbling back into the barricade separating the area from the rest. "Pridric had no choice but to reject me. To hate me."

Dania came to him and slapped him hard, forcing his head to the side. The physicians' eyes bulged in terror. Tavelo turned silver glowing eyes at her, then shrunk back. Dania glared furiously at him.

"Is that pity?" She yelled. "Do you think Pridric wanted that?" She stepped back. "I always knew something didn't seem right. Pridric never discussed our clan. But they seemed to have an iron grip on him, even on Earth."

She clenched her fists and went back to stand by the physicians.

"I'm sorry for striking you. Please accept my apology, Emperor Tavelo." She bowed.

"Stop!" Tavelo straightened his posture and went over to the bed. He placed a hand on Pridric's cheek. "You did nothing wrong. I needed that. Deserved it." He removed his hand and brought his attention back to the physicians. "Can it really be repaired?"

"Not fully. We can only do so much during her gestation period. The rest we can complete two years after she spawns."

The first physician sat on the nearby stool. "This will be a dangerous birth."

Tavelo and Dania left the medical wing, into the main corridor. Both remained silent for a long stretch as they walked, nodding to passersby who addressed them. Halfway to the throne room, Tavelo halted. Dania came up next to him.

"The Strana spy in the palace." Tavelo stared ahead. "I think they are trying to snatch him and take him back into their fold."

"Pridric would fight this time." Dania frowned. "They either brainwash him or," she turned to him. "They'll kill him. Especially now that Pridric carries an Endaga spawn."

"That is my conclusion as well."

"Why do they hate your family so much to this extent? I don't understand it."

"Neither do I."

Tavelo resumed walking and Dania followed.

Their silence spoke to a mutual agreement. They would protect Pridric at all costs.

For the first time, three generations of trade merchants converged under one roof. The inside of the community building had additional furnishings to accommodate their number. Two more conference tables, along with snack and beverage stations, filled the room. Instead of the merchants helping themselves, four servants waited for their requests.

Commissioner Polp didn't want any interruptions or distractions during the meeting. On the massive wall behind him, the holoscreen displayed the Cellaxa Trade insignia. As soon as all parties were seated, he would begin his presentation. He noticed the divide at each table.

The elders sat at one, the Earth coven leaders at another, and their offspring took the last.

He expected as much.

They had their own entities with different trade products. A few similar goods, but distinct features made them custom. Even the elders' experience seemed low, many not yet six hundred years old. Again, children. Every last one of them, in his opinion. The new generation, mere infants.

He sighed heavily, adjusting his deep purple robe, almost black. A custom made Endaga wardrobe he ordered for the occasion. The velvet-like fabric from Earth felt smooth and lavish. Embroidered gold lines ran vertically down the sleeves and front. The puffy upper sleeve part gave him full motion or his arms.

An Endaga tailor of the Earth coven told him the design came from the planet's Renaissance period.

The matching hat had a plume sticking out from one side. He felt important. And fancy.

Servants moved swiftly towards the tables with drinks in hand atop trays. They distributed the non-alcoholic fare to everyone. No spirits until after the meeting. A slight taste permitted during intermission if they all behaved. Which, by the furrowed brows and scowls, made it unlikely.

Again, Pridric and Tavelo remained absent. He understood that. Having an emperor roam the streets for a simple merchant meeting would cause chaos on the streets. The logistics alone made him shudder. He glanced over at their proxies. Chancellor Rayne and Armon, the vampire. Armon's age put him on the same level as the elders.

I'm sure they don't like that little tidbit.

The low voices ordering snack platters from the servants died out, and the room went silent. Only their shuffling while the merchants heaped food items on the miniature plates echoed.

They shouldn't be stuffing their faces either.

The trade commissioner scoffed inwardly.

With a drink and plate in front of each attendee, the trade commissioner clapped his hands for their attention. They all focused on him.

Good, good.

"A lovely morning to you all. I appreciate your participation in this meeting. It will be extensive and last the day." He heard groans. "Important matters that involve our planet's commerce takes time."

"As long as we're done before evening meal," Master Boresso said, tersely.

"If it does not, we will bring service here." He stared the woman down. "Is that acceptable? Good." He didn't give her a chance to counter. "Now, let's begin." Her eyes glowed red as he turned away.

Hmph!

The holoscreen's image changed to display three documents, side by side.

"As you can see, there were major differences in trade documents. The first is the standard contract the merchant families have used for centuries. The center is from the merchants dealing with Earth goods. On the end is also derived from Earth trade, yet it has new tiers that benefit Earth. This document the offspring created."

Soft hissing and angry whispers spread.

This marked the first time seeing each other's contracts. A transparency rule he implemented during the individual talks. He found the children's' negotiation skills promising. It needed work just like their parents' confusing verbiage.

"Trade should benefit every party involved. No need for underhanded tactics." He eyed the new Master Strana. Pravin raised his glass as if toasting him, his irises glinting red. "Or other shady dealings that do nothing for the greater good."

His glare found Master Boresso still miffed.

"It's clear that the Earth coven merchants took sections from the original and made it their own. The problem stems from certain regulations weren't translated in kind. Whereas, your offspring created a new one without any input transferred from the old."

Holograms of the three forms popped up in front of each person for better scrutiny. More frowns from the elders followed by amusement from the youngest merchants.

"Such innovation on the infants' part." Master Dakien laughed. "There is room for improvement."

The offspring bristled at the term. The trade commissioner stifled a chuckle. They shouldn't be surprised after all this time. None had yet to turn one hundred.

"So, what?" Master Callesi asked tentatively. "You want us to adopt their methods?"

The protests got an octave higher. Commissioner Polp held up a hand to squash it.

"I'm merely pointing out each one's strengths and weaknesses. No need to worry about brainstorming a new contract. We've already done so."

The screen changed yet again to a new document. Its pages overlapped, creating a stacking illusion. The same replaced the holograms with scrolling enabled. He saw fingers swiping through the documents.

"The trade commission took all of your contracts into account and assembled a new standard with room to customize for your businesses."

A deafening silence blanketed the room. He felt mounting fear and rage mingling in the air. The competition for dominance had begun.

The original plan, suggested by Emperor Tavelo, for shipments on the West docks split and reroute to the East, eventually got scrapped. And rightly so. Gauging the animosity in the room, that scenario would be detrimental to trade.

The new configuration worked best.

"According to these documents, we are banned from using the East docks." Master Strana said.

"Only in cases of emergency. That is correct," Commissioner Polp replied.

"And we must get permission from?"

Master Strana's glare seared into him.

"The bay owner you wish to use."

"So we must ask those children for access?" Master Callesi frowned. "This is absurd."

"The same goes for them if they needed to use the West bays." Commissioner Polp severed his gaze from Master Strana. "This goes both ways. I see no problem here."

"Neither do we." Holnar glanced over at the other coven leaders. They nodded in agreement. "As long as you don't interfere in our business, we won't have our hands in yours."

More tweaks were made to the final forms before the meeting ended with an hour left until evening meal. In a rush to get home, they fled from the community building to their transports waiting outside. When it seemed the end was in sight, they had called ahead. A slew of transports lined the streets outside the building. The trade commissioner watched them scurry like insects to get away.

He turned to see the offspring rising leisurely from the table. They walked towards the doors, bowing, and saying thank you to him. It took him off guard.

"Wait." He stopped them from reaching the threshold. They turned to him. "I wanted to praise you for your candor and patience. This was no easy thing to accomplish. I wish you great success and hope you bring prosperity to Cellaxa."

"No need to worry about that." Chase gave a smile. "We intend to do just that. This may not be our birthplace, but it is the home of our origin."

They continued to the streets below.

Commissioner Polp felt a sense of pride. It soured a bit thinking about the past deeds of the Strana and Boresso clan. Would they use their usual tactics on their younger spawns and their offspring?

I need to find a suitable penalty to deter such acts.

He turned to his assistant, who blended in with the servants.

"Make sure you send all the recordings and forms to the Emperors." The assistant nodded. "What is your take on this?"

The assistant cocked his head and set the stack of dirty plates on the side table before him. He wiped his hands on the tablecloth.

"I think the separation would be good for the elders. They will see how differently this new generation of merchants work. A cautionary tale, if you may."

"Ah, yes." Commissioner Polp rubbed his chin. "Let's have the reroute start immediately. Which shipments are arriving soon?"

The assistant pulled a mini tablet from behind his back where he had it tucked in the waistband. He scrolled through the incoming manifests.

"Earth goods from houses Greiger, Ambrook, and Durante."

"Are those bays operational on the East?"

"I believe Greiger is still in construction."

"Speed it up. And make sure the docking stations are fully operational as well. We don't want any last minute issues with ships landing."

"A smooth transport?"

"Always."

"May I make a cruel suggestion?"

Commissioner Polp gave him a curious stare.

"Oh? What did you have in mind?"

"Let the Earth shipments go through the West docks. When it is clear the elders cannot handle the logistics, we will have the goods transported to the East docks for proper receiving."

"Why, that's ..." The trade commissioner's lips curved into a devious grin. "Genius. I like it. It will put a craw in their ego."

"Take them down a notch. Especially the Stranas . They're determined to absorb Ambrook contracts."

"Pfft!" Commissioner Polp waved dismissively. "Master Strana needs a personality adjustment."

"I will contact the construction company to redo the timeline." His assitant turned to lift the plates.

Commissioner Polp clapped his hands.

"You have more pressing matter to attend to. Leave those for the actual servants."

"Of course." The assistant tucked his mini tablet under one arm and exited the building. "I will send you a report when the details are finalized."

Commissioner Polp eyed the untouched liquor being stored back in the cabinets. He approached the servants in charge.

"May I have a glass of that one before you're done?" He pointed to a bottle of dark liquor.

"Of course, your grace." The servant holding the bottle turned to get a glass tumbler and poured it halfway. "Will this suffice?"

"Oh, yes. That's plenty." He took the glass from her, stepping out of the way so they could resume their work. The harsh liquid burned as it went down, the heat easing out to a soothing warmth. "Ahh!"

The meeting never calmed down enough for him to permit spirits. He counted his stars for averting a bloodbath. One thing he noticed over the past two centuries since the demise of the clans. Their brood were not as civilized and cordial when they assumed the master roles.

Even Dakien and Endaga bordered on ruthless, though nowhere near what the new Strana and Boresso engaged in. It hurt him internally to see how they all had fallen.

"The rest is up to you, Emperor Tavelo."

He raised his glass, then finished it.

Handing the glass to a nearby servant, he too left the community building. There was trade to run.

The grey stone of the bridge matched the gloom of the sky. Its curve sat twenty feet above the river below. Gurgling sounds of water rushing between the rocky shoreline soothed the mind. Muted sunlight turned the water into a layer of glassy waves.

Tamar breathed in the fresh air, tilting his head up. He pulled his robes tighter to stop the chill. Olivier walked beside him in silence, taking in his surroundings. Only two other couples strolled along the riverbank on the bridge. Not quite midday, most people were at home relaxing before afternoon meal.

"Have you decided to let someone else be kind to you?" Olivier blurted unexpectedly.

Tamar glanced at him while still facing the sky.

"Huh?" Then he understood. "That's not what it was. I just needed…" he couldn't find the word.

"I would have comforted you. Why didn't you come to me?"

"Because." Tamar lowered his head. "You wanted more than that."

"Is that a bad thing? You know I've always pined for you."

"I wasn't ready." Tamar hung his head. "I didn't want to burden you with my shit."

Olivier laughed, holding a hand to his chest as tears squeezed from the corners of his eyes.

"Tamar." He straightened his posture, wiping his eyes. "We have been entangled in each other's shit for a long time."

"Hehe, true." Tamar smiled. "And you still want me after all this?"

Olivier stepped in front of him, forcing him to stop. They locked eyes.

"I will always want you." Tamar tried to turn away to hide his tears. Olivier gently bring him back to his gaze using two fingers. "You should know that."

They continued walking until the bridge ended at the main road that crossed it. To the left were the sectors leading to the new merchant houses.

Olivier nodded that way. Tamar hesitated for a moment before relenting.

After forty minutes of walking, they reached the Marchand estate nestled by a sparse forest. Coven members guarded the entrance. Olivier walked up and they opened it for him.

"All good so far?" Olivier asked the guard on the right.

"Quiet as the dawn," he replied.

Olivier and Tamar maneuvered the halls, nodding to people on the way. A few of the women took in Tamar's presence as a sign and gave him a knowing stare.

What the hell? He brushed it off. I mean, I do want to. It's why we came here. He had no shame in getting what he wanted.

For so long, he simply did what others told him, not caring about his own state of wellness. He liked mating. It killed time and made him feel better afterwards. Nothing spectacular. He rarely climaxed and even then it seemed lackluster.

They finally reached Olivier's chamber located in the farthest corner of the compound. No other chamber could be found in the hallway.

Tamar entered cautiously.

A dark room with a bare two square foot window letting in minimal daylight. Its shine gave the room a hazy glow. Heavy drapes covered the other window and the walls around it. Black bedding with sheer white sheets peeking underneath added to the aesthetic.

Close to the bare window sat an enormous bed with the mattress at Tamar's waist. He looked for a step stool because how else would anyone get on it?

When he turned to inquire, he saw Olivier pulling his tunic over his head. The cloak and robe long gone. Tamar stared in awe at Olivier's physique. Bryhels and Boresso's were known for their stocky bodies.

Built for combat and manual labor.

He had never noticed how much taller Olivier was until now.

Broad shoulders, a barrel chest with six-pack abs, and biceps that could lift a boulder. Tamar felt his mouth salivate. This meant Olette wasn't some skinny violet. The twins were matched in height and stature, their clothes now interpreted to slim them down. Make them less intimidating.

"Why are you staring at me like a piece of meat?" Olivier asked, startling Tamar from his stupor. "I'm not waiting any longer."

The moment Olivier touched him, Tamar shifted into female form. It surprised even them how fast it happened. He stripped her naked in seconds and tossed Tamar onto the bed. Where she would need stairs, Olivier simply climbed on.

Tamar glanced at Olivier's cock emerging from the folds and felt her eyes bulge at its size. Rumors about his sexual prowess among the coven wenches came to light. I guess it wasn't all lies. She caught Olivier's eyes. He grinned.

"What? You act like you've never seen a big one before." His eyes glinted. "And we know that's not the case."

Tamar opened her mouth to speak and didn't get the chance. Olivier grabbed one of her legs under the knee and dragged her to him. He leaned over, entering her at the same time. The girth of his member felt like a trench being dug inside her. She gasped, crying out in pain.

"Almost," Olivier breathed in her ear. His sinister tone made her tense. "No. don't do that." He repositioned her body so that she couldn't again and it slid in further. "That's better."

"Ahh!!" Tamar turned her head. "Fuck!" She tried to breathe.

"Exactly." Olivier rose above her, pushing his hips so that her thighs wrapped around them. "You'll never experience mating like this with Innego."

His eyes glowed a brilliant blue.

"Or anyone else."

Each thrust sent Tamar into a plane of euphoria and pain. Olivier was right. She had never been taken like an animal in heat.

And she liked it.

Evening meal in the royal dining hall grew tense as Manel stared at Tavelo with an animal lust. Gallic averted his gaze, not wanting to make a scene. Tavelo halted his fork midway to his mouth. He lowered it and glared at Manel.

"Stop! You're making everyone uncomfortable."

"Hmm?" Manel grinned. "Am I not tempting you enough?"

"You shouldn't be trying at all. I've already told you no."

"No to what?" Master Endaga asked.

"Yes, what indeed?" Maxellia snorted.

"I proposed we mated to create a hybrid," Manel replied sweetly. Utensils clanked onto plates as they dropped from people's hands. "A Volshin and Kataling. What do you think it would be like? Would one gene dominate the other?"

"That is," Maxellia yelled, "madness!"

Everyone sat horrified by the idea. They stared at Manel as if he had gone insane. Again.

"Absolutely not!" Tavelo answered, his irises blood red. "Stop asking."

"Where does such a notion even come from?" Maxellia cried out.

"One of your father's list of experiments," Tavelo snapped.

Manel frowned.

He didn't like the way everyone's expression turned sour. Megen leaned back from the table's edge, folding his arms.

"I've said it before." Tavelo picked up his fork. "There's no reason for any of you to continue his will. Hasn't Cellaxa and the royal family suffered enough atrocities?"

"It has nothing to do with that," Manel muttered. His lips drew back, showing clenched teeth. "That's not what I'm doing!"

"Then why?" Master Endaga's eyes widened as he spoke.

"Curiosity?" Manel's face turned playful, his head tilting to one side.

Tavelo shoved the fork in his mouth, not wanting to entertain the idea any longer. Innego's lips went thin and became a lopsided grin.

"Yeah. We really shouldn't go there." He turned to Tervan sitting quietly at the end of the row. "Though it's probably too late for that."

Manel's gaze landed on Tervan.

"Ahh. Tavelo, your son is mated to a Kataling." This time, Tavelo dropped his fork. Manel placed an elbow on the table and leaned forward, his chin resting on the back of his hand. "With Tervan having possibly dormant Volshin abilities, I might get my hybrid after all."

Tervan's face paled. He kept his head lowered, not wanting to see the glee in Manel's eyes, feeling it in the air.

"Manel!" Tavelo warned him.

The corners of Manel's eyes crinkled.

Innego already regretted hinting at the possibility.

The bright rays of grey gloom struggled to squeeze through slit openings in Tervan's heavy curtains. He lay in bed watching the dim light move across the room, casting shadows. His breathing stayed slow and steady. A routine he began the moment he woke up in a mild panic.

Reliving the conversation at that evening meal, heightening his anxiety. Calm. Closing his eyes, Tervan took a few deep breaths before opening them again. His vision adjusted to see the hazy gloom permeate the room. Everything in the barely furnished chamber looked heavy.

Why did I decorate it like this? Caden's hand slid over his chest, pressing her naked body closer to him. He glanced at the weighted blanket keeping them both warm. That's the reason. Caden made him feel grounded. My own sense of security.

The small bump of Caden's belly against his side brought fear.

"What is it?" Caden whispered. Her warm breath caressed the side of his face, heating his ear. "You feel tense." She squeezed tighter.

"You missed the awful conversation last cycle during a royal meal."

"Hmm?" Her body relaxed.

You shouldn't feel so safe with me!

"Apparently the old ruler had a wild agenda for ancient ones. Emperor Manel's been trying to coerce my father into making it a reality."

"What kind of horror is he promoting now?" Caden mumbled, not seeming to really care.

"A hybrid." Caden went still. "Of Kataling and Volshin."

"Is that so?" Her squeeze was not gentle.

"I may be a dormant Volshin."

Caden stayed silent for a long time. Tervan got nervous when her grip loosened.

"I never thought about that," she breathed. "I only wanted to be with you."

"I know. We're not some experiment for Emperor Manel to exploit."

Caden's leg slid between his as she rolled onto him. She locked her eyes with his and folded her arms under her chin. So beautiful! The extra weight showed in her face, making her cheeks a bit puffy.

Her skin had a healthy glow.

"We're not. It's not about what they want."

Tervan stared into her amber irises, seeing the tiny spokes within. He bent his head and gave her a quick kiss before smacking her on the side of her ass.

"We have to get up. There's much to be done."

Caden smirked. "You mean more spying in the palace?" She rose to straddle him. The blanket fell behind her. The air grazed Tervan's chest. "I really don't want you getting in more fights with thosee imperial guards." Her expression grew dark.

Tervan turned his head.

"Why does everyone continue to harp on that?"

"Because it was foolish on your part." She slid from the bed, letting the room's coolness attack his now exposed body. Come back! He wasn't ready to release her yet. "I'll join you today." She looked over her shoulder as she walked to the wardrobe and winked. "Keep you out of trouble for once."

Her recent bouts of cheekiness shocked him. She showed it to no one else. In public, Caden was brooding, secretive, and rarely spoke. With him, laughter added to the mix.

Tervan reluctantly swung his legs from under the blanket, planting his feet on the plush carpet surrounding the bed. He would never tolerate having bare floors that retained the cold. Wiggling his toes, he stood and walked over to Caden.

No one addressed the topic at morning meal. Innego gave Tervan an apologetic stare.The same one he gave every time he saw him. He noticed his father didn't look at him the entire time. Emperor Manel's creepy gaze stayed glued on him and Caden.

A diabolical expression of longing that bordered on sexual.

At the end of the meal, he grabbed hold of Caden's hand and fled from the room. Ignoring the protest of his father who rose to stop them from leaving.

"That was rude," Caden chided him.

"Don't care. Not dealing with their drama today."

"Then, can you slow down and ease up on my hand?"

Tervan halted.

He turned to her with wide-eyed shame.

"I'm sorry." He loosened his grip, seeing her hand had turned pink from being squeezed. His other hand caressed her cheek. "I never want to hurt you." He leaned over so their foreheads touched. "Forgive me."

"No." Caden's eyes glowed softly. "You have to do better than that to make it up to me."

Tervan let out a small laugh. "Hah!" He straightened his stance. "You're right."

They strolled through the palace, taking in the sprawling gardens on the other side of the wall windows lining the halls. At a leisurely pace, they covered the first half of the west wing. When Tervan noticed the time, they headed back towards the east side for the next meeting.

Nearing the narrower corridor that linked the two wings, Caden yawned. The long walk may have been a bit much. A group of imperial guards were walking in the opposite direction towards them. Tervan recognized the man in front.

Well, shit.

He felt Caden's demeanor shift, stiffening.

"Oh, if it isn't the East emperor's inept spawn," the leader laughed. "Done with your royal duties? Off to babysit?" he smirked. "You can at least handle that, can't you? Since you're so poor with swords."

"Clear a path," Caden demanded. "We don't have time for your jokes. We have an important meeting to attend."

"Shut it, you worthless beast!" The man's outburst froze Tervan. "Just because you laid with that Volshin emperor's spawn doesn't mean we have to listen to you."

Caden's eyes turned red, her fangs growing as she stepped forward, meeting the man's stare. Before Tervan could pull her away, the head guard shoved her back.

"Move aside," the head guard ordered. "We have jurisdiction on the west."

Caden's body went backwards.

She regained for footing too late to stop Tervan. He crashed into the head guard, pushing him into the others. They flailed their arms to prevent falling. The head guard barely got his footing back when Tervan punched him in the chest.

He felt his fist make contact with the breast plate under his robes. A dent in the metal showed when the head guard whipped off his cloak.

"Endaga trash!"

The head guard attacked him viciously, not giving him an opening to strike. The other guards moved to join. Caden extended her talons and went into a squat position. They backed off, not wanting to deal with a morphing Kataling.

"What is the meaning of this?" Lendor yelled from the end of the corridor.

Which startled Tervan.

The head guard took advantage, reaching behind him to pull out a short blade. He shoved it right between the ribs under Tervan's armpit. With a battle cry, he pushed him into the wall.

"Stop!" Lendor flashed forward.

Caden let out a shriek, tearing the head guard from Tervan. The blade went with him as he slammed into the opposite wall.

Tervan felt his body suddenly go weak as his temperature rose. Something inside him bloomed like an explosion.

Oh no! Are you shitting me?

Every vein in his body felt like needles flowed through them. Did that freak emperor manifest this when he spoke about it?

The way his bones shifted, sending a pain he couldn't describe, he knew what was happening. That asshole! The last thought he had before his mind went blank.

When he raised his head, clutching his wound, his vision turned multicolored. Wings protruded from his back and a different kind of cry came from his lips. Even he inwardly flinched at the high pitch. He pushed himself off the wall, heading for the head guard getting to his feet.

His moment was short lived.

Lendor got between them and rammed a syringe in Tervan's neck, pushing the plunger as he did. Tervan's body stopped as if turned off by a switch.

Blackness engulfed him.

"Pick him up!" Lendor commanded his guards. "Get him to the royal physician!" He whirled on the imperial guards. "I hope this pettiness you entertained was worth being expelled from your positions."

The head guard seethed. His eyes glowed red as he stared down Lendor. The others stood immobile, shocked at his words.

"It's a small wound!" the first yelled. "If he can't handle a short bout of conflict…"

"You murdered him in plain sight," Lendor snapped. "The only reason he lives is because it triggered his ancient blood." He watched Caden silently follow his guards carrying Tervan. That alone frightened him. What is that child thinking? He brought his attention back to the imperial guards. "If he had truly expired, both emperors would have executed you immediately."

More guards arrived and circled the culprits. Lendor turned from them and headed to the royal medical wing.

"Take them to the dungeon. I will have Megen deal with them later."

He didn't look back at the struggle that ensued.

The sound of angry shouts and bodies clashing let him know they were resisting.

How stupid.

By the time he reached the royal medical wing, the head technician had notified Tavelo and Eterenia. He didn't want to wait for them to arrive, but knew he had to explain the situation. The physician leaned over the scan and turned his head to Lendor.

"You stopped his Volshin form from completing."

"Was I supposed to wait until he took out the corridor with his size?"

"I doubt he'd have grown that much, not being a hundred years old yet." Caden glowered at him. The physician gave him a confused glance. "Why are you upset? You're not that much different."

The doors slid open to let Tavelo and Eterenia inside the ward. Lendor saw Tavelo's eyes widen in fear as he zeroed in on the wound. He turned to him. The physician walked over.

"Emperor Tavelo," he bowed his head low then raised it. "Rest assure, we are stabilizing him. You know quite well what kind of death he experienced. He is sedated."

Eterenia's fangs and talons grew. Drool filled the corners of her mouth.

"Who did this?"

Tavelo's eyes had turned silver, causing Lendor and the technicians to step back. Her action terrified them. Lendor knew he needed to extinguish her rage for now.

"Do not fret." He raised a hand, signaling for her to remain calm. She took offense. I get that. "The guards in question are being sent to the dungeon."

"I want their heads on a spike!" Eterenia cried out.

Tavelo went rigid. Stunned by the suggestion, knowing how their parents' bodies were displayed on the palace grounds.

As if realizing it too, her expression fell.

"As their superior, Megen will judge them. Since

Tervan is still with us, execution would be an over-reaction. Please see reason."

Lendor glanced back at Tervan's unconscious form. Then he looked over at Caden's slightly pro-truding belly.

Gods of Cellaxa! What will happen now?

CHAPTER TWO

Booming Commerce

With news of a new planet to trade with grew amongst the other systems, Earth goods became popular as novelties. For contact information and delivery, they had to go through Cellaxa merchants. Commissioner Polp voiced his excitement every time an order confirmed in the books shipped.

Business boomed.

That also meant policing the bad doers cropping up from their trade system's outer regions. Nefarious races sniffed around, looking for an angle to cut into deals. As the lead merchant clan, part of the Jaubros' responsibility lay in keeping tabs on the situation.

Master Jaubro assigned sectors for his top family members to cover all contracts, shipping, inspection, and fund transfers.

Nothing left unturned.

Master Jaubro used a finger to swipe across the tablet set before him on the six-foot dark wood desk in his study. Muted sunlight crept through the sheer drapes over the picture window behind him. The hover lights in the ceiling corners flickered, ready to go out as another light source came.

A lounge chaise and two high-back chairs graced the room for furniture. Desedon's steps struck silent on the plush neutral carpet.

"Do you need assistance at the moment?"

Desedon asked, stopping halfway into the room.

Master Jaubro looked up from the tablet at him. He seemed agitated.

"No. I think you should take a day or two away from your duties. I'll be fine. Go see how your mate is faring."

Desedon's body relaxed a bit, then quickly bowed. "Thank you. I shall return at your command."

Master Jaubro watched him perfectly pivot and exit the room. He felt guilty for keeping him an extra week when his mate, due any day, may give birth without his presence. This time, he would be there to witness his offspring brought into the world.

Desedon didn't speak about his family, having a sense of strict, unwavering discipline and loyalty.

He turned his attention back to the tablet and frowned. The influx of Earth goods he found fine. Where the merchant groups housed the products, he didn't quite appreciate.

Granted, the coven leaders took possession, as they should. But it left the West docks practically void of them. The old guard wasn't getting any action like before, when the coven companies had no choice in using their credentials.

Thank Trade Commissioner Polp for that.

Master Jaubro didn't chastise the youngsters for being industrious, ambitious. No. It was pure envy that consumed him and the other merchant leaders. Instead of nurturing their success, they saw rivals.

He let out a long, breathy sigh, closing his eyes.

A knock on the door frame made him open them.

Chancellor Rayne leaned against the frame with his arms crossed. He wore plain clothes in stark deviation from his usual Ambrook attire. Wearing a white tunic, brown jacket and pants, with short boots, he liked like a commoner. His hair hung in loose waves, brushing the shoulders of his jacket.

"Omaris. What brings you to the Jaubro stronghold so early in the day?"

The man uncrossed his arms and entered.

He sat in one of the chairs across from the desk, running his fingers through his thick hair to neaten it. Master Jaubro smirked. *He looks like his brother.*

No mistaking the genes of that bloodline.

The only difference between him and Omeron was the Kataling strand. Omaris didn't have it.

"I feel our coven merchants are being penalized for something, and we have no idea why. Lord Pridric has entrusted me to handle operations of the Ambrook Holdings entity."

How observant! Master Jaubro could do nothing except laugh, startling his guest.

"Is this amusing for you then?" Chancellor Rayne tilted his head, his eyes flickering red.

"In a way, yes." Master Jaubro cleared his throat. "Stand down, you brat. Don't make me hurt you."

Not dissuaded, Chancellor Rayne leaned back in the chair, not averting his gaze.

"You started it when you addressed me by my name and not my title."

"Then you should have come presenting yourself that way." Master Jaubro waved a hand at his attire. "Is this to appear humble? Or are you not taking this seriously, after all?"

"I worked the docks this morning. Is it a crime to dress for the task at hand?

"Omaris…"

"Chancellor Rayne."

The two men stared at each other for a moment.

"Absolutely not." Master Jaubro's eyes went red. "I will not call you that. You will always be Omaris Strana, no matter what Earth name you adopted."

"A name I have been accustomed to for over two centuries, equal to my life span on Cellaxa."

"But you are no longer on Earth. This is your home. Even Omeron kept his true name."

Chancellor Rayne inhaled deep through his nose, his chest puffing out, and let it out slowly. Master Jaubro saw him calm down and commended him.

"Better? I'm sure this tat isn't what you came for."

"Why antagonize me then? I'm not a child."

"Hmm? I beg to differ. Enough." Master Jaubro waved the thought away. "You're not being penalized. We're merely dissatisfied with no longer being involved in Earth trade. It all must go through your channels."

"You can't be serious." Omaris deadpanned.

"I'm being frank with you."

"No one is stopping any of you from trading yourselves. You can send your own representatives to Earth and negotiate. Plenty to go around."

"You say that."

"That is true. If you don't want to give us business and pay the finders' fee, then that is your option."

"Well, haven't you grown into a bunch of greedy merchants?" Master Jaubro snorted.

"We learned from the greediest of all." Chancellor Rayne's eyes turned pure red as he smiled.

"Yes." Master Jaubro raised his hand and ran a finger across his bottom lip. "Indeed."

The Jaubro clan holding dominance over the other merchants came as no secret. His brother and their father before him ran their trade with an iron fist. They never let another clan surpass them, joining hands with Boresso and Strana, at times, to sabotage the Endagas when they seemed on the verge.

"Fine. We'll do just that. Thank you for the tip."

"I surely didn't have to tell you that," Chancellor Rayne spat.

The moment he left, Master Jaubro went back to the data on his tablet. Knowing the Trade commissioner would try to stop any interference regarding the coven shipments, he schemed a way to avoid it.

New shipments from Earth entered the west docks and the merchant workers scrambled to get them to the family holding blocks. Within hours, problems with instructions arose. Crates of products back logged on the docks awaited a certified unpackers.

Master Dakien marched down the boardwalk to the family locker and snatched the manifest tablet from the loading technician. He scanned the information, his eyes turning to slits the more he read. Looking out at other family crates sitting in limbo, he turned to the loader.

"Is there anyone here who can decipher all this?"

"Not at this dock. We don't want to take chances ruining product from mishandling."

"If we could get one of the Grieger merchants here, they can assist."

"What you're saying is, we can't process these through our docks and have them delivered."

"Essentially, yes."

How sneaky.

He knew it came from Commissioner Polp. Of course, the Elder families would charge a holding fee. Master Dakien had qualms about making the younger merchants pay out of spite.

"Load them into the locker and contact the Grieger clan for transport instructions," he ordered his workers. "Make sure they are secure. I don't want any accusations that we tampered with any of it."

"Yes sir!"

The unloader pointed to the other shipments for Ambrook and De Luce.

"Do you want the same message relayed to the other merchant heads?"

That would be the considerate thing to do. Did he really want to help the others in the same boat? As he contemplated, he caught sight of Masters Jaubro and Strana heading in the same direction. They spotted him. Damn! Putting on a winning smile, he turned to greet them.

"Come to see the Trade Commissioner's carnage?"

"What's the meaning of this?"

Master Jaubro demanded of the unloader.

"I'm sure Master Dakien can fill you in. I shouldn't have to explain the situation more than once."

The unloader walked back to the main docks to check on another shipment coming in. The three merchant leaders stared after him in disgust.

"Well?" Master Strana addressed Master Dakien. "What madness is this?"

"I suggest you take a look at the manifests and see for yourselves," Master Dakien answered.

They went to the row of shipments congesting the boardwalk and retrieved the tablets from the dock workers. After scanning the data, they both seethed. Master Strana stared out at the ocean, his irises shining silver with rage. Master Jaubro merely sighed in defeat.

Commissioner Polp got us all good.

Master Dakien smirked.

❀ ❀ ❀

Yutel squinted at the dock hand coming towards his merchant locker. The man wore the new west docks implemented uniform. Grey tunic, brown cargo pants, and black suspenders. He stood out among the east dock workers wearing blue tunics, black leggings, and grey suspenders. In his hands, Yutel could make out hard copies. Oh?

Other workers kept their gaze on his approach. Chiron came over from his company's locker and stood next to his father.

"What do you think this is about?"

"Not entirely sure." Yutel pulled his navy jacket together out of habit, letting it go when the buttons wouldn't reach the holes. "I have a suspicion, though."

The west dock worker stopped a few feet from them and pulled out a thin digital slate from the top. He handed it to Yutel.

"We have shipments at the west docks that require a specialist to process them. The Greiger products from Earth are being held at the Dakien lockers. Please read the document and send an acknowledgement. I will come back and get your instructions."

The worker then headed for the Ambrook and De Luce holds. Yutel could hear him giving the same spiel to Chancellor Rayne and Armon. He looked down at the slate and read it. When he finished, he handed it to Chiron while stifling a laugh. He finally burst out into a loud guffaw. Workers flinched from being startled out of their wits.

"This is hilarious!" He slapped Chiron on the shoulder. "I'm sorry. We were going to do the same to your companies. Now that I see how it went for our elders, that plan is scrapped."

Chiron's eyes bulged in fury then he gave his father a side glance. On the other side, Chancellor Rayne and Armon had grins as well.

"So, what do you want to do with your part of the shipment?" Yutel asked. "I could do a one-time waive of the process fee for separating the goods."

"I thought you said that plan was being scrapped."

"After this. You need to negotiate better."

Yutel took the slate from him and tapped the acknowledge icon. The west dock worker checked his wristband and headed back to him.

Yutel nodded to Chiron.

"I'll take two representatives, one from each of our holdings, and a small crew." Chiron saw the other merchants gesturing to their workers. "Or, we could just combine forces to get our merchandise."

Yutel glanced over at him. Smart. As if reading his son's mind, the other two merchants followed the west dock worker while tapping their slates.

Chancellor Rayne crossed his arms as he stood next to Armon, who seemed all too happy to be a part of the plan.

"I know what you're thinking," Armon addressed the dock hand in a singsong tone. "Shall we converge on the west docks and take possession of our goods?"

"If you could arrange that by end of day, we would appreciate it. The crates are blocking an entire section of the boardwalk." The west dock worker replied. "We can't move any more until those are gone."

I guess we better hurry, then." Chancellor Rayne looked over his shoulder as Baltise and Adelia walked out of their hubs. "I'm sure Master Strana is livid about now."

"When is he not angry about something?" Yutel snorted.

❁ ❁ ❁

The goods inspector stopped his checklist and stared at the crate next to the one he worked on. He scrutinized the company insignia, not recognizing it. Memories of the arms dealers previous attack popped into his head. Not this time.

He pulled out his scanner and ran it along the edges of the crate. No weapons detected, he sighed inwardly with relief. That didn't deter him from logging the delivery code to take a look at later. It seemed Cellaxa's business grew more than usual since the arrival of Earth goods. None of the new products interested him. He didn't see the appeal.

"Where do you want me to move this one before sending it to the merchant's hold?" A dock worker had his hands on the hover carrier, ready to load the crate. "We're going to have another bottleneck from Earth shipments. Someone forgot to do a reroute to the East docks."

"Hmph." The goods inspector forced himself not to frown. "Alright, move it to the other side of the boardwalk. I'll need to contact Commissioner Polp."

The dock worker's head straightened in surprise, his eyes leering at the crate.

"Is it weapons?"

His hand gripped the carrier's handle.

"No. If that were the case, I would have alerted the imperial guards. I already scanned it."

"That means nothing," the man spat. "It could still be weapons. Just not the kind we think."

"In any case, you need to move it far away from the other shipments."

The dock loader pushed the button to lower the bottom shelf of the carrier and slid it under the crate. Checking that it was secure, he raised it off the ground and used the remote control to maneuver it ahead of him towards the boardwalk.

Master Endaga watched the interaction from his holding block across from the delivery stations. He also eyed the crate dubiously. Many new trade deals saw unfamiliar goods flowing through.

The Trade Commissioner had confiscated four restricted products so far. Not significant for most planets, but too many for Cellaxa. They were the prime standard for other galactic merchants, having strict regulations that prevent such things.

When the dock worker settled the crate in its temporary place, he saw the merchant insignia from his vantage point. A lower merchant house trying to move up in the ranks. He became certain the goods in the crate came from a planet they had never done business dealings with.

Knowing the inspector would be busy for the next few hours, he took the handheld device his doljas called a smart phone and hit the auto call for Innego.

"Father, it's early morning," Innego complained. "Please tell me it's urgent."

Master Endaga could tell by the croak in his son's Innego probably still laid in bed with some random lover fast asleep at his side. He wondered why Innego accepted the position as royal inspector.

"It could be. There's a shipment on the West docks that doesn't quite pass the smell test. Initial scan shows no weapons."

"That means nothing!" Innego echoed the dock worker. "I'll be there within the hour."

"Are you sure?" Master Endaga smirked. "Not too busy servicing the help?"

"Not funny." He heard the hurt in his son's tone.

"I know. I'm sorry. To be fair, you created such expectations by your behavior."

"True." A long pause followed. "Your disappointment in me is noted.

Master Endaga reared from the phone, shocked at his words. The line died as he opened his mouth to respond. He pursed his lips, feeling stung.

That's not what I meant!

Innego tossed his phone on the bedside table then rubbed his face with both hands. He glanced down at the sleeping form next to him. Tamar's eyes fluttered, as if having a bad dream. Tavelo would strangle him if he knew they were mating.

Not out of love. Well, not that kind.

He loved Tamar as family. Their mating resulted from Tamar' emptiness after losing his guardian and being defeated in battle. More comfort than affection.

He leaned over and whispered in Tamar's ear.

"You have to wake up, my sweet. I've been summoned to the West docks."

"Uhn." Tamar squeezed her eyes shut, curling further into a ball. "What time is it?"

"Too early." He kissed the corner of her lips. "Come." He smacked the side of her buttocks through the sheet.

Tamar flinched, finally opening her eyes.

They went over to the mini wash station by the dresser and wiped themselves down. Tamar shifted back to male form. Neither spoke while dressing, Innego donning royal robes over his battlesuit. Better safe than sorry. Merchants were touchy these days.

"Are you feeling okay?" Innego asked, placing a hand on the middle of Tamar's back. "You weren't sleeping well." Tamar exhaled, then nodded. "Good. I worry about you."

The two exited his chambers. Innego turned left at the end of the corridor towards the main palace while Tamar went right towards his chamber. Not far, in the shadows, he sensed Tervan watching them with a murderous stare.

The clanging of metal, waves smacking against the wharf, and Volshins shrieking in the air, made Innego's head hurt. He squinted in pain, holding the side of his head. His blue and silver royal robes swayed behind him, the slight wind forcing the front to cling against his body. His father stood in the Endaga holding block conversing with one of his assistants, another cousin.

"Greetings, family," he called out on approach. "Father."

His father caught him off guard, grabbing him by the front of his robes and steering him to the side.

"Don't you ever say something like that to me and hang up," his father seethed. "Not once have I ever voiced disappointment."

Innego sagged in his grip.

He stared at the ground, not sure how to respond. Smacking his father's hand away, he stepped back.

"My apologies. I assumed that was the case. It won't happen again."

"Innego!" His father's eyes turned red.

"Where is this sketchy shipment?"

Innego turned away, ignoring his father's rage.

"Don't make me hurt you, child."

Innego glanced back. His eyes widened in fear. The rest of the family workers had moved to the rear of the holding block. He raised both hands in the air.

"I'm sorry. So sorry. Please, father, calm yourself."

For a moment, thinking his father would come at him, he braced himself for an assault. None came. His father's eyes reverted to normal, filled with sadness.

"Don't dismiss my words," his father chastised.

"I'm sorry." He straightened his posture, feeling his shoulders slumped.

"The shipment is over there, isolated from the rest." His father pointed to it. "No one has touched it since. I don't think the inspector even notified the merchant house who ordered it."

Hmm? Not suspicious at all.

Innego gave the crate a side eyed glance.

"Guess I better go enact my duty."

"We will talk later." His father's hands were tight fists at his sides.

"Of course." Innego waved as he walked off. "I'll see you soon."

As he stepped onto the main docks, four royal guards fell in step behind him. Workers gasped in surprise and made way for the procession. Halfway down, they created an open path. The goods inspector fumbled to one knee, bowing his head. Innego rolled his eyes in exasperation. He hated the rules of royalty. He motioned for the man to stand.

"Please, I am not someone important enough to receive such a greeting."

"Surely, you jest, Royal Inspector." The man clutched his tablet to his chest. "What brings you to the docks this early in the day?" He frowned. "Have I done something wrong?"

"No, no." Innego waved a hand. "I was informed of a nefarious shipment."

He pointed at the crate.

"Ah, yes. I didn't have time to go over its manifest, so I had it put there. As you can see," the man nodded at the overfilled docks.

Innego hissed.

"What is the meaning of all this?"

"Someone forgot to attach reroute instructions for goods meant for the East dock."

Sighing in defeat, Innego nodded.

"Send me the crate's manifest."

A guard handed Innego his tablet and the goods inspector tapped his own. The received documents icon blinked on the bottom of Innego's screen. He opened it and stared in confusion at the goods list.

"I will inspect the contents myself. Carry on."

"Of course, your grace." The man bowed again before resuming his work.

At the crate, Innego checked all the markings. He looked over the initial scan images on his tablet. No, not projectile weapons. Something else. He zoomed in closer. A handful of damaged goods were seeping liquid. He turned to a holding bay worker.

"Bring the merchant head and his proxy here."

"Yes, your grace." The worker ran towards the merchant house's bay.

Innego gestured with two fingers in the air for his guards to come closer.

"I think, these pods have explosive components," he said softly, so only they could hear. One guard hissed, showing gritted teeth. Another gaped at the crate. "We need to tread carefully as not to cause a panic on the docks."

"Why would a merchant think they could get away with bringing these in?" his first guard asked.

"Oh, because they're being sneaky." He zoomed out to the second layer of the scan. The pods were encased in gourds. "They've hidden the goods in food stuffs."

The merchant head and his proxy arrived at the crate, stunned at Innego's presence. They appeared nervous as they bowed on one knee before rising. Innego noted the stocky build of the head merchant, his dirty blond hair unkempt, yet his suit tailored. The slender proxy had similar features, with dark circles under his eyes.

They haven't slept in days.

"Lord Innego," the proxy stuttered. "What brings you here?" He glanced at the tablet screen. "Is there a problem?"

The guard's hands went to the hilt of their swords. Innego motioned for them to stand down.

"Of course there is. You know why I'm here. Did you really think you could get these past inspection?"

"Why, it's only decorations made from edible items," the merchant head said, laughing.

"Then if I were to pierce one, you're confident of its nature?" Innego nodded for a guard to unsheathe his sword. The proxy's eyes grew large. "Yes?"

"Wait! We have no idea if they're stable."

The proxy raised his hands to block the guard from approaching.

"We only wanted to find a way to defend our planet," the merchant head yelled. "These will get rid of any enemy without loss of life on our side."

"This is madness." The first guard shook his head. "It's good we stopped this one in time."

Innego's eyes glowed red.

"I have a feeling this won't be the last we see."

A Fierce Empire

Tervan paced the length of his chamber, his fists swaying with each steps' motion. Seeing Tamar and Innego together made him furious. He had known that might be the case* and still found it unacceptable. For his father's cousin to take advantage of Tamar's pain.

He halted in the center of the room and scanned it to kill time. The limited furnishings glared at him. An overly large bed, an armoire, some side tables, and a lounge chaise. That's all he had since he rarely occupied the space.

Caden leaned on the door frame with both arms crossed. She also stared at the bare room. They spent more days in Tervan's chamber these days. Letting her arms drop, Caden walked over to the bed and flopped backwards on it.

"I saw it too." Caden sighed. "I don't like it."

Tervan went to sit beside her. Their combined weight made the mattress sink down.

"Should I out them? Tell father what's going on?"

"You think he doesn't know?"

"My father," Tervan snorted. "He has selective observation skills."

"Would it anger him?"

"Hmm." Tervan stared at the giant chandelier high in the ceiling. "I would think so."

"Then you should wait until after the morning

meetings. No need to have our emperor up in arms before dealing with the royal family."

"We're a royal family," Tervan retorted, giving her a side glance.

Caden struggled onto her elbows, the sunken mattress causing him to lie slanted.

"I meant the crazy one." She eyed Tervan. "I'll never forgive him, or his siblings, who furthered the situation. They're all insane."

"That is an understatement." Tervan rose and the mattress slowly sprung back into shape. Caden went lopsided and regained her balance before getting up. "I guess we should get going."

They left together. Tervan still felt anxious. He forced himself to focus on the meetings. Confronting Innego and Tamar in front of his father would be no easy scene.

The last morning meeting ended, and everyone fled the conference room towards the main hall for breakfast. Tamar and Innego had left with the first wave and stood conversing in the corridor. Tervan decided to make his move.

Innego laughed at Tamar's joke, tilting his head back with his eyes closed. On instinct, he caught Tervan's wrist that flashed before his eyes and wrenched it back, forcing him to the side. When Innego hit him with an open palm to the chest, he finally saw Tervan's face skewed with rage, as slid backwards to a stop.

"Get away from him." Tervan said coldly.

"I won't tolerate you coming at me like this. Hurting you would make your father sad."

"As opposed to what you're doing?" Tervan spat.

"What is the meaning of this?" Tavelo came upon them with Caden not far behind.

"Did you know your cousin has been mating with Tamar in secret?" Tervan straightened his posture.

Tavelo's eyes grew red as he stared at them.

"I am only easing his pain. Giving him comfort. Is that wrong?" Innego shrugged.

"Is this some kind of sick retaliation?" Tavelo snapped.

"For what?" Innego turned to him. "I'm only indebted to you, cousin."

"You will end this…"

"That is not up to you." Innego barely got the words out when Tervan moved to strike. With one hand, he evaded the blow by hitting Tervan below the clavicle. He heard the sharp exhale of breath. "I warned you."

"Stop." Tavelo commanded right as Caden held her talons under Innego's chin.

Tamar stood silent with clenched fists.

"Come away." Tavelo looked to all of them.

Caden retracted her claws, leaning close to Innego.

"I don't condone what you've done. Treating Tamar like one of your random whores."

Innego smirked, walking away, not paying Tervan or Caden any mind. He glanced back at Tamar.

"I'll talk with you later."

They left Tavelo and Tamar alone in the corridor. Tavelo stepped towards him and halted when Tamar flinched, moving back.

"None of you bothered to help me. You didn't see how much pain I was in. No one came to comfort me. You were asleep. My mother could have come out of the cage you left her in, but even she didn't bother to check on me." Tears streamed down Tamar's face. "But Innego did. He was the only one who broke through the fog. He didn't ask me anything. Just said, you're not okay."

Tamar glared at Tavelo. A fury mixed with sadness emitted from his very soul.

"Everyone thinks he took advantage of me. Like I was some weak animal who needed to be coddled. You're wrong." His gaze bore into his father's. "I pinned him down with every ounce of sorrow I had.

He probably could have pushed me off, but he knew I wouldn't stop. He wasn't the one who initiated our relationship. I did."

Tavelo remained stunned. He didn't dare move. Tamar wiped his face with one hand.

"I decide when it's over. Not him."

Tamar walked off in the opposite direction. He would not be attending morning meal with the rest of them. Out of the corner of his eye, Tavelo spotted Maritze off in the shadows. Her stricken face told him she heard every word.

"It's not like we're getting an award for being amazing parents," she said, with her head lowered.

"I wish I could fix it."

"It's too late for that." Maritze resumed her journey towards the main hall.

Tavelo covered his face with both hands. Seeing Tamar's distress hurt him more than he thought.

For the umpteenth time, more than he could count, Tavelo endured the screams inside the medical wing. Inside the birthing room, Pridric thrashed in agony. The technicians struggled to hold her down so they could get her feet into the newly installed stirrups.

Thin rivers of blood streamed from her womb. Tavelo went to her side, and with brute force, held her still.

Pridric's eyes became kaleidoscopes, glowing in the dim lighting. Her screams grew as the child's head crowned. The gelatinous pouch surrounding it broke as it slid out. A medical assistant caught the newborn in the swathing cloth and held it up for the other to spray off the mess.

Within seconds, Pridric's body arched off the table as she unleashed a blood-curdling scream. The technicians and Tavelo stared wide eyed as a second head emerged.

"Again?" a technician yelled in awe. "Is there some royal setting for twins?" He grabbed another swathing cloth and went to catch the second child. When the head only emerged halfway, he frowned. "This one is stuck." He tossed the cloth on Pridric's bulging stomach while he tuned out her screams. "We'll have to pry it out."

Tavelo saw the man's hands move towards Pridric's inner thighs, his fingers splaying wide. They slid around the tiny head and into her womb. Tavelo's vision blurred, hearing a hard suction sound as the technician gently pulled. The moment the newborn's head cleared, it wailed, creating a sonic wave.

Not to be outdone. The first one joined in.

Tavelo barely managed to grab the birthing table's ledge to stop himself from falling. Pridric abruptly fell silent, her body sagging down onto the slab.

"Hurry, she's bleeding out!" The head birthing technician yelled.

"Almost." The assistant kept a steady hand as he continued to pull until the legs came free. "There you go." He grabbed the cloth and wrapped the newborn in it. Another tech took it from him to rinse the child off.

The other technicians rushed to care for Pridric. Tavelo, slumped in a daze, watched them work until an assistant nudged him.

"I'm sorry, Emperor. You need to move so we can work properly."

"Oh, yes."

Tavelo staggered out of the room and into the hallway. He had never attended the birth for any of his children. Seeing how much pain and suffering Pridric went through, and hearing Manel's awful event, for that matter made him feel guilty and ashamed. They endured such pain alone. He looked down at the front of his robes splattered with Pridric's blood.

"I'm sorry," he whispered. Tavelo slid to the floor and brought his knees close to his chest. He cried into his hands, leaning his head against the wall. "I'm sorry."

Only immediate royal members, their palace guards, and the servants working attended the announcement in the East throne room. Tavelo watched the magistrate saunter over to the basinet that held his newborn twins, not yet two weeks old. The room bore the West's red and black colors contrasting the East's silver and blue. It hurt Tavelo's eyes. He squinted, keeping his focus on his spawn.

"With the birth of a new generation comes the confirmation of a new regime. By royal decree, Pridric Strana is named Empress of the East. May they reign supreme with Emperor Tavelo Endaga. Here, the children of the East empire are so declared their successors."

The magistrate anointed the twins' foreheads with smeared dots of blood. Manel rolled his eyes at the wordiness of the decree. Tavelo felt the same. The ceremony concluded, and he braced himself for the congratulatory procession. One by one, the royal members came up to praise him and get a glimpse of the twins. As their numbers thinned, his royal guards moved to the doors, ready to shut them.

Family members, the royal council, and personal guards remained. The magistrate sat with the royal council by the window wall covered by heavy drapes to block out the rising sun.

"Now that we have a moment," the royal physician stood from his seat amongst the council. "My team has compiled the data on Empress Pridric's condition."

Manel cocked his head. He glanced over at Tavelo with intrigue. The royal physician continued.

"We have confirmed our initial findings. The extraction procedure of an early fetus bordered on unnecessary brutality. It and the womb were literally destroyed, torn apart."

Gasped erupted. Manel's eyes glowed red. Tavelo could imagine him reliving the horrid experiments his father conducted on him.

"What madness are you spouting?" Eterenia cried out. Her horrified expression clear.

"Also, as determined, the empress is indeed a Volshin." Another round of angry gasped cut him off.

"Pridric? A Volshin?" Master Endaga turned to Tavelo. "How is that?"

He stopped, knowing the answer.

The royal physician eyed his audience. They seemed to clam up, getting the hint.

"The second procedure that followed the extraction had one purpose. To eliminate the ability to shift into Volshin form. Vital organs necessary for the transition have either been ripped apart or removed."

"Stranas were experts in Volshin medical care. I would assume they continued it despite their goal to rid their bloodline of them." Master Jaubro said.

"Or that being the very reason they continued it," Master Endaga added.

"Yes," the royal physician said. "They are the only ones who could do so much damage with such precision. Though brutal, it was done meticulously."

"Can it be fixed?" Dania asked in a whisper. "I know we discussed it before, but realistically." Her eyes pleaded with the royal physician. "Are you confident?"

The royal physician rubbed the bottom of his chin. He glanced around at the royal council, stunned by the revelations. The magistrate gave him a stern glare.

"Reversing the damage will take time. Am I confident we can achieve this? Of course. The problem is that the empress may never regain their Volshin ability." The sound of air sucked through gritted teeth erupted. "Forever incomplete. Empress Pridric will never fly."

A sharp pain the size of a boulder hit Tavelo in the pit of his stomach. The cruelty of those words. He couldn't muster the strength to tell Pridric that when they awakened. He looked up, and found everyone who saw his distress understood.

"That is why he is stronger than most," the royal physician blurted out. Tavelo turned to him. "Once the repairs to their anatomy are complete, the empress can tap into their Volshin power."

"In other words," Lendor said, "Pridric will be a menace with infinite strength."

"More or less," the royal physician shrugged. "It's the best-case scenario."

"I'll take it." Tavelo leaned back onto his throne. "How long?"

"Realistically?" He nodded to Dania. "Five years, give or take two. It's a complicated task."

"That's more than reasonable," Master Jaubro added. He turned to Manel and his siblings. "The Stranas' and the previous regime created similar medical technologies for Katalings and Volshins. Each specialized in one or the other. Over the centuries, they chose not to share their techniques or data."

"So, the only ones who could successfully reverse this are the Strana clan?" Tervan crept from the shadows in the back of the room. "And we all know they would refuse."

"Are we," Lendor glanced around the room, "not divulging these to anyone outside this room?" He addressed the royal physician. "The Stranas won't be given a chance to explain their actions?"

"We shall let them be." The royal councilman, on the end, replied. "For now. They will be punished accordingly when the time is right."

A hostile atmosphere came with eyes of red fury.

Manel sat sideways in the plush chair of the newly decorated meeting room. Eleven more like it surrounded the large oval table made of tempered glass. No longer a dull, uninspiring room, Dania and Pridric had worked with the royal interior designers along with Lendor to give it more life. He approved of the change. Bringing his knees up, he set his legs on the edge of the seat and nestled in.

Wearing his casual kaftan, his hair wild atop his head, he didn't appear royal in any way. Gallic also dressed down, in only a tunic, leather pants and an open robe cinched at the waist.

I know I said an impersonal meeting.

Tavelo admonished them.

He blinked a few times to adjust his vision. Tired after two hours of consoling his twins before the start of his day. Dania came right on the verge of him giving up. The newborns had yet to open their eyes. The royal physician advised him to be patient. He noticed his own attire and tsked. His dark grey sleeveless robe, over a plain black long-sleeved one, was no better.

It might as well be loungewear.

"Did all of you simply roll out of bed?" Eterenia laughed. Behind her, Lendor arrived in similar garb as Gallic. "Were we supposed to dress down for this?"

Tavelo and Manel stared at her pristine red robe and coiffed hair. Innego snorted as he passed her, wearing an imperial jacket over a plain black body-suit. His sword hung loosely at his hip in its sheath holster.

"Oh, you didn't get the memo?" Dania walked in, her hair undone and the white robe sporting a yellow stain smeared along the left shoulder. "No one has time to spruce themselves up so early."

Tavelo pointed at the stain.

Dania gave him a small smile.

"Not from your little imps. They're angels. This

is from Manel's tiny creatures."

"When did you…" Tavelo asked, confused.

Manel glared at her.

"Oh, Grasilda came with them not long after you left." She smirked at Manel. "Such mean little demons."

"Let's get this over with," Manel snapped.

Obviously offended.

"Well, I expect them to be unruly." Eterenia said.

Tavelo let out a loud sigh, getting everyone's attention. He sat in the chair opposite Manel on the other end of the table. The rest took their seats, Master Endaga and Jaubro arriving moments later.

"Cellaxa has suffered a downgrade in trade points over the centuries." Lendor began. "After talking with Commissioner Polp, it seems the decline started long before Emperor Manel's takeover."

"Exactly," Manel said with an indignant burst. "I was trying to fix it."

Everyone balked at him. Master Jaubro placed a hand on the side of his face, his index finger and thumb framing his jaw. Tavelo tried to find words to counter and failed. There were too many.

"Yes, well," Lendor glanced at his tablet. "Your methods proved unsuccessful."

"How do we remedy the issue?" Eterenia asked. "We're still in the restructuring phase of merchant bays and the docks."

"Oh, that's simple," Armon spoke, raising his hand. "We need more clients and bigger contracts."

"And how do you suppose we get more clients?" Master Endaga asked.

"We have almost triple the amount of merchant hubs." Armon spread his arms wide. "Time to get out there and snag some buyers."

Tavelo noticed Master Jaubro frown before relaxing his face. Eterenia seemed to catch it too. The head merchants still viewed them and their offspring as incapable business dealers.

Even though they brought new trade to Cellaxa, the disrespect lingered.

As if sensing the mood, Master Endaga folded his hands on the table.

"I know many dominant clans seem reluctant to work with you. Please know house Endaga would be honored to teach you the advanced techniques of trade we've developed over our lifetime."

The corner of Master Jaubro's mouth twitched. Tavelo realized in that moment, a gauntlet had been thrown. Tension filled the room.

Innego stared at the housing complex's third level in the bowels of the ghetto. Clusters of buildings just like it blocked light from reaching the streets. Different colors marked each level with a family insignia for scanning on its left side. The hues ranged from a mustard yellow, to rusty red, then pale blue. He frowned at the dilapidated state of the neighborhood.

This needs to be remedied.

Chancellor Rayne and Yutel stood next to him on either side, with four royal guards behind them. They too seemed upset by the sight. Innego went to the front entrance and selected the insignia matching the third level marking. Beside it the family name Loengir in raised blue letters had faded over time.

On Earth, they were called the Brownlee Coven. The first battle with the imperial fleet diminished their numbers, resulting in the coven's destruction. Survivors scattered, not willing to shame themselves by accepting help from the other covens. They went to Earth as a group of thirty, then rose to nearly a thousand strong. Only the couple of hundred that were left returned home.

"What do you think?" Innego asked Chancellor Rayne while they waited for the acceptance chime.

"They need to get out their funk and start being

merchants." Chancellor Rayne glanced up again, checking for any movement in the small windows of the third level. "They essentially stopped after their defeat. Even we could only do so much to help them with trading their domestic goods."

"It was a heavy blow," Yutel added, matter of fact. He tugged the front of his robe to loosen the fabric a bit over his large chest. "I agree. They better get their shit together."

Innego smirked at the vulgar Earth term being spoken on Cellaxa. The populace didn't know what to say about having another race's language mingle with theirs. It needed time for acceptance.

The chime sounded, followed by black metal double doors squealing open to an abyss. Motion lights flickered on, a few out completely, giving the foyer a gloomy haze.

At the end lay the lift, sitting open. A monstrosity of shiny metal with a single door that slid to one side. The group loaded in, taking up an eighth of its space with the ceiling twenty feet above them.

They all winced at the door screeching closed.

"That's annoying." Chancellor Rayne tapped the side of his temple. "I know we're in the ghetto, but this is ridiculous."

The lift lurched hard as it ascended, forcing them to find stability against the sides. Before it stopped, they managed to find their balance and group back together. They wanted to show some resolve and unity. When the door slid open, they tried not to gasp. Even the royal guards' hands twitched, wanting to cover their mouths in awe of the scene.

Paltry furnishings in barely usable condition scattered the communal area. Heavy drapes worked as doors covering the entryways to the other rooms. Chipped dining ware sat neatly arranged in the glass armoire. The occupants either moved around lethargically or lounged with not a care, their worn attire showing hints of past glory.

A few raised their gaze towards the group as they stepped onto the matted carpet once plush.

Yutel's fists clenched, his lips drawing back to expose teeth as he hissed. His irises grew red.

"Who gave you this pit to live in?" He seethed. "This is unacceptable!" No one answered.

From the drapes in the back right corner, a hand moved it over to reveal a gaunt man wearing a white long-sleeved tunic, a corn silk vest, and brown leggings. His brown hair, cut just below his ears, ended in deep waves. A few wisps fell into his amber eyes. Innego recognized him after scanning his face for a moment.

The son of Count Brownlee, Windsor, sauntered over to stand in the center of the room. No one from the other covens had seen him since the burial rites for his father and the fallen. Innego saw the anger etched in his soul. Count Brownlee's arrogance, not listening to reason during the battle, is how they ended up losing so much.

Windsor's fists pressed into the sides of his thighs. He didn't look at them as he spoke.

"We are grateful to have even this. What would you have us do? Our clan refused to take us in. There was no place for us to go."

"That's where you're wrong!" Chancellor Rayne snapped. "Our arms are always open to you."

This time, he raised his gaze, eyes glowing red.

"We don't need your pity or charity!"

Yutel moved in a flash, too fast for Windsor to block the blow. His body went sailing into the three people occupying a loveseat. They caught him before he went over, turning hateful glares at Yutel.

"Stop your own self-pity!" Yutel yelled. "What are you doing?"

"This has gone on long enough." Chancellor Rayne sighed. "You need to establish the Brownlee Corporation here on Cellaxa and start pulling your weight."

"What for?" Windsor cried. "We're not fit to run any trade, let olone be claimed as part of our clan!"

"Is that what the head of your clan told you?" Innego walked past Yutel and grabbed the man by the collar out of his family member's clutches. "Do better," Innego said, gritting his teeth. He shoved him back and towered over him. "Get dressed and bring your head of finances with you."

Windsor balked, ready to argue, then closed his mouth. He struggled to his feet, giving Innego a final angry stare. A woman sitting on the floor, against one of the couches, rose to follow him through the drapes he came from. The rest of the family fell silent, not wanting to draw attention to themselves. They failed by doing that alone.

A royal guard placed two fingers under his nose and glanced to his right at a young man passed out at the foot of a plush chair. Dark stains on his disheveled clothes appeared to be dried blood from meat. Another stain spread from the center of his crotch out past his thighs.

Innego stomped over and backhanded him. He tumbled a few feet before jumping, startled, onto all fours, eyes glowing red. His fingernails morphed into talons that pierced the carpet.

"Clean yourself up!" Innego turned to the rest of the members in the room. "All of you!" He stared down at the unclean man. "You think you can take me?" He challenged him.

The man immediately backed off, falling back on his butt in shame. He took stock of his condition and winced, turning his head away.

"You've let yourselves fall into despair." Chancellor Rayne shook his head. "Is this the legacy you wish to leave behind? It doesn't matter what our clans say or think about us. We make our own fortune."

The West throne room's cold, vast emptiness made Tavelo's skin prickle. He leaned further into the high-back chair near the platform and stared up at Maxellia and Lenri. The sisters huddled together in front of a holoscreen.

Their bodies stretched sideways over the thrones, so their heads met a few inches apart. They wore their usual attire, as did Tavelo. Best to keep with royal appearances in the throne rooms. The royal guards stayed close to the walls, out of the way.

Silence felt just as cold, with no one saying anything for the past few minutes. Tavelo squinted as nervousness crept in. Beside him in the other four chairs, Innego, Master Jaubro, Eterenia, and Dania squirmed, ready to flee or fight.

As the holoscreen winked out, the sisters straightened themselves in their seats. Maxellia grinned.

"I got bored." Her mouth curved into a sinister smile. "So I went over the the last few battles records."

"She asked that I assist." Lenri said proudly. "After going over the possibilities of new threats with new trade deals, we have decided."

In the center of the platform, Manel, slumped on his throne, equally bored, perked up. He too sensed a foreboding. Gallic stood behind him and inhaled silently.

"I think we should reinstate our battle maidens," Maxellia announced. Lenri nodded in approval. "They can be a front line of defense after the ancients."

Tavelo forced himself not to let his mouth gape open. Innego snorted, covering his own. Master Jaubro glanced over at Desedon with a knowing expression. Only Dania seemed to go eerily silent.

"Oh?" Manel lowered his hand from his face and sat upright. "Do we still have those?"

Lenri and Maxellia's heads whipped towards him, and they gave him deadly glares.

"What makes you think they disappeared?" Maxellia snapped. "Did you think they went into the void after your failed coup?"

Manel frowned. His disdain for them grew since the two royal houses came to be.

"And how do you propose we do that?" Manel asked.

The two haughtily sat back on their thrones.

"A competition," Maxellia replied.

"A battle royale, if you will," Lenri added.

"How intriguing. And the winner is determined, how?"

"The last one standing gets to choose one of us in a final battle." Lenri smirked as she said it.

"Not much of a victory then," Innego quipped.

"What was that?" Maxellia leaned forward, her teeth bared.

Master Jaubro raised a hand, signaling her to back off.

"There needs to be a better incentive for the top contenders. No battle maiden is coming out of the shadows for the chance to throttle one of you."

This time Tavelo's serious expression broke. A grimace followed by laughter erupted from him. Even Manel threw back his head and let out a guffaw.

"Yes," Eterenia interjected as she competed with the laughter. She could see the sisters get flustered. "There should be tiers of victors and a prize for each. I'm not really familiar with the warriors, though I've heard a few stories from my former maids."

"Right?" Innego cocked his head. "When was the last time Cellaxa had Battle Maidens in service?"

"Centuries," Master Jaubro replied. "Veterans still train them. The new generations have yet to prove their worth."

"I will send out a decree." Maxellia turned to Manel. "Is that acceptable to you?"

"I'm riveted with excitement." Manel let his arms dangle off the throne's armrests. "It would be curious to see how many come to the surface."

"Then the arena needs to be inspected and prepared for the event." Dania finally spoke, her eyes still seemed focused somewhere far away. "As for an incentive." She paused, then looked down. "Nothing overtly tangible."

"No one wants some medallion or statue that will sit useless." Tavelo said. He tapped the bottom of his chin. "A plot of land, perhaps? A title?"

"A royal position?" Eterenia added.

"How about you brainstorm this a bit more and let us know the logistics?" Tavelo addressed the two sisters. "And what prizes would stir interest."

Maxellia and Lenri rose from their thrones and stepped down. They walked past everyone and through the doors with Maxellia's royal guards in tow. Master Jaubro and Innego followed. Dania stood slowly, as if afraid to move. A flash of resolve in her eyes told Tavelo that wasn't the case.

Tavelo met Manel's gaze.

Those amber eyes stormed deviously.

High Stakes

Tavelo left the West throne with Eterenia and found Innego waiting for him.

"What's going on? I thought you were heading out to the docks for another surprise inspection."

"Hmm? But I went and did you a big favor." Innego crossed his arms, the sound of his leather sleeves rubbing together filled the space. "You'll thank me later. Come." He nodded his head for them to follow.

Tavelo and Eternia expressions grew skeptical before doing so. They walked for a while and Tavelo realized he had not been in that part of the palace. Even after years of living there, there were too many areas still a mystery. Innego led them to a sprawling banquet hall, recently cleaned and serviced. The bare minimum of furnishings made it appear unending, the cloths and dining ware stark white.

Inside, close to one hundred Brownlee coven members sat dejected at the round tables, pushing their food around on the plates. The servants looked away, their anger visible. Tavelo walked in as Innego stepped out of his way.

"What is this?" Tavelo yelled. "Are you so far gone that you dishonor the food prepared by my servants specifically for you?"

Silverware clanked against plates. The hall fell into a dark, deeper silence.

Tavelo scanned the room and his gaze landed on Windsor. Then it hit him as he took in the scene. The glaring contrast of the coven members amid the white proved jarring even for him. They resembled charcoal sketches on a blank canvas.

His outburst seemed to shame them into eating. Windsor tried to hide tears of rage as he fervently consumed the items on his plate.

"They're reluctant to be seen as heathens despite being near starving," Innego whispered in his ear. Tavelo turned to him, startled. He had not heard his cousin move. "This is better than how I found them."

Tavelo's eyes widened. If this was them cleaned up, he couldn't imagine what they were before. Yutel and Chancellor Rayne arrived to stand beside him.

"Yes, it was quite disgraceful," Chancellor Rayne said. "I made sure they were all at least washed."

Yutel snorted.

"That was the least of our worries." He eyed the man who had previously soiled himself. "The way they're living is the problem."

"I wondered what happened to them after arriving back home," Elerenia said. She covered her mouth with the sleeve of her robe. "They may have washed, but there's a distinct odor coming from them."

"Base soap," Chancellor Rayne replied. "The only thing they could afford, apparently."

Tavelo cringed. Not one to judge, yet even the poorest dock workers managed to add some herbs to cut the antiseptic scent. He scrutinized their clothes.

"Where did you find them?" Tavelo asked. He dreaded the answer.

"The Southern ghetto district." Yutel's irises gleamed with a flash of red.

Guilt gripped Tavelo.

All the other covens established hubs on Cellaxa, gaining contracts. Not once did he reach out to find the Brownlees to see how they fared. Of course, the

Loengir clan turned them away.

"I'm sorry." Tavelo looked out at them. "As your emperor, I should have made sure you were alright." He turned to Innego, Yutel, and Chancellor Rayne. "What do you think?"

"If your remedy is for them occupy the palace until they get on their feet, then I agree," Chancellor Rayne replied.

"They cannot live in that container." Yutel said, vehemently.

The anger in his tone conjured images of violence in Tavelo's mind. No doubt the demand of washing came with brutality. He saw the looks on the coven members' faces and Windsor ready to protest.

"I won't hear dissent from any of you! That is my decree! You will be vacated from that abode and your belongings brought here."

Chancellor Rayne leaned closer to him.

"I recommend their belongings be sorted before the return. Some of them are..." He grimaced, unable to finish.

"Just take it all and dump it in the incinerators. Make them start all over." Yutel shrugged.

Horrified by the notion, Windsor shot up from his seat, eyes glowing red. His finance assistant grabbed hold of his shirt sleeve to stop him from moving further. Tavelo understood better than anyone. What few items they clung to were precious, having abandoned almost everything to return home.

"That's not going to happen." Tavelo stared Windsor down. "You should know me better than that." He waited for Windsor to unclench his fists and sit down. "Now finish eating. Take all you want. The first thing is to get you acclimated to the palace."

"I guess we'll give them the trade lecture another time." Chancellor Rayne slapped Yutel's shoulder and motioned for him to follow. They exited the hall.

Innego gave Tavelo a side glance.

"I did good, right?"

"You did. Thank you."

Tavelo lingered before leaving.

Innego motioned for two of the servants near the entrance. They bowed their heads as they came within a few feet of him. He gestured for them to come closer. Leery, they obeyed. He leaned in.

"When they're done, march them straight to the communal bathhouse. Take their clothes and have East palace robes for them."

Both servants seemed to perk up with enthusiasm. Innego nodded, and they returned it with theirs. Confirmation that they, too, had the same sentiment.

Searing pain invaded the dark beneath Pridric's eyelids. She squeezed them closed tighter, trying to alleviate it, and ended up causing an aching pulse. Her nostrils flared at the floral scent in the air. She could feel her body embedded deep within the plush mattress, hugging her whole body.

Moving her fingers to get the feeling back, Pridric forced her eyes open. The eyelids peeled apart like adhesives, making her wince. Too much light flooded in as she made out someone coming towards her to the side of the bed.

"Empress Pridric," the woman said. "So good to see you awake."

Everything looked blown out.

Pridric couldn't make out the servant's face. Just a hazy, white silhouette floating around. Opening her mouth, her lips pried apart with a dryness like glued paper. She could feel their tattered skin.

"Come. Let's get you up." More servants surrounded Pridric as they placed a hand behind her head and gently lifted. 'It would be good to do your hair and go for a stroll."

Pridric remained upright only because the woman held her there. Her entire body felt like an immovable boulder. Heavy, stiff. Even her hair weighed down her head, making her neck hurt. A servant pulled the covers away, and together with the head attendant, they swung her body around so that she sat sideways on the edge.

A maid came with a wet cloth and wiped down Pridric's face, neck, and arms. While the head attendant dressed her in intricate robes, the outer one a heavily brocaded blue and silver, another maid handled her hair. After combing, then brushing it, the servant pulled the front back from her face and braided it in a style that crowned her head.

"Slowly, Empress Pridric." The head attendant helped the other bring her to her feet.

The sheer weight of her body and the robes on her legs made her swoon. Sharp static pain shot through them. She hissed through her teeth. The servants didn't let her falter, their grip firm. They kept her there until she felt stable.

"Ready, Empress?"

Empress.

Pridric made a sharp intake of air. Memories of Tavelo begging desperately for her to accept the title before he ravished her. Everything after that became a blur. Snippets of lucidity, yet she still couldn't decipher them.

As she walked past the mirrored armoire, she caught a glimpse of her eyes. Despite her cloudy vision, they sparkled brighter than anything else. Two swirls of multicolored kaleidoscopes beamed.

What's happened to me? Pridric cried silently. Did Tavelo's Volshin DNA override mine?

The troupe stepped out into the corridor and the two attendants released her to walk on her own as they followed close by. Two royal guards came along. Sun rays slanted through the wall windows, giving the corridor a yellow glow.

Not quite midday. Pridric sighed.

Sparse foot traffic made it easier to relax. The few people strolling the halls bowed to her. Some in awe, others with worry.

I probably look horrid. I feel horrid.

Movement on her left startled her.

She turned, squinting, to see what caused the commotion. That scent. That presence. She knew it better than her own. Tavelo's fingers went behind her ear and ran through her hair as he drew her close.

"My beautiful Empress," he breathed as his lips covered hers. Their kiss lingered. Pridric's anxiety melted away. Tavelo disengaged and stared into her eyes. "I'm glad to see you awake."

Pridric fought back tears of exhaustion. Her body had already met its threshold after only a half hour of walking.

"I'm tired," she whispered. Her eyes reflected in his and she saw the many colors up close. "I'm sorry."

Tavelo's hand slipped away. He stepped back, scrutinizing every inch of her.

"I will come check on you later."

He turned and resumed his walk, with a procession of guards following. Pridric realized he would be on his way to another morning meeting. Without a word, her attendants guided her back to her room, the same route as before.

Inside her chamber, Dania waited, leaning on the foot of the bed with a floating basinet. She started to rise until she saw Pridric's face. A frown formed.

"I heard you had awakened." Dania pushed off the bed and walked Pridric to it. The attendants bowed and left the room. "Maybe it was too soon to let you move around."

"I can't stay in bed," Pridric cried defiantly. "I won't be bedridden!"

It sounded more like a sob than a yell.

"There's no rush." Dania set her on the side of the bed. "Lay back down."

Pridric tugged on the heavy outer robe, feeling for the clasp to undo it. Dania smacked her hand and removed it for her. When she swung her legs up and lay upright against the headboard, Dania used the fob in her hand to bring the basinet closer.

"At the very least, you must see your adorable spawns."

Pridric's eyes widened.

She peered into the basinet at the two bundles wiggling in their sleep. Tears brimming in her eyes, she used a finger to rub their cheeks. They both yawned, the one on the left raising their tiny fists in the air. Then their eyes opened. Pridric reared back at the glowing kaleidoscopes. She folded over in grief, her tears falling onto the blanket covering them.

"Don't fret." Dania caressed the top of her head. "They need time to adjust, just as you do."

"I don't understand," Pridric wailed. "Why are they not well? What's wrong with me?"

Dania stiffened. Pridric turned to her and saw the rage brewing within her.

"It's from what your clan did to you long ago."

A heavy thump beat in Pridric's chest, almost pitching her forward. She clutched the front of her robes. Those memories she kept at bay. Never allowing them to resurface. Then it struck her. How does Dania know? If she did, then Tavelo knows as well. The sudden urge to sleep hit her.

"You're not ready to come back yet." Dania caught her head as it fell back, stopping it from hitting the headboard. "Maybe a few more days."

Pridric let Dania ease her back down and pull the covers over her. She fell into a deep sleep.

"How is she?" Tavelo asked Dania, standing in the nursery. Although designated for his royal twins, other infants were present. "I didn't like the way she looked earlier."

Dania turned around to face him. He noticed her expression and nodded.

"She needs more time. I think she won't awaken again for another few days." Dania paused, checking on the twins in the basinet. "She saw their eyes. It almost did her in."

"The royal scientists are researching a remedy." Tavelo clenched his fists. "I won't forgive the Stranas for this." His eyes glowed silver for a split second. "If only I could narrow the punishment down."

"Why?" Dania's brow raised. "Implement all the options. There is no need to limit your vengeance."

Tavelo tilted his head.

"I feel you have some suggestions of your own."

"I never enjoyed being in their circle. Like Chalayl, I was slated to be sent to another clan for the sole purpose of breeding. Every day among the Stranas made me think of fleeing."

"I'm glad you didn't." Tavelo went to her side and tickled his new offspring. "Nor Omaris."

Dania couldn't contain her anger, letting her eyes go red. Her lisp drew back.

"We would never leave Pridric or Omeron in that pit of hell."

Her conviction surprised Tavelo. Then he thought about it. The Stranas were capable of great evil. He couldn't imagine what Dania witnessed before their elders sent them away.

A month of being freshly washed and fed lifted morale in the Brownlee coven. They attended daily meetings with heads of other covens in rotation to get up to speed. Small plates of half-eaten food littered each table. The white cloth stained with spilled drink and remnants of messy consumption.

Holnar Bryhel and Chancellor Rayne took turns relaying information from a holoscreen displayed on the far wall.

Windsor listened without interruption.

He contemplated what he and his coven wanted. On Earth, retail sales were king. The Brownlees had profited greatly until their fall. Years of freedom from the rat race of commerce left them complacent in their plight.

Do we really want to go through all that again? He stared at the table before him during another meeting. The logistics of running a business swirled in his head and he cringed. So much work!

"Are you really not paying attention?" Holnar asked tersely.

Windsor looked up to find everyone staring at him. Holnar's face flushed with disdain.

"Not particularly, no." No sense in lying. "I don't think we can do it."

"What?"

Holnar's tone bordered on fire and brimstone.

"This. Re-establishing our business. Going up against our elders. We don't have it in us anymore."

"Oh? And you speak for everyone in this room?" Chancellor Rayne asked.

To Holnar and Chancellor Rayne's surprise, the entire room nodded. Windsor smirked, meeting Holnar's gaze. The two seemed confused by the response.

"What would you have us do? Go into the same market as our clan? They already have the contracts for every proprietor on Cellaxa. We would only be subsidiaries with no real say in goods."

"True." Chancellor Rayne pursed his lips.

"How about this, then?" Innego entered the room, having listened outside the door. "I had a feeling you may be reluctant to come back into the fold." He walked past Holnar and Chancellor Rayne. "I propose you work under me as dock inspectors."

Windsor gave him a surprised stare, then scanned the room at his people for a reaction. They didn't reject the idea. He sniffed hard, sitting back in his chair while folding his arms. Innego's sly expression made him wary, but he felt inclined to listen further.

The spy walked through a hall he shouldn't be in, careful not to draw attention to himself. He wore a uniform designating him as a lower house royal guard. His cover while infiltrating the East Palace on behalf of the Strana clan. Having to wear the blue and silver getup angered him. He adjusted the sash at his waist where his sword hung attached. Even the scabbard bore Endaga colors.

He rounded the corner at the end of the hall into a larger corridor. Royal members littered its width, with traffic going both ways. The usual amount of people during midday taking walks to gossip. Which is why he chose it. Information had all but sealed close to the emperor's main chambers. No one said anything outside their duties. That alerted him some major event had occurred.

Keeping his head down, he slunk among the masses, his ears honed on their voices. After nearly a half hour of eavesdropping, he got a hit.

"When do you think they will introduce the new empress?" A woman strolling with three others asked.

"Well, she still needs to recover from giving birth to the royal twins," the woman on her left replied.

"I did hear it was a difficult delivery," the one

behind the first said. "They almost lost her."

"To think, a Strana and an Endaga would be mated." The first woman sighed. "Maybe that will stop the infighting."

"Hmph!" The woman behind her turned her nose up at the notion. "I doubt it."

"Please, ladies." The fourth woman chastised them. "We shouldn't speak so casually. Have you forgotten?"

"Oh!" The first two covered their mouths while their gaze darted around them.

"There's a spy in our midst," the fourth woman whispered.

The spy frowned. Though he himself had not been made, his presence was. Now it made sense. The royal investigators had narrowed the leaks down to the emperor's wing. He ducked into an open chamber, making sure no one was inside, and waited for the procession of women to pass. Another few minutes and he stepped back out, heading back the way he came.

Being off duty, he left through the servants' entrance out to the edge of the palace grounds. The midday sun barely created enough light and warmth through the bluish gray sky. The forestation ahead grew dense, trapping in moisture. Wet leaves and twisted branches covered the muddy forest floor. There he tapped the wristband he kept hidden in the folds of his robes. He plopped on a large boulder to wait for his ride.

A small transport carriage came into view down the overgrown foot path. The spy jogged towards it, pushing low hanging tree branches out of his way. He entered the open door, having to step a few inches up where it hovered above the ground.

Inside, Master Strana's assistant sat on the bench to his right. He eased down on the other across from him right as the carriage took off.

"You must've learned something good to contact me so urgently," the assistant said.

"Yes. It is dire, indeed."

"Speak."

"Tavelo Endaga has taken an empress. It has not been announced."

"Is that so?" The assistant's eyes narrowed. "I wonder why."

"The new empress has given birth to twins."

The assistant's head snapped up, his eyes glowed blood red.

"No."

"The new empress is Pridric." The spy pushed himself further into the back of the bench seat, scared by the assistant's sudden murderous aura. "I think they are keeping her hidden from other parts of the palace."

"I will relay your report to Master Strana. Do not wait for a reply. Proceed as planned."

"Is there a timeline?"

The assistant's irises turned silver.

"The first chance you get, kill that thing and its spawn."

"As you command." The spy relaxed. He watched the assistant also regain his composure and eased back. "I will send word when it is done."

"No. You will leave the palace immediately. Do you really think they won't suspect you if both are found murdered?"

"Of course. My position would be forfeited in the palace."

The carriage came around to the end of the footpath, where it picked him up. He exited it and bowed to the assistant.

"Don't get caught before then." The assistant hit the close button, and the door slammed shut.

The spy waited for it to disappear before turning towards the palace. As he walked, he went through scenarios to implement his plan.

Taking a bite of the fruit he plucked from a nearby tree, Tervan sat perched on a branch, watching the spy leisurely walk into the palace. The tiny, winged creatures nesting above squeaked at him for invading their space. He paid them no mind.

His observation of the spy in action came the moment he saw the roster of royal guards assigned to the East Palace.

A Strana rarely went into military service. When they did, it was to become imperial soldiers for carnage and glory. Not this one. He opted to be a servant, switching his role before the blood-letting rites to make him an imperial soldier.

A poor plan. Tervan snorted, causing flecks of juice and fruit to fly. Too hasty as he saw it.

Tervan didn't need to hear what transpired in the carriage. He had already assessed the spy's role. He would let the spy make an attempt, but never allow him to succeed. The royal investigators needed to catch him in the act. He leaped down, landing softly on the mushy ground.

Should I report this?

Tervan tossed the fruit core behind him. Knowing his father, he would close ranks, alerting the spy.

But I have to tell someone!

He thought hard, running through everyone in contact with Pridric and her new offspring. One kept circling around.

Dania.

Trade Wars

Commissioner Polp perused the daily reports for the week from both docks. His wide-screen monitor hovered in front of him. Using one finger, he swiped through them, frowning more as he went. *Are they mocking me?* The contract and inspection issues stemmed from the elder merchants. *Why go to such lengths to gain status over their own children?*

It didn't make sense.

He pulled his puffy sleeved robe tighter around him and leaned back in his plush swivel chair. A chill swept through the small palace office he claimed nearly a century ago. The two hundred square feet made for the perfect hideout. Only a desk, his chair, and the monitor furnished it. Cool air drifted down from the ceiling vents.

To his surprise, a young man rapped on the door frame. Commissioner Polp saw his reflection on the screen, then turned around to greet him.

"And what can I do for you?"

Windsor, wearing the same clothes as before, stepped into the room.

"Greetings, Commissioner Polp. I've been assigned as your new assistant."

"Ahh, the trainee my head assistant told me about. He does need the help, as do I." Commissioner Polp gestured to him. "Come. You can see what I see. Tell me your assessment." Windsor leaned over to see the screen better. "I should get you a chair." He looked around, even though he knew there would be none.

"It's fine."

He watched the young man's eyes move with the flow of text. After a few minutes, he stood straight and let his arms hang at his side.

"It seems the West dock elders circumvented parts of the contract. With inspections ramping up, they've found a loophole."

"Indeed. What do you think I should do in this situation?" Windsor's possible answer intrigued him. He waited patiently as the young man crossed his arms. "Take your time."

"I would say nothing for now. These appear to be one offs. Like they're testing the waters to see how far they can take it."

"Hmm, hmm," Commissioner Polp nodded.

"On Earth, they have a saying. Three strikes and you're out. And third times a charm."

"An obsession with the number three."

"I guess so. Never thought of it until now."

"So we give them three chances to correct their actions." Commissioner Polp rubbed his chin. "That seems to be three too many in my book."

"But, at the same time, you don't want to antagonize the elder clans. Especially the top ten."

Commissioner Polp snorted.

"Ever since the emperor Manel's taming, they have regained some confidence. With the return of their young ones, it has turned to something else."

"Jealousy," Windsor blurted. "Envy. They were set in their ways. Now they see new opportunities they should have."

"Well, that's on them. I will not have my authority scoffed at." He stared up at the young man. "I'll need to report this to the emperors."

He tapped the transfer icon on the screen. It winked out, descending onto the desk until flat.

"Please join me. It's part of your training."

He pulled a ten-inch tablet from the folds of his robe and tapped the screen. It came to life with the documents displayed in a fanned succession. Satisfied that the data transferred correctly, he put it back to sleep and into his robes.

They exited his office and made their way through the winding palace halls. Both emperors would be in the dual throne room this time of day, taking a break from morning meetings. Royal house members and guards walked the corridors, killing time until afternoon meal.

Commissioner Polp took in Windsor's overall demeanor. He heard about the coven's plight from Innego. Knowing how Loengir operated, he agreed with the young man's decision. That still didn't make what their family did to them right.

The slums? Such cruelty!

Two Imperial guards flanked the giant double doors of the combined throne room. The commissioner bowed his head, Windsor following suit. On the other side of the room, the caller yelled out.

"Trade Commissioner Polp and his assistant have arrived for an audience with the emperors."

He could see Emperor Manel and Tavelo wince, their mouths downturned at the oral assault. It was a bit much, in his opinion.

"Greetings, Emperor Manel, Emperor Tavelo." The commissioner bowed as he stepped to the edge of the platform. "I believe my new assistant needs no introduction."

"All the same," Manel's gaze bore down into Windsor's back while he bowed. "I want him to take this seriously."

"My apologies, Emperor Manel." Windsor raised his head. "I am Windsor Brownlee of Loengir clan, son of Aker. We ran the Brownlee coven on Earth."

Tavelo gave him a forlorn look. Manel's brow scrunched, as if he found the young man distasteful.

Well, that's a rough start.

Commissioner Polp sighed heavily.

"So, why have you come here?" Manel's stare never left the young man, despite addressing the commissioner. "Is it that dire?"

"It could pose an issue," Polp replied.

He handed his tablet to the guard coming towards him. They placed it on a data platform near the foot of the thrones. The documents displayed in midair, spanning half the room.

"Please, see for yourselves."

The guard tapped the tablet screen to spread each document out. Tavelo's hand clenched while Manel simply glared at it. Oh! The commissioner took a step back. *They are not amused.*

"And your plans to remedy this?" Manel asked.

The commissioner nodded to Windsor.

"I suggested we do nothing for now. Apply the three-strike rule."

"What nonsense is that?" Manel leaned forward, baring teeth.

"Calm yourself," Tavelo chided him, raising a hand to stop him. "This may work."

Manel sat back with a dubious expression. Gallic mimicked it, not buying it either.

The clan elders were too proud to back off. They would easily fall into an imperial trap. And it seemed Tavelo had an idea which clans were first in line, as did he.

Dania moved around the nursery, checking stock on the changing cloths, wipes, and unsullied infant gowns. Her cream-colored robe, with a sheer overlay, swished along the floor. The long sleeves that widened at the wrists brushed the top of each cabinet as she passed.

Quiet.

She relished it, knowing it would be short-lived once the babies awakened. Rays from the setting sun gave the room a golden glow as it slowly dimmed.

The other infants had already been picked up by their parents' or the servant in charge. Only Pridric's remained. She sat in the chair next to their basinet and felt her body slump. Taking a few deep breaths, she finally relaxed.

"Was it that bad?" Pridric asked at the entrance.

Dania looked over and tried not to flinch at those kaleidoscope eyes glinting in the light. Pridric wore simple blue and silver robes, her hair undone. She went over to her twin boys and leaned into the basinet.

"And how are you, my little demons?" Her hushed tone made Dania tilt her head in awe. She had never heard that from Pridric. "Have you tired out poor Dania?"

"Huh?" Dania shook her head. "Those precious things don't make any fuss. It's the other ones."

Pridric rose a bit and turned her head to Dania.

"Oh. Manel's?"

"Did you have to ask?"

They both smirked, letting a small laugh escape their lips.

Pridric straightened her posture and turned around as two arrows sailed past her head. She froze. Her eyes widened. She saw Dania bend to the side, avoiding the one headed straight for her. Dania's focus shifted to the hall behind her and saw two pairs of feet laying toes up.

A servant guard appeared in the doorway.

"Pardon my intrusion, Empress." The guard bowed. "I have a message for you."

"And who would this message come from?" Dania rose to her feet.

The royal guard's eyes went red as he sneered.

"Master Strana sends his regards."

He advanced into the room in a flash, his body

position crouched low, catching them off guard with not knowing his plan of attack. When he got a few feet from Pridric, Dania stepped between them, bringing her fist down onto his shoulder blades. He stumbled forward, allowing Pridric to kick him back. His instant recovery surprised them again.

The royal guard whipped out two arrows and fired them off before either could move. Seeing their projectory, Pridric went to push the basinet out of the way. The arrows hit right as it tipped over. Dania closed the gap between her and the assassin, landing a blow to his head. He spun around from the impact. Following a full rotation, the bow fell from one hand and a short blade replaced it.

Dania couldn't stop her momentum and felt the cold metal sink into her right side. He knocked her out of the way, forcing the blade's release. Blood splattered on his robes and the side of his face. With no delay, he moved forward while Pridric was still in free fall, the basinet hitting the floor.

The high-pitched screams of the twins made him wince in pain. Pridric took advantage of his falter and went down on one knee. She punched him in the solar plexus, causing him to bend forward. Blood flew from his mouth as he gacked. Yet, he didn't waste the opportunity. His blade went into her back, right below the shoulder, stopping him from flying back. He pushed deeper to reach the main artery located in the front.

Bent over beneath him, Pridric grabbed hold of his arms and pulled. Sensing his arms were about to be snapped off, he released his hold. Dania had him by the hair and flung him into the side wall. More blood sprayed out of his mouth. He fell to the floor. To their surprise, he scrambled to his feet, grabbing his bow and ran from the room.

Dania could hear royal guards yelling, their boots striking the marbled halls. Tervan arrived, his expression one of malice. A few scratches on his face let her know he had been fighting.

"I'm sorry," he spat. "He got away from me." He turned to the royal guards behind him. "Stay with the Empress. I'm going in pursuit."

"Tervan!" Dania extended an arm to stop him. "Don't..." She watched him pivot towards the assassin's direction and flash step down the corridor. The move caused her wound to expand. "Damn it!" She winced, clutching her side to stop the bleeding.

On the floor by the basinet, Pridric heaved, her breath raspy. She lay on her side with one elbow propping her up. A small circle of blood appeared on the side of the basinet. The twins had stopped wailing.

Oh no!

Dania saw the rage in Pridric's eyes.

Two royal guards were tossed aside as Tavelo forced his way through the cluster at the entrance. His demeanor matched Pridric's. He went to the basinet and looked inside. His expression fell. With great care, he gently lifted one of the twins out and cradled him. Blood trickled from a gash on his forearm.

Relief filled his face as he pressed the baby to him. He looked down at his brother laying still, in shock from the ordeal. The arrows had missed their mark. The one that grazed the first, stuck through at an angle while the other sat mere millimeters above the other twin's chest.

"Get the royal physicians!" Tavelo ordered.

The two guards he pushed down, regained their footing, and hurried out the room. Using the commlink would alert the main palace of the incident. It already looked dire, with royal guards down and more coming to assist.

"Tervan is in pursuit," Dania said, breathless. "His words." Tavelo's lips pursed. "I did try to stop him."

"Like that?" Tavelo glanced at her wound.

Tamar came into the room and took the baby

from his arms. Tavelo opened his mouth to protest.

"Take care of your empress!" Tamar shouted as she ripped the arrow out the basinet to retrieve the other twin. "What are you doing?" Her angry tone made them all flinch.

Tavelo finally focused on Pridric. His expression of malice returned.

"This wound is deep." He gauged how far it went and determined a few more centimeters and it would have punched through her chest. "They'll pay for this," he seethed. Pridric grabbed the front of his robes, her grip like a vise. "I'm here."

Dania turned away from the tears streaming down Pridric's face. That sense of weakness oozed from her very soul. The blow to the assassin didn't do as much damage compared to if she were at full strength.

I didn't fare any better! Dania chastised herself for not noticing the assassin earlier. She kept watch of Pridric's surroundings after Tervan alerted her to the potential threat.

A royal physician arrived with four technicians. They went to the task of treating her, Pridric, and the infant's wounds. The atmosphere turned hostile. Every guard seemed to take the blame for allowing the event to happen. And that a fellow guard was the culprit. Dania understood that feeling well.

❀ ❀ ❀

The assassin made it to the other side of the palace. He barely stepped out from the servants' entrance into the evening gloom when a sword swung at his head. Bending backwards, he avoided a beheading, and flipped all the way over to face his assailant.

Innego stood, sword extended. His eyes glowed silver. *I may be in trouble.* The assassin twirled his short blade and gripped the handle.

"It looks like you had a hard time." Innego didn't

give his usual combat smile. "Shall I relieve you of your suffering?"

"I'm not suffering. Just had a slight misstep." The assassin wiped blood from his mouth.

"Is that so?"

"That thing and its spawn will be taken care of in due time."

Innego moved without warning, his lightning speed forcing the assassin to defend mindlessly. Not getting a moment to make a plan of attack. He felt the skin on his arms, chest, legs being sliced open.

Damn it! He's too fast!

"That prey is mine!" Tervan yelled as he slid to a stop at the entrance. He came out, his sword drawn. "Step away."

Innego didn't acknowledge him, pushing the assassin further towards the palace. Tervan flashed forward to strike the assassin in the back. He dodged to the side, forcing Innego to step away to avoid Tervan's sword.

Now's my chance!

The assassin sped towards a nearby tree and climbed up. Innego turned to see him already high above. Tervan screamed in rage, running after him. The assassin snorted. Giving the two a victorious grin, he leaped from tree to tree, disappearing into the darkening horizon.

"Fuck!" Tervan turned to Innego. "If you were going to interfere, you should have struck him down with the first blow."

The way Innego's silver eyes turned on him made Tervan shrink inwardly. He had never seen such a stare from the womanizing leader.

"I would say the same to you since you decided to do the same. His death was imminent."

Innego sheathed his sword and went back into the palace. Tervan stared into the distance. The assassin may have gotten away, but the Strana clan had much to answer to.

Trade representatives from every empire in the three systems arrived on Cellaxa via commercial transport. Its sleek silver alloy glinted as it passed over the docks. Their official ships scattered outside its orbit remained in standby formations.

Commissioner Polp felt the corner of his lips twitch. The last gathering with them happened over five hundred years ago, when he was still under his father's tutelage.

His robes fluttered in the gust of wind created from the transport's landing. It added to the already chilly breeze accompanying the gloom. Grey clouds darkened the sky, refusing the sun's rays. He stared at them, wishing silently for rain. Windsor stood with authority beside him wearing new clothes. *Thank the founders!* A simple dark brown suit with a white tunic and short boots made him look like a merchant again.

"Are you certain the venue we booked accommodates all of them?" Commissioner Polp asked.

Windsor raised the tablet attached to his hand looped under its handle. He pulled up the venue's layout where the newest wares Cellaxa offered would be showcased.

"Sixteen dignitaries and their proxies. I think it may be too big,"

"Let's hope the merchant leaders are on their best behavior for the exposition."

The transport's ramp extended. Creatures of various races, wearing expensive robes and military uniforms, descended. Commissioner Polp could tell they were going to be difficult and demanding. At the bottom of the ramp, they congregated, making pleasantries while sizing each other up.

"Let's get them there and this whole ordeal over with," Commissioner Polp told Windsor.

They made their way to the group. A good five of the representatives turned to give disdained looks at them. Commissioner Polp noted who they were.

Windsor appeared to do the same.

"Greetings, guests! It is a pleasure to meet you once again." Comissioner Polp exclaimed.

"Where is your father? Is he not facilitating this?" A representative in elaborate robes asked briskly. He stared at him dubiously. "Who's the authority here?"

"My father has retired," he replied tersely. He fought to contain his anger. "I've been in charge of the trade commission the past four hundred years."

"Hmph. That doesn't make you competent."

Windsor stepped forward.

"If you are not here to make a trade proposal, we can have another transport escort you back to your ship. Just know that you will not be allowed to depart until the others are finished with their bids."

Dead silence blanketed the group. The representative's eyes narrowed. When no one else voiced any concerns, Windsor gestured towards the boardwalk.

"If you would follow us, a vehicle waits to take you all to the expo."

Such professionalism!

Commissioner Polp praised him. He needed to find a fitting reward after the dignitaries left.

A fifty-capacity double level transport normally used for military units sat curbside at the end of the boardwalk. Everyone filed in and the pilot engaged the engines right when the doors sealed.

Despite its size, the vehicle sped through the first sector. The passengers didn't see much scenery until it slowed down entering the city.

Ahead on their left, the venue came into sight. A circular structure of white slate with a dome made of green tempered glass. Merchant transports littered the backside. Commissioner Polp saw the merchant elders and coven leaders.

Good.

The transport eased to a stop in front of the entrance. Commissioner Polp and Windsor exited first.

Each guest followed in a single file, looking around, taking in the area. The double glass doors slid open to the sides, letting them enter four at a time.

Inside, products of every kind sprawled throughout the multi levels. The bottom floor had bigger items in the center. Along the curved walls, every merchant stood with their wares. The buyers let out collective gasps at the collection.

Commissioner Polp felt a sense of pride.

He commended the setup, knowing infighting occurred on who would get the prominent bottom level. Bryhel got the honor, showcasing new tools and machines. Which made sense, considering their size. Eight levels in all, with two merchant clans on each, gave the representatives a nice spread of goods to feast on.

Servants awaiting the arrivals spilled out from the side doors on each level. Lady Dania had researched the delicacies for the races and created a generous array of foods they could all enjoy.

"Please, browse. Take your time. Negotiations are open." Commissioner Polp raised both arms and waved them forward. "Merchants, be courteous."

He watched them flow along the exhibits, scrutinizing every product. By the hour mark, heated arguments erupted.

"We demand exclusivity!" The fourth empire representative said to a planet representative from the second quadrant. "You don't even have enough business for this product's uses!"

"Your people don't get to have a monopoly," the other spat back.

While they squabbled, their proxies fought each other with the merchant leader. Eterenia Jaubro looked put out by the situation. The same happened at every level. The Dakien clan seemed amused by the fight for deals, while the Endaga clan moved about uncomfortably.

A bidding war ensued.

Seventy percent of the new products came from Earth. Not having seen anything like them in their systems, the representatives wanted to snatch them for their own purposes. Commissioner Polp smirked. Cellaxa would keep the reins.

"That is not up for debate," Eterenia finally cut the two representatives off. "Why should I limit my business to one with a marginal gain when I can get three times the revenue if I go broad?"

"We would generate equal business with third party dealers," the fourth empire representative said. "The numbers would build over time."

"Meanwhile, no one else can get it because they have to wait for it to go through your acquisition system," the other retorted.

"Exactly," Eterenia replied. She glanced over at Armon handling the proxies. "Please make a more reasonable bid." Armon nodded to her.

The waterproof attire created by the Endaga clan had three different representatives vying for rights. Since they made the product jointly with the Durante coven, Tamar and Master Endaga tried to fend them off.

A foreboding pricked the commissioner. He turned to see Master Strana scanning the levels as if listening to every word. His gaze fell on him. An icy stare like a knife went through his chest. In the next instant, Master Strana's focus went elsewhere.

Windsor frowned, seeing the exchange. The Stranas would be up to no good. He gave the commissioner a warning stare. Neither could do anything until they knew the outcome.

Every port on the docks saw multiple cargo lifts crammed into their spaces. Massive orders flooded through Cellaxa over a short period of time. The dock workers did their best to keep up, moving them to their designated merchant's holding area. Whistles and the banging of cargo being transported drowned out the voices of proprietors making last-minute deals.

Exhaust fumes drifted into the air, mingling with the ever-grey clouds. No sun again for the second week in a row. Master Strana peered at the sky. Although the sun remained hidden, its strength still affected the eyes. He squinted to lessen the strain on his retinas.

The proprietor before him prattled on about unfairness regarding negotiatons for multiple contracts. That didn't concern him. Of course it wasn't fair. Master Strana let out a sigh, disrupting the man's flow of words.

"How about this?" Master Strana sneered. "I'll get you two shipments of your choice. What can you do for me?"

"Is it a guarantee?" The man asked, dubiously.

His eyes widened in anticipation.

"Have I ever not guaranteed an order?"

His gaze made the man step back in fear. He cleared his throat and tugged his jacket down before matching Master Strana's stare.

"I will waive delivery fees and discount the transport." He tilted his nose up. "On transfer of goods, obviously."

"Yes." Master Strana cocked his head, amused. "I want a no harm negotiation clause." The proprietor and his proxy raised their heads in surprise. "Just a precaution. In case something goes awry." They frowned. "Or this conversation is over."

"No, no!" The man waved his hands in front of him. "I will make sure my proxy gets it to you by end of day." He leaned forward. "When can I expect the goods?"

"After the clause is signed."

Master Strana smiled sweetly.

When he didn't speak further, the man and his

proxy took the hint and walked off. Master Strana pinched the bridge of his nose and glanced back at his assistant standing behind him.

"Find out how many pieces are in the Endaga, Durante, and Dakien shipments."

"May I ask the plan?"

Master Strana glowered.

"You may not. I will let you know when you get me the data."

"My apologies. Of course." He brought his tablet to eye level. "What numbers do you need?"

"At minimum, five from each. That should satisfy that greedy horder."

Master Strana averted his gaze to the Endaga bays. A twinge of guilt caught him off guard. His brow furrowed. What for? He couldn't say he wasn't doing anything wrong. Old habits die hard. Then he recalled the report from the spy. All the effort his family put into keeping Pridric and Tavelo apart ended up in vain. How did Pridric manage to spawn any children with such a damaged body?

"Master Strana?"

He looked over at his assistant, staring at him with concern.

"I'm heading back to the homestead."

"I'll have this done by midday."

Master Strana grabbed his full-length black coat off a cargo box as he left the bay. His long strides covered twice the steps of everyone else around him. As he passed the Dakien bay, he tilted his hat to Master Dakien. The man gave him a nasty look as he did the same.

He snorted.

"That was uncalled for," he muttered to himself.

"Because we don't trust you, Strana." Master Callesi called out, emerging from the back of his bay. "You can't blame us, either. For all we know, you're scheming to screw us over this very moment."

For some reason Master Strana's gaze panned

over to the Endaga bay. Master Endaga stood staring intensely at him. The two men locked eyes.

"Just as I thought." Master Callesi tsked. "Your clan can never leave well enough alone. They don't deserve the strife you cause them."

"I know that!" Master Strana replied in a low tone, baring teeth.

He severed his gaze from Master Endaga and resumed his walk to the end of the docks, where his transport waited. Inside, he settled into the first swivel chair and tapped the screen on the back of the divider between him and the driver. It displayed the calling tree. He found his assistant's contact.

It pinged twice before the man answered.

"Mater Strana?"

"Look into Callesi as well as Sapienti."

"A grudge?"

"The same total as the others."

"They must have angered you good."

"Get it done."

Master Strana disconnected the call. The screen went blank, then replaced by the family insignia. The Strana clan only went after the lower merchant clans. Meaning none in the top five. To go after Callesi would no doubt cause a stir, their clan being fourth in line behind them. The same for Bryhel who ranked second or third, switching with Strana often.

The transport stopped in front of the Strana homestead. He scanned the multilevel structure that spanned nearly five thousand square feet. One of the largest homes on Cellaxa that equaled a fifth the size of the palace. A dark grey fortress of stone and metal, ominous no matter the time of day. The over-sized double doors of the entrance opened outward to create the illusion of entering an abyss.

A fitting home for monsters.

Master Strana stepped out and waved the driver away. The transport had to go back to retrieve his assistant, and the proxy left behind tallying the cargo inventory. Two sentries on each side of the entrance bowed as he passed them. He tossed his hat on the table in the foyer and his coat to a servant standing by near the main corridor.

He felt agitated. Not only with the unease of backstabbing his fellow merchants. What needed to be done with Pridric weighed on him. The Strana clan vowed to eradicate the ancient bloodline from their own. He never asked why. It had been in place for centuries. By his father's decree, any Strana found to have ancient blood or attempted to mate with one would be slaughtered.

Hypocrite!

Master Strana entered his private chamber and plopped onto the edge of his bed. He stretched his long body sideways across it, resting his head on his bicep, using it as a pillow. He focused on the empty wall. The only furniture in his chamber was that of necessity. He had no need for extra material things.

Trade. Revenue. Strana dominance.

Those, his father raised them all to prioritize. He never wanted to be head of the clan. With his father and older brother's demise at the hands of Emperor Manel, no one else stepped up. As the obvious next in line, he had no choice. And he decided to be ruthless. That was the only way to survive in the emperor's new era of bloodshed and slavery.

Jaubro. If only he could find a way to surpass them. The backlash from going after them would destroy the Strana clan. Master Jaubro proved more cunning than his brother, the previous leader.

Enough!

The wall lit up, displaying a holoscreen feed from his assistant's tablet. He slid halfway up onto one hand planted flat on the bed. A grid of information from each merchant clan's invoices overlay each other. An illegal hack he would gladly pay the fine for. His eyes narrowed.

Time to make a deal and have a bit of fun.

CHAPTER THREE

Competition

Holoscreens popped up in the sky above every sector across the planet. Their brightness lit up the early morning gloom. People outside squinted at them. Those inside went to the nearest windows. An announcement in bold letters with a background of fireworks gave a festive vibe.

Join the Battle Maiden Competition! To be held on the third moon cycle at the palace arena. Sign up to see the list of prizes! All spectators welcomed.

Dock workers stared at it in awe. They were never allowed to attend palace events. Even store owners had been barred. Now it seemed the royal house had lifted that restriction.

The merchant families outside the top ten stared at it with trepidation. What was the point of the competition? Whose idea was it?

The message stayed until a few sun rays cracked through the clouds. It faded out before disappearing completely. Young men scratched their heads while the older generation grinned with anticipation.

Battle Maidens dominated the combat forces. Women warriors fiercer than any imperial soldier. Although some families still trained for them, the numbers dwindled after Emperor Mallen decreed their services no longer necessary.

In the East palace study, the usual group of women sat gathered drinking tea.

Eterenia sipped hers slowly, trying to mask the nervous jitters in her hands. Dania and Maritze stared each other down while Adelia and Grasilda kept to themselves.

"Will you enter, Eterenia?" Maritze spread one arm over the back of the loveseat she occupied. Her mouth curved into a sinister grin. "I would love to beat you down to a pulp in the final rounds."

Adelia sputtered, flecks of tea flying from her lips. Dania glared at her. Eterenia leaned forward and set her cup down on the center table. She sat up and met Maritze's stare.

"That's presumptuous of you to think you can."

"Yes, quite the statement," Dania sneered.

"Oh come now. Your mother was a great battle maiden. Yet, she never sent you for training."

"What does that matter?" Eterenia cocked her head. "Real combat trumps training."

"Oh ho!" Maritze laughed.

"I think you underestimate the dedication that goes with being a battle maiden." Grasilda paused, sipping her tea, not looking at any of them. "Some may find your words insulting."

A silence fell on the room.

Maritze smirked at Eterenia.

"Well, if it's insult you crave," Adelia huffed. "None of you have really done much fighting. If anyone could probably take out my mother, it's me."

Adelia closed her eyes as she brought her cup to her lips, smiling haughtily. Her blonde hair, back to its illustrious color after overcoming years of abuse, framed her face in big curls.

She resembled a doll.

Dania's mouth gaped open, ready to counter, yet nothing came out. She sat stunned by her words. Eterenia looked confused, not sure how to respond either. Maritze finally burst into laughter, throwing her head back. The sound echoed, causing the other women to wince.

She let her neck rest on the top of the loveseat as she finished, calming herself. When she rose it, her eyes gleamed.

"Now that, I would give funds to see."

"Adelia," Eterenia said softly, "a great fighter you may be, and I recognize that, but I think you're being naïve." She gave her a gentle smile.

To which Adelia lowered her cup and locked eyes with her.

"What? You think I can't take you?" Her snappy tone made Eterenia jerk upright. Adelia's gaze didn't waver. "Like she said, you're not a battle maiden. I can try my hand at it, too."

"Well said, child." Grasilda nodded in agreement.

"Wait." Adelia looked over to Maritze, then Dania. "What about you two?"

Dania seemed to shrink inward, her expression going blank. Maritze laid her other arm out across the loveseat and settled against it.

"I was once a battle maiden in training and so was Dania. We forfeited our status when we left Cellaxa." She turned to Dania. "Now we can reclaim our titles."

"I don't really need or want any of the prizes," Dania replied softly.

"Pfft!" Maritze dropped her arms and leaned forward. "Who cares about that?" Her voice rose. "I just want to get in the arena and prove my worth. If I can take down the beast, Chalayl, I'll call it a win."

"Chalayl?" Adelia exclaimed.

"Ahh, the last great battle maiden who completed her initial training." Grasilda let out a sorrowful sigh. "A title she never wanted."

"She's been out of the loop for centuries. Surely she's not as formidable as before," Adelia said.

The other women glanced at her with pity. She reared back in her seat.

"The competition is all the masses are talking about." Tavelo stared out the wall windows as he walked the main palace corridor with Innego and his uncle. Four imperial guards followed. "I heard Adelia told the other women she could take her mother in a fight."

The group reached the dual throne room, where the doors sat open. They walked towards the platform where Manel and his siblings were already seated.

"Hah!" Innego blurted. "That's a bold declaration."

"Is she really entering the competition?" His uncle frowned. "Battle Maidens are not ones to trifle with."

"But, there hasn't been any in service for what, nearly a millennium?" Innego asked.

"And yet, our women are coming out of every crevice to meet the demand." Manel laughed. "I would pay handsomely to see mother and daughter take each other out."

Tavelo gave him a nasty stare. Manel grinned, resting his head on the palm of a propped-up elbow.

"This will give the ones in training a chance to prove themselves," Maxellia added. "A way to put all their skills to use and bring glory to their houses."

"Isn't Tamar's mother one?" Lenri asked. "And Eterenia'mother was one as well." She smiled at Tavelo. "Sounds like fun."

"I'm trying to dissuade them," Tavelo snapped.

"What for?" Megen sat on the far right throne, his massive frame overflowing with both legs wide apart. "I say let them. It'll strengthen their bond."

"And what's going on with the prizes?" Lendor pulled up the announcement on his tablet. "A com- memorative cape with the battle maiden insignia? Really?"

"I agree with the trade credits," Master Endaga said. "Useful."

"The station in the royal guard is only appealing to a handful of these competitors."

Innego leaned over Lendor's shoulder.

"But, better than most of the other ones."

"Yes. A pick of mates from the top families seems to be a popular perk. The women are clamoring for information on the candidates." Manel snorted. "Such whores ready to throw themselves at any man with status."

"That's not…" Tavelo cried out, then stopped himself. He took a deep breath.

"Am I wrong?" Manel's brow raised.

"Manel." Maxellia leaned forward so he could see her. "Many of us don't have your level of lust and debauchery."

"Wait?" Tavelo held up a hand as Manel's eyes turned red like ripe tomatoes. "Let's not do that." He turned to Maxellia and Lenri. "You can't say that when the main prize is simply your selfish need to do the same."

Master Endaga settled in a seat just below Tavelo's throne.

"He's correct in that assessment. A final challenge against one or both of you? What exactly does that accomplish?"

"If you merely want to feel pain during a fight, I will gladly assist," Megen said.

Four more guards entered the room flanking Pridric. Still recovering in female form, her heavily embroidered blue and silver robes seemed weighted, the hems dragged across the floor as if being pulled.

Her kaleidoscope eyes jarred everyone.

IncludingTavelo.

"Empress Pridric. So good to finally see you in attendance." Manel scanned her entire body.

Pridric met his gaze and shuddered.

"Stop that!" Tavelo stood from his throne and took Pridric's hand to guide her to the throne beside him. He caressed her cheek. "How are you feeling today?"

"Tired. But I refuse to stay cooped up in my chambers." Pridric gave him a tiny smile. "At least I'll have some entertainment soon." She glanced over at the announcement hovering in the air before Lendor. "I have a feeling Dania will enter after thinking it over a bit."

"She hates fighting," Tavelo replied, leaning back from her.

"Exactly. That doesn't change the fact that she's good at it."

"Hmm?" Manel dropped his arm onto the sides of his throne. "Should we actually set down a few wagers for this thing?"

Tavelo glared at him again. Maxellia's face glowed with excitement.

Ugh!

※ ※ ※

Olette perused the mate candidate images on her tablet with their stats below each one. She pulled the heavy handwoven blanket tighter around her, the bulk of it covering the entire chair. It cascaded over her bare feet, keeping them from touching the cold floor. A thick coil of hair fell into her face and brushed the tablet, moving the first image down.

"Huh. Must be a sign." She scrolled past his profile. "Wasn't too keen on a Jaubro, anyway." His flawless features, accompanied by too many accolades, turned her off a bit as well. "Next."

Beside each profile sat an icon with the words 'place your bid'. She noticed the high number on the last one. There would be a one in twenty chance of her getting him if she put hers in the running. And then she would have to make it in the top twenty-five to claim him.

The others came from Dakien, Loengir, and Bryhel. Her tablet's light made her face glow an eerie light blue in the dark room. She couldn't see anything beyond it and liked it that way. No one had come near the corridor outside to disturb her.

Her finger stopped on a Bryhel candidate. The blank expression on his face let the rest of his features shine. Olette leaned forward.

So beautiful and manly!

Thick dark hair past his shoulders framed a slightly tanned face with blue eyes. He wore a simple white tunic and what appeared to be a denim blue work apron or overalls. Good with his hands.

She bit her lower lip.

Her gaze fell on the bid count. Five others vied for him. She recognized the code numbers from the other higher bids.

"Oh, you wenches aren't serious about him." She tsked. "You'll only take him if you can't get the top ones." She ran a hand down the screen. "Don't worry, Krenan Bryhel. I want only you."

Olette tapped the bid icon. Her code appeared with the others. Bid successful displayed at the bottom. Now to get in the arena and beat a lot of women to make it to the top.

"What are you doing on the other side of the house in the dark?" Olivier asked from the doorway.

Olette jumped, causing her tablet to slide off her lap, hitting the floor.

"Don't do that!" She snapped, picking it up. The light beamed across the room and landed on her brother. "Give some warning, at least."

"Hmm? Were you doing something scandalous?"

"Of course not!" Olette gathered the blanket above her ankles so she wouldn't trip. "I was going over the competition info."

"You're not seriously going to compete?" Olivier pushed off the door frame. "These Cellaxan women are on a different level."

"I'm Cellaxan," she said hotly.

"Born and raised on Earth," Olivier countered. "Have you told father yet?"

Olette's eyes narrowed.

He would surely disagree. Forbid her, even.

"I'll let him know when the time is right."

"What prize are you looking to gain?" Olivier asked, before scanning her up and down. "You," he zeroed in on the tablet, "are you really?" He clamped his mouth with one hand. "Are any of them any good? I won't let you mate with some deluded half-wit from those clans."

"If you must know," Olette chided him, "Our clan has also put up a prospect or two."

Olivier dropped his hand and frowned.

"And that means what?"

"Seriously." Olette walked past him, out into the corridor. "If we don't have pride in our own clan, how are we supposed to convince others?"

The Bryhel clan's lower foundry bustled with activity. Workers flowed between workshops while servants kept a steady supply of drinks and finger food to fuel them. A mixture of machines whirring and shouting to overcome it reached a high pitch that made Olette wince.

She pushed her way against the traffic coming towards her. Only a few followed her direction. The edges of her robes got pulled as they caught on the fabric of passersby. At the clearing ahead, she stopped to catch her breath, not realizing she had exerted herself.

To her left, she saw two women coming out of a small room. Their demeanor contradicted the plain faces and robes. They carried themselves like royalty, though clearly not. The first one, a slender brown-haired hussy with not much bosom or backside to entice anyone, rose her nose in the air.

"He's not much to look at, is he?" She asked her companion. "He does have some muscle."

"He's no Dakien, for sure." The other woman sniffed. "And he's just an assembler."

"Yes, I would rather have an engineer."

"Well, he's merely a last resort."

"If it comes down to it, I'll take the trade credits for my family." The hussy walked past Olette and gave her the stink eye. "Looks like the gene pool got tainted."

"That's probably why the new generation of Bryhels are so tiny." The friend scoffed at her.

Olette continued, not acknowledging their petty jests. She also took stock of the two women and concluded they too would fall in the first round. She had nothing to worry about regarding them.

The small room held two workstations. A man striking a metal cylinder, curving it to a perfect shape with a mallet, occupied the one on the left. The other sat empty.

There he is!

Easily six feet eight inches tall, he had adjusted his station platform right at his waist, so he didn't have to bend over. His bicep muscles bulged as he worked. Strands of dark hair, soaked in sweat, clung to the sides of his face. He wore the same attire as his profile image.

He finally looked up and saw her. His arm in mid strike lowered slowly.

"Please don't stop working on my account," Olette said, raising her hands palm out. "I didn't come to disturb you." She watched him step away from his station and stand in front of it. "I wanted to see you in the flesh."

Krenan wiped his brow with the back of his forearm. She gestured to the chair between the stations. It barely held his well toned ass, which she noticed instantly. He cocked his head, catching her gaze.

"Are you here to say nasty things nicely, to hide your disappointment as well?"

"Hah!" Olette moved closer to him. "Unlike those inferior creatures, I chose only you."

"Is that so?" He reached over to the empty station

where a bottle of hydrating fluid sat. He took a huge swig and exhaled sharply. "Why do you want me?"

"Is that a trick question?"

"I don't hold much status. My parents didn't want me after I failed at engineering. They sent me to the workshops before I turned twenty."

"Yet, you learned how over the centuries." Olette smiled deviously.

"Hm? I'm only a hundred and twelve," he replied, sensing her prying joke.

Olette leaned over and placed her hands on his thighs. So meaty! She pressed lightly, then met his eyes. The blue seemed to shift from bright to stormy.

He's holding himself back.

"You have a great physique for a mere assembler." Her lips grew warm as she felt his breath against them. "I would love to get my hands on it."

"You already have." He didn't avert his eyes. When he did, she slid her hands off. "You have other competition."

"They have no chance against me. I already claim you as mine."

"Don't you have to win first?"

He took another swig.

Olette smiled. "Do you not have faith in me?"

Krenan's eyes changed to sheer lust. Not the playful kind. Olette felt her inside tighten, forcing her to clench her own thighs shut to avoid the moisture that suddenly spread from seeping out. His stare moved down, zeroing in on her crotch.

He knows what he's doing!

"I'll hold you to it, then. I look forward to seeing you after the competition."

"How scandalous you are," Olette whispered, slowly backing out of the room. "Until then."

Krenan set the bottle back on the empty station and returned to his own to finish working. His eyes never left hers until she stepped outside the door's view.

Olette's entire body shuddered. Her gait became stiff as she left the workshop, not daring to let her thighs separate before reaching the outside.

Pregame gatherings for battle maiden teams at the merchant homesteads started a week before the event. Adelia decided to join the Dakien's instead of Jaubro. She stood in the back room of one workshop of many with four other women.

They glowered at her, checking out every inch of her small frame compared to theirs. Near the door, Master Dakien's assistant and Yutel crossed their arms and waited for them to finish being rude. The two together were a wall of muscles in nice suits.

"Are you done?" Master Dakien's assistant asked when it went on too long for his taste.

The women glanced over at him. They remained a few feet feet away from Adelia.

"What can this puny thing do?" The first woman, easily a good six inches taller than her, narrowed her gaze. "The wind could carry this one off."

"Can she even fight?" The burly woman on the end added. She too stood taller than Adelia.

What are they feeding these bitches?

Adelia met her uncle's eyes. He got the message and tried to stifle a laugh. The woman with biceps the size of her thighs wearing a tight fitting dress that barely went above her knees stepped forward.

"Do you have anything to contribute to the Dakien clan's might?"

She towered over Adelia, daring her to move.

Adelia let the woman get inches from her and stared unflinching into those menacing eyes.

"I assure you," Adelia unballed her fists curling on instinct. "I'm more than capable of bringing down my enemy."

The two women stayed like that for a long while.

No one else spoke. They finally backed away from each other, not severing their eye connection.

"I like this one." The burly woman pointed to Adelia. "That still doesn't mean I approve." She addressed her. "If you lose in the first round, I will slander your name throughout the territories."

"You will do no such thing!" Yutel snapped.

Master Dakien's assistant raised a hand to stop him. He approached the women.

"We have heard of your victories on Earth from other members of our house and Jaubro. I've doubts about your fighting skills." He gestured an arm out towards the four Dakien women. "They are Battle Maidens in training. I do hope you understand this."

"I do. Which is why I want to fight under my father's clan, not the other."

Yutel dropped his arms, his expression serious.

"By joining us, you will have to face your mother in the later rounds. I heard she will enter."

"Why does everyone fret about that? My mother is not invincible. Her mother being a former battle maiden is of no consequence."

"That is true," the fourth woman said, tapping a finger on her chin. "Eterenia is soft compared to her." The others stared at her. She gave them a side glance. "She would be easy to knock out."

"I didn't say all that." Adelia's irises turned red. "My mother is a force to be reckoned with. She is no easy feat to conquer in battle."

"I can attest to her mother's skills," Yutel added. "Underestimating Eterenia Jaubro will be your downfall."

Master Dalien's assistant let out a heavy sigh. He scrutinized the five women. Adelia could see his thoughts by his expression alone. This is all the Dakien clan had to offer as battle maidens.

The historian predicted a low count. She felt a sense of woe at the state of the planet's forces.

"That goes for any of you." He made sure he met everyone's eyes as he spoke. "If any of you don't make it past the first round, it will look bad for our clan." They all nodded. "Good. Now, what prizes are we aiming for?"

"The trade credits!" Two of the women yelled.

"A mate!" Said the other two.

"Glory." Adelia didn't yell like them.

She had no need. Master Dakien's assistant stared at her with newfound respect. "I want to prove not just to the Dakien and Jaubro clan but all of Cellaxa that us Earth born children are worthy of status like everyone else."

"Hmph! Then you better do well, small one!" The first woman exclaimed.

Adelia felt the corner of her mouth twitch. She tried to stop the smile. As she raised her gaze higher, she saw the other woman sputtering. Oh hell. They all unleashed laughs. She peeked at the younger of the women who wanted a mate. That one won't make it.

These women may be a hundred years older, even two, but she could tell by their muscle structure and demeanor how well they could fight.

None of them had been in a real one.

Rows of spectators waited in line to enter the newly renovated arena centered in the palace grounds. The stone walled corridors leading the way in and out were isolated from the rest of it. There was no entry into the corridor from the sides. No secret passageways in case of emergency.

Muted sunlight greeted the midday hours, breaking the gloom. A perfect day for bloodshed. Maxellia grinned, watching the seats fill up. She and Lenri sat on thrones on a raised platform over-looking the fighting area. An oval space covered in a thick layer of white sand. She fought to contain her excitement. Lenri fidgeted next to her.

In the royal boxes, Tavelo and Pridric took their seats along with Manel and Gallic. Maxellia frowned at Tavelo's look of disdain for the event.

As an emperor, he should be thanking me!

She recalled the number of contestants. A mere three hundred. Not enough by far. Veterans totaled less than one hundred. This is why they needed a competition. To assess Cellaxa's true might.

Heightened conversations about what would commence rose the sound decibel. Battle Maiden certifications were usually conducted in private sessions with the trainer and candidate. All of Cellaxa will get to see them in one shot.

"Are you placing any bets, sister?" Lenri didn't look up from her tablet. A list of the contestants with their stats and a credit number displayed on the screen. "Not that I'm biased in any way."

"Oh?" Maxellia leaned over to get a better look. "I think you're going to lose more credits than you'd like with those." She saw a familiar name further down. "Well, except for that one. She's a guarantee."

Within the hour, a royal guard came to her side and whispered in her ear.

"Your grace, the spectator seats are full. The holo-screens are set on the outer perimeter for those who could not get in."

"Excellent." She tapped Lenri, breaking her away from her tablet. "Time to start this." To the guard she nodded to him. "Tell them to open the commlinks."

"As you wish, your grace." He gave a short bow with his head and left the platform.

Lenri stowed her tablet under her throne and settled into it. The chime of the PA system made the audience look up, pausing their conversations. Maxellia watched them sit correctly in their seats and wait for her to speak. She rose, spreading her arms wide.

"Cellaxa! Welcome to the first Battle Maiden competition!" Excited roars shook the venue.

Yes! She let it wash over her.

"We are entering a new stage for our race. New trade, new decrees. Means new powers envious of our success will come to challenge us. We must be prepared!"

Maxellia lowered her arms as Lenri stepped forward to stand beside her.

"There will be three rounds with one hundred contestants in each. The top twenty-five left standing of each round will compete against the winners from the others." She motioned to the royal guards below. "Bring them in."

The ten gates along the outer rim of the oval opened and the contestants filed out, climbing the stairs to the center stage. Women of every size and shape peppered its entirety.

"This first round incorporates the unknown. New trainees and Earth born Cellaxans. The second will be those who completed their training or have battle experience. Veterans and seasoned fighters make up the last. The first official round will determine the top twenty-five.

In the final, only the top five will move on to fight against each other or challenge my sister and I for the title of Supreme Battle Maiden."

Gasps of surprise followed by an upheaval of approval made the sisters smile. Maxelllia stared down at the contestants.

"The first initial rounds." Her sinister grin spread. "A battle royale." The arena went silent as contestants looked around, appearing confused. Then the atmosphere shifted. "Begin!"

The sound of battle cries and bodies crunching against each other filled the air. Blood flew. Less than a minute had passed, and a handful of contestants were already on the ground. Maxellia and Lenri stood stunned, not sure if they had made the right decision.

They slowly backed against their thrones and sat down to watch the remaining display of carnage.

Eterenia chose to sit in the spectator stands to watch the bout. Her hooded cape concealed her head and face. From her seat in the upper section on the tenth level, she had a straight view.

Seeing the way Adelia moved swiftly to take out the first five women who targeted her from the start made her chest tighten with anxiety. Further into the fight, a sense of pride swelled.

I wouldn't mind giving her a good battle.

Next to her, Tesul and his sons watched in awe. Addie gripped the rail he leaned over and shouted words of encouragement.

"Take her down! Watch your side! Go for it!"

His older brother shrunk in embarrassment in his seat. "Addie, sit down," he hissed, looking around to make sure no one saw them.

"Let him be." Tesul crossed his arms.

He didn't need to shout for Adelia. Eterenia could see the adoration on his face.

Two imperial guards stationed on each side of the arena kept an accurate body count. When the number of competitors still on their feet reached twenty-five, they called the match. The sand, now splattered with blood, settled.

Every contestant on the platform looked crazed, covered in blood, and panting. No one moved as they waited for the signal to leave.

The horn signaling the end of the round startled the arena patrons. On the holoscreen floating above, the time flickered, showing less than an hour had passed. Among the winners, she noticed a handful of Earth born Cellaxans in the mix. Proof that it didn't matter where they were raised.

The next round would start after the next hour once the sand was cleaned. Each bloody clump got thrown into a bin for extraction processing.

Not one drop to be wasted.

"I wonder how that would taste?" A spectator in the row above asked.

Eterenia's mouth downturned at the thought. She knew certain people would line up for it. As she looked up at Maxellia and Lenri whispering to each other, it became clear the blood would be sold as a souvenir.

"All that sweat and saliva mixed in." The person beside them frowned. "Maybe if it ages for a while."

Addie made a retching sound. He sat down in his seat. Eterenia stood.

"Please send Adelia my congratulations."

She then made her way to the exit aisle.

Her time to fight came after the next and she needed to prepare mentally. The veterans round included true battle maidens.

Maxellia walked from her throne to the edge of the platform. Her glowing red eyes stared at the remaining contestants to show her disgust at their level of fighting. Some returned her gaze, equally offended by her action.

Good. Let that anger fuel you.

"The first round is complete. Winners, return to the waiting pens and replenish. Your time to fight real warriors grows near."

The imperial guard on the left end tapped his earpiece. His voice boomed through the arena.

"Contestants able to stand are to report to the satellite medical bay. All others will be transported by technicians. Please make sure to watch your step and let the collectors finish their task."

The winners were allowed to leave first, followed by another fifteen to twenty staggering behind, clutching their wounds.

What a sight to behold!

Maxellia snorted as she turned away and went back to her throne.

"That's going to taste awful," Lenri blurted.

She watched the collectors sift the sand with long handled nets. They tossed the clumps in a basket carried on their backs. "Are you sure they're worth anything?"

"Absolutely." Maxellia settled back. "The coordinator I assigned took a poll. If we can get a full mini cube, the preorders are set."

"With this much bloodshed," Lenri propped an elbow on the armrest and laid her head in her hand. "I think we should have plenty."

❀ ❀ ❀

Olette and Adelia passed each other on the way to the winners holding pen. They simply nodded to each other, doing the same for the four other Earth born Cellaxans joining them. The ire coming from the other winners made them more determined to prove themselves. A segregation occurred in the pen the moment they entered.

A large spread of fruits, vegetables, cured meats, and sweets lined the far wall. On the adjacent table, sat massive carafes of hydrating drinks in assorted flavors. Olette smirked and headed for it first. She scanned the winners and found the hussy alone. Her friend didn't make it. Adelia came to her side and nodded at the group.

"They sure don't like us."

No one except the coven members were getting drinks and food. The others sat glaring, waiting for them to move away. The hussy whispered with the two women flanking her on a bench seat. She glanced at Olette a few times.

"Those bitches don't have enough skills to take us." Olette took a bit of cured meat, tearing it like a heathen. "All they can do is gossip to feel superior."

The hussy shot from her seat, heading towards her. An arm swung out and knocked the woman back against the benches. The two women scooted to the sides, leaning out of harm's way.

"Enough." A Cellaxan woman stood in the center where she had swatted the hussy. "We need to rest. This pettiness means nothing. The next fight we face far more seasoned warriors than us. Do you think they have time to trash talk fighters at our level?"

The woman went to the food table and grabbed a platter to fill. Sporadically, the others rose to do the same. Within minutes, the winners began putting more fuel into their bodies. A medical group came in to check their wounds while they ate.

"By the way," Olette tapped Adelia. "What was with those five cunts coming at you like that at the first horn? They gunned for you hard."

Adelia shrugged. "I guess I hurt their feelings?" She bit into some fruit. The juices squirted, covering her chin. "Not really sure."

"You called them entitled trash at the participation banquet last week in front of their family and the mating candidates," a Durante coven member replied.

Olette let out a hardy laugh, startling others in the room. Tears formed in the corners of her eyes. She finally regained her composure and wiped them with the back of her hand.

"And yet," she waved a piece of meat in the air. "You took them all down in the first ten minutes. Not one of them got back up."

"What you did to her friend," Adelia nodded at the hussy slumped on the bench while a medical technician checked her. "Was borderline disrespectful."

"Hmm?" Olette's eyes narrowed. "She deserved it. So did that one. I just couldn't get to her fast enough."

The hussy met her gaze. Both of their eyes glowed red. Bring it! Olette thought. *I dare you.*

❀ ❀ ❀

The second round proved boring.

Many of the fighters tried to appease the crowd with over the top maneuvers that resulted in minimal bloodshed. The bout went on longer than it should. Accusations of not taking the competition seriously flew from the spectators.

Realizing they made an error in judgement by showing off instead of beating their opponent, the fighting shifted. Twenty minutes after the audience turned on them, the required number rose victorious.

Still, the spectators seemed unhappy.

Maxellia pursed her lips in frustration. She almost stopped the round midway because of the lackluster performances. Lenri gripped her throne's armrests in anger, leaning forward ready to drop down into the fray. She waited until the platform cleared, the collectors not having much to do.

"Come sister. I have a new plan." She motioned for Lenri to follow her. "This will not do."

"Such a disgrace!" Lenri scratched the tip of her wound showing at her shoulder.

"Stop that!" Maxellia smacked her hand away. Lenri's expression turned to shame. "Why do you not get it healed? There's no reason for you continue harboring that scar."

"Stasi…My Valkyrie finds it sexy," Lenri muttered.

Maxellia rolled her eyes at the sappy sentiment. The two reached the anteroom available only for the royal family set behind the throne platform. She plopped down in one of the plush chairs and let her head fall back. Lenri sat across from her in another.

"Well? What are you thinking?" Lenri asked.

"Since it's come to this." Maxellia raised her head to look at Lenri. "The veterans have no desire to choose any of the prizes."

"Except the one." Lenri grinned.

"Yes. They want to get a shot at taking us down."

"Then the next round?"

"Let's mix it up. Make it fun."

"And so very bloody." Lenri reached towards her scar and stopped when Maxellia glared at her.

"I wonder how many of those brats will rise to the top."

"I wouldn't underestimate them." Lenri frowned. "I watched their fighting. They are formidable."

"Such a shame Adelia won't be going against her mother."

"As much as many wanted to witness that," Lenri shook her head. "We would be held accountable for if it goes awry."

Maxellia drew her lips in with disgust. That was the last thing she wanted.

An imperial guard appeared at the entrance. His demeanor gave away his own disappointment.

"How much time before the next round?"

"Oh. Make sure the winners of the last bout are ready within the hour."

The guard tilted his head in confusion.

"Your grace?"

"Trust me." She smiled at him. He flinched though he kept his ground. "You'll like it."

❀ ❀ ❀

Olivier moved sideways down the narrow aisle to his seat in the stands. Tamar, Chiron, and Caden, already seated, found empty ones on the twentieth level, giving a perfect view of the arena's platform. He could make out Tesul and his sons farther down. Across the way, in the royal boxes, he saw Tavelo and Pridric surrounded by guards.

"To think, we're here to watch hundreds of crazy women beat each other to oblivion." Olivier dropped into his seat. "This is worse than the dungeon fights for guardians."

"Uhh, I believe your sister is one of them," Tamar said, pointing at the sand pit.

"I still can't believe she advanced."

"Well, you missed one hell of a fight." A Brownlee coven member above them leaned over. "What she did to that one fighter." He shook his head in awe. "I think a grudge was involved."

"Really?" That intrigued Olivier. He knew his sister fought dirty when she felt wronged.

"Put her down in the first ten minutes."

Olivier opened his mouth to reply then saw his father approaching.

"You're late," he chastised him.

"You just got here yourself. I watched you enter." His father sat next to him. "It will be a while before she's up. I came for the veterans round."

"Huh?" Chiron snorted. "Why would you want to watch those old biddies trying to restore their glory?"

"Watch your tongue."

"Regents Maxellia and Lenri are coming out," Tamar yelled. "Looks like you got here right on time."

Maxellia and Lenri took their place at the edge of their royal platform. The arena fell into a hush.

"There's a change in plans," Maxellia announced. Murmurs erupted. "The last round did not satisfy our cravings. Thus, the next will be the winners of the first against those of the second."

Loud cries of surprise and outrage assaulted them. Lenri seemed amused.

"We know you want to see the final round. But do you really want the last round to be etched in your memory?" The crowd's yelling subsided.

Agreements flowed in the air and Maxellia felt relieved. She turned to the imperial guards.

"Bring them out!"

Fifty women emerged from the gates and climbed onto the sand. They scanned the arena confused as to why they were back on the fighting platform.

"The veteran fighters do not wish to claim any of

the prizes." Maxellia spoke through the commlink. "So this round will determine the winners for those."

"May you fight with honor, dignity, and emerge victorious." Lenri then walked back to her throne.

❀ ❀ ❀

The brute from the pregame meeting stared Adelia down. Two others equal in size stood behind her.

"Looks like I get to break you in half, Earth girl." The woman puffed out her broad chest and spat to the side. "I'll show what a real battle maiden is."

Adelia's eyes widened at her declaration.

Olette laughed.

"Oh wow!" She smacked Adelia on the shoulder. "As they say on Earth, clean her clock."

"Gladly." Adelia turned away from them.

Olette eyed the hussy stretching each arm, her gaze focused on her.

"It's time for you to pay for what you did to my cousin," the hussy sneered.

"Careful. I'll do the same to you if you push me."

Olette's eyes glowed silver.

The horn blew, signaling the start of the round. Spectators began shouting, demanding bloodshed. They would get their wish after the previous match.

Adelia barely got into a stance when not only the brute, but two other contestants charged her. The first one to get within a few feet of her pulled back their lips and growled, "Jaubro," baring teeth. Saliva dripped from her mouth. Her fist came towards Adelia's face.

She never knew how much the lower merchant clans hated her mother's until living on Cellaxa. Adelia let the woman get a little closer then weaved to the side, bringing her knee up into her ribcage.

Right as she bent over in pain, Adelia delivery an upper cut to the other one not far behind. Her head snapped back, and her body hit the sand.

Adelia swirled around in turn to block the brute's arms, attempting to encircle her. She head butted her, yet the brute wouldn't budge. The two locked eyes. With a swift drop to the ground, Adelia brought the brute with her, pushing her lower body up so that the brute flipped over and landed on the top of her head. She heard the impact.

Not willing to let her recover, Adelia Punched her between her shoulder blades and lower back. The brute's eyes rolled up in their sockets. Sensing movement to her side, she struck out one leg and connected with the first assailant's face. Dead center, the kick sent the woman flying back a few feet. She landed flat on her back, out cold.

Olette had her hands full with multiple fighters as well. Among them, the hussy. She had already taken down four others and two mid-tier warriors. *I'm not impressed.* To her surprise, the hussy brought down the fighter in front of her who got within striking distance of Olette. She grabbed the woman by the hair and used it to spin her body around and toss her to the edge of the platform. Strands of her hair clung to the hussy's hand.

She pushed the other woman in stride next to her so hard she rammed into another fighter. Their heads hit, knocking them both down. Olette moved to dodge her, but the hussy was faster than she anticipated. She kept in step, managing to get her hands around Olette's throat. Her eyes gleamed as she lifted her off the ground, Olette's feet dangling a few inches above it. She brought her other hand back in a fist and punched her in the face.

"How does that feel, you Bryhel mongrel?" She shook Olette's neck. "You don't get to pick that shitty assembler."

Olette spit blood in her face. The hussy went to punch her again. She let go of one of the hussy's forearms, using the other as leverage, and got her in the side of the head first. The hussy staggered, not loosening her grip. No matter. Olette extended her talons and sliced through the bend of her arm, nearly severing it at the elbow.

The hussy howled; her grip gone. She stepped back as Olette landed on her feet.

Blood splattered over the front of her leotard and Olette. The crowd cheered, seeing it on the holoscreen. Her and Adelia's fight drew the most attention.

"I think you deserve some special treatment," Olette seethed.

She roundhouse kicked the hussy in the abs then flashed towards her right as she hit the sand. With one hand, Olette took hold of one of her legs and yanked her towards her. The first stomp between the hussy's legs made her scream in pain.

"That's right. Your cousin liked it too."

Olette stomped her foot multiple times until she felt the pelvis give. The hussy lay unconscious. She secured her grip on her ankle and hauled her into the air. With a loud growl, Olette swung the hussy's body up and released it.

Other fighters looked up and calculating the hussy's fall, moved away. Her body hit the sand with a resounding thud. The one arm barely stayed attached. Both her legs were broken, splayed in un-natural positions.

The horn blew, ending the round.

"The Winners Round is complete!" The imperial referee announced.

Adelia scanned the other winners left standing. She caught Olette's stare. Both raised their heads in defiance, their mouths downturned.

We won!

"What, and why?" Tamar whispered.

"I agree," Caden said. "That was uncalled for."

"Oh, that was tame compared to what she did

to the other one," the Brownlee member said. "This one got off easier."

Olivier feigned shock and leaned into his seat.

"I always knew my sister had a sadistic streak. This is what happens when you give her free reign."

"That's no excuse for such violence," his father exclaimed. "I can't condone something like that."

"You don't have to." Olivier pointed to the giant holoscreen floating in the center of the arena. "The masses approve."

They listened to the roar of cheers as the image zoomed in on the two Earth born coven women standing victorious among battle maidens.

The regents wasted no time giving the winners their accolades. The imperial guards who served as referees corralled them to the upper platform where Maxellia and Lenri sat.

"Winners, line up!" The first guard ordered.

They made a curve along the edge. Some had a hard time bowing due to their injuries. A servant came out of the hidden door with a stack of fabric.

"Congratulations on proving your worth." Maxellia raised her hands, palms up. "And your might. Today you can now call yourselves Battle Maidens."

A guard took a square of fabric from the top of the servant's stack and flapped it loose. The dark grey cape had a wide hood and, on the back, the long-forgotten Battle Maiden insignia in black and red. They went down the line, dressing each winner in the cape. When they reached the end, the servant left the stage empty handed. Lenri stood.

"You will all receive trade credits for your families." The second holoscreen changed to show a grid of twelve men. Lenri gestured a hand at it. "These fine specimens have been put up for bidding by their clans. Those with winning bids can claim their mates."

"Face the crowd and bow!" The stadium guard commanded.

The images captured would go in the evening news feeds.

"Report to the medical bays for treatment. You are free to stay and watch the final veterans round." The guard gave them all a pitiful stare while scanning their bodies. "May you bask humbly in your glory."

The winners were escorted single file through the hidden door and down a corridor that slanted steeply. This was the royal route to the arena floor. A few of the women stumbled.

Exhaustion crept in.

Maxellia and Lenri waited for the all-clear signal from the other guards by the fighting platform.

"The round you've been waiting for will commence in two hours. Prepare yourselves." Maxellia felt the vibrations of the cheers as she stepped down. Lenri left her throne and came beside her. She leaned closer. "I'm starving," she whispered.

Maxellia nodded. The crowd dispersed, with only a few scattered sections occupied by people pulling out bundles and baskets of food.

They came prepared!

Olette and Adelia slumped against the farthest wall, their capes tossed to the side. After arriving at the medical bay, the head physician turned them away. The bays were full. He sent them back to the holding pit with four medical technicians. They checked them both, administering pain killers and sealing gel on the deepest wounds.

When he finished, they glanced at each other. Four other coven members came and sat with them. No one said a word for a long time.

"So," Adelia spoke. "Was it fun for you as well?"

Two of the women gave her horrified stares. Olette laughed. The Boresso coven winner cocked her head.

"You have a strange sense of fun, Adelia. Fighting the imperial guards in the last battle felt easier than this." She leaned back using her arms to support her.

"Really?" Olette smiled lazily, the pain killers working. "I had tons of fun."

The Brownlee coven winner frowned.

"You need therapy. What you did defied dignity and logic."

"She deserved it," Olette snapped back. "They both did."

"No one deserves that!" The Jaubro winner turned to Adelia. "Don't you agree?"

Adelia answered by wrapping an arm around Olette. She squeezed her shoulder in solidarity.

"Come. Let's get some food, a drink in us, and take a short nap before the veteran's bout."

Adelia struggled to her feet, pulling Olette with her. The spacious room felt cavernous with only the winners.

❀ ❀ ❀

The royal chamber had a spread of food and drink for the taking. Yutel didn't bother to address Tavelo and Pridric before barreling in, heading straight for the table. Holnar sighed in defeat seeing him attack the fare. Tavelo simply ignored him.

"I am surprised Adelia fought for trade credits under Dakien," Holnar blurted out.

"Hmm?" Yutel turned his head to him. "Why? Jaubro doesn't need them."

"True." Pridric tilted her head. "Still. It surprised me as well."

Yutel and Holnar averted their eyes from hers. Those kaleidoscope swirls unnerved them.

"You need to sit your daughter down for a hard discussion," Yutel addressed Holnar.

"I'm disturbed by her," Tavelo clawed for the right word, "fighting technique."

Holnar grabbed a glass of spirits and tossed a big swig down his throat.

"Is she sexually repressed?" Yutel asked while chewing a piece of cured meat.

"What?" Holnar frowned. "What does that have to do with her…" He stopped. "She's by no means a virgin."

"That isn't a factor."

Tavelo gave him a knowing glance.

Yutel nodded. "Right. It's about satisfaction. A horde of bad lovers just frustrates you."

"She did make a bid for a mate," Holnar muttered.

The others blanched at the thought. They sent their silent condolences to the candidate.

❀ ❀ ❀

Not one empty seat could be found in the arena as the holoscreen counted down to the veterans round. The second round had trained battle maidens but the ones arriving were the real deal. They either fought in the last war or completed missions by royal decree.

Sanctioned killers.

Maxellia tried once again to contain her joy. To see the returned glory of battle maidens was her life-long dream. Lenri had only been in service for less than a decade before their father declared royalty would not be lowered to such titles. He also stripped Maxellia of her duties.

The countdown ended with a loud buzz and the crowd cheered. Maxellia and Lenri stood before them patiently waiting for the decibel to die down.

"I welcome you to the fourth round with our seasoned veterans. The Battle Maidens of lore." Maxellia's eyes burned red. "Destroyers of enemies."

"The top five have the opportunity to challenge my sister or I if they so choose." Lenri smiled. "Let them out!"

The gates opened for fifty scantily clad women to file out. Some climbed the stairs to the platform while others leaped onto it from the ground. They assembled within arm's reach of each other. No need to spread out when they were fighting so close.

"What," Tamar stuttered, his eyes wide, "are they wearing?"

Olivier clamped a hand over his mouth then slid it over his face. Adelia frowned, embarrassed. In the royal boxes, Gallic averted his own gaze away from the platform. Manel glanced over at him and stifled a laugh.

"Oh." Pridric got out, her stare fixed on Dania.

Among the fifty, a handful stood out.

Maritze sauntered out wearing bikini bottoms that barely covered her buttocks. The flimsy, loose fitting spaghetti strap top with a shimmering green, bronze, and rust gradient design did nothing to cover her breasts. Her hair sat wild on her head as if she had already finished a fight.

Eterenia found her old battle suit and cut the legs and sleeves off. It was now a black leather shorts bodysuit that clung to every inch of her. The ankle boots made sure everyone could see the length of her legs. A black ribbon secured her blonde hair in a tight ponytail.

Dania's white unitard criss crossed her mid section, exposing skin. The wide strips at the top, though tight, struggled to hold her bosom. She wore fingerless gloves and her hair fell loose down her back.

Grasilda's unitard sported one leg with tears along its side. A swoop design cut out right under her breasts. She too had her hair undone, the thick ash blonde strands flowing against her face from the breeze behind her.

Maritze turned around to address the woman approaching.

"Chalayl the beast. We knew you would come."

Chalayl didn't speak. She stood still, her fists clenched at her sides. The two-piece outfit resembling strips of cloth, displayed her full figure. She clearly felt the eyes of the crowd scouring her. The off-white cloth covering her breasts didn't allow them to move. Her shorts left nothing to speculate.

"Without those fancy clothes, we see what you are," another competitor scoffed. "You've come to prove your title? The beast of the Boresso clan?"

"Enough!" Eterenia snapped. "You talk big for someone who won't be standing soon."

"Hah!" Another competitor snorted. "Listen to the privileged Jaubro brat. "Your mother was a great battle maiden." Her eyes glowed. "You're not her."

"Are you done?" Grasilda asked in a soft tone.

She looked up at Maxellia and Lenri. They got the hint. Time to start the round.

Maxellia paused as she started to speak. She turned to Lenri, giving her a devious smile. Lenri's expression turned to surprise.

"Let's make this worth everyone's wild." Her lips spread wide. "Battle Royale."

The competitors stared at her in awe while the crowd's cheers tapered off for a split second. Roars of encouragement rained down on the arena.

The atmosphere shifted to murderous intent.

Maxellia didn't get the last syllable of, "Begin!" before the sound of flesh against flesh and talons ripping skin, engulfed the arena. Blood flew everywhere, turning the white sand shades of red, pink, and black. A den of monsters occupied the platform.

Within twenty minutes, their numbers went down by half. Bodies littered the sand.

An opponent came towards Chalayl, her eyes glowing red with both hands out to grapple her. Devoid of expression, Chalayl let the woman get within a few inches. Her fist hit under the woman's chin, knocking her head back. The body arched as it got lifted into the air by the impact.

As it rotated, Chalayl delivered another blow, kicking her in the side, changing its trajectory. Instead of flying backwards, the woman's body veered left and went outside the sand pit. She landed with a thud.

Maritze swiped her talons across a competitor's face, gouging the flesh. The woman screamed, holding her hands in front of her face, not daring to touch the wounds. Bood spurted.

"Chalayl the beast strikes again," she said as she kicked her opponent in the chest, sending her flying back into another wounded woman trying to escape Eterenia's clutches. "Nice form."

Chalayl pivot towards her. Maritze knew she had talked big game regarding her but seeing her up close changed her mind.

"Oh, ho! I'm not messing with you." Maritze dodged her blow by a hair. She turned, grabbing a competitor who just put down her prey and swung her towards Chalayl. "Here, play with her."

Chalayl plowed through the woman, sending her to the ground with broken arms and ribs. Maritze was long gone, engaging in a fight farther away.

The crowd's cheers rose to an almost unbearable level. The bloodlust in their eyes gave Maxellia and Lenri chills. Though many came to see Chalayl, they became impressed by Grasilda's brutality. As the oldest battle maiden in the pit, she dominated. And it seemed she wasn't using all her force or skills.

At the hour mark, the horn blew to end the round when only five remained. Barely out of breath and covered in blood, Chalayl, Maritze, and Eterenia halted their attacks. Dania wet her fingers with her saliva and wiped her opponent's blood from her thigh. Grasilda didn't have a drop of blood or any wounds on her.

"The winners of the battle royale!" The announcer shouted through the commlink. "They will now have the option of taking the prizes or challenging the royal siblings!"

Maxelllia rose to stare down at them.

"Who has the gall to take me on?" She smiled with evil intent. "Are you frightened?"

The winners stared at her with disinterest. Not acknowledging her cockiness. When the silence went too long, her eyes went red. The crowd instigated the challenge.

Suddenly, a voice rang over them.

"I will take you down, if you so wish."

Grasilda met Maxellia's gaze.

The crowd roared. The other winners gaped at her in awe. Maxellia smirked, throwing off her royal robes. In a short cropped sleeved red dress that came just at her thighs with a thick rope belt, she landed a few feet from Grasilda. Her leather sandals dug into the sand.

The two women locked eyes. Grasilda's turned silver with utter hate. Maxellia let out a laugh.

"You have a score to settle with me? Is that it?"

"You may have been a battle maiden before," Grasilda said. "But you are no combat fighter."

Maxellia grew angry. She leaped towards her, not giving her time to react. Or so she thought. Grasilda moved with lightning speed, coming around behind her to hit her in the lower back. Maxellia managed to get enough space between them to lessen the blow.

Grasilda was already back in front of her. Maxellia blocked her flashing blows, connecting one, only to have her take it without the flow of strikes stopping.

Maxellia reached down and grabbed hold of Grasilda's ankles. She pulled, and to her surprise, the woman let her. She understood why in the next second where her body got tossed over Grasilda's body. The shock loosened her grip. She corrected her body so she could land on her feet.

Grasilda stood, then looked behind her at Maxellia. Right as Maxellia got into a defensive stance, the old battle maiden was on her, each blow deadlier than the next. Maxellia tried to get her arms up to block them. She tasted her own blood.

Lenri jumped down into the sandpit, heading straight for Grasilda. Maritze and Dania blocked her. She sent a flying kick to Dania's head. Dania caught her by the ankle and slammed her down onto the sand. Maritze came to stand over her.

"No, no. If you want to play, we'll gladly oblige." Maritze rose a foot to stomp her in the chest. Lenri pushed up from her shoulders and back flipped out of range. "Stay still, you brat."

This time, the crowd went wild.

Tavelo and Pridric watched in horror at the scene. Maxellia went face down. Grasilda straddled over her and grabbed her by the hair, lifting it up to the crowd. She raised a fist to deliver a blow to the back of her head.

"That will be enough." A man's voice echoed.

The crowd went silent. Manel had Grasilda's wrist in his hand. "My sister deserves many things. Punishments even. But I will not allow this." He turned to the referee. "Call it."

Terrified, the referee spoke into his commlink, attached to his ear.

"Grasilda is the new leader of the Battle Maidens! This concludes the competition!"

For a second, one could hear a pin drop. No cheers or applause. Maritze let Lenri up. Her and Dania had given her a few bruises and broken bones. Still, the tiny thing stood regally beside them.

Grasilda stared at Manel's hand. He sneered as he released it. Fear gripped Gallic.

Olette made her way through the main halls of the Bryhel workshops with her father. She could tell how skeptical he felt about her chosen mate. They navigated the foot traffic in silence. At the small room her new mate shared with another assembler, she stopped at the door.

Krenan sat wearing a half face shield, anti-static gloves, and a leather apron at his workstation. The other once again left unoccupied. Olette wondered if that assembler ever came to work. He halted his soldering on a piece clamped under a zooming lens. He shut it off, set the needle nosed iron down on its stand and lifted his shield off his head.

"Lord Bryhel." He straightened his body. "It is an honor to meet you."

Olette glanced at her father. Holnar took stock of the young worker. No frowns emerged. Olette thanked the heavens for that.

"My child has chosen you as her mate. As such, it would be convenient if you moved into our stronghold under the Marchand Company."

"That makes sense. I am merely an assembler here. I'm not sure what skills I can offer you."

"Father," Olette turned to him. "He has many ideas for product improvements."

"Is that so?" Holnar stared him down. "Then why are you not part of the engineering sector?"

"As a disowned spawn, the managers don't take my suggestions seriously, in addition to my rank."

Olette saw her father's eyes glint red with fury.

Exactly! She yelled in her head.

"That is not how we operated at Marchand. If you have ways to make a superior product, then I want to hear it."

Krenan's expression went blank. He looked down at the floor for a moment.

"It doesn't bother you, I have no family lineage to boast?"

"As I said," her father waited until his head rose

to make eye contact. "We do things differently in my home. Since you will be my daughter's mate, that makes you part of my family."

"Will you accept coming to my home? To take me as your mate?" Olette batted her eyes shyly. Her father grimaced at the blatant show.

Krenan stared intently at her. There it is again! The way he looked at her, as if digging into her soul.

"That was the agreement, was it not? You said you would come to claim me after you've won."

Her father seemed to watch him in surprise, his eyes wide. He glanced over at Olette, then pursed his lips. What was that about?

"I need to finish this piece first." He turned the soldering iron back on. "I won't be accused of not finishing my work."

"Of course." Her father replied. "I wouldn't have it any other way. My aunt is unforgiving. We will wait."

Olette observed Krenan's delicate handling of the piece despite his large hands. He completed his task in twenty minutes, then cleaned his area. After storing the tools in the bins behind him, he wiped down the station with a disposable sanitizing cloth.

"Do you not have your own toolsets?" Her father asked angrily.

"I'm not allowed, since I do not have any funds of my own. What little I do earn is taken for room, board, and meals."

Olette had seen her father angry before. This time, it frightened her. She knew why. There were tales of the clans not paying the young interns. They were to be grateful for the privilege of knowledge before getting an assignment.

Nothing had changed.

"Let's hurry. Get your belongings and meet us outside the gates."

While Olette and her father stood by their transport, a ruckus came from the doors. A few workers began taunting Krenan as he walked out of the Bryhel workshops.

"Good riddance," one said.

"Your work wasn't all that great anyway."

"Having you in assembly was a waste of time for everyone."

"Now we don't have to hear your stupid ideas berating our skills." The last one spat at his feet.

Krenan sidestepped it, ignoring the insults. Olette felt her father tense.

"I'm sorry you had to witness that," Krenan said as he got closer.

"Get in." Her father spat, turning to the transport. "We're leaving."

The ride home felt stiff. They engaged in small bits of conversation. She wanted to go back and teach those workers a lesson in brutality. Krenan slid a hand across her thigh. She looked up and met his gaze. His expression told her no. She frowned, looking away.

"I know what you're thinking," her father said. "And he's right to discourage you."

The transport arrived at the front entrance. Krenan stared at, trying to hide his astonishment. He stepped out with his satchel of meager belongings thrown over his shoulder. The string pulled tight on his fingers while holding it.

"I've never gone outside the Bryhel workshops except to to pick up shipments at the docks or deliver a demo to the main house."

"Well, this is your home now." Her father held his arm out. "You have free rein to do as you please. This is not a work prison." A coven member came up to Holnar and whispered in his ear. "If you'll excuse me. I have a situation to attend to."

Olette waited for her father to enter the home and disappear before taking her mate by the arm.

"Come. You need to get settled in our part of the home. My chamber is rather large, but we can fill it with more things to make it feel more comfortable."

His silence made her body tense again. He didn't look at her. Just walked silently by her side.

Inside her chamber, he set his satchel down near an armoire on the right side of the wall. He pushed the door shut so hard it slammed. She jumped and glanced back at him. His expression changed from blank to … Olette backed away on instinct, not sure why fear gripped her.

"Since you kept your promise to claim me, it's only fair I give you a taste of what you've won."

She stood rooted by the end of the bed, her eyes widening the closer he got, removing his clothes. When he stood less than a few inches from her, she had to look up at him. She hadn't realized his height. How tall he truly was. He undressed her while she stayed in that state, her gaze unwavering. He cupped her face in his hands.

"You'll let me do whatever I want, won't you?"

Olette blinked. He kissed her deeply.

An explosion filled her entire body. Her thighs clinched together as she felt her juices flow. He picked her up with ease as if she weighed nothing and laid her on the bed. He disengaged his lips, creating strings of saliva. Olette's breathing grew harder.

"Wait," she whispered, not sure why she said it.

Krenan pried her legs open, wrapping them around his hips as he entered her. She gasped in pain, feeling the girth of his cock force its way in. She had never had one of such size. For a moment, she thought she had made a mistake. Then it slid all the way inside. The pain turned to something else. Her back arched as her cry got caught in her throat.

"Ahh," he breathed, throwing his head back. Then he locked eyes with her. "You'll endure this."

His thrusts were hard, his strokes long and vigorous. Her body responded, yet she felt the need to run. It bordered on too much. Her eyes rolled up in her sockets for a moment. She clawed at his chest, trying to push him away and consume him at the same time. Tiny specks of blood formed where her partially extended talons punctured his flesh.

"I...can't..." She again tried to get away, only to have her body slide further against his hips, allowing him better leverage. "Please," she breathed.

He didn't answer her. Instead, he took one hand and wove his fingers into hers. She endured it for hours, multiple times, before he finally became spent past the late hours of night into morning.

A soft knock on the door startled Olette out of a restless sleep. She groggily rose her head from the pillows.

"Enter." Her voice sounded raspy.

Olivier walked in and stopped halfway. He took stock of her appearance and snorted, clamping a hand over his mouth.

"You look like you've been rode hard, sister."

She tossed one of the smaller pillows at him, then eased back down.

"You wouldn't understand!" Olette bunched a pillow under her chin. "He was relentless," she mumbled.

"Oh, I bet." Olivier moved closer to the bed. "He's not some random inferior coven man with no skills." His eyes scanned her playfully. "Serves you right for underestimating him."

"I did no such thing! I just," she frowned, "wasn't prepared."

"Well, I came to inform you that because you missed evening meal last night, you are required to attend morning meal. To formally introduce your mate to the family."

"Oh!" Olette went to raise her head and felt light-headed. She lowered it back. "I forgot."

Olivier laughed as he walked out of the room, closing the door behind him.

In the hallway, he ran into Krenan. The man appeared unassuming. An ordinary worker. Until he got closer. Olivier immediately saw something deeper. He patted him on the shoulder as he passed.

"Good job. Keep her in line."

Krenan paused, then smirked.

Hostile Acts

The worker's communication screen displayed the disturbing scene taking place near a client planet. Commissioner Polp made note of the carrier ship's location as it moved to block the Cellaxan transport. *What are they up to?* He watched their convoy fly down to the surface while the transport pilot sent urgent messages to the space dock.

"Contact our ship. I want to know what that planet's trade liaison is doing."

Two ships from the space dock arrived on the scene, parking themselves in flanking positions next to the transport. More messages flowed between them and authorities planetside.

"Pilot is on screen." The trade worker said.

The main screen on the far wall lit up. Commissioner Polp saw the frustration on the pilot's face.

"What is the situation?" Polp asked.

"Sir!" The pilot leaned closer to the screen. "Another race arrived saying our shipment is counterfeit and that they have the true goods. We already sent our manifest."

"And what did they say?" Commissioner Polp felt a lump in the pit of his stomach.

"That they needed to verify it. A security envoy was dispatched to prevent us from leaving."

"That's unacceptable." He stood straight. "Keep me informed."

"Of course, Commissioner."

The screen went black. Behind him, the doors slid open. Innego and Windsor entered.

"I tapped into the feed on my way here." Windsor showed his tablet screen. "Who would be so bold as to interfere in our trade?"

"Counterfeit?" Innego crossed his arms. "That planet knows better. This isn't the first time we've delivered goods to them."

"Something smells rotten." Windsor scrolled through the data on his tablet. "A high-level member getting incentives under the radar."

"Oh!" Commissioner Polp grimaced. "Someone wants to encroach on our business instead of establishing their own contracts."

"I've identified the ship, your grace," the trade worker announced.

"Yes, who are these miscreants?"

"A carnivorous reptilian race like the ones who attacked us. From the same system, three planets away." He frowned. "Their ship is being granted access while our transport has been denied."

"Send this message to the planet." Commissioner Polp glared at the screen. "Due to the mistreatment and blatant disregard for our contracts, your business with Cellaxa is hereby dissolved. No other deliveries will be forthcoming. Any goods slated for such are subject to resell. Refunds up to fifty percent can be negotiated."

"The hell they can!" Innego's eyes narrowed. "They get nothing." He swung an arm out.

"It will add insult to injury. If they're so adamant to cut us out and do business with that race, they will suffer the consequences. We, on the other hand, must conduct ourselves according to trade laws."

Innego pursed his lips in anger.

Windsor mirrored his expression. I get it. The commissioner watched the message get sent.

"Wait for it." Commissioner Polp smile widened.

The three went over to the catering table and took their time eating small fruits. They drank sweetened brew, chatting away.

In less than an hour, the main screen came back to life with the image of an apparent dignitary. His shiny multicolored cape stood out against his pale face and dark hair.

"Commissioner Polp. I received a disturbing message from your department. Please tell me the meaning of this."

"Are you feigning ignorance?"

"I assure you…" A guard tapped his shoulder and whispered in his ear. His face flushed, his eyes widened in disbelief, and his glance turned icy. "I see." He brought his attention back to the screen. "There has been an accusation of counterfeit goods. We are simply going through protocol."

"And when has Cellaxa ever done such a thing?"

The dignitary sputtered. "We're doing our due diligence. The accusers have come to show proof that they have the correct shipment."

"Then we are done here. Release our ships. Refund negotiations for next deliveries will start once the current goods are resold."

"Wait! We never said we wanted to sever our contracts. If you do this, it will be a breach!"

"No. you purposely blocked our shipment. After over six hundred years of exclusivity rights, you are the ones who breached it."

"This can be remedied if you would be patient for a moment." The desperation in his tone didn't sway the commissioner or Inngeo. "We'll have the other race's ship moved so yours can dock and complete delivery."

"Why should we deliver at all at this point? Would you not have already received the other merchants' in lieu of ours?"

"That's not what we're doing!"

"Double dipping." Windsor interrupted. "Getting

two shipments from the same manufacturer with different contracts."

"I had no knowledge of this. I, too, am trying to figure out what is going on."

"You have thirty-six hours. If the situation is not remedied by then, my decision stands."

Commissioner Polp gestured for the worker to disconnect the feed. He turned to Innego.

"I believe he's in a panic."

Innego nodded. "Whoever initiated this farce will be severely punished." Then he smiled. "Unless it is, as you say, someone higher up the chain. Then he would have to tread carefully."

"This must be reported to the emperors."

Innego and Windsor winced.

Commissioner Polp understood the sentiment. Manel was easy to read. Tavelo, on the other hand, always seemed to be an enigma. The three made their way to the dual throne room. Their meeting time drew near.

After the report, Manel's irises turned a dark, juicy red. Tavelo's went silver. Not necessarily rage, yet on the verge. The royal council huddled near the far right of the throne platform. Their hushed voices stern. Manel rested the side of his head on his propped-up fist.

"So, these carnivores want to play with us?" He crossed his legs, tapping his dangling foot in the air. "Not very smart, are they?"

"They took advantage of an opportunity, betting on it going smoothly." Tavelo folded his hands on his lap. "I think we should wait and see what happens."

"Hmm?" Manel glanced over at him. "Are we not going to teach them a lesson?"

"Brute force isn't always the answer, Manel."

"Since when?" Manel's brow furrowed.

Tavelo exhaled slowly.

"I have a feeling they will come to us. When they

realize they picked the wrong planet to try this on."

"Yes, it seemed we were not singled out."

Commissioner Polp caressed his chin.

"This was a random act. They didn't check the contracts. Information on the goods' route got intercepted." One of the royal council members piped up. "Emperor Tavelo is correct. They will come to beg forgiveness."

"And try to glean every bit of information on our trade system," another added. "Find the contracts we have and go after them behind our backs."

"Dastardly creatures." The first councilman spat.

"How shall we greet them, then?" Manel asked sweetly.

"With suspicion and a hint of malice," Tavelo replied. "We let them know we find their behavior unacceptable. A small show of force."

"And if they decide to bring an armed force to rebel?" Windsor inquired.

"If red it bleeds, then indeed we feed," Manel responded.

The room went silent. They could always use more blood cubes.

❀ ❀ ❀

The convoy ship eased into the designated slot on Cellaxa's west docks. A bulbous shaped vessel with black and red shades mingling together to give it a murky, unclean aesthetic. How ugly. Commissioner Polp's lips went thin. It fit their personality in his mind. Six royal guards accompanied him. They also scrunched their faces at the visitors' ship.

Dock guards surrounded the ramp extending from the open hatch. A group of tall scaly beings in fancy robes came down. The one in front had what appeared to be a gold crown, though its crude design blended with its head. Twelve visitors in all stepped onto the platform.

Beside him, Innego peered beyond the visitors into their ship. The way his face went blank alerted him to be aware of more to come.

The translator device attached to the leader's robe at the shoulder jumbled before getting the correct words.

"Greetings, Cellaxan. We are glad to have this opportunity to meet." That last words came out smoother.

"How many of your forces did you bring with you?" Innego asked.

Commissioner Polp stiffened. The royal guards went into defensive standby stances.

"I'm not sure what you're referring to," the leader replied.

"If the first thing you're going to do is come to our planet with armed forces and lie about it, you need to turn around and leave this system."

The leader's gator-like mouth curved to reveal sharp tiny teeth.

"I assure you, the only guards I have brought with me are a small unit of fighters to ensure my safety." It raised its hands up, the webbed fingers spreading. "Nothing of concern." It met Innego's gaze. "Maybe one hundred or so."

Commissioner Polp forced back a gasp.

"As long as they stay on these docks, in your ship. We won't have any problems." Innego stepped away from Polp and positioned himself with the royal guards flanking him. "Let's be cordial moving forward."

"Of course."

The leader's head tilted forward less than an inch. Not considered a nod or a bow. Commissioner Polp glared. An act of insincere respect. They won't acknowledge anyone's title here. He glanced at Innego and realized he too understood.

"Please, this way." Commissioner Polp gestured with a swing of his hand towards the boardwalk.

"We're to escort you directly to the palace."

The group followed his entourage, with four of the royal guards, moving back to take up the rear. Commissioner Polp kept in stride with the leader while Innego and Windsor stayed on either side of the other visitors. They filed into the large transport, and it sped off.

"What an interesting view," the leader spoke about the landscape scenery. "Is the land barren? Where is your vegetation?"

"We don't grow much in the city limits," Commissioner Polp responded. "We like to keep undeveloped sectors in case they are needed later."

"Such a waste of territory. I believe every part of a planet should be utilized for gains." The leader turned to Commissioner Polp. "I mean no disrespect. Of course your emperors see fit to do as they please."

Innego's demeanor to tense. That remark irked him as well. Their blatant audacity was not lost on anyone.

Tavelo and Manel stood waiting at the palace's main entrance with forty imperial guards, Gallic, Master Jaubro and his assistant, Desedon. A servant held up the communication sphere, relaying the feed from when the visitors arrived for the ride over. The overcast reflected how the emperors felt.

Master Jaubro, whose shipment had been the one in question, kept a blank expression.

He's clearly angered.

Tavelo struggled to keep himself from blurting out obscenities at the sphere. Manel had no such restraint, and it took a lot of coaxing from them to calm him. His eyes remained red.

The transport had arrived to a hostile welcome. More imperial guards surrounded the group as they stepped out onto the palace grounds.

"Emperors Manel of the West and Tavelo of the East!" The head of the imperial guards announced for the visitors. "Bow down and show your respect!"

Everyone went to their knees except the visitors. Again, they all did the head tilt, this time holding their arms crossed before them. Manel bristled. Tavelo slid a hand behind his back and pressed. Manel glared over at him, but kept still. When the others rose, he could see the anger on their faces.

"Greetings to you, rulers of Cellaxa. May I ask what you have planned for this visit?"

"I beg your pardon?" Tavelo said, using the Earth term with a venomous tone.

"Since we are here, wouldn't a tour of your abode be in order?"

"You want to stroll our city? For what exactly?"

"We would like to get to know you better." The leader did that smile thing that made Innego twitch. "Trade would go better if we understood what kind of race we are dealing with."

"Is that so?" Tavelo stepped down and faced the leader. Their eyes met, being of equal height. "Then we look forward to an invitation from yours to do the same."

The way the leader's snout snapped shut without an answer gave him one regardless. No one spoke, causing an awkward silence to linger.

"What an excellent idea." Master Jaubro's tense voice said. "Let's take a stroll." He glanced over at Innego. "It's good to get out of the palace for some fresh air."

The leader sniffed, his snout's nostrils flaring.

"It's quite acrid with the smell of your waters. To each its own."

"This way," the imperial guards' head ordered.

Manel and Tavelo walked with the leader and Commissioner Polp. Master Jaubro and Desedon followed while Innego and Windsor mingled with its entourage. The guards split in half, covering the front and the rear. An equal space of one hundred feet between them and the group.

They headed down the stone path of the palace onto the main thoroughfare leading to the city. Small banter included more quick jabs at Cellaxa itself from the leader.

"Such a gloomy atmosphere. Does it not hinder production? With a lack of sun, I can see now why your vegetation effort would suffer."

The leader got no response, and they seemed bothered by it. *Ahh. It's trying to bait us.* As they reached the bridge that went over the river, Tavelo started the real conversation.

"We need an explanation regarding the shipment you tried to block." Tavelo nodded towards Master Jaubro. "It is their contract you messed with."

The leader and the two behind him sized up Master Jaubro and Desedon. The one to the leader's right spoke for the first time.

"It doesn't seem a meager shipment would affect your bottom line. I am not seeing what the fuss is about."

"Yes," the one on the left interjected. "Surely it's unimportant. The goods were delivered eventually."

"There is the principle." Tavelo replied.

Master Jaubro clenched his fists.

"Blindsiding legal trade with false accusations is bad business. One in the industry knows better."

"The same could be said about veterans in the trade. You should always safeguard your products."

Movement from a visitor in the middle, caught Tavelo's eye. He followed Innego's stare to see it walking over to whisper in the leader's right-hand companion's ear. Then it stepped back in place.

An imperial guard ahead of the group frowned at his communication wristband. He tapped on it a few times, which alarmed Tavelo.

"What is it?"

"I'm having trouble connecting with the guards watching the visitor ship on the docks."

Tavelo looked over to the guard with the sphere

and saw it had gone dark. He stopped a few feet ahead of the leader and turned to face him.

"Explain why my guards can't communicate with the ones at the docks."

The leader gave him a confused look.

"Is something wrong?" The leader asked concerned.

Gallic slowly drew his sword. Manel bent one leg forward, ready to flash towards him. The royal guards went on full defense.

"What exactly did you come here for?" Tavelo moved back from him. Something about his body language made him feel hostile. "How you answer determines if you and your people leave here intact."

The leader didn't like his tone. Its eyes narrowed, showing only its slitted pupils in yellow irises. Its entourage changed their demeanor to match.

"You know, after surveying this planet," the leader held out his hands, palms up. "I feel it needs restructuring. New leadership perhaps?"

Tavelo heard multiple engines closing in. Small vessels covered the sky above. Fighters jumped out with weapons trained on the group. The leader and his entourage scattered out of the way to give them easy access to the Cellaxans. Some fighters never made it to the ground.

Two Volshins shrieked as they swept across the sky, knocking them into the river. Another swatted a handful of ships, sending them down as well. A small tidal wave slapped against the bottom of the bridge as they fell.

Nothing stopped Manel from launching towards the leader. The two beside him moved to be sacrificial shields. He gave them their wish, slicing through them with extended black talons. Manel pushed them out of the way and grabbed the leader by the top of his head.

To his surprise, a long, thin metal rod went through the leader's back and hit him in the chest. He leaped away before it went deep.

The remaining ships maneuvered to pluck the enemy in the river into their open bays. Long cables dangled from their hatches and the survivors grabbed on, clambering up into them. Tavelo eyed their fast retreat, confused by the sudden attack, followed by a hasty abandon.

The leader's entourage held their own against the imperial guards as they made their way to the edge of the bridge. Oh, they can fight. Tavelo didn't move. He watched the action at arm's length. Another ship swooped by and hovered above them. Grappling arms extended and scooped them up into the hatch. It sealed shut and sped off back towards the docks.

"Don't let them leave!" Innego yelled.

The Volshins gave chase, trailing at least a mile behind. They won't catch them. Tavelo could see the difference in distance. They waited too long to turn back around. Manel let out a shriek, drool dripping from his mouth.

Static came from the communication sphere a royal guard produced. It finally cleared to show the west docks in chaos. The visitors fought to keep the royal guards away from the convoy ship as the smaller ones flew into its open underbelly. Katalings climbed the beams to ram the ship.

A group of visitor fighters aimed their weapons at the docking clamps, destroying them to let the ship loose.

Innego yelled in frustration. Tavelo understood how he felt. An opportunity for bloodshed had sailed.

"What was that?" Commissioner Polp exclaimed.

"A test run." Tavelo turned to them. Manel gave him a crazed look. Then he straightened his posture. "They had only gathered minimal intel. This was to see our response and what they would encounter if it were a real attack."

"A smart strategy," Master Jaubro said. "But they're in for a rude awakening if they try again."

"Oh." Tavelo's eyes went silver. "They'll be back with an entire army."

"How stupid!" Innego spat. "Their plan would have failed if we killed them all."

"Do you really think they came here without a contingency plan?" Tavelo asked.

Manel checked the shallow wound on his chest and glared at the blood seeping through his tunic.

"They will not be so lucky."

They watched the convoy ship break away from the docks and punch through the thick clouds. Tavelo could easily order the land space missiles launched and take down the main ship. He thought about it for a moment, then decided against it.

No. Let them try again. Manel appeared to read his mind. A devious grin spread across his lips.

"I like the way you think, East Emperor." His voice dripped with lust.

Gallic tensed.

Tavelo rolled his eyes in exasperation. Master Jaubro's brow furrowed.

"Stop that!" Tavelo finally said. "Save it for when you drain the life from that pompous reptile's body."

"Mmm." Manel smiled. "That's even better."

Their royal guards had the same sentiment.

Everyone felt cheated.

Seeing Pridric outside of the palace walls for the first time sent mixed feelings in Pravin. His love for her went deep, yet he despised her for fawning after that Endaga. And now he is emperor!

When the neighborhood renovators came with one of those gaudy statues to place in front of their homestead, he refused it. Not tolerating anything that signified their clan as ancient bloodline carriers.

From his seat in the arena's supper deck during the battle maiden competition, he could see Pridric's kaleidoscope eyes. It solidified their father's, and the generation before him, that the blood line needed cleansing.

Despite every attempt to destroy her womb after extracting the embryo created from Tavelo and her, she somehow still got impregnated. The option of mating with a Strana no longer a factor. Though if the strict protocols were eliminated, he would have taken her.

Master Strana sat up from slouching in his chair and stretched his arms in the air. His shoulders felt stiff from throttling insubordinates earlier.

The spy's failure to eliminate Pridric and the damnable offspring she spawned angered him. He had to activate another and hope they completed the task. The thought sent a pain in his chest.

Stop! He had to keep his resolve. The reputation and respect of his clan were at stake.

He remembered when his father brought in an exiled royal member and gave him one of his sisters. The mating resulted in two offspring, Omaris and Omeron. Luckily, only one had Kataling blood and could shift into one of those creatures.

They were not treated well, and in the end, their mother died in their fifth year during childbirth. That child lived for only a few hours. The previous Master Strana, having signed an agreement to keep any offspring, tortured Omeron when it fancied him.

Dania along with their sense of justice didn't offer them any favors either. They were constantly trying to protect Pridric from the family. Their actions only made things worse for Pridric and Omeron.

Everything about how they were treated was wrong. He knew that. But the clan expected him to uphold their traditions and laws.

A light rapping on his door made him stand.

It opened for his assistant. The man seemed worse for wear; his eyes lackluster as if sleep deluded him.

"What do you have?"

"The skirmish on the docks came from that race visiting who tried to block the Jaubro shipment."

Pravin stared in shock.

"They came to start a fight?" He yelled. "And those emperors let them leave alive?"

"About that. From my spy network, it seems Emperor Tavelo made the decision since the fight hardly constituted as one."

"So when they come back," Pravin began.

"We reap the spoils," his assistant finished.

"I still don't like it."

"Of course."

Pravin moved closer.

"And what about the spy in the palace? Is he set to execute his mission?"

"They are waiting for the right time. As you know, Tavelo keeps her tethered."

Holnar burst into the Boresso workshop, shoving lab workers out of his path. He grabbed the back of the lab coat of the man leaning down over Chalayl ready to punch her. He spun the man around and lifting him off the floor, tossed him into a workstation covered in beakers.

Glass shattered and flew everywhere. Chalayl propped herself off the floor with one arm. She wiped blood from her nose and mouth, smearing it across her face.

The workers moved to attack, surrounding him from all sides. He clenched his fists and spread his legs arm's width apart. His expression dared them.

"What is the meaning of this!" Master Boresso came into the room along with her two assistants. "Explain why you're in my clan's home attacking my people?"

Holnar turned his red eyes towards her.

"I will when you explain why you allow Chalayl to be tormented and beaten. Or maybe it's under your watch and you sanction it."

"How dare you…"

Master Boresso stepped closer, then halted. She glanced down at Chalayl struggling to rise. A dark bruise spread above her ankle. The blood on her face began to dry. "Get up! You call yourself a battle maiden. The only good thing you were useful for was winning those trade credits."

Holnar met Master Boresso's gaze.

"Chalayl will not live here any longer."

"That is not up to you."

"As she is the mother of my children, you're wrong." He turned to the nearest worker. "Move."

The man didn't budge as Holnar closed in,. They drew the same breath. Master Boresso waved a hand.

"Let him pass."

Holnar went over to Chalayl. He helped her stand and bore her weight against his body.

"This ends now. Understand?"

Chalayl nodded. She didn't look at her aunt, keeping her head down.

"Fine. Take her if you wish." Master Boresso turned her head away.

"You never wanted her in the first place," Holnar spat. "Find some other clan member's child to torture for fun."

"You don't get to slander me in my own home," Master Boresso returned his bloody stare. "Child."

Holnar, holding Chalayl tight to him, walked past her through the door. He gave her one final glare before heading down the hall. There wasn't an ounce of respect for her in them.

Master Boresso remained in the doorway. The pain in her chest rendered her immobile.

The man Holnar had tossed rose from the floor, brushing off pieces of debris. Another worker helped him check to make sure he didn't have any wounds.

"We should invoice his coven or whatever for the damages." He smirked. "At least we don't have to worry about that whore messing up another sample."

The man's body embedded four feet up into the opposite wall. His eyes rolled up in their sockets. Everyone else in the room backed away, creating a wide circle around Master Boresso, who stood in the center. Her silver eyes burned with hostility.

"Never have I sanctioned any of you to harm that child. Let me be clear. Discipline is not the same as beating." The man's body slowly peeled away, dropping face down on the floor. "Clean this up."

She turned and walked off with her two assistants.

When a page rushed in to report Holnar's arrival in a tirade, she knew why. If not him, then one of Chalayl's children would come to take her. After that first shameful incident in the other workshop, they vowed to rescue her from the clan.

Seeing the way Holnar disrespected her home and the workers, she realized Chalayl had a support system she never received from her own family.

Attack On Cellaxa

Manel squinted at the sky, focusing on a blotch in the clouds. He flicked his taloned thumb and forefinger together. Their clicks sounded like glass cracking. Wearing his black battle suit with a red swath of cloth across one shoulder, clasped at this hip, he reminded Gallic of his previous self.

The only difference was Manel's length of hair and leaner physique.

"I need communications to scan the orbit," Manel instructed an imperial guard stationed at the bottom of the throne's dais. "I think we have visitors."

"Of course, emperor." The guard bowed and left the room.

Gallic walked up to stand beside him.

"Who would be so delusional to attack us?"

He peered out at the horizon.

"Besides those arms dealers from before?"

"Oh. Them." Gallic's lips went thin.

The holoscreen opposite the throne flicked on. Tavelo's face filled the display. Manel could see its reflection in the window.

"You see it too?" Manel's irises shifted from red to amber as he tried to contain his rage.

"I'm going to fly up and take a look," Tavelo replied.

Manel tilted his head over his shoulder, surprised.

"Is that wise? Don't you need a chaperone?"

Tavelo opted to ignore the jab at his previous landing event.

"Make sure the weapons crew is ready if needed."

Manel waved a hand to dismiss it. Gallic could tell that would be Manel's next order.

The holoscreen split and the communications tech appeared next to Tavelo.

"Emperor Manel." The tech frowned. "There seems to be a vortex opening right above the…"

The technician's image scrambled, then turned to white noise before winking out. Residual audio continued to crackle through. A rumble from the sky spread. The clouds brightened on the opposite side of the sun, hitting the palace windows, causing a glare.

Manel's eyes went wide as he stared at it. They heard the technician let out a yell before the feed cut out. Gallic's sight locked in on what looked like a tunnel of light barreling towards them. He turned to see Tavelo disconnect his feed.

With one arm, he grabbed hold of Manel and leaped to the side, tumbling down to the floor right as the blast hit.

Its beam spread across three quarters of the room, scorching everything. An imperial guard lay flat, face down, the entire right side of his body exposing flesh that sizzled. They managed to avoid most of the attack, only a few inches from the edge of its projectory. A gaping hole in the far wall allowed a view of the forest outside. The blast carved a path, destroying the trees.

Manel tried to push Gallic off him and was denied.

"Stay down!" Gallic cocked his head to one side. Listening. Within seconds, he heard the inevitable. Air strikes. "They're bombarding us from orbit."

This time, Manel knocked him off and climbed over the debris to the open space where the window and his throne used to be. He stood on the jagged edge, staring at the now darkened sky.

Gallic brushed off his uniform and joined him. They could see ships enter the atmosphere.

Lendor and Megen came rushing to the throne room and stopped in their tracks, seeing the damage.

"What madness is this?" Megen went to inspect the hole leading to the forest.

"Do we have confirmation of who did this?" Lendor asked, helping the wounded guard to his feet.

Gallic made out the shape of the incoming ships.

"Visitors is right. It's them."

The holoscreen came back online with the tech.

"I have an incoming message for Emperor Manel and Tavelo."

Manel whirled around, his eyes blood red.

The reptilian leader came onscreen.

"Your race is a menace to all, yet we came to assess you in good faith. The overaction to such a small skirmish is telling. Wounding the delegate of a potential client shows a lack of respect for order. This is your punishment and a chance to prove you can do better in the future."

The feed died, replaced once more by the tech.

"Tavelo must be seething right now," Gallic said.

"He's not the only one," Lendor nodded to Manel.

"A fleet of one hundred ships has appeared outside the planet," the technician announced.

"Taught a lesson?" Manel jumped down from the wrecked platform. "Prove we can do better?"

Gallic saw the crazed expression and knew he could do nothing to stop Manel from going on a rampage. He wouldn't want to either. The insult hit deep. There would be no negotiations this time.

Wide strands of enemy fire rained down on Cellaxa, targeting the docks and the palace. Tavelo walked out onto the front steps of the East palace and glared at the ships making a landing. His uncle and Innego pulled him back right before one hit five hundred feet in front of him. The blast left a crater in the stone.

Tavelo's eyes became a kaleidoscope of blues, greens, and yellows. He moved forward, ready to morph. Innego clamped a hand on his shoulder, stopping him.

"No! You need to stay calm."

"Pridric is out there," Tavelo yelled.

"I know. But first you must ensure the safety of those in the palace."

Tavelo tried to pull away.

Then he halted, straightening his posture. He turned around and went back inside the palace. Innego and his uncle followed him to the defense room two levels below the center of the palace. He flung open the doors.

"How many ships are up there?" He asked.

An operator tech leaned his head over the side of his workstation.

"By our count, they have one hundred."

"Shoot down every other ten."

"As you command, emperor."

The technician nodded to his counterpart.

The two went back to manning their stations.

"And raise the shields for the palace. I almost got cremated by a blast."

"My apologies, emperor Tavelo. We will get it done." A soldier at a station farther back replied.

Tavelo left the room and headed towards the West palace. Midway there, he ran into Manel and Gallic.

"We were careless, Tavelo." Manel's left eye twitched. "We assumed they needed time to regroup."

"Yes, they proved us wrong." Tavelo nodded to the window beside them.

A horde of uniformed reptile fighters surged onto the palace grounds.

"Shall we?"

Gallic and Innego held their hands up in protest.

"Hold on!"

"Wait!"

They shouted in unison. Gallic stepped between Manel and Tavelo.

"The last thing we need is the two of you tearing up the grounds in full ancient forms."

"Let's try brutality first," Innego added.

Master Endaga took a few deep breaths before he addressed the emperors.

"I'm going to have to agree on that."

Manel chuckled as he walked off. Tavelo turned and fell in step with him. Together, they went outside to greet the enemy.

❀ ❀ ❀

The first blast blinded the royal transport pilot, causing him to swerve from its point of impact. Pridric got jostled inside. The transport tilted sideways and skidded onto the crumbling road, sending sparks.

When it stopped, Pridric kicked out the damaged door and climbed out to the top. Above, smaller fighter ships lay a blanket of fire as they came in for a landing.

Pridric checked on the pilot slumped unconscious in the front. The left side of his face had deep contusions from debris that flew through the window. His royal guards clambered out, followed by the rest in the second transport behind them.

Enemy fighters charged towards the group from all sides. Pridric stared in disbelief at the reptilian warriors. Why? He couldn't fathom what they were retaliating for. Their leader started it. Realizing his guards only possessed swords, he braced for hand-to-hand combat.

The fighter leading the enemy's first wave spoke as he got closer.

"You wound our leader and insult us. This is your lesson."

Pridric's eyes widened in mocked shock. He gave the fighter a confused look.

"Your leader insulted our people first. I see no justification for you to invade our home."

"Trash like your race have no right to address us so casually."

The fighter got close enough to swing his curved blade at Pridric's neck. He bent back and weaved to the side, sinking his extended talons into the back of the enemy's ribs. To his surprise, the enemy merely grunted and knocked Pridric from him. His talons came out, dripping blood. He got pushed into the front of the transport.

Without missing any opportunity, four more enemy fighters came for him. Pridric scanned the area, taking in how his royal guards were holding up against a horde, outnumbering them five to one. More ships went flying past toward the docks. They always target the docks. He could see a thin trail of smoke coming from the palace.

Don't worry about me, Tavelo.

He met the four fighters midway and fought them head on. The wounded enemy moved to strike him from behind. The pilot grabbed him by the back of the head and punched his talons through the top. He let the body drop and climbed out of the transport.

"I will guard your rear, Empress." The pilot pulled his sword from behind the broken seat and unsheathed it. "Emperor Tavelo would kill us all if you were harmed."

The pilot struck down an enemy trying to come at them from the other side. Pridric felt the tension ease a bit. They weren't out of the woods yet, but he could see victory.

❀ ❀ ❀

A barrier activated at the sight of the enemy above kept the west docks from getting damaged. Manel had scientists in the defense sector create it after the last battle. Workers observed enemy ships getting crunched or exploding as they careened into it.

Volshins in the sky picked them off when they fell. The small number of enemy fighters that made it through before the shield went up faced an angry mob of dock workers.

"Shall we kill them all?" A Boresso merchant asked a Jaubro merchant across the way. "Drain them dry for the cubes?"

"Hmm. Let's bring them despair first, then wait to hear from the palace. I'm sure the emperors have something in store for them."

Hearing this, the enemy fighters scattered throughout the docks, attacking the workers. They didn't allow them to form a defense. Their advances were short-lived. Two Katalings stomped out onto the boardwalk. Their nostrils flared, followed by puffs of misty snot. Red eyes with no whites bulged.

A group of enemy fighters charged, trying to cut through the first one's thick hide. That only made it angrier. It lowered its massive head and speared them with its horns. The second turned and rammed into the rest of the fighters. Blood flew upward, then splattered the ground around the enemy bodies on the ground.

"I feel like getting my hands dirty," an Endaga merchant said. His words shocked the others as he pulled off his jacket and flung it into the bay. "Just a little."

"In that case," the Boresso merchant said. He, too, removed his jacket.

The Callesi and Strana women merchants did the same, revealing flowy blouses. They rolled up their sleeves and tied their hair into buns atop their heads.

"Ancient ones shouldn't get all the fun."

The Strana merchant pouted.

An enemy leaped from a rafter straight towards her. She looked up and frowned. She didn't have time to dodge it fully. It sliced her shoulder. With the enemy still bent forward from his momentum, she spun around and sent her talons through both sides of him. He gagged on his own blood when he tried to rise. Her talons skewered his arms in place under the pits.

"That's what you get for trying to be sneaky."

She wrenched her talons out, nearly severing the enemy in pieces.

"No fair," the Dakien merchant sighed. He flashed into the mob of enemies on the right. "I wanted to slice that thing in half before it landed."

On the edge of the palace grounds, Tavelo and Manel encountered a horde of thirty reptile fighters coming at them in a formation of three rows, the back fighters carrying guns. The first wave had handheld weapons resembling battle axes and spiked clubs.

Tavelo stifled a snort. Reptiles wielding those kinds of weapons seemed comical. He turned to Manel. He didn't find it amusing at all. Since they both promised not to morph into their ancient forms, they drew swords instead.

Tavelo knew how deadly Manel could be with one and he proved his skills many times over. The enemy would be in for a treat.

Right as the first row clashed against them and their imperial forces, enemy ships laid down a layer of firepower around them.

"That's dirty!" An imperial guard shouted. "But we're the ones in the wrong?"

Manel turned his back on his opponent and ran towards a volley of missives. With one swing of his broadsword, he knocked them back towards their ship. They hit their target, and the ship tilted down, explosions scattering across its underbelly. His prey caught up to him, believing they had the element of surprise.

Without missing a beat, Manel's sword continued its swing and sliced through the enemy's torso. It came out the other side clean. The enemy stopped, not sure what happened. Then its eyes glazed over. The top half of its body slowly slid forward, landing on the ground. Its bottom half stayed standing a few seconds more before it too collapsed.

Tavelo flashed through a cluster of ten enemy fighters hellbent on surrounding him for the kill. Another group lay beyond them, ahead. Nice. He waited until they closed in before squatting and thrusted forward. Two in a row got skewered, along with a third behind them. He yanked out the sword and severed the legs of the closest enemy.

The others drew back.

Tavelo stood up in the disrupted circle, his sword dripping blood from the tip as he held it by his side.

"Come now," he breathed. "You can do better than that."

He flicked his sword with a wrist twist, sending an arc of blood into their faces. Angered, they came at him at once, fury in their eyes. Tavelo laughed.

How stupid!

"Keep most of them alive," Tavelo ordered. "We want to make sure we send them back as a warning."

"You're being too nice again, Tavelo." Manel shoved his blade into an enemy's neck, and twisted. The sword's width cleaved off its head in a jagged line. He met Tavelo's gaze. "If you insist."

Imperial guards corralled the rear row of enemies away from Manel and Tavelo to let them take care of the others. At some point, the reptiles tried to retreat. They had no such luck.

"I feel," Manel stretched his arms, streaked with blood on his forearms in the air, "like they aren't serious enough." He tilted his head back over his shoulder to look at Tavelo.

"Oh, they were serious enough. It just turns out they're delusional." Tavelo spat enemy blood from his mouth. "Their blood needs some doctoring up."

"I think, they deem themselves superior and have never had their asses handed to them." Innego added. "The way they felt insulted when they were the ones doing it." He shook his head. "The audacity."

Nearly a hundred enemy bodies lay strewn across the palace grounds, some in the forest. Only a few were dead. Tavelo spotted Gallic watching an enemy twitch in pain. His hand gripped the handle of his sword.

"Don't." Tavelo glared at him.

Gallic hesitated, then let his hand fall to his side. The disappointment in his eyes spoke volumes.

"What do you want to do with the survivors?" Master Endaga asked, wiping his talons off on a nearby enemy's body. "You need to send them back with a message."

"First," Tavelo walked to the palace, "we need to check on the ships in orbit."

"Ah yes." Manel followed him. "Your little plan to disrupt their formation."

Innego pointed to the sky.

"I think it worked.

Dark shadows formed in the sky before flaming ships burst from the clouds, heading into the ocean. Two of them were on course to hit parts of the city. Volshins used their power to shove them off course. Tavelo's wristband emitted two sharp beeps.

He wiped the blood from the small screen.

"Their leader wants to have a talk." He took the steps a few at a time and landed in what used to be a section of the main corridor.

"How about we convene in that chamber ahead?"

People in the halls gave the group covered in blood a wide berth. With heads held high, they strolled through like the royalty they were.

Inside the chamber, Tavelo waited for the royal soldier to connect the feed. Within minutes, the holoscreen on the wall lit up and revealed the enemy leader. His expression exuded horror and disdain.

"What kind of monsters are you?" He tsked, his thick tongue jetting out for a second. Gallic tensed with malice at the action. Manel glared at the screen. "To go so far and target our ships that are only standing by. Is that your policy? To kill the innocent as it suits you?"

"Tell me where these innocent bystanders are." Manel leaned forward in his seat. "If I find one, I will send my condolences."

"I want…" the leader began.

"You don't get to ask for anything." Manel's eyes turned a fleshy red. "We don't care what you want."

Tavelo held up a hand. "You will collect your dead and wounded, then withdraw." He sat back against his chair. "We shall allow you to retrieve your ships from our ocean."

"Make no mistake," Manel interjected. "If you ever come here again, we will drain every fallen body and use the remains for compost."

The leader's horrified expression intensified. They reared back from the screen.

"Have we made ourselves clear?" Tavelo added.

"This will not stand." The leader replied indignantly. "I will order my fleet to do as you ask."

Gallic swiped a hand across his neck at the royal soldier and they cut the feed. Manel slumped in his chair. Tavelo motioned to the soldier.

"Send word to the docks to cease their attacks." His eyes lit up, full of rage. "And find my Empress."

Unity

Across Cellaxa, enemy fighters scoured the streets and the docks, engaging with citizens and royal guards spread out among the territories. The initial shock of being invaded gave the enemy a winning start. Buildings were damaged, people wounded in the streets, and no sign of it letting up.

Until the merchant families snapped out of their stupor. The elites' guardians defended the homes. In three hours, the tables turned, seeing the enemy struggling to get a foothold.

Master Strana and his entourage headed down the streets leading towards the palace. He assigned his best fighters to guard the homestead when he saw more ships coming in for a landing nearby. They were more than capable of making sure the enemy had no footing when they came.

The Strana stronghold would not fall.

Not on my watch!

When he found the main walkway torn up with a massive hole in its center, he leaped across the tops of buildings to get closer. A cluster of enemies out to the north caught his eye. He motioned for his group to follow his lead. As he moved in, he witnessed the gruesome scene.

On the street below him, Pridric took on two fighters. The ferocity of his attacks stopped him in his tracks.

Black talons extended, eyes a kaleidoscope, with his blond hair billowing in the wind as he struck an enemy across the face, slicing it in sections, Pridric looked like a monster.

Such beauty!

Four more enemies descended upon Pridric. He held them off, pushing the fist fighter away from the imperial guards behind him.

"I never knew Pridric to be so monstrous and brutal in battle."

"He is a Strana," his assistant said matter of fact.

Out of the corner of his eye, he saw an enemy take a step back, holding a metal spear with jagged teeth on its tip. They drew their arm behind them, the spear aimed at Pridric. Master Strana gripped his assistant's shoulder, digging deep into the flesh. His eyes turned silver.

"I will not let him die this way!"

A split second from releasing his hold, Master Strana bolted forward, his body a blur. His assistant watched him change direction, heading for the spear wielder.

"Hurry! We must protect Pridric and Master Strana." He charged down with the rest of the clan in tow. "Stop being so rash," he chided to Pravin under his breath.

The spear wielder launched his weapon right as Master Strana plowed into them. The spear lost some of its momentum, giving him enough time to pivot away and catch it before it struck Pridric. He fell backwards into his chest, holding the shaft just below the tip.

Pridric stared at him in awe, not daring to move. His brother stood straight and tossed the spear to the side. He turned his head to glance back at him.

"You need to be more aware of the area around you." Master Strana saw Pridric step back, confused. "I know." He turned around and cupped his hand against the side of Pridric's cheek. "I frighten you.

But it shouldn't be this way." He dropped his hand and turned back to the enemy getting up, shaking his head. "I'll handle this brute."

Pridric whirled around in time to see a Strana knock an enemy that came close to him ten feet away. The imperial guards' leader gave him a shrugging glance. Thankful for the assist, Pridric continued their efforts to either kill or drive the enemy back.

The pilot heard the familiar chirp of the transport's comm-receiver. He cut down an enemy and made his way to it. With difficulty, he leaned into the front and tapped the accept icon. The screen flickered, showing a distorted image within the cracks.

"By Emperors Tavelo and Manel's decree, all fighting must cease. Allow the enemy to retreat. Retrieval will commence by nightfall."

He glanced back to see tiny lights blinking right below the enemy's right ears. They immediately went into defense mode, assuming they would not be granted such a reprieve.

Pridric dropped his arms, exhaling loudly. He walked towards the enemy now clustered together in a circle formation.

"Leave this place." Pridric gestured to the bodies on the ground. "Take your dead with you." He turned to six of his guards. "Make sure they do not stray from the path."

"As you command, Empress," they answered in unison.

When the enemy marching down the walkway finally disappeared in the distance, Pridric's legs buckled. He felt all the strength leave his body as he fell. Arms caught him inches from impact. His brother locked eyes with him before they closed.

Master Strana helplessly watched Pridric start to convulse. He held on tight, feeling his body shift beneath him. When Pridric lay still, sweat covered her face. Dark lines ran under the skin of her arms and went up around her cheeks.

"What is happening?" Master Strana yelled.

A royal soldier knelt beside him.

"The Empress is not yet fully recovered. This much fighting could have killed her. Emperor Tavelo will not be pleased."

"The decree has been made." The pilot stood over them. "I suggest we wait until nightfall and the enemy fleet is gone before we report this."

"We can't stay at this location for that long," a royal guard said.

Master Strana stood, still holding Pridric. The pilot saw the look on his face and raised his sword.

"If you're about to suggest what I think you are, the answer is no. Emperor Tavelo has specifically advised to not let you anywhere near the Empress."

"And yet," Master Strana's eyes went red. "I have. Our clan is the only one who can help her."

"Put her down," the royal guard demanded.

Master Strana lowered his head so that his eyes resembled slits.

"Take her from me."

The pilot and the rest of the royal guards stared at him, then assessed the other Strana members, ready to take them out if they tried.

Master Strana grinned.

"Follow us." He leaped up into the sky and landed on the building above. He stared down at Pridric. "I finally get to take you home."

To avoid being seen, and the damaged streets, the group of royal guards and Strana members went along the rooftops until they reached the Strana Homestead. Master Strana sucked air through his teeth when he saw the front of the grounds scorched black with gouges in the landscape.

Wounded family members lay on the ground being treated by their medical staff.

The head of the workshops came out to greet him and stopped.

He eyed Pridric's unconscious body, limp in Master Strana's arms.

"We need to get her to the medical lab. She started convulsing. Her body is…"

"Practically destroyed," the man finished. "And yet, somehow, it managed to spawn new life."

His assistant went over to the holoscreen on the foyer's main wall. A feed of the planet's chaos played. The royal decree along the bottom, advised the citizens to remain indoors until the enemy had vacated.

"It appears the fighting has died out. The dock workers corralled the enemy towards their ships."

A family member came bursting out the side door. His flustered face fell on Pridric.

"We got that thing's body? When can we start dissecting it?" He stared at her with disgust, then a gleam of lust, thinking about operating on her. "Give it to me."

The member went sailing into the wall, blood spurting from his mouth as he hit. He fell to his knees, gasping. When he looked up, he scooted back against the wall.

Master Strana lowered his leg, bending it at the knee before planting his foot flat on the floor. Pridric never left his grip. The man who greeted them shook his head in pity at the lab member.

"Such ignorance. I'm glad our young leader has finally realized the old master's ways made us monsters. There is no reason to continue a legacy of fear and loathing among our own."

Master Strana clutched Pridric tighter. Her royal guards' leader relaxed his fingers atop the hilt of his sword. The man glanced over at him, focusing on his hand.

"I understand your apprehension. And it goes without saying, Emperor Tavelo will be angry."

He gestured for Master Strana to follow him to the medical wing.

"That's it?" The lab member yelled, rising from the floor. He followed them to the medical lab. "We just throw it out the window because our leader was too weak to carry it out?" His eyes went red. "Do you know how long we waited to gut that abomination?"

The group halted.

Workers inside brought their attention to the fray. Right as the group turned around to stare in awe at his words, the assistant flashed towards him. He punched him with talons extended in the abdomen, sending him up into the air. The lab member's body hit the ceiling, then crashed down with a loud thud. Blood seeped from beneath him.

Master Strana turned silver eyes to the workers in the medical lab.

"Who else dares to harm her?"

Frowns creased their faces. It's true, he indeed encouraged those actions. Forced them, even. Regret hung heavy on his soul. Two lab techs came forward and motioned him to the examination pod. He carried Pridric over and laid her inside.

The system lit up, engulfing the pod in a pale blue light. Multicolored tendrils of light swirled above her body. On the hologram behind, displayed a map of her entire biological system. It divided into layers to show each level. From skeletal to veins and muscles.

Pridric's royal guards stayed outside the doors, observing. Master Strana stood a few feet away from the pod with a worried look on his face.

Yelling along with the sound of fighting in the halls made everyone alert.

A voice surfaced over the din.

"I must implore you to calm down! There is no danger to the Empress here!"

The royal guards backed into the room and made way for the oncoming people. A Strana member walked backwards with both hands up at chest level. He stopped near the center.

Tavelo stepped into the bay, his Volshin eyes glittering in the light.

"What do you think you're doing," his gaze fell on Pridric, "Strana?"

Behind Tavelo, the royal physician and Master Endaga came around to get a look at the situation. The royal physician went closer to the pod, marveling at the technology.

"We have the means to repair the damage." Strana's head of medicine explained as he came into the room. "Is that not what you desire?"

"Your people did this to her," Tavelo seethed.

"Yes." The man's head lowered. "We sadly are responsible for that."

Tavelo hesitated.

He had come barreling into the Strana stronghold intent on killing every clan member if he found Pridric wounded or dead by their hands. Master Strana could see all of it and turned to him.

"You have every right to assume the worst in us. We haven't proved you wrong." He met Tavelo's glare. "Am I bitter that she chose you? Of course. Pridric should have been mine. I knew long ago she would never love me the way she does you. My clan thinks I'm weak for not following the tradition my father and the one before him started." He clenched his fists at his sides. "I never wanted to harm her. Pridric will always be precious to me."

Tavelo glanced behind him at the four technicians ignoring the scene, focused on diagnosing the issues pertaining to Pridric's condition. His eyes reverted to normal, and his talons retracted.

"She must be transported to the palace once she is stable."

The royal physician moved even closer.

"I will stay to supervise the procedures. The Strana's medical knowledge should be witnessed." He turned to the head of medicine. "Would you be willing to send a team to work in the palace?"

The head of medicine pressed his lips together, exhaling slowly.

"You want our technology."

"We want to be able to save Katalings and Volshins the right way." The royal physician replied harshly. "If we knew more about their anatomy in detail as your clan does, we could have fixed Emperor Manel properly."

"Fixed?" The head of medicine and his workers gave him a puzzled stare. "Emperor Manel?" His eyes bulged. "Is that why he seems to be in flux all the time?" His eyes narrowed. "What did you do?"

"What we could!" The royal physician snapped.

The head of medicine's head reared back at the verbal assault. Then he addressed Tavelo.

"Emperor Tavelo. Please allow us to reverse the evils we laid upon our own. Entrust your Empress to us." He bowed his head and lifted it. "We may not be able to make her whole, but she will be healthy."

"If that is what needs to happen at this moment," Tavelo stood conflicted.

"Your instincts are telling you not to leave her here." Master Strana grinned. "I don't blame you."

"Your grace, if I may." Pridric's guard leader made a bow and waited.

"What is it?" Tavelo tilted his head towards him.

"The enemy is in the process of leaving. Roads need to be repaired as they go. This situation, though not ideal, is the best option. The Empress can be transported when it is deemed safe."

"Then your unit will stay here along with the royal physician." He met Pravin's eyes again. "I'll trust you. Bring my Empress back to me, where she belongs."

Master Strana watched Tavelo and his imperial soldiers leave. He turned his focus back to Pridric. The royal physician rose from his leaning position and glanced over at him.

"Your mind must have broken witnessing what

they did to her. I can see hints of it oozing from your being. You had no way to stop it. You realize that?"

Master Strana tightened his fists.

"I didn't even try."

"And you would not be standing here now." His assistant patted him on the shoulder. "Your father had no qualms about making his own children suffer. He would have crippled you at the very least."

Master Strana leaned over, causing the hologram to flicker, and softly kissed Pridric's lips. He slowly rose and addressed the head of medicine.

"Fix her." He turned to the royal physician. "I will arrange for a team to accompany you back to the palace. They will assess what methods you used on Emperor Manel."

"I appreciate it." The physician gave him a nod and resumed observing Pridric's treatment.

Master Strana and his assistant left. They walked down the corridor, seeing the damage done by Tavelo's rage. At the door of his chamber, Pravin pushed it with one hand, easing it open. A poisoned arrow came sailing towards him. He could see the liquid coating the head the closer it got.

His assistant caught it as it got within inches of its target. The assasin's brow furrowed before he went to escape out the window. Before his assistant could get to him, Pravin had the assassin by the neck. He held out his hand and gestured for his assistant to give him the arrow. The assassin's eyes widened with fear.

"Which one is it?" Pravin asked. "The one that drops the victim dead on the spot? Or the one that causes excruciating pain before the body gives out?"

The assassin glared while struggling in his grip.

"Your father would be disgusted. You have dishonored our clan by letting that thing carry our bloodline."

"No." Pravin took the arrow placed in his hand and rammed it into the assassin's chest. "Our predecessors did that when they decided to cleanse it."

Pink foam grew around the assassin's mouth, growing in volume. He writhed in pain, not able to scream. Verifying the poison had a lingering effect, he nodded to his assistant. The man went over to the drawers on the far wall and retrieved a needle with red liquid. He tossed it like a dart to Pravin who plunged it into the assassin's neck.

His writhing finally stopped.

Master Strana released him.

"I think it's time for me to address the clan. This ends now." Pravin walked back out.

"I agree, Master Strana." On his way out, he grabbed hold of a servant and whispered instructions, nodding towards the assassin. "We can't have such disobedience in our home."

Chalayl defended the Marchand homestead from the enemy as repayment for Holnar letting her stay. She didn't feel comfortable there, but knew not to be ungrateful. Some of the members stared with disdain when she walked through the halls. Whispers of her bad parenting skills came up often.

I know that!

She smashed in an enemy fighter's face. The bones made a crunching sound as they broke. Her pink dress, torn ragged up to her thighs, was drenched in blood.

The royal decree came through the global feed, and she backed off, letting the enemy scurry away. She stood panting. All around her, members of the coven ran around tending to each other.

Making sure no one noticed, she went to the side of the homestead where she had stashed a big satchel to carry on her back.

She got far enough away so Holnar nor any of his people could pursue, then leaped atop buildings until she got to the edge of the city. Beyond the outskirts lay cavernous mountains. No civilization for miles. The enemy had not gone there because of that.

A presence behind her made Chalayl turn around, ready to drop the backpack for a fight. Omeron stood before her. Blood, still slightly wet, smeared on his face and the front of his tunic.

"What are you doing?" He stepped closer to her.

For the first time, Chalayl moved away from him. He frowned.

"Please, just forget that you saw me."

"But I have." He stared at her, waiting for her to meet his gaze.

"It's better this way." Chalayl stepped farther. "No one will feel the need to defend me."

"We never saw it that way."

Chalayl raised her head and locked eyes with him. She felt the tears sting before filling her vision.

"Please. Let me go." Her voice came out in a rasp.

Omeron flashed forward. Grabbing her by the neck, he pulled her to him so their foreheads touched.

"Only if you promise me, you'll keep yourself safe. And come back." She nodded in defeat. "Come. Let's find you a suitable hideout."

"What?" Chalayl lifted her head. "Why would you…"

"I need to know where you are. No one else needs to." He slid his hand from her neck. "I may not trust you. But you must trust me this time."

Chalayl stared in surprised, then wiped her face. "Okay."

They ran towards the mountains at lightning speed. At the third one on the horizon, Chalayl pointed to a cavern far up, almost secluded from view. Omeron didn't like its location but relented when she wouldn't back down, commencing to climb up to it. Using their talons, the two reached its mouth. The cavern ran deep, nearly the size of a master bedroom.

Chalayl dropped the backpack. Its weight made a thud on the stone floor.

"This will be my new home." She felt his glare at her back. "For now?" She winced, not daring to turn around to look at him.

She opened the bag and took out a square bundle with a button on its side. Pushing caused the cube to inflate until it formed into a bed. Chalayl shoved it against the far wall of the cave. She took out two portable lanterns and set one at the foot of the bed and the other near the head.

When she stood from setting the last one, Omeron came behind her and lifted the torn dress over her head. He tossed it out and spun her around to face him.

"Don't," she cried. "You don't want me. I'm nothing but a dumb beast who doesn't know how to do anything right."

"If you had just asked me," Omeron cupped her face with both hands. "I would have been your mate."

Chalayl's eyes widened. Then she hung her head, ashamed of what she had done to him. She could have any man she wanted. Yet, she didn't think he could ever want her.

Omeron stripped naked and met her gaze once more. He caught her off guard when he picked her up and tossed her onto the bed. As he climbed over her, grabbing her leg under the knee and pulling her to him, his eyes glowed golden.

"This time, you will endure my desires."

Chalayl had no chance to reply. He entered her roughly, his thrust that of a hungry animal. The way she liked it.

For weeks, Holnar tried to find out where Chalayl had gone. After the enemy jumped through a vortex, disappearing from Cellaxa space, he went to check on her. Most of her belongings were still there, yet no sign of her.

He went to the Boresso clan to inquire about her.

"So she's missing," Master Boresso said flatly. "Maybe this is for the best."

"What if she's wounded?" Holnar snapped.

"You think she can't take care of herself? She's a battle maiden."

Holnar got up from his chair in the sitting room.

"You really don't care one way or the other. I should have known this would be a waste of time."

"You assume a lot, don't you, child of Bryhel?"

"It's not an assumption." He glanced back at her as he left the room. "I know it's true."

He passed the clan members from the last time he came to rescue Chalayl. They glared at him all the way to the main entrance. Outside, standing near the transport, her children waited for him to report. He shook his head.

"She couldn't have gone far," Olivier said loudly. "Where would she hide?"

"Why is she, is the question," Olette replied.

"You may not want to hear this," Chiron interrupted. "But, I think she needs to be far away from all of the crap she's been through." He turned to Caden. "Yeah, she's not getting the mother of the year award, but you're precious to her whether you believe it or not."

Holnar took a few deep breaths.

"Let's wait then. I'm sure she'll come back on her own." He waved a hand at them. "Let's go. I don't want to be around this place any longer."

Caden lingered and stared menacingly at the Boresso homestead. His eyes turned red for a split second, then he followed the others into the transport.

Holnar felt a chill in his spine. He prayed the boy wouldn't do anything stupid.

CHAPTER FOUR

Retaliation

The five systems' trade organization received Cellaxa's report on the reptile race and sent them a scathing admonishment. A message of solidarity came to Cellaxa with a guarantee of resolution.

Emperor Manel and Tavelo sat on their thrones in the dual room and read it on the holoscreen. Their royal council stood in attendance, looking hostile at the words.

"What will they do to remedy this?" The first councilman asked.

"Indeed," the one next to him said. "They have no shame. Why would they listen to the trade federation?"

"Because they want to keep doing business," Tavelo answered. "And they can't if their license is revoked."

"They should have thought about that before targeting us," Manel snorted.

"I have a suggestion." The council on the far end piped up. "The federation will no doubt restrict their movements. We can impose sanctions of our own."

"Hmm?" Manel sat up. "Please enlighten us."

"Cellaxa has nearly a third of the galactic trade contracts. We work with our suppliers and clients to add tax for all shipments set up by them."

"Is that a standard trade practice?" The first councilman asked Commission Polp.

Commissioner Polp sat in the section near the bottom of the throne platform. He raised his head and stared at them in horror.

"Absolutely not. We would be subjecting ourselves to punishment as well."

"I don't want them getting off with a slap on the wrist," Tavelo said vehemently.

"Nor do I," Manel added.

"I'm sure our commissioner will find a solution." The second councilman said.

"Whatever we do, it cannot be traced to us." Commissioner Polp frowned. "They need to pay for the damage they caused. Twice."

"Cellaxa has never been targeted so much in over three hundred years." The third councilman sighed. "We would have expanded our trade eventually, even without the new contracts with Earth."

"With greater success comes more enemies and competition," the other councilman finished.

"And we were almost done with the East docks. Now we have repairs needed for both." Commissioner Polp slapped his thigh. "This has set us back by four moon cycles."

"What would speed things up?" Tavelo asked.

"If the clans would add resources and funds, that would help."

"Are they not doing that?" Manel asked angrily.

Commissioner Polp's face flushed pink.

"Well, the Endaga and Dakien clans contribute." Commissioner Polp cleared his throat. "I believe the others feel there's no need."

Tavelo stood and walked down the four steps to the bottom of the platform.

"I'm leaving. I have more important things to do. We can deal with the other clans later. Keep coordinating with the Endagas and Dakiens."

Manel watched him go. He looked down at Commissioner Polp. The man shrunk from his gaze.

"As long as any underhanded deeds are not traced

back to the trade federation, I see no problem. Those wretches should know it came from us in the end." Commissioner Polp opened his mouth. "Do you understand?"

He swallowed hard and nodded.

"As you wish, Emperor." He looked over at the councilmen grinning with approval.

Tavelo hastily walked the palace halls towards the royal medical wing. As promised, the Strana clan sent a team of their lab technicians to show the royal physician and his assistants their technology.

Pridric remained unconscious to ensure a safe procedure. The way they explained it to Tavelo, she would need multiple rounds to repair her body.

He rounded the corner of the medical hallway and went straight to the pod where Pridric lay. Her face seemed etched with pain.

"Is she not properly sedated?" He asked, forcing the group of physicians to abandon their banter over a hologram displaying layers of tissue. "Why is my Empress in pain?"

One of the Strana physicians turned around and walked over to Pridric's side.

"We can't know what parts need attention if she can't feel anything. Trust me. It is tolerable. She is not suffering."

Tavelo balked at him. The royal physician came to him with both hands at his chest.

"I know this is hard for you, Emperor Tavelo. Please be patient. I would never let any harm come to the Empress."

Tavelo turned back to her sleeping body, seeing her fingers twitch.

I should have protected you better.

When Tavelo left, the royal physician went back to explaining the results of his medical team's work on Emperor Manel. The Stranas listened in horror, not sure how to react any other way.

They could see all the evidence from the previous emperor's experiments that the royal physician tried to reverse.

"Did he start tearing his child apart at birth?" The first Strana tech asked, his eyes wide.

"I believe he waited until Manel's tenth year," the royal physician replied. "By his fiftieth, he was subjected to DNA altering in order to breed more of the bloodline."

The Strana medical leader pointed to the backbone structure that connected to the core.

"How much damage affeced his memory? I'm surprised Emperor Manel knows who he is, or even where."

"That's..." The royal physician gave him a pained expression. "I'm not sure because we don't ask him. But, on occasion, it seems he has little recollection from a year before his reign to his time of restraint."

"So he has no idea what travesties he caused across Cellaxa?"

"Oh, he hears all the stories."

"And what?" The Strana leader asked. "He just simply pretends to know?"

"Something like that, yes."

"And these?"

Another Strana pointed to the womb structure and the pinpoints of his Kataling shift.

"We did the best we could." The royal physician and his team looked off in defeat.

"You need to convince Emperor Manel to come so we can repair all of this."

The Strana leader walked over to the nearest workstation and sat. He rubbed a hand over his face and exhaled sharply. His clan were the ones who treated the ancients.

Studied every centimeter to ensure full recovery. When the split happened and ancients were hunted, the Stranas refused to help any of them. They first focused on ridding their own bloodline of Volshins to eliminate any threats to themselves.

And they did it well.

Regret seeped into his soul. He knew what they did was wrong. Yet he still went through it under the previous masters' decrees. All of their decisions were made out of fear. Fear of the unknown concerning Volshins. Which led to the rise of Katalings.

"Are you alright?" The royal physician looked around at the Strana team.

They seemed to snap out of their brooding. The leader propped up his elbow and leaned his head against the palm. He stared at the hologram, then at Pridric.

"We need to hold a medical exam for all ancients. I have a sinking feeling in my gut that tells me there's more damaged ones than we think."

"That's probably true. I will address this with the emperors at the next dual meeting."

The Strana leader raised his brow in amusement. "How does that work?"

"This planet had dual rulership. It begs to assume they had a shared throne room for the masses to see. That's where the midday meetings occur."

"Ahh! That makes sense. Well, the sooner we can implement the examinations, the better prepared we'll be when a race takes their envy out on us."

The royal physician nervously wrung his hands while nodding, contemplating.

Were both emperors so unstable that their own physicians feared them? He also looked at Tavelo's scans while the others were occupied with Pridric's treatment. His clan's neglect of caring for ancients was partly responsible for Cellaxa's strife.

❈ ❈ ❈

Manel's eyes narrowed listening to the royal physician's suggestion for wide scale examinations. Though it sounded plausible, he knew that include himself. He didn't want that kind of scrutiny. The truth would be known. Things were fine the way they were.

What did it matter if he couldn't remember much of his reign?

He glanced over at Tavelo also struggling with the inevitable outcome. At the same time, they both realized it needed to be done.

"I suggest four stages," the royal physician continued. Manel glanced down at him. "We can make sure you and the royal families are first."

Manel flinched. Tavelo reached over and clasped his hand over his, the gesture startling him. Gallic tensed up as the royal physician kept talking. He also felt dubious about having Manel being examined.

"I understand your hesitation." The man finally wrapped up.

"Do you?" Manel leaned forward. Tavelo's grip restrained him from going further. His eyes burned, indicating they had turned red. Fury filled him. "Are you perhaps waiting to confirm your suspicions to try and dethrone me?

The councilmen, Commissioner Polp, and the royal physician gasped as one, horror-stricken.

"Absolutely not, your grace!" The physician bowed his head.

Tavelo pressed Manel's hand harder.

"Calm down!" Tavelo whispered tersely.

It needed to be done. Manel got that. He didn't like it. Too many opportunities would arise to eliminate him as incompetent, or a detriment to the empire.

It's not my fault!

"Your plight is no fault of your own," the first councilman said. "Your father did as he pleased, regardless of if it harmed his own. That you lived through all of it is miraculous in itself."

Manel eased back. His eyes reverted as he breathed deep. Tavelo let go of his hand.

"Fine. We will send out a decree."

"I thank you." The royal physician lifted his head and left the throne room.

Tavelo leaned back over.

"It needs to be done. We have no idea how much those years of torture affected the ancients' biological structure. You had Volshins flying around in that form for weeks on end, sometimes months. The same with Katalings."

"I'm not denying that." Manel placed his elbows on the armrests and steepled his fingers. "The masses already despise me. This will only make it worse."

"You didn't slaughter them indiscriminately," Gallic said. "I don't understand why they're being so ungrateful."

Manel looked over at him. Gallic pursed his lips at his disparaging stare. He essentially told him to shut up. Sometimes he wondered about his mate. Tavelo sighed heavily in exasperation at him.

"If I may," a councilman raised a hand, stepping out from the others.

"You may not!" Manel replied heatedly. The councilman halted, not sure what to do. "Just because I appointed you after getting rid of those other parasites doesn't mean I trust any of you."

"Yes. And we are grateful. But Emperor Manel, you need to keep any findings contained. I am merely suggesting such a team dedicated to doing so."

"And who would this team be?" Manel snapped.

"Since it is obvious we are not worthy of such a position, might you use Emperor Tavelo's cabinet to facilitate?"

It never occurred to him to use Tavelo's people instead. He gave a small smile, terrifying everyone in the room.

"I commend you for such insight. Thank you."

"Of course, my lord."

The councilman stepped back, visibly shaken.

Manel scanned his eerily quiet siblings occupying their thrones. Especially Maxellia. Innego, Master Jaubro, Desedon, and Master Endaga seemed to be lost in their own thoughts.

"Speak!" Manel finally shouted, unnerved by the tension in the room. "Say your piece."

"Yes, I did try murdering you," Maxellia said. "Tried to have you dethroned." She met his gaze. "Because of all this. My whole intention was to put you out of your misery. That you would no longer be a pawn. I felt you had spiraled out into a dark descent."

"We know your secret now." Lindor said softly. "It became apparent over time. You need this. Let them fix you. Reverse all the horrid things our father ordered the labs to do to you."

"I've no doubt, your Volshin powers being laid dormant were of natural causes," Master Jaubro addressed Tavelo. "The fact that shifting is excruciating tells me someone manipulated your body at birth." Master Jaubro tapped the tips of his fingers together. "Too many secrets is what led us all astray."

Manel suddenly felt weak.

All his anger and frustration drained from him. Gallic sensed it and placed a hand on his shoulder. Flashes of himself as a child prodded and dissected while his father watched gleefully behind the barrier. His cries to him falling on deaf ears.

His body convulsed. Gallic came around to stop him from pitching forward out of the throne. Uhn! Phantom pain from memory hit him. He struggled to catch his breath. Tavelo got his legs and helped Gallic lay him down.

"No!" Manel heard the gargled muffling of his voice. He didn't want anyone to touch him.

Why can't I speak? Tears blurred his vision.

"St...ahh...pa..." he trailed off.

Megen pushed Gallic and Tavelo out of the way.

He stood over him then knelt on one knee, placing a hand on Manel's chest. They locked eyes.

Wait! Manel screamed silently.

A pulse of energy slammed into him. His body arched off the floor as his eyes rolled up in their sockets.

His strangled cry escaped his lips. Then waves of euphoria crashed forward, easing the pain. He slumped to the floor, his breathing easier. Which made him cry even more. Like a wounded child. He hated it when Megan did that, because it made him feel vulnerable and weak. Everything his father raised him not to be.

"It's alright, Manel." Megen whispered. "No one in this room is judging you." Megen slid his hand over Manel's face. He closed his eyes as his fingers grazed his eyelids. "Sleep."

Eterenia fumed at the information on her small holoscreen regarding Emperor Manel's medical examination results. She couldn't wrap her head around how she felt about it. For so long, his actions fueled her hate. The death of her mother, the way in which he murdered her from his own mouth.

Was it all a lie? Did they expect her to feel sorry for him now?

She paced the length of her chamber biting her thumbnail. Her eyes turned red as her head shook to stop her rage. The door opened and Tavelo came in while his guards stayed outside. His expression conveyed his worry about her opinion. He stopped a few feet from her and waited.

"Why? Why did they let it go this far? Did he do it?" She shouted. "Those horrible things he said he did to her?" Tears streamed down her face. "Either way," she sniffed.

"He doesn't want to dwell on if he remembers or not. There's nothing he can do about it. What would you have him do?"

"I don't know!" Eterenia yelled. "I just. What's wrong with these people?"

"We can't let anyone know this." Tavelo's voice turned menacing. "I'm not forgiving him for what he's done, but I will protect him with all I have."

Eterenia reared from him. "I understand, Tavelo. You don't have to treat me like an enemy."

He winced.

"I'm sorry. I didn't mean to sound hostile."

"Does that mean my son needs to be examined as well?" She saw Tavelo look away for a second. "When did you do that?"

"Not long after I became emperor and learned about Manel's issue."

"And?"

She clenched her fists, bracing for the answer.

"It's up to you if you want him to be treated."

Eterenia's shoulders slumped.

My poor child!

Then she flash backed to Manel climbing on top of her like some crazed monster. Her hands clutched her abdomen on instinct.

I'll never forgive you for that.

Construction to complete the Eat dock merchant bays resumed. New signs replaced the damaged ones. Metal pegs reinforced the sections of the boardwalk. Dock workers moved about, carrying loads on transport carts. For the first time in a month, the sun bore down on the planet through fluffy clouds. The heat made hauling things harder.

"Why can't we have gloom during days of labor?" Yutel asked.

Chiron came out from the back of the bay sans jacket with his shirt sleeves rolled up over his forearms.

"Because the weather doesn't answer to our whims, father." He bent down to check the cargo sitting on a transport cart outside their bay. "Besides." He turned to Yutel. "You could use some exercise."

"Watch what you say."

Yutel glared down at him.

He surveyed the area. Trade did not stop when ports got blown to bits. Ships still landed to deliver their wares. The damage came at minimal costs for the merchant covens. With most of the structures still unfinished, any upgrades were easy to add.

"Have you heard anything about your mother?"

Chiron paused his inspection and shook his head.

"If she were in any kind of danger, I think one of us would know."

Falson walked towards them accompanied by Demetri and Chiron's nose wrinkled.

"Stop that!" Yutel whacked him on the back of the head. "Don't antagonize them."

"He's a pompous ass," Chiron retorted.

"No," Falson said. "That would be you."

Chiron stood. Yutel used two fingers to push him back. He gestured for Falson to stay put.

"What brings you here, Falson?"

"My father wishes to have a word with you. Something about a coordinated shipment."

"Ah, yes." Yutel tugged his jacket down. He stopped to address them. "Don't forget, there's a meeting to go over the bay assignments."

"Hasn't that already been established? The old clans can keep their west dock locations and we take the East. It makes sense."

Chiron went back to inspect the cargo.

"Don't be late." Yutel walked off.

"It's because some of the old clans," Falson said playfully, "want to use these docks as well."

"Tough luck. Why do we have to let them come and abuse us?"

"I think the trade commissioner wants to have a mixture to balance out the two."

Chiron stood, finished with the cargo.

"Maybe. I don't trust them. Even the Endagas. They've changed from what I heard."

"You can only kick a sleepy bear so many times before it swipes your head off." Demetri scanned the docks for possible hostiles. Chiron rolled his eyes. "Contrary to what people think, Emperor Tavelo has always been a menace. Talk to any who did business with the Durante coven and they'll tell you the same."

"I guess we should get ready soon." Chiron flexed his pectoral muscles. "You can probably skip, not having anything to do except be pretty and whine." He shot him a mocking smile.

"Better than a big dumb animal with more brawn than brain," Demetri shot back.

Chiron moved towards him.

Demetri wrapped his hand around the hilt of his short blade attached to his hip. A hand from behind karate chopped Chiron's left shoulder. He fell to one knee, clamping his hand on the spot where it landed.

"Stop this foolishness and be useful." Holnar towered over Chiron. He looked over at Falson and Demetri. "Same for you two. Go help with manifests for incoming shipments."

The two left with Demetri glancing back once at Chiron.

Commissioner Polp checked the set up in the meeting hall. He counted the number of tables and chairs again, despite the servants having done it twice themselves. His assistant stood near the wall where the holoscreen waited to be turned on. Unlike the first time, where the clans segregated themselves from each other, he arranged the merchant leaders' seats so they'd mix.

Again, he instructed the servants to hold off serving spirits until after the meeting's first round. There were going to be hurt feelings. He understood the hesitation on both sides. Drinking won't solve the issues.

The doors opened for merchants to flood in. They stared at the name plaques proximity to each other. Furrowed brows and comical smirks followed. After all that coordinating for that small enemy attack, they still wouldn't trust their fellow merchant?

They're all practically related at this point! Commissioner Polp cried out in his head.

Once everyone had a seat, the servants went to the tables to take their orders. Many balked at the denied request for alcohol. He dared one of them to demand it. The coven leaders in attendance didn't make a fuss. Neither did their offspring.

"Please settle in," commissioner Polp yelled. "We will get underway as soon as the servants are done. There is much to go over."

Not waiting to sugar coat the inevitable, he quickly nodded to his assistant. The man tapped a few icons on the virtual pad and a diagram of the docks side by side displayed on the holoscreen. Angry gasps, outburst of surprise, and the rearing back in the seat were the immediate reactions.

Most of it came from the merchant clans.

"As you can see, I have reconfigured each dock to combine the strength of your businesses."

"What is the meaning of this?" Master Bryhel shouted. "Our docks have been on the West since the start of our clan."

"Not true." Commissioner Polp watched her mouth gape open. "It was originally on the East for good reason." He walked in front of the holoscreen and faced them.

"The merchant bays were assigned a dock based on the products and services. Heavy goods such as building materials, devices, and machinery came through the East because the terrain into the towns was flat and easier to maneuver."

Master Dakien nodded. "That does make sense. Right now, we have to lift the heavier goods into a different transport and set it on the outskirts to get them delivered."

"Correct. We are eliminating that hardship." Commissioner Polp continued. "That means all the consumable goods came through the West. As you will conclude, it's because all the shops and eateries locations are centralized in the nearby cities."

"So, what you're saying is, you didn't reassign merchant bays out of spite," Chase blurted.

"Also correct. I am here to maximize Cellaxa's potential. I would appreciate your cooperation."

"Fine," Master Boresso huffed. "I see the reason. Are we to coddle the others?"

"What makes you assume we need coddling?" Armon asked sweetly, though his face showed the opposite. "We're quite capable of running trade."

Commissioner Polp pursed his lips. The Boresso and Strana clans would be the ones to cause trouble on the docks. Yet, he saw no hint of resistance from the Stranas. As if sensing the same lack of reaction, Masters Jaubro and Callesi glanced over at them.

"No objections, Master Strana?" Commissioner Polp regretted asking it.

Master Strana, with arms crossed and his head down, the wide brim hat hiding his face, looked up. He noticed everyone staring at him.

"Why would I? This makes things easier. Rejecting

the new assignments out of some entitled sense of ownership is ludicrous. WE don't own the docks. The monarchy does."

The room went silent as if they had all been slapped in the face with harsh reality. Commissioner Polp saw on the merchant clan leaders' faces that they had forgotten. They ran their businesses by the grace of the emperor. Regardless of how many millennia they used those docks.

"Oh!" Olette raised her fingertips to her bottom lip. She turned to Chase. "Did you know this, fearless leader?"

"I did." Chase didn't look at any of the merchant leaders. "I wanted to confirm who owned the docks."

"Business savvy as ever," Holnar snorted.

Commissioner Polp stepped to the side of the holoscreen so they got a full view of the grid.

"Dakien and Bryhel will move to the East docks. That gives room for Endagas expansion on the West. That is long overdue. Callesi will downsize and have smaller bays on both docks per their own recommendation."

"Wait!" Master Boresso jumped out of her seat. "That option was never discussed. How is it that Callesi is allowed to have port access at both docks?"

"Sit down," Master Jaubro said calmly, giving her a side glance.

When she eased back in her seat, Commissioner Polp resumed his presentation.

"Marchand and Ambrook will be on the West. Grieger will split with larger goods going through the East docks." He paused. "To answer your question, Master Boresso, there's no need have your products on two docks. Even a substantial load only takes up five hundred cubic meters."

Master Boresso seemed put out by the meager explanation. The bay already had too much space, but her clan refused to let it go. They could easily switch with the Loengir clan, who had a smaller bay that barely accommodated their wares. She looked up and caught his gaze. He made sure to convey to her that he thought the same thing.

Done making Master Boresso feel a touch of fear, he turned his attention back to the holoscreen.

"Those are the major moves. Everyone else will remain in their current bays. We want to get them fully functional by the start of the next year cycle."

Grumbling erupted.

A short timeline, yes. He had no doubt they could pull it off if they just hunkered down and facilitated construction duties. Such laziness. He felt the elder merchant leaders had become complacent over the centuries.

Old Enemies

Tavelo went over the sanctions report levied against the reptile race on the holoscreen in his throne room. It split the images between the report and Manel on his throne with a smug smile. They agreed the enemy were the ones needing a lesson in trade, but he didn't want Cellaxa to look like the bad guys. Going past the lesson into outright prejudice.

"This is going to get traced back to us," he finally spoke. "That's not ideal."

"As I have said before, the only ones who'll see it for what it is are those reptiles. The trade federation won't know a thing. Commissioner Polp reassures."

"I still don't like it." Tavelo rested against the back of his throne. His blue and silver robes slid across the armrests. "Those reptiles are the type to retaliate after being retaliated on for their own actions."

Manel side glanced upwards, contemplating. He met Tavelo's eyes.

"What do you want to do then? We showed them the error of their ways. Essentially warned them to tread carefully."

"We need the dock barriers fully operational. Have the imperial weapons technicians check the cannons."

"Yes. We don't want to be caught off guard."

"But we will be. That's the problem."

Manel smirked.

"You think they will bring more of their fleet?"

"Absolutely. A full invasion."

That angered Manel. His eyes turned red and he gripped his armrests. Movement behind him let Tavelo know Gallic had drawn near in case Manel went off the hinges.

"There will be massive damage at the start." Tavelo continued. "Our priority will be to safeguard the citizens. The dock workers and merchant clans are capable of defending themselves."

"How much damage are you willing to allow, Emperor Tavelo?" Manel asked mockingly.

"This isn't funny and your question offends me."

Manel seemed to pout. His regression had slowed, and he progressed back to his previous self before going insane. It disturbed Tavelo and others in the palace.

"My apologies. I only jest."

"What is your suggestion?"

Manel's expression turned maniacal. His red eyes reverted to amber, and he smiled sweetly.

"One hundred units of imperial and royal guards stationed at every planet's entry point. The moment any of those ships land, they will get closed in."

"I like that plan." Tavelo felt impressed. "Are you going to utilize the ancients?"

"Each sector has Katalings for ground combat. I think we're good on that."

"I'm worried about Volshins being blasted out of the sky."

"Tavelo," Manel leaned forward a bit. "I feel you may not realize that the Volshins of Cellaxa are far more versed in aerial combat than you."

Tavelo glared at him, his eyes glowing. Manel sat back, laughing.

"Why does everyone harp on that one incident?" Tavelo rested the side of his head on a propped-up fist. "If you must know, I am very efficient in combat. We won't get out of not joining the fray."

"Who says we're not? I always thrive on eating any enemy that dares to bring harm to Cellaxa."

"Then it's settled."

Manel cut his feed, leaving the report to expand on the holoscreen. Tavelo looked it over once more and felt dread in the pit of his stomach. The enemy didn't act reasonably. He harbored a guess they would come full force with a monstrous intent.

※ ※ ※

The chatter received within the palace's communications room made Innego's skin prickle. He stood behind a soldier at their station, looking over his shoulder at the screen before they sent it to the holoscreen on the far wall. Following the trail of conversations, he finally hissed in anger.

He recognized the signature of the party the reptile race talked with. The arms dealers who were banned from trading with Earth.

What could those two be talking about?

"Sent a copy to my tablet address," he instructed the soldier.

A soft ping alerted him it received the data. Innego stood and walked out, headed towards the dual throne room where the midday meeting would be well underway. He was late yet again. The doors sat open, so he went in and sat next to Lindor.

"What excuse do you have this time for being late?" Tavelo asked. The rest of the occupants turned their attention to him. He grinned proudly and stood.

"Glad you asked, Emperor Tavelo." Tavelo's eyes went bright red, almost glowing. He hated when his family called him that. "I have been keeping tabs on our spy channels and came across something sinister in the communications from the next system over."

"And that would be?" Maxellia asked haughtily.

"It seems," Innego went over to the holoscreen's module and laid his tablet with the copied data on its surface. It displayed for all to see. "Our reptile friends have been meeting with our favorite arms dealers."

Tavelo and Manel reared back in their thrones. The royal council whispered to each other angrily. Master Jaubro frowned.

"You must be joking!" Pridric cried out.

"They wouldn't dare!" Polp exclaimed. "To ally with those..." he couldn't finish.

"I had a bad feeling about their next move."

Tavelo regained his composure and stared at the screen.

"If they actually bring those cretins along, we will need to boost our forces," Windsor said. "Why would those arms dealers come back for more after we sent them off crippled?"

"They're another race that didn't get the lesson." Manel replied. He sighed, slumping in his throne. "I guess this time we'll have to annihilate them."

"Any hints of a timeline?" Master Jaubro asked.

Innego scrolled through the data.

"Nothing concrete. By the way the conversation went, they're gearing up for something. A mass order of weapons from the arms dealers means the reptiles are advancing their firepower."

"Great." Tavelo sighed. "Reptiles with guns."

In the early hours, right as the gloom brightened to light grey from the sun trying to reach the surface, sirens blared across Cellaxa, warning that the enemy drew near. A vortex swirled angrily as another in the planet's orbit spewed out fighter ships.

Two different races attacked. Volshins swooped around to take care of the reptilian invaders headed for the open lands. Imperial ships gave chase to a familiar group of enemy.

"So they've teamed up."

Tavelo walked down the palace steps that led to the courtyard. "Those beings really do hold a grudge." The hem of his robes dragged behind him, slipping off the last step onto the ground. "They truly didn't get the lesson."

"The arms dealers?" Pridric came to stand beside him. "After we sent them off with little mercy?"

Back in male form, Pridric looked more majestic, beautiful. Tavelo stared at him for a moment, taking it all in.

"Hmm." He averted his feasting gaze. "We're getting real tired of having to defend Cellaxa from the same culprits time and again. Repairs of the damage to the territories and the docks is getting tedious."

"I truly regret having dealings with such petty creatures." Pridric frowned. "It's all my fault."

"Don't you dare!" Tavelo chastised him. He looked up. "They'll come towards the palace."

Pridric walked past him to the center courtyard.

"I'll take a unit of imperial guards and stop them on the main thoroughfare at the edge of the city."

"Don't overdo it."

Tavelo knew his words fell on deaf ears.

Pridric had only shifted back a year ago. He wouldn't be in top shape for an all-out battle.

"I'm not bedridden," Pridric snapped. He tapped at his wristband. "You should have more faith."

Within minutes, an armed unit of twenty imperial guards rushed out the palace side doors and formed a barricade around Pridric.

Tavelo watched them head to their destination. His uncle stood behind him three steps up.

"What will you do about that" He pointed to the sky. Four enemy ships and another two from the arms dealers sped towards the palace. "I think they are planning to ram the upper level." He glanced down at him. "Again."

The outer walls and part of the roof were recently

rebuilt. To have them destroyed a second time made Tavelo fumed. Not this time. He tapped his wristband to connect with the control room.

"Yes, your grace?" A garbled voice asked.

"Target those ships and shoot them down. Make sure they don't land on the palace itself."

"Of course, your grace."

The feed ended and Tavelo turned to watch the cannons protrude from the ground behind the palace. Their long barrels swerved around, then stopped when they locked onto their targets.

One of the reptile ships dodged the first blast, leaving the other two vulnerable. They went down on the other side of the palace walls. The remaining arms ship tilted sideways and circled around to force the cannons to track it.

"How clever," Master Endaga mocked them.

Tavelo snorted. Right as the ship came back around, the blast of the second cannon clipped its wing. Fighters jumped out, a few landing not far from Tavelo and his uncle. Master Endaga sighed.

"Shall we clean up this mess?"

"Wouldn't dream of doing anything else."

"What about Manel and the others?"

"Oh, I'm sure they'll have their own bout of fun soon enough."

Tavelo removed his outer robe, and the long-sleeved one beneath it. He tossed them onto the steps. In a simple tunic and black leggings, he went toward the enemy coming around the bend. His eyes glowed silver.

Master Endaga made sure to steer clear in case he decided to morph into Volshin form.

Master Jaubro stared at the enemy fighters rush through a breach in the West palace's side wall. Innego kicked one of them back through it, causing them to knock down their comrades like dominoes behind them.

"Again?" Master Jaubro punched the first enemy that got within his reach, plowing them to the floor. "This is who those reptiles joined forces with?"

More enemy fighters came through, forcing Innego to back away. It gave them enough berth to flood the hallway.

"This," Innego looked towards the docks in the horizon, "is no mere fight. This is indeed an invasion."

The loud decibel of voices inside the control room drowned out the sounds of stone cracking as the room shook. On the center holoscreen, they saw two more vortices open near the East dock and over the new communities.

The enemy ships made dark splotches in the sky.

Manel stepped into the hallway with Gallic. Both had their swords drawn.

"So they brought an entire fleet along with those mongrels to try and take our world. Hmph!"

He sliced the first enemy to come near him in half at the waist. The torso skidded past him while the lower half dropped to the floor. Gallic bent down and stabbed the one that was coming behind the first in the chest and lifted them up. He braced his back leg and tossed the body over his head. It smacked against one of the giant pillars.

"Trash." Gallic regained his stance.

"Yes. And I don't tolerate it in my presence." Manel stepped forward.

Master Jaubro and Desedon cleared his path to the enemy. Innego's back was to him, so he didn't see. Manel cut through the enemy forces coming around the opposite of him.

Blood splattered the entire left side of Innego. It stunned him immobile, some of the blood dripping into the corner of his eye. The enemy, in the process of advancing, moved to retreat.

"No," Manel drawled. "This time you don't get to flee."

The whites of his eyes turned black, the irises bright red. He shifted to a smaller Kataling form as he entered the outside and started mowing down the enemy.

Innego slowly lowered his sword and let both arms hang at his sides. Master Jaubro walked over to him and patted his clean shoulder.

"My apologies. I should have warned you."

Dark grey smoke drifted from the west docks. Enemy ships pummeled the ports and hit a slew of ships docked in the spaceport. Clients ran horrified to take cover in the merchant bays. A few enemy ships got through the barrier as it sealed off the area. The ones left outside were at the Volshins' mercy and they gave none. Their talons ripped through the hulls as they flew by, bursting in flames on their way down into the ocean.

On the docks, Katalings greeted the enemy along with royal guards. Still, their numbers surpassed them and the Katalings were driven back twenty to one. The entire sector got covered in an enemy swarm like insects.

The Endaga and Callesi merchants locked their clients in the bays with their own workers and went into the fray. They prioritized making an opening for the Katalings to take down the majority of enemies near ports occupied by delivery transports.

They must protect the goods at all costs.

An enemy leader in the group of arms dealers gestured for another of the reptiles to join them as they headed straight for a dock.

"Come. We will take all the products from their

clients' ships and claim them for ourselves."

Half attacked the hull with sharp weapons to breach it. The other half tried to pry open the hatch to get access to the ramp. A loud ping rang out from the seal being broken. They pulled on the edge, opening it up enough for them to get in.

The first row of enemies went flying backwards, their bodies full of holes. Eight aliens in mechanic jumpsuits stood in an arc with laser rifles spraying a barrage of firepower. One of them raised his goggles above his eyes.

"Did they think these ships were empty?"

He saw an enemy charge forward and shot them in the chest. They fell back onto more clambering up and they went down in a cluster, hitting the ground. Pools of blood spread.

"Now we have to repair all this damage," the one on the end sighed.

"Hey." The mechanic in the center slapped the one next to him in the chest with the back of his hand.

"What about them?" He nodded to an enemy group still digging into the hull on the other side, oblivious that their companions had fallen. "Shall we blast them too?"

"Wait" The first mechanic yelled. "Let's use the fire feature instead. There's enough holes as it is."

"Agreed."

They split into two groups of four. The enemy at the hull didn't have time to turn and assess their fate. The four aimed their rifles. Scorching flames engulfed the horde. Getting away proved futile as the mechanics laid it on thick, not leaving an inch unburned. The other four did the same to the rest at the opened hatch.

From across the way, another group of enemy fighters witnessed the act and seemed to rethink their strategy. Too late. The hatch of the ship looming above them opened.

An alien wearing a battle suit under a military coat stood brandishing two circular blades, one in each gloved hand. Beside him, another dressed identical held a weapon resembling a wide mouth cannon on swivel arms attached to his coat's shoulder clamps.

The enemy halted for a moment, seeing only two assailants. They were thirty strong. With a sharp pivot, they rushed back towards the ship, determined to claim it. As the first handful got closer to the bottom edge of the ship's hull, the one with the circle blades leaped out the hatch. His body sailed gracefully, twisting into a back flip. He extended his arms when he got directly above them.

He landed behind them, exposed to the second wave coming towards him. Blood flew in every direction, splashing against the back of his black coat. He dropped into a defense stance, one leg bent forward, his arms raised at chest level. Behind him, enemy bodies lay scattered in pieces.

On the ledge of the hatch, another aimed the cannon at the enemy. The cannon's barrel glowed a blinding hot white. He hit the firing button. A blast expanding to eight feet wide hit the enemy dead on, stopping them in their tracks.

The Endaga and Callesi merchants tried to hide their grins as they struggled to keep control of the West docks. It would take some time to get rid of all the enemy, but they had the means to succeed.

Defeat was not an option.

The rest of the top merchant families coordinated with each other to take back each sector, dispatching their assistants to the cities and towns. For the first time in nearly a millennium, they would to fight together.

Masters of Boresso, Dakien, and Bryhel went to secure the West docks. Members of the Endaga clan and the Brownlee coven headed for the East.

Master Bryhel changed course, leading her clan fighters to the East docks instead. Something nagged at her, and she realized it stemmed from how their clan treated the offspring who returned. Holnar left Cellaxa at barely an adult age. His struggles on Earth were unknown, even foreign to them. And she didn't bother to ask so she could understand.

The closer to the docks, the more her anxiety intensified. The swarm of enemy fighters on the ground and their ships blotting the sky enraged her. She could barely make out the bays. Katalings fought against a horde that outnumbered them two-fold. Dock workers used tools to defend themselves.

Only carnage greeted her.

She spotted Holnar stabbing an enemy with his talons and viciously ripped them out, cascading blood. Darean stood next to him, doing the same. They focused on the enemies in their bubble. Master Bryhel saw a dark shadow above.

An enemy with a spear came hurling towards them. She frowned.

They still haven't learned to check every angle in battle.

In a flash, she got between them and shoved them to the side. They stumbled to the ground, startled, as she pivoted one leg behind her and caught the spear's shaft with one hand.

The enemy growled at her, turning his body mid-air to force her grip loose. Instead, she used brute force to swing it at an angle and threw them, letting it go. The enemy went into a cargo carrier on the opposite side of the boardwalk.

"Pay attention!" She yelled.

They regained their stance in time to counter the two enemies that got pushed along with them. After dispatching them, Holnar turned to his aunt.

"What brings you here? I figured you would be at the West docks to defend the Bryhel bays."

"Boresso and Dakien can handle that side."

"Oh?" Darean raised a brow. "We're friends now?"

"Stop being childish." Master Bryhel scanned the perimeter. "And, how did this dock get overrun so quickly?"

"They came from everywhere," Holnar replied. "I think they really are trying to invade us."

She watched a Kataling crunch on an enemy arm and tear it off. Another chomping on their head cut their anguished screams short.

"We need a better strategy." She grimaced at the damage. "Are the goods still safe?"

"None of this is safe." Master Callesi came down the tattered boardwalk to stand with them. "It's not just a strategy we need." He pointed at the ports farther out. "First thing is to secure the client ships and block off that area."

"Then we can start getting rid of these creatures," Chiron added. His clothes were coated in blood. None of it seemed to be his. "I'm a bit pissed off. We just got these parts of the docks finished."

Another horde of enemy fighters charged for them. The Volshins circling above dodged ships that clustered together to ram them out of the sky. With no active barrier, the enemy zipped around, dropping more fighters onto the docks.

At least two Volshins had been shot down and were now wounded in the water. Enemy ships fired on them, thankfully missing when they submerged.

"How dare they!" Master Callesi seethed.

The atmosphere shifted.

Even in the throes of battle, the Cellaxans saw that and became fueled with rage. In an instant, they turned ruthless. Like a sea of monsters, the dock workers and merchants killed indiscriminately. The enemy tried to regain control and found themselves in a dire situation.

Though they outnumbered the Cellaxans, they could not match the malice that consumed them.

As if understanding the need, many of the dock

workers plowed through the enemy and formed a blockade in front of the delivery ports. They stood their ground, not letting a single enemy go through. With nowhere else to go, they became prey for the Katalings.

Masters Boresso and Dakien arrived on the scene with their entourages and immediately joined in the fray. That surprised the enemy, allowing the merchant clan members to decimate entire hordes. Master Dakien took out four fighters attempting to break into a bay. When he turned around, blood flew in his face.

An Endaga merchant stood behind an enemy that had snuck up on Master Dakien. His talons protruded from the enemy's neck. He yanked them out and let the body fall.

"I'm forever in your debt, Endaga." Master Dakien gave a nod.

"I don't need repayment. Our clans are bound by blood. We should always protect each other." A sense of shame hit him as Endaga's words hit him like a stone. The Endaga's brow furrowed. "We don't have time for that!"

The number of enemies thinned, but still far too many for their taste.

"Yes, you're right. We must clean this up first."

Master Dakien shrugged off his cloak and abandoned it on the boardwalk. He removed his jacket and rolled up his sleeves. The giant biceps bulged against the fabric.

"Let's do this the right way."

"With brute force?" Endaga tilted his head.

"Always."

Master Boresso glanced over her shoulder and caught Dakien and Endaga's exchange.

When she saw the coat and jacket come off, she snorted at the ridiculousness of it. Then she looked down at herself, stopping midway towards another enemy. She gave a side eye at a clan member ruining their attire.

With a heavy sigh, she removed her coat and set it gently inside a busted crate. The first enemy to approach her received a taloned punch under their chin. She stared at the tips peeking out the back of its head.

"You dare to come here and think conquering our world would be easy?" She scoffed. "Know your place." She pulled out her talons and kicked the enemy's body out of the way to let the next one come to her. "Yes, come to your doom." She waited patiently for the three enemy fighters to charge.

Roaring, baring their teeth, the trio ran to her.

"Please save some for me, Master Boresso," her assistant begged as he sauntered close to her. "I can't hold the title as your bodyguard if I let you do all the fighting."

Master Boresso didn't turn. She merely pointed to a wave of enemies coming from the other side of them. Without saying a word, he pivoted towards them and took off in a flash to halt their advance.

An arms dealer pushed their way through the three to stand before Master Boresso.

"You remind me of Pridric's whore. He showed her to us once."

She bristled at the creature's vicious tone. The clan had treated Chalayl badly. She knew that. What she wouldn't stand for was the enemy demeaning her niece.

"All that muscle." The enemy turned his head and spit on the ground at her feet. "Disgusting."

Master Boresso flexed once, and flash stepped to the enemy. They blocked her blow by crossing their arms. Not to be denied, she brought up her knee, knowing he would block that too, and punched them in the side of their head. The enemy staggered off balance.

"That child is not for you to mention, ever."

The enemy recovered quicker than anticipated and punched her back. She skidded to a stop a few feet from him and wiped blood from the corner of her mouth. Master Boresso threw her head back and laughed. The enemy, thinking that was an opening, moved to give a finishing blow. She straightened her stance, red eyes glowing, and knelt on one leg right as he got close.

Her fist went through his abdomen. The two locked eyes. She twisted and watched their life fade from their eyes. Bored, she removed her fist and wiped the blood off on the back of the enemy's uniform.

"Pity. I wanted to hear him howl."

The Jaubro and Strana members in charge of shipping, and already on the west docks, made their way out towards the center where Masters Boresso and Dakien engaged the enemy. After securing the dock workers and cargo on that side they decided to lend a hand.

Master Boresso turned to look them both up and down. Master Dakien tilted his head in amusement.

"Decided to get your hands dirty?" Master Boresso berated them.

The Jaubro leader checked his person, glancing at the torn fabric and blood on his clothes.

"I'm not sure what you are implying." He gave her a side glare. "Is our cargo not important?"

"You show up in the middle of the fray and dare to accuse us of not fighting?" The Strana woman scoffed. "We helped keep the enemy at bay while the dock workers secured the shipments." She raised her arms out to show her own torn attire and injuries. "Go protect your strongholds. We can handle this."

The Jaubro leader smiled. He saw the enemy move to take advantage of their infighting.

"See. Even they have no interest in latecomers." He turned in time to punch his talons into an enemy that came up behind him. "What is your plan?"

Master Dakien laughed heartily. The Endaga met the Jaubro and Strana leaders' eyes, chastising them. They looked away, shrugging in defiance.

"Fine. My apologies." Master Boresso scanned the area again. "We need to get back control of this dock." She glanced back at Master Dakien and pointed at the landing pads getting damaged. "First, we stop that."

"Leave that to us." The Jaubro leader stepped closer. "I already have an idea for them." He turned to the Strana member. "Are you joining in or staying down here?"

"Let's switch out," The Endaga suggested. "I'll go with you." He addressed the Strana. "Think you can take over my light work?"

He nodded to the group of enemy charging in his direction.

"It would be my pleasure." She went to meet the enemy head on.

Master Boresso clenched her fists and her jaw tight. She could see the injuries they sustained. They would need to feed off at least four of the enemy to seal their wounds and another ten to fully heal. She felt the guilt of knowing how long they were fighting compared to Dakien and herself.

"Then let's push them back and feed to our fulfillment."

Another horde of enemy rushed forward. The insult of her child and the clan itself fueled her rage.

❀ ❀ ❀

Pridric tried not to let his fatigue show.

His strength diminished rapidly as the battle dragged on. The enemy coordinated flawlessly, complimenting each others movements. When one arms dealer advanced, a reptile was not far behind on the other side.

His body felt hot, as if his blood boiled under his skin. His vision shifted, turning everything multi-colored. Howling in rage, his body morphed. Wings spanning two feet on both sides sprouted from his back, splattering blood all around him. The shriek that emitted from his mouth made the enemy drop to their knees, covering their ears.

Flapping his wings once, he launched into the first group of enemy fighters. He had already been wounded. Deep stabs, broken bones, and contusion had sealed with clotting blood. With every enemy he took down, he drained them as much as he could before another attacked him.

He couldn't drink enough enemy blood to force his body to heal faster.

A loud thud within his body followed by a deep pounding halted his rampage. Evey ounce of energy he had left him. The wings retracted as he stumbled.

He managed to strike a blow with his talons under the chin of an enemy right before his body faltered. No amount of forced movement or words stopped him from falling to his knees.

An enemy took the open, ready to gut him like an animal. Pridric's eyes glazed over as he fell backwards.

The enemy's blow never came. Pridric lay facing the sky and saw a blur of colors out of the corner of his vision. He watched the enemy's head fly off to the side.

"Pridric!" A man's muffled voice called to him. "Pridric! Get up!"

He turned his head to the voice and couldn't make out the man's face.

"He's down. Help me get him up. We need to protect him above everything else."

Tavelo. Pridric sent his thoughts to him without thinking.

Roren, Master Strana's assistant gathered Pridric in his arms and backed out of the fight zone with other members covering them. He was glad to have made it in time to rescue him. When they got far enough away, he turned around and ran. Master Strana had headed to the docks along with the other merchant clan leaders.

He offered to check on Pridric at the palace, knowing Tavelo would be fighting alongside Emperor Manel. Neither thought Pridric would be out alone with a small unit of imperial guards.

"You're still too stubborn for your own good," he said to him. There would be no answer. "Stay like this until we get to safety," he wished out loud.

An enemy horde in pursuit inched closer, enough to be in range of their weapons. A combination of laser fire and arrows whizzed past his head. One arrow hit its mark right between his right shoulder and arm. Refusing to lose his grip on Pridric, he squeezed harder.

The sting of the wound closing over the shaft made him wince. He could feel the sticky wetness bloom, soaking through his jacket. Each move of his arm pulled at it.

The Strana stronghold loomed up ahead.

We can make it!

The enemy behind them spread out to try and cut them off. More of the Strana clan came out to engage them. Roren finally stepped foot on Strana soil, the other foot raised to take another step.

He felt the arrow go through his back and fly out the front of his abdomen. Not a regular arrow, it had a spiked tip and a longer shaft. It's momentum continued and struck the clan member before him.

His foot stomped the ground, trembling from the weight of Pridric bearing down on him. The member ahead staggered before dropping.

I will not fall!

Within minutes, the rest of the enemy entered the grounds and were immediately outnumbered by Strana fighters. Three came to help him and the fallen member. One took Pridric from him and ran into the building.

"Come on," the one helping him commanded. "Stay focused. You do not meet your demise here."

Roren nodded. His vision had blurred. He felt off kilter, nauseous.

"The fight is taking too long to end. We need all the fighters we can muster." The member glanced over at him. "Don't close your eyes. I don't want to deal with Master Strana's wrath."

Why would he?

Roren gave a tiny smile as his soul filled with sadness. Master Strana wouldn't care one way or the other. He remembered when, not long after he became leader of the clan, he cornered him with a proposition.

Master Strana sat slumped in a plush seat with his legs spread eagle and arms stretched across the back. His head flopped over the top and he let out a deep sigh. The meeting with the elders of the clan had gone longer than he liked. His assistant stood in the center of his chamber awaiting instructions after he regained his composure.

"I want to wrap my talons around all their necks." Master Strana didn't raise his head or open his eyes. "Is this what my father dealt with on a daily basis?"

"Perhaps." Roren turned from him. "Do you want a drink?" He looked over at the tray sitting on a side table near the window. Four bottles of liquid and two glasses sat on it. Two were definitely alcohol. "Which would you like?"

An uneasy silence fell in the room. Master Strana lifted his head. He could feel his eyes boring into his back.

"Do you still pine for me?" Master Strana asked.

The question startled Roren, but he didn't show it.

"Are you asking because you want some reliable pet?" He sensed animosity. "Or because you've finally given up on Pridric?"

He glanced over his shoulder and saw Master Strana's eyes flicker silver.

"The reason doesn't matter. Do you still pine for me?" He asked again.

"I do." Roren replied softly.

Master Strana leaned forward to remove his jacket, then tunic, and pants, kicking his boots across the room. He eased back into his previous position, waiting.

"This is your only chance to get what you want."

Roren looked away, contemplating his answer. His love for Pravin would not be returned. He understood that. Pridric would always be first. Mating with the Master may mean something over time. It's the only choice he had.

Not turning around, Roren slowly undid his shirt, shifting as he went. In female form, she removed the jacket and tunic together, then the rest of her clothes. She took a few deep breaths and turned to face him.

His eyes roamed her body as if inspecting it, making her feel inferior.

"Come. Show how much you want me."

The assistant went over and climbed atop his lap. To make sure she couldn't change her mind, he pushed her down roughly on his erection and grabbed the back of her head by the hair. The sex could only be described as brutal, with no passion or empathy for her pain.

And she endured it to the end.

Why think about that now?

As the member helping him got them over the threshold of the Strana home, Roren thought about the three children he spawned for Master Strana. They would worry about him if they saw him like this. Not once had Master Strana spent more than five minutes at a time with either of them.

A medic rushed over and took custody of him. He led him down to a holding chamber where they staged less critically wounded. Roren sat on an empty slab bed and rested his head against the wall. The medic brought over giant shears with rounded curve blades. He snipped the back end of the arrow in his shoulder and pulled it out from behind the tip.

The flesh ripped as it got free.

Roren snapped his teeth together and forced down a scream, only letting a short grunt escape.

"Sorry I don't have time to give you a painkiller." He took a bottle of sealing foam from his lab coat and sprayed it on the wound. "I'll be back once we're caught up with the worse off."

"I understand." Roren closed his eyes.

Pain enveloped his whole body. He embraced it, allowing a wave of false euphoria to take him.

A Horde Of Carnivores

Enemy ships hovered over the palace, unleashing a bombardment of missives to crack the shield. Each impact caused a ripple of prisms across its surface. The fighters who got inside before it was erected, were now trapped with the imperial guards and both emperors.

Hence the reason for the onslaught. The enemy realized those fighters would be lost if they couldn't get to them in time.

Should have thought about that before you came here! Innego chastised them.

An enemy charged, brandishing a short version of those deadly black spears. Innego moved forward and went under its arms, forcing it sideways. When he came up, the two locked in a face-to-face struggle.

His sword bore down on the spear's shaft.

He saw the rage in the arms dealer's eyes. Neither could budge the other. A stalemate of strength. Innego noticed a glint of surprise.

Ahh. They assumed he would be easier to handle. People always underestimated him. He had no need to show off his skills except in battle. Doing drills and practicing his swordsmanship felt like a waste of time. He'd rather pursue a nice pair of thighs and bosoms to dive into.

He pushed harder and the enemy's feet dug into the soil. The second he thought to move down, the enemy's eyes trail with him. Damn! The fighter was smarter than it looked, tracking his every motion.

The tip of a sword punched through the enemy's chest, forcing Innego to bend backwards to avoid getting stabbed. He pushed off and slid to a stop a few feet away. The enemy head butted the person behind him and went to snap the sword in half with a slicing motion of its hand. The sword slid out and swung across its neck, severing it.

The head went flying.

"It looked like you needed assistance." Tervan wiped blood from the cut on his forehead. He tsked at his hand, covered in his own blood. "That piece of shit!"

"I didn't." Innego frowned. This was the second time someone interfered in his fight. He pointed to Tervan's head wound. "You deserved that for not assessing the situation."

"I was getting tired of watching. That thing was not backing down."

Innego couldn't argue with that. He tried a few scenarios in his head. All had the enemy anticipating his move.

"Fine. Stay out of my way."

"I would, but," Tervan nodded at the horde of enemy surrounding them. "I don't think they want to let us through."

Innego frowned. He scanned the perimeter and counted how many enemy fighters were in the first row of the enclosing arc.

"Down," he ordered Tervan.

For a second his young cousin hesitated, then crouched into a low squat. Innego's sword swiped over his head and struck a third of the enemy as they moved in. Enemy bodies cut in half fell, disrupting the formation. Tervan pivoted while still down and attacked the other side of the arc.

The two had killed at least half of the enemy, yet they couldn't seem to get ahead.

Frustrated, Innego jumped backwards from the horde to get some distance. Tervan beside him. Innego checked himself and Tervan. They both had Injuries. The enemy didn't give them time to drain any for refueling and to heal.

A loud boom followed by the ground before them splitting the arc of enemies in half, forced them to move to either side. Five ended up on Innego and Tervan's side. Kneeling on one knee, Megen rose, dragging his gigantic sword off the ground. Innego saw the glowing red eyes as he went into a stance.

"Move!" Innego grabbed Tervan by the arm and pulled him out of harm's way.

Where Innego could cut a few enemies with his sword, Megen was next level. The enemy left on the larger side of the crevice swarmed him. He waited for them to get almost too close and swung. Limbs and torsos scattered in the air, raining blood on him.

Tervan stood with his mouth agape. Innego's turned down with envy.

You monster.

❀ ❀ ❀

This is taking too long.

The thought went through both emperors' minds as they fought at the palace and its surroundings. Another vortex had opened for more enemy ships to invade Cellaxa space. It gave the enemy fighters on the ground more confidence. Strengthening their boldness to attack even the unarmed.

Ancient ones were having a hard time protecting their wards, so combined forces to defend a shelter with multiple families inside.

No one could approach the docks.

Volshins defended the skies while dock workers and merchant leaders tried to lessen the damage.

The enemy were set on dominance.

Not while I still breathe. Tavelo vowed to himself.

275

Over my rotten and decayed body! Manel cried out.

The two stayed in human form, not wanting to shift unless the situation became dire. Morphing alone would cause mass destruction and not ideal. The current state of affairs started to look that way. They frowned in frustration.

"What do you want to do now?"

Tavelo asked Manel telepathically.

There was a long pause before Manel answered.

"We have no choice. In order to rid Cellaxa of these vermin, we must unleash all our military resources."

"I don't want to show our hand so soon."

"I agree. But the enemy has pushed us to a brink."

They both looked up at the sky covered in enemy ships blocking the clouds. Eight days of fighting had taken a toll on the citizens. The docks received heavy damage on the fifth day after the enemy found a way to crack the shields.

Tavelo slid to a halt on the East side of the sector with at least one hundred imperial guards before him engaged in battle. Manel did the same on the West side with Gallic defending him.

Tavelo stared at the enemy swarming the land and sky. A thought came to mind.

"I have a proposal." Tavelo's eyes narrowed. "On Earth, they call it salting the land."

Manel smiled. "I know that term. It's what I was thinking about as well. Though not to that extent."

"It will cause more damage to the planet. Though not as much as us when we go on a rampage."

"True." Manel went silent again. "Shall we?" A devious smile spread across his face. "End this?"

"Yes, let's" Tavelo stripped off his robe.

"Megen!" Manel sent to his brother, as he removed his clothes. *"Prepare to spray down the area."*

The silence grew deafening until heanswered,

"Understood."

Tavelo sent a message to his uncle.

"We're going ahead."

Within minutes, the planetary feed crackled.

"All citizens, prepare for spraying of the enemy. The emperors are on the move. Those in the royal vicinity take shelter."

The two emperors shifted to their ancient forms as the imperial soldiers nearby scrambled to safety. Enemy fighters turned to see the giant creatures loom over them. Their puny weapons would do no good. Yet, they still fired upon the emperors, the arms dealers stabbing their spears to try penetrating the underbellies.

Each step of Manel's Kataling body caused the ground to shudder, deep craters forming under his hoofs. He engulfed multiple prey at a time, draining the bodies until only husks remained. It did little to heal the deep wounds except stop the bleeding. A few more feedings would help them close.

Tavelo squashed an enemy unit as he stepped forward. More met their doom the same way before he took to the skies, screeching with rage. His Volshin body overshadowed four ships. He swatted two down to the surface while his tail whipped around and knocked one towards the horizon.

The force of wind from his wings flapping kept other ships away. Using his talons, he grabbed the last ship and tore it open. Amid the explosions, he picked out a handful of enemy fighters and shoved them in his mouth. Blood dribbled down his long snout as the bones crunched.

Cannons rose from underground across the planet. Unlike the ones already out sending missiles to knock out enemy ships in orbit, these had a shorter range and deadlier ammunition. The barrels had multiple holes in a plate that rotated. They glowed a fiery blue, engulfing the barrel until it looked like one giant beam.

The cannons adjusted their positions, targeting the enemy ships in the sky, and fired.

A laser light show of blue streams criss-crossed

the skies, moving slowly in arches. Enemy ships exploded in rapid succession, careening into each other or falling to the ground in pieces. The surface below got pummeled with debris.

The Volshins fighting above dove into the ocean long before the blast. A few got hit with random pieces that fell.

With the first round ended, black smoke drifted in the sky. A scent of smoldering flesh and metal filled it, making people cough as it reached them.

"Commencing second round."

The planetary system announced.

To the emperors' surprise, the enemy's fight shifted. Their ships retreated to rendezvous with the remaining ones in orbit. The fighters on the ground desperately tapped their wristbands to request a rescue as they fought to keep Cellaxans at bay.

Manel reverted to human form, naked, covered in blood. His red gorged eyes gazed at the carnage in his wake and the enemy before him attempting to run away.

He addressed his imperial soldiers in the area.

"Let none leave alive." He commanded viciously. "Eat what you like. Leave the rest for harvesting."

Tavelo swirled along the sky, clearing the air by knocking the damaged ships down. He circled around and landed on the East side of the palace. Reverting as he touched the ground. The blood of the enemy mingled with his own all over his body. He frowned in disgust, wiping some of it and ended up smearing it more.

He didn't need to order his imperial soldiers into action. They did so on their own. He watched them go after the retreating enemy. Many got rescued. Beamed up from where they stood into passing ships that kept going off the planet.

"Damn!" Tavelo didn't want to let any of them get away. His wounded body wouldn't allow him to shift back into his Volshin form.

He felt drained.

As emperor, he could not show weakness. So, he stood firm, regulating his breathing.

Above him, the skies slowly cleared. Only a few enemy ships crippled along until a main ship located then beamed them up.

Tavelo took a few more deep breaths to calm himself. It's over. His kaleidoscope eyes burned with fury.

Strategies for retaliation swirled in his mind.

Pravin burst through the stronghold doors into a din of chaos. Clan members rushed to help the wounded and clear away debris. The front part of the stronghold outside gave evidence to an intense fight. Holes the size of boulders littered the court-yard. The majestic statues lay broken along the walkways.

Inside, his family scrambled to fix things.

He maneuvered through the corridors to the medical bay. More than twenty members languished in the holding area. While quickly scanning the room, his gaze fell on Roren slumped against the wall farther back. He rushed to him.

"What's the meaning of this?" He cried out, grabbing hold of his shoulders. "Why are you hurt? Why are you not being treated?"

Roren opened his glazed eyes.

"They're treating the worse off first. My wounds aren't dire." His voice came out as a whisper.

"Why are you hurt?" Pravin repeated. "I can't take you being hurt." He bent his head, sobbing, and rested it on his chest. "I never want to see that."

Roren hesitated to touch him, not sure what to do in that situation. He used his good arm to hold Pravin's head and caress his hair.

A medical technician came in and stopped in his track, shocked by the scene. Pravin lifted his head and glared at him.

"You will treat him right now! Understand?"

"Of course, Master Strana. I'm here to escort him."

"He should not have been left to wait!" He stood; eyes glowing. "This is the mother of my children. Their life takes precedence."

The medical technician bowed his head.

"Please forgive my mistake."

When Roren tried to slide off the slab, he went down. Pravin caught him, lifting him in his arms. He motioned to the technician.

"Lead the way."

He adjusted his weight and carried him to the operating room.

Roren let himself be cradled in Pravin's arms. The medical technician wasn't the only one shocked. He didn't think Pravin cared about his wellbeing. Certain that he would only look for him after the chaos died out and needed him to resume his duties regardless of injury. It was his turn to ask.

"Why are you being kind to me?" He whispered.

Pravin laid him on the table while the technician activated the scan.

"I know I've treated you badly. I've no excuse for that. But, I never want to see you hurt. You spawned children for me. Whatever you may think, I do care for you. Very much so."

Roren felt taken aback by his words. All this time. Nearly two centuries! And I was wrong? Tears filled his eyes and slid down the sides of his face.

"I know." Pravin moved hair from his forehead and stepped back so the technician could do his work. "Please forgive me."

The medical technician gave him a sedative. He didn't wait for it to kick in before scrubbing the dried sealing foam from his wounds. He could see Pravin frowning.

Roren laughed a little inside.
He found his reaction endearing.

The docks smoldered. As far as the eye could see, both sides looked to have been destroyed. Shimmers of the broken shields served as evidence of the fight. Not long after the announcement for the second round of spray, the enemy turned tail to run before another came. Since the enemy fled, the next round didn't happen.

"Citizens. Have your fill. Leave all others for harvesting."

That alone made the enemy desperate to get off Cellaxa, finding themselves prey to the population.

Too late for that!

Master Callesi stood with Master Bryhel. Both scanning the layer of dead enemy bodies on the ground. He guesstimated the count and concluded it would be a good amount to harvest.

And that's just from this area.

"Should we negotiate for a share of the haul?" Master Bryhel asked.

"Of course. We did most of the work."

"Their blood isn't exactly tasty, but I guess served with some herbed bread that should cover it."

Dock workers began gathering the dead and making piles in the center for easier removal. Though relieved the battle ended, they still remained hostile about being invaded. How they handled the bodies with utter disrespect showed how they felt.

"I can't imagine what the emperors are feeling right now," Master Callesi said.

"Oh. Something unprecedented will happen." Mater Bryhel replied. "We've not seen this much devastation in over a thousand years. We will surely answer the call in kind."

Master Callesi snorted.

The enemy had poked a sleeping monster.

"I almost feel sorry for them," he laughed.

"Surely, you jest."

"Of course. They will get what they deserve." He swept his gaze over the docks. "This will not stand."

After The Carnage

Tavelo and Manel walked along the aisle of the harvesting bouse lined with carts of dead enemy bodies piled high. The workers processed them by stripping off all the armor, boots, and other clothing. They put it aside in giant bins for later repurposing assessments.

At the end of the aisle sat four large metal squares ten feet high. A receptacle on the front had a handle to open it by pushing the door down.

The head of the harvesting facility came up to them and bowed.

"Greetings Emperor Manel, Emperor Tavelo. I am honored by your presence."

"How does it look?" Tavelo asked.

"Oh, we shall have a good harvest." The facility head extended a hand to the piles already stripped. "I'd say we'll be able to fill an entire mega cube."

"That's all?" Manel exclaimed. "Huh!" He glanced around at the haul. "All that work for this."

"Stop complaining," Tavelo chided. He turned to the facility head. "Please, start the harvesting."

"You're going to watch the process?" The facility head asked, cautiously but with excitement.

"Yes," Manel answered. "We want to see every last one of them sucked dry."

The facility head and the workers nodded in agreement. They understood completely.

A group of four workers manually pushed the first pile of stripped bodies in front of the harvester of the end. The sides of the machine went from dark to opaque for the emperors' viewing pleasure. Whirring erupted as the conveyor belt dragged the bodies in.

First, it tore off the skin. Making an incision along the back of the body. Pinching clamps took hold of the flaps and pulled, exposing the muscle and tissue. A second wave of lasers cut into each section. Robotic arms tore it away until only the skeleton remained.

Then the mess got deposited into the main bin where a grinder waited below. An air power wash helps to collect any excess blood.

The grinder went slow, keeping all the nutrients intact. A long pulverizing method that turns the meat into slush. It emptied into a vat via a sieved shelf to separate any clumps that didn't break down. In the vat, it purified the fluid of any harmful elements.

Two workers attached a ten square foot cube to the end of the harvester, making sure the spout aligned with the output feed. Within minutes, the harvester released its product. Red liquid filled the cube, stopping shy of the top by ten inches.

"Almost got a full cube on that one," the facility head mused. He motioned to the workers stripping the bodies. "Add more to the rest of the piles. We'll see what's left over at the end. Get a smaller cube if necessary."

"If that's the case," Manel began, "Make two smaller cubes and present them to us."

Tavelo turned to him. "I didn't think of that."

"Always keep a memento of your spoils," Manel said with a smile.

"Of course, Emperor Manel." The facility head addressed the workers. "You heard the emperor's request."

Royal guards carried over two chairs and sat them at an angle by the harvesters to ensure the emperors could see the now clear sides of each machine.

Manel and Tavelo settled into them.

When Pridric, Innego, and Maxellia arrived, they fetched more chairs.

Maxellia looked up at the not quite full cube and her brow furrowed.

"I'm assuming adjustments are being made?"

"Yes. We may get our own mini cubes with the leftover pile," Manel replied.

Pridric stared at the carts of arms dealers they separated from the reptiles. A few of the piles the workers blended while others were not to create three different products.

"Are we going to increase its volume for the masses?" She asked. Her shimmering eyes showed malice. "I would like to have at least small samplers for the citizens."

Tavelo shook his head in awe. Again, he had not thought of that either. Manel snorted.

"You haven't adapted to being home, I see," Manel chided him. "It's all about the blood."

"I had forgotten." He called to the facility head. "Can we split the haul for that?"

"Indeed. What a wonderful gesture." He bowed, his workers following.

The next pile went to the second harvester and so on until all four machines had one butted against it. Maxellia's eyes widened in delight watching the process. Pridric remained stoic, making it a point to witness the enemy's demise.

Tavelo tried to reassure her it was not her fault. Yes, she had been the one who contacted them on behalf of the humans for trade. Their actions were beyond her control. He could see the blame in her eyes as she flinched at the skin being pulled off.

He placed his hand over hers. She flipped it and squeezed his.

"It shouldn't have ended this way," she whispered.

"They were greedy," Manel said.

"And stupid," Innego added. "Their leader will

probably be contacting us soon."

"To request their dead, I'd guess," Tavelo smirked.

"Should we make a sample for them too?" Maxellia laughed. "A gesture of condolences?"

Absolutely not!" Manel answered. His eyes glowed for a brief second.

The harvesting took six hours.

The royal group would periodically get up and walk around the machines, getting a closer look. A break two hours in saw imperial guards take the role of servants and fetch food and drink for everyone, including themselves. The facility head distributed shot glass sized testers.

"Not too bad." Innego sipped from the blended taster, then passed it on to Pridric. "It has potential."

Pridric took a sip, swishing it around her mouth before swallowing. Her mouth down-turned, unsure about how she felt about it. She gave it to Tavelo.

"Well, we knew from the start it wouldn't be spectacular," he said after his taste.

Manel took it from him and raised the almost empty glass up to the light. Its color seemed heavy, not a bright ruby color. The light didn't penetrate it. He took a sip.

"I guess if I need something to whet my palette." He frowned as he passed the last of it to his sister.

Maxellia tossed the remains down her throat, not bothering to savor the taste. Her eyes went red with disgust. She handed the empty shot glass to the worker beside her.

"Best to just cook with it instead of drinking it."

"The royal chefs will know what to do with this." Innego waved a hand at the cubes filling up.

With the last pile harvested, and the smaller cubes from the leftovers done, the facility head and a worker walked over to Manel and Tavelo, each holding a mini cube.

"Emperors," the men knelt on one knee.

The facility head raised his cube.

"I present these spoils of battle to you."

"Rise," Manel ordered.

They placed the cubes in their hands, and the two men stepped back. Tavelo handed his to Pridric.

"For my Empress."

He kissed her hand as he let it go.

"Now that we've finished all that," Innego said, standing. "What is our next move?"

Manel's eyes darkened. Tavelo and Maxellia leaned away from him. His golden amber irises turned a shiny bronze. The workers and imperial guards tensed, not sure if they were safe. No one had ever seen his eyes do such a thing.

"I feel," Manel's voice breathed with a sultry tone, "the need to return the lesson."

Maxellia's eyes widened in fear.

Gallic, standing off in the wings amidst the shadows, hung his head and nodded. He seemed not surprised. Tavelo pondered the meaning, when felt his insides flip. Then he grinned, letting out a grunt before bursting into a full throaty laugh. Manel joined in.

Everyone watched the two emperors' maniacal laughter go on for a long while. When they stopped, both their eyes glowed an electrifying red.

Cellaxan battleships, many not having been in service for centuries, filled the skies. They ascended into orbit towards the open vortices, waiting to take them to the enemies' home worlds. A massive force not seen in over a millennium. This time they would take the fight to the vermin who dared invade them.

Driving off the enemy was not enough to satiate Cellaxa.

Manel and Tavelo stood on the palace vestibule overlooking the horizon. They smiled with pride at the ships equaling only a third of their military.

No need to go all out.

That alone would devastate a planet.

"Such magnificence," Manel breathed. He turned to Tavelo. "Don't you think?"

"Impressive. I never knew Cellaxa had such a thing." Tavelo marveled at the sight.

Behind them, Manel's siblings, Pridric, Innego, and Commissioner Polp stood in awe.

"One turn deserves another," Megen said. "They will feel our wrath."

"You wish you were on one of those ships, don't you?" Innego asked Manel.

"I do," Manel tilted his head down while still staring at the ships.

"Your duty is to stay and be ruler of our people," Megen quipped, turning away. "I will bring you back a souvenir."

He left them to rendezvous with his ship. Manel eyed his disappearing back with envy.

"This is an unprecedented event, your grace." The historian appeared with four of the royal council. "A milestone to be recorded. I believe the last time Cellaxa went out to conquer or retaliate spanned some two millennia ago."

"Makes sense." Tavelo pointed to the sky. "Yet, these ships were maintained."

"Of course," a council member replied. "We are always being targeted by ambitious races. We must stay vigilante and respond accordingly."

"Should we have sent a warning?" Lendor asked playfully.

"Hmph!" Maxellia glanced one last time at the sky and headed out.

Frothy saliva oozed from the reptile leader's mouth. He seethed in outrage at nearly a thousand ships emerging from the vortices surrounding his planet. The Cellaxa insignia blazoned on each one made his blood boil.

How dare they? And without warning.

The fleet he sent to take control of Cellaxa's docks had not yet returned. Was this in response to such a meager attack? Those blood suckers should have been easy to dominate with an entire fleet. The first was merely a test.

He marched over to his office communication station and slammed a taloned paw on the console. The operator flinched, leaning away from him.

"Open a channel! I want to have a few words with them."

The operator's talons moved across their console to try establishing a connection. It succeeded.

"I want to …"

A message sprawled across the screen.

This is your answer.

The connection then severed. A thousand beams of light shot forth from the Cellaxan ships and pierced the planet's stratosphere. They scorched the surface, demolishing every structure they hit. His head raised in horror as multiple beams sped towards him.

Across the planet, they spared nothing. Cellaxa showed no mercy.

No ground units were deployed.

Only a mass blanket of firepower. When the bombardment stopped, the planet's auditory system got hacked. The commander of the fleet regurgitated the enemy's spiel delivered to them.

"Following your actions and disrespect for our monarchs, we felt it necessary to teach you a lesson. We hope you will reflect on your wrongdoings and await your apology."

The reptile leader crawled out of the rubble that

used to be his command office. A communications technician sat on a pile of debris holding a ten-inch tablet displaying reports.

"What now?" He climbed over to the technician. "Are they making any demands?"

"No, leader." The technician turned the tablet so he could see. "They are leaving."

Onscreen, the Cellaxa fleet reversed course into vortices opening behind them. Darkness swallowed them and they winked out of sight.

The leader stood on broken pieces of structure that crunched under his feet. He stared at the horizon and took in the destruction left in their wake. Smoke replaced the clouds, covering the planet with acrid air. He could taste burnt metal and ash.

Everywhere he looked, there was carnage. The horizon seemed vast, and it shouldn't be. He saw all the tall buildings decimated, clearing the view. In the distance, he heard the echoes of screams, cries for help, anger.

Far more damage than his race had done on Cellaxa. This attack came as extreme prejudice. It hit him that he had indeed made a mistake. They poked the wrong monster. The communications technician got his attention with a wave.

"Sorry to disturb you, leader."

"What is it?" Fear gripped him.

"The galactic trade federation has sent a notice of suspension."

The leader's expression crumbled. This wasn't supposed to happen. His tattered robes flipped in the wind picking up. A bad judgement had turned deadly. And his people now paid for it.

The arms dealers were ready for the Cellaxa fleet when it appeared in their home world's space. They positioned hundreds of ships around the planet's circumference. Ground troops lay in wait on the surface, anticipating an invasion. Non-combatants were evacuated off the planet. Only military forces remained.

Nevertheless, the sudden vortex that appeared first took them off guard. The ships didn't wait to clear its edge before unleashing their missives. More popped up, outnumbering the enemy ten to one. That didn't deter them from returning fire. While the attempt to keep the Cellaxan fleets at bay worked, Most of the bombardment did its job, reaching the surface.

The enemy forces took shelter in fire resistant bunkers to wait out the storm.

Megen took in reports and data images displayed on the ship's bridge holoscreen. He stood on the command dais with his arms crossed. The fleet had beaten the enemy forces that attacked Cellaxa home.

Which meant their numbers had dwindled. He wondered if the enemy noticed how his fleet slowly moved forward, choking their ability to maneuver anywhere except planet side.

"Open the channel," he commanded his communications tech.

Within minutes, a second screen appeared in the right corner of the main. The scaly, face of their race's king filled it. Their glassy black eyes expressed pure murder.

"You find yourselves clever?" The enemy king spat. "We knew you would come. No honor."

Megen refused to entertain his prattling as he repeated a similar message crafted for them.

"For your disrespect and actions against the planet Cellaxa and her emperors, this is a teaching moment. It would be in your best interest to reflect and atone for your deeds."

The king leaned forward, baring his sharp teeth.

"You talk to us about disrespect! After your own people interfered in our trade business!"

Megen's eyes glowed red. He smiled crookedly.

"Since it's clear you don't feel the need to repent, Cellaxa deems you unworthy."

"We will cut you down before…" Megen cut off the feed.

"Have we finally reached the planet's access point?" He asked his pilot.

"All ships are in position. The enemy is locked in."

He nodded to the communications technician, who opened a channel to the fleet commander.

"Send down the battalions." He instructed.

"As you command, General Megen," the fleet commander responded.

Each ship's docking bays opened, letting rows of fighter ships shoot out to the surface. The enemy came out of hiding to engage. Already a smoldering array of damage, the enemy managed to keep their footing on unsteady ground. For every Cellaxan ship, a group of soldiers descended on the enemy. With no fear of civilian deaths, both sides went into full combat.

Good. That's how it should be.

Megen turned away from the screen.

"Is my ship prepared?" He asked his specialist as he passed him.

"Your imperial unit awaits you." The specialist bowed his head. "May victory be yours."

Megen walked down the corridor leading to the ship bays. He had one mission to fulfill at the request of Manel and Tavelo. They didn't need to ask.

The enemy would feel his wrath regardless of an order. Seeing the enemy king's rage at being invaded solidified his decision.

He also felt Pridric did not have any fault in the matter. Yes, dealing with them in the first place was bad judgement on his part.

From his studies of Earth, he agreed they were not ready for such advanced weaponry. Sometimes trade required higher risks. And one never knew what the outcome would be until it played out.

At the lift, he hit the icon to open the door and stepped in. It automatically shot to the lower bowels where the loading docks were. He went through the doors as they parted and marched to his ship. The pilot stood at the ramp, bowing his head.

He raised it as Megen approached.

"Your grace, we are ready for battle."

"Let's go."

Megen went inside. The pilot followed.

The pilot went to his station and began the launch sequence.

"Coordinates set for the capital. Fleet ships in the vicinity will clear a path."

"Shields?" Megen asked.

"Our attacks have weakened the dome around the palace by fifteen percent." Megen gave him a skeptical stare. The pilot squirmed and addressed the engineer who came on screen before him. "I think the General is wanting a solution."

"If you have no qualms about getting harmed and having a damaged ship," the engineer said. Megen's furious gaze made him clear his throat. "The ship can handle being rammed. The integrity would drop by half, but the impact would penetrate that shield in conjunction with continuous blasts."

Megen liked the sound of that strategy. He glared at the pilot.

"Are you on board with that?" He scanned the faces of everyone on the bridge. "All of you?"

The move could end up being a suicide run. But it would annihilate the entire palace and destroy most of the capital when the ship exploded. A successful maneuver meant the ship landing inside the shield and careening right into the palace. From there, his unit could spread carnage into the capital.

"We are at your command, General Megen," a soldier replied from his station. "We trust you to bring us to glory. As you always have."

Megen smirked. He had only lost one battle in his life. Against his father. Any other enemy he deemed inferior to that man's madness.

"Then prepare for victory." Megen nodded to the pilot, who returned it before focusing his attention back on his task. "Brace for impact. We attack the moment the hatch opens inside that dome."

The ship launched into the fray, avoiding enemy fire that went astray as their own forces forced them to the sides, creating a safe corridor. It sailed undeterred towards the shield dome around the palace. Megen noticed the capital sat unprotected.

Cellaxan fire rained down on the dome. He glanced at the counter on the weapons tech's screen. Another ten percent, putting the shield's integrity at seventy-five. Good enough.

"Coming in range of ramming maneuver."

Megen saw the shimmer of the shields right before his ship plowed into it. Power flickered in and out. Sparks flew from consoles. He could hear the hull start to buckle as the ship forced its way through. The tail end cleared the shield, and the ship shot forth right into the top level of the palace.

The holoscreen blew out, exposing the bridge to the air inside the palace. The only thing holding the structure intact was the ship. Enemy troops emerged from the deep shadows of the damaged walkway and charged forward. The hatch below opened with a thunderous clank, the broken gears snapping.

Megen's soldiers flooded the walkway to meet their combatants. On the bridge, they climbed over the main console to join them. He checked his wristband to make sure the scan of the palace gave him the route to the throne room.

To conserve his energy, his team cut down any enemy closest to him.

They made a direct line to their destination and weren't disappointed when they reached it. The throne room doors sat partially open; the mechanism apparently damaged from the impact. It had been in the process of sealing.

The one seated on the throne was not the king. A doppelgänger. Megen glimpsed the ruler being snuck out. He concluded he would have to deal with his replacement. A menacing foe, showing his air of authority. Clearly a family member or of high status. Someone the king trusted, yet deemed dispensable.

His red robes flowed over the armrests. In his lap, one of the long piercing spears rested. He slid from his seat, discarding the robes, and stepped down onto the floor. His soldiers immediately engaged with Megen's. Only the two monarchs faced each other. No one interfered and prevented others from doing so.

"That thing sitting on your throne sent a lowly military soldier to do its bidding?" The fake king spat saliva at his side. "Who are you supposed to be? A great warrior?"

Megen tilted his head.

"Did it ever occur to you that our Emperor had family? Did you not look into that? Did you not say you knew of our planet?"

"We tried to trade with your kind. That is all we needed to know."

"Hmm. Then let me introduce myself." Megen threw off his own cloak to stand in his black battle suit. "I am Megen, Eldest son of Emperor Mallen. Brother to Emperor Manel and General of the Cellaxan forces." He saw trepidation spread across the warrior's face. Then it turned hostile. "Oh?"

"So you forfeited your claim to that monster? That means you lack ambition." The warrior gave a devious smile. "I will gladly end your suffering here."

The fake king proved faster than Megen thought.

Its spear came at a deadly speed. He barely dodged it by leaning sideways. He pivoted to get around him and found himself denied. The warrior anticipated the move, driving an elbow into Megen's side as they both turned in a dance. He took it, not letting himself react to the pain. Tumbling out of range, he got back to his feet.

Megen only had a split second to draw his sword before the spear came down. Its heaviness numbed his fingers for a moment. He adjusted his weight to relieve the sensation. The warrior twirled the spear above his head and brought it down again.

This time, Megen matched his speed. To his surprise, their fight sped up until he found himself moving faster than he liked.

He's got me caught in a whirlwind! Confirming his suspicions, the spear suddenly veered off to the left and came back before Megen could stop it. The hit sent him into the wall on the right of the throne. He tasted blood and spat out a mouthful.

Something's broken! Not life threatening.

He forced the tissue to close and stared at the fake king, smiling in confidence as he raised the spear, pulling it back. Launching it at such close range meant it would impale Megen to the wall.

Should I chance it? Megen weighed on getting impaled to trying to dodge it. The spear would knick his shoulder or the side of his head. Letting it go through, he could then pull it out. If it didn't hit a major organ and kill him instantly.

Or.

In a flash, Megen flung his sword in a low swing. The moment the spear released, the fake king's legs were cut open above the shins. He fell backwards. Megen slid to the floor, feeling the tip of the spear graze the side of his head. The deep cut spewed blood, flowing into his right eye.

He wiped it away in time to see the fake king back on his feet.

The wounds seeped, then fused together from a spent mini torch in his hand. When did he do all that? The fake king tossed the torch and charged, wielding Megen's own sword. The insult in itself drove Megen into a rage.

With an ear-piercing shriek that scared everyone in the room into a standstill, Megen morphed into Kataling form. His soldiers immediately abandoned their fight and fled the room as his body filled a third of it. The fake king stared up at him, horrified. The enemy soldiers in the room, now trapped, hesitated.

Megen took one step, shaking the room. The floor caved in where it landed, snapping the fake king out of his stupor. Grabbing an abandoned spear, he moved to strike the giant creature looming over him. He stabbed its underbelly, erroneous to claim victory, hearing Megen emit a high-pitched squeal.

Megen engulfed the king's head in his mouth and chomped down, severing the head. The fake king's body stayed standing for a few seconds. His grip steady on the spear stuck in Megen's leathery hide. The only thing holding it up.

The loud crunch as Megen chewed echoed.

A nearly clean skull came flying out of Megen's mouth, hitting the floor and rolling. With a swift turn, Megen dislodged the spear, sending the body with it, and brought his attention to the enemy soldiers.

Determined to fight with honor, they rushed him.

It was a decent meal. Enough to heal his wounds when he finished them off.

CHAPTER FIVE

Rebuild

A summons by Emperor Manel never boded well for anyone in Omaris' eyes. And not just him. His brother Omeron as well. He walked the palace halls in silence, nodding to royal members as they passed. His attire was of the same high quality, though of a distinct style.

He had grown accustomed to Earth suits. The black jacket and pants with a white shirt and red tie were standard Ambrook colors. He would usually slick back his hair but decided not to this time.

At the throne room entrance, he met Omeron. His brother wore a tight-fitting black tunic, dark grey pants, and a buttonless black jacket, showing off his physique. They went in together and stood before Manel and his siblings, sitting on their thrones while the royal court caller announced them.

"Omaris and Omeron Strana as summoned," they said, backing away as he bowed.

"Ahh, the twins of Strana where one is a Kataling, and the other is not." Manel leaned forward. "Were you ever told how that came to be?"

Omaris tilted his head in thought.

"We know that our father was mated to one of the previous Master Strana's sisters in some sordid deal and she died not long after our fifth year." He brought his focus back to Manel.

Lendor clasped his hands in his lap.

"Hmm. Your father was exiled from the palace by our father when he failed to produce suitable offspring for our bloodline. Tossed out for having insufficient seed."

"A broker on the outskirts of the city made a deal with Master Strana. He bought him for a meager sum." Maxellia's expression soured. "His intentions were no better than our father's."

"That makes both of you royalty." Manel gave a devilish smile. "And of ancient bloodline in addition, since Volshins derive from the Strana clan."

The two brothers frowned at the revelation. Omaris knew of it in the back of his mind, but never delved into the details.

"I understand you weren't treated very well in the Strana homestead." Manel sat back. "Maybe you could serve the palace instead of the Stranas."

"I serve Empress Pridric of my own volition. Of course, I am not really needed in a royal capacity."

"Yes, taking over the Ambrook company is your new priority," Lendor said.

Manel glanced down at Omeron.

"And what about you? I'm sure we could find a position worth your time. Or will you serve the Stranas once more?" Omeron's face grew hesitant. "I heard he wants to address the subject with you."

"I have not served them in over two centuries for good reason. I have," he paused. "more important responsibilities now."

"Chalayl Boresso. I suppose I should congratulate you for snagging her." Manel saw the way Omeron stared at him in fury. "I did apologize to Caden for my indiscretions."

"I'll never forgive you for that," Omeron said through clenched teeth.

"Nor should you." Manel waved off the topic. "What is your answer?"

"We need to think about it," Omaris replied. "I want Empress Pridric's suggestion on this."

"That's fair. Just remember." Manel met their eyes. "You're of royal lineage. Use it to your advantage." He addressed Omaris. "You have no mate. Maybe it's time you found one. You could have any royal you want." Manel glanced over at his sister. "Maxellia has yet to be taken."

Maxellia's head snapped up, and she turned to him, enraged. Omaris' expression intensified it. He looked mortified. Manel frowned.

"Is my sister not to your liking?"

Omaris fervently shook his head. "Oh no, Emperor Manel. That's not the reason I hesitated."

"Granted, she doesn't leave much to be desired."

He could feel her fury come at him like a wave.

"I assure you, it would be feasible if she felt inclined." Omaris averted his gaze. Omeron's horror didn't leave his face. "I believe in mutual encounters."

Maxellia turned her nose up at him, tilting her head to the side with indignation.

"Good to know." Manel gave a devilish smile. "The offer still stands."

"I'll keep that in mind." Omaris bowed his head and waited until Omeron did the same.

They raised their heads and left the throne room.

Strolling the halls, Omaris could feel Omeron's tension. He let out a sigh.

"Did you really have to look like that the whole time?" Omaris chastised him.

"The thought of that creature coming at you with a hint of lust terrified me."

"Oh, come on." Omaris gave him a side glance. "She just needs attention. Maxellia is quite stunning."

"And a menace. What did he mean by not yet taken?" Omeron looked dubious. "There's no way she's untouched."

"You think so? I think it's probably true." Omaris grinned. "Who in their right mind would approach her for mating?"

Omeron's mouth opened to reply, then he clamped his lips tight. Whatever it was, wouldn't have been nice, Omaris concluded. He thought about the way the Emperor Mallen treated the royal family. His own children. It led to him remembering their own upbringing in the Strana household.

Between him and Pridric, he wasn't sure which one got treated worse than the other. The previous Master Strana was a monster like their father.

"I did get an invitation from Master Strana to talk over our roles in the Strana clan." Omaris broke the silence. "Will you go?"

Omeron slowed his stride.

"Yes." His tone sounded heavy. Like the answer was a burden. "Though he never lifted a finger to help me or Pridric, I know he isn't like his father."

"You're better than I," Omaris said. "I won't let him off the hook that easily."

"Won't you talk to father? He's waiting for you."

Omaris' lips pressed thin as he exhaled through his nose. He remembered witnessing the reunion between Omeron and their father. The way they greeted Caden and his child with outright disgust before feigning to accept them.

"I will, eventually. He didn't protect us either in that house." Omaris clenched his fists at his sides.

"I know," Omeron said softly. "We all need to heal, I guess."

They came to Dania's chamber and found Pridric inside. No doubt hiding from the imperial guards and Tavelo. Dania scanned their attire, as he knew she would.

"We were summoned by Emperor Manel,"

Omaris informed her.

"Oh?" Dania straightened her stance over the raised playpen housing the royal twins. Though not yet five years old, keeping them contained made it easier. "What did he want from the two of you?"

"That seems ominous," Pridric added.

"It was regarding our royal bloodline." Omaris saw them both draw back, hissing. "He wanted to know if we would be interested in serving the royal courts or the Stranas."

Dania's face turned vicious.

"I will not serve the Strana clan ever again." She averted her gaze. "Afte the horrors they committed against you and Pridric. Never." Her slow emission of the word felt razor sharp.

Pridric's lips thinned.

"You already serve me. Why would he ask that?"

"Do I really?" Omaris gave him a telling stare. "My role is for the Ambrook coven. You have your own servants and the royal council now."

"That's true, but." Pridric struggled to find the right words.

"And Omeron has Chalayl and a newborn to care for soon," Omaris continued.

"Ahh, yes!" Dania exclaimed. "I am glad for you. And Chalayl. I worried about her."

"Really?" Pridric's blue eyes glowed as she turned her nose up. "I still don't have much sympathy for her." She eyed Omeron. "No offense. Her rebellion against being mated into the Strana clan though me, then in the end, she still wound up with a Strana."

Dania cringed. Omaris tried not to react and grabbed hold of Omeron's wrist. Pridric's harsh words stung. He always chastised his master for such unfiltered bursts.

"We do have an invitation," Dania changed the subject. "I'm interested in what your brother has to say for himself after all this time," addressing Pridric.

"I think he wants to change the clan."

Pridric went back to attending her spawns.

"That will be an uphill battle." Omaris went to a chair and sat down. "My sources tell me a faction of the clan was none too happy when he called off your assassination.".

"Your father ruled with an iron fist and kept that decree in place for so long. He made so many faithful to the cause." Dania frowned in disgust. "And they nearly succeeded."

"Volshin births dwindled by sixty percent. All it did was hurt the clan." Omaris shook his head.

"Master Strana wanted to experiment like the emperor. He wanted to see if he could make a Kataling."

Omeron leaned against the side wall and slid down to the floor, resting his forearms on his knees. He looked comfortable there, which disturbed Omaris. Dania gave him a strange look, seemingly feeling the same. That's how they always saw him inside the Strana homestead.

Even on Earth, Omeron opted to stay in the lower bowels, not wanting to engage with the coven elite.

I want him to find some sense of peace.

New dock construction proposals flooded in from the planners in Cellaxa's trade commission headquarters. With so much damage to the West docks and the East still being built, they decided to start from scratch. Dock assignments were locked in. The planners realized a new configuration to make proportionate bays according to the merchant shipments.

Commissioner Polp presented the ideas to Emperors Manel and Tavelo during the midday meeting in the dual throne room. The royal family, along with Tavelo's cabinet members and Empress Pridric, went over the details on the holoscreen.

"While it's true the East docks are incomplete," Innego began, "we had made much progress. Four of the merchant bays were fully functioning."

"It is a shame." Master Endaga sighed.

"That said, improvements work best when you

have a clean slate." He leaned back in his seat. "Our clan needs bigger accommodations, anyway."

"We must build with reinforced infrastructure," Manel added. "The shield is not enough."

"It would have been if activated in time," Lendor countered. "Why was there such a delay?"

"Let's not dwell over that. What's done is done." Commissioner Polp waved a dismissive hand.

Manel sat leaned to the side, his head resting in the palm of his hand. He tapped his temple with a finger, frowning at the multiple plans fanned out on the screen.

"None of these create a flow of productivity." He glowered. "I've always wanted to strip the docks and start over. It's cluttered, overcrowded. Nothing moves well."

Commissioner Polp let out a gasp in agreement. He felt the docks hindered trade as well. He glanced over at Emperor Tavelo and became startled by the look of frustration on his face. As if it irritated him that he had not thought of the solution first. That can't be! How childish.

"That is ideal," Emperor Tavelo finally spoke. "It would have to be in stages. A strategy to determine which bays would be first."

"That's obvious," Manel snapped. "We start from the ports and work our way out towards the end of the boardwalk." The room went silent. Manel raised his head and turned to Tavelo. "I wasn't trying to be insulting. I know you realize that's how it's done. I was addressing the others."

"Of course." Emperor Tavelo didn't seem to be eased by his words.

Master Jaubro seemed to fidget at the proposal. As the known top merchant clan, he probably felt his should take priority. He too would agree with Emperor Manel. The Jaubro clan's bays were in the first few sectors, but closer to the center. To start there meant multiple reroutes around it.

"Whoever is first will need a temporary bay for business." Windsor stated.

"We can build one on each dock so they can house it during construction." Innego said.

"What do our coffers look like?" Manel asked the treasury councilman.

The woman pulled out her tablet and tapped it open. She perused the data on her screen.

"We have generated threefold in revenue over the past five years."

Manel dropped his arm and sat up straight.

"Then I propose this." His eyes smoldered with pride. "Since our current docks, even reconfigured, cannot accommodate the flow and expansion of traffic, we will build two more. On the North and South."

Silence spread. Those about to protest clamped their mouths shut. Tavelo looked over at him in awe.

There it is again! Commissioner Polp was certain this time. Emperor Manel's proposal made his skin prickly. It fascinated him.

"Surely, you're not serious," Master Jaubro blurted.

"Do I appear to have said it in jest?" Manel's eyes grew red.

"Are there truly enough funds for that?" Pridric asked, incredulously.

"Yes," the treasurer replied. "With much more left in reserve."

"Then that's settled." Manel again stared at the plans on the holoscreen.

Commissioner Polp went and removed his data stick from the platform. The holoscreen went blank.

"I will have the planners create new ones based on your suggestions, Emperor Manel." He turned to Emperor Tavelo. "Will you be sending your recommendations to my office as well?"

Emperor Tavelo smiled.

"Of course. I should have a few ideas to you by the next moon cycle."

The commissioner left in a hurry, excited to get started. Four spaceports on Cellaxa! The possibilities on expanding trade were endless.

Inside the throne room, Tavelo and Master Jaubro seethed in silence. Their brows scrunched in thought.

And it did not go unnoticed by Manel.

News of additional docks' being constructed spread, causing high levels of excitement. Although only a few of the top merchants will have ports, the emphasis lies with smaller merchants who rarely got a chance to make dealings on their own. They usually went through a proxy of the top merchants and received only sixty percent of their profit.

This would change the class system, elevating those in poverty out. With every citizen able to live comfortably, Cellaxa had the potential to surpass expectations.

Tavelo understood that. Even as one of the top merchant clans, the Endagas struggled. Because of this, they horded their funds, amassing wealth, yet never using it. Afraid to lose any of it.

The surveyor walked ahead of him towards the southern shore. Not as vast, it showcased choppier waters and a jetty. Jagged cliffs lined each side. The water crashed against the rocks.

Further out on the horizon, it glimmered.

"I have never been inclined to see the Southern coast." The surveyor held the sides of his navy blue robes up so that it wouldn't drag across the dark sand. His ankle boots lost their shine from being rubbed by the sand. "Such magnificence. I don't want to ruin the view."

"Then find a way not to," Tavelo suggested.

"Hmm." The surveyor tapped his bottom lip with a finger.

He scanned the area, the pupils of his dark grey eyes expanding. A small breeze tussled the hair sticking out from under his woven cap. "These docks will be smaller in scale." He turned towards the jetty. "Maybe we could build off there and still keep the shore's aesthetic."

"It is beautiful." Pridric stared at it lovingly. "I could vacation here."

The surveyor whipped his tablet from inside his robes and pulled up the new plans. He scrolled through, stopping on a few possible designs then back. He landed on one and turned it to Tavelo, holding it up.

"This may work. We need to modify the lower section to wrap around the bottom of the cliff."

Tavelo scrutinized the schematic of the build. True, it looked plausible. He wanted something grander.

"It's a bit simple. The sand is a dark, rich color. The docks should complement it."

"You're right!" The surveyor detached a stylus from inside the tablet's bottom and began sketching on the design. He glanced at the surroundings multiple times while doing that. "Give me a moment."

Pridric wandered off to the beach line, letting the foaming water wash over her boots. The hem of her robes got wet. She didn't seem to care. Tavelo watched her face become serene.

"We will also need temporary housing for merchants when there are overnight or delayed shipments."

"Of course, your grace." The surveyor didn't look from his tablet. "There!" He pushed the stylus back into it and turned it again for Tavelo to see.

The sketched overlay enhanced the design. Tavelo's mouth curved down, impressed.

"Yes, send this to the treasurer and Emperor Manel."

The surveyor beamed with pride as he flipped the tablet back and began his correspondence to send. Tavelo walked over to stand next to Pridric.

Her waist length blonde hair almost floated straight out in the gust of wind coming off the water.

My beautiful Empress.

"You're staring again," Pridric chided, giving him a side glance.

"I can't help that." Tavelo wrapped an arm around her shoulder and placed his hand against her cheek. "You enchant me."

"I wonder what the North looks like. Do you think Manel has the same aesthetic?"

Tavelo's eyes narrowed.

He recalled the report from the other surveyor that the North couldn't sustain life due to its weather and barren terrain. He didn't relay the information as he was supposed to. For some reason this felt like a competition, and he didn't want to give his opponent a heads up.

"I doubt it. Even if he does, that shore would differ greatly from this one."

Pridric turned to him. The look in her eyes told him she suspected him of doing something sketchy. You're not entirely wrong. She tilted her head and waited for an explanation.

"There's nothing to tell. I've done nothing wrong. I promise." Tavelo kissed her softly.

The skepticism didn't go away. She let out a sigh and averted her attention back to the crashing waves. Silver blue water rippling on the deep reddish-brown sand reminded him of the colors of Tuscany on Earth. This dock's build he would see to himself.

Cold. Desolate.

Black sand along churning grey and white waves that reached twenty feet in height. They crashed against craggy rocks scattered down the coastline. The waterway spanned out in the shape of a skeleton keyhole, the arch reaching around the beach's edge.

Dead trees lined the rest of the way into the ocean. The roar of a waterfall signaled where the drop began.

Manel, the royal family, and imperial guards followed their surveyor to the shoreline. The harsh wind beat at them, yet they all ignored it, finding it refreshing.

The surveyor clutched his navy robes tight to his chest as he scanned the site. He wore a knitted hat with flaps that covered his ears. A few wisps of his dark hair stuck out. His grey eyes matched the color of the waves.

"Do you wish to see the build prospects?" He hesitated, releasing his grip on his robes to retrieve the tablet inside. "There were only five that suited this region."

"Yes. Tavelo forgot to tell us about your report." Manel's expression remained dark the entire trip. It now bordered on hostile. The surveyor went pale. "No matter." He too took in the land. "I'm sure none of them would work."

"The materials must be weatherproof," Lenri said.

"As well as the ports, if they end up facing the wind," Lendor added.

Maxellia walked past the surveyor to the shoreline. She breathed deep, inhaling the crisp arctic air, and raised her arms out.

"I think it's perfect." She turned to Manel with a grin. "Don't you?"

"Absolutely." Manel joined her, clasping his hands behind his head. "No need for extravagance like the others." He turned to the surveyor. "It should be simple. Streamlined for efficiency. Modern and blends with its surroundings."

"Like camouflage?" The surveyor removed his tablet from his robes. His navy blue kaftan beneath was buttoned all the way up around his neck. "Only authorized ships will be guided in for docking?"

"Correct. You understand my vision." Manel smirked. Tavelo did him a favor by not sending the report. Better that his family saw it firsthand. "I want it to be more advanced. A pillar of strength equal to its brutality." He lifted his arm towards the Northern Sea.

They all stood watching the deadly rapids while the surveyor sketched. Megen went towards the bluffs. The weight of his massive size footsteps dug his boots deep in the sand. The royal family felt at ease in the frigid environment.

Once the surveyor finished his work, he walked over to show Manel. The others gathered around. Manel's eyes glinted with approval. His siblings showed similar delight.

"This is perfect."

The surveyor breathed a sigh of relief. He made a few notes on the sketch.

"Will you be personally overseeing the build?"

"We all are," Maxellia answered. "This will be our legacy."

"A new steppingstone." Lendor said.

Manel glanced sideways at the sky, a sloppy grin on his face. He knew what Tavelo was thinking. Would it come to that? The rest of the royal family didn't calculate threats the way he did. After nearly two hundred years of reign, he learned to read the space, even in his deranged state.

Tavelo. How naïve.

"I want the technology implemented before the construction starts."

Manel finally turned away from the beautiful chaos of the waters.

"To prevent delay when the structure goes up. I see." The surveyor made more notes. His fingers grew almost white from the cold. "I need to check the other side for a moment. Is it possible to have a transport retrieve me?"

"How long do you need?"

"About two hours."

"Then we shall wait."

Manel signaled his imperial guards to set up the gear they brought it in case the trip lasted longer than anticipated.

"And put on your gloves," Manel snapped at the surveyor.

The man's eyes went wide as he flinched.

"Of course, Emperor Manel."

Tucking the tablet under his chin, he retrieved a pair of navy gloves from the pockets of his kaftan and pulled them on. He clenched his fists tight a few times to get blood circulating.

"I will accompany you," Megen told him. "I want to see how secure it can be."

"I appreciate the assist, Lord Megen."

The two went off towards the cliffs. Manel and the others sat on plush cushions arranged under a windproof tent. A gallon sized metal thermos of hot beverage sat in the center with portable heaters. Half the guards sat along the floor of the tent while the rest stood outside. They would rotate every half hour to keep warm.

Manel stared at the shore.

This dock would surpass the others. And not one top merchant would have a bay in it. He took one of the collapsible cups from the tray, popped it open and dispensed a drink from the thermos. He took a sip, feeling the heat warm his throat and hands.

Tavelo would be envious.

The top merchant clans resumed their annual meeting after decades of not communicating with each other. They filed into the conference building and broke out the drinks and food they brought with them.

No servants or guardians were used for this clandestine endeavor. All of it got spread down the middle and they helped themselves to the first round of spirits.

Master Jaubro, sitting at the end of the table, his usual spot as the top merchant leader, set his empty glass down before him.

"Let's discuss the new dock construction."

He met everyone's gaze one by one.

"I really don't see the problem," Master Strana piped up. "Having updated bays is ideal." He glared down at Master Jaubro. "What seems to be the issue?"

"Are you being snide, ignorant, or naïve?" Master Boresso asked.

The others focused their attention on Master Strana. He reared back in disgust. When Master Jaubro called for the meeting, he knew the others felt the same apprehension. An unwarranted response, in his opinion. But he also knew where it stemmed from. Fear.

With their younger counterparts now doing trade on the same level, their status would diminish. Jaubro, Strana, and Bryhel would no longer reign as the top three. He was fine with that. Trade on Cellaxa had gone stagnant for centuries.

Despite the horrors of Emperor Manel, he implemented new rules that both heightened and hindered business.

A double-edged sword.

"We can't let our businesses lose their standing!" Master Callesi burst out. "Our clans have dominated for over half a millennium."

"We are considered the standard,' Master Bryhel

retorted. "Your clan stands to lose as well."

"The Strana clan is secure. I've no fears about our revenue."

"Then you are being foolish," Master Jaubro said.

"I attended the meeting with the emperors and not once did they address our clans having docks on the Southern and Northern shores."

"Because there would be no need." Master Endaga took a swig of his drink. "We already have bays on the East and West."

All eyes fell on him. He glanced up from his drink. Master Strana gave him a warning look. The last thing he wanted was for the others to gang up on him. The Endaga clan already had the upper hand receiving a larger bay on the West.

"Oh. I see greed has won you all over." Master Endaga set his glass down. "My clan will always be your target to make yourselves feel adequate."

Master Jaubro slammed his fist on the table. Cries of outrage erupted around him.

"How dare you!" Master Bryhel yelled.

"What nonsense are you spouting, Endaga!?" Master Dakien shouted.

"That has never been the case!" Master Jaubro locked eyes with Master Endaga. "My clan has never wished you ill!"

"Is that so? Can you all say that?"

Master Endaga's eyes glowed red.

The room went silent. Master Strana fought his urge to antagonize them. Instead, he chuckled.

"I know I can't. Our sabotage was quite blatant." He tilted his head. "And I wish there was a way to fix that. Your clan didn't deserve any of it."

The others stared at him in confusion, awestruck by his admission. Master Endaga's mouth gaped open for a moment. He closed it and looked away. Master Jaubro looked uneasy.

You won't admit it! Master Strana's respect for him grew less each day.

Not that I had much in the first place.

"Enough!" Master Jaubro reached for the nearest carafe of spirits and poured himself another glass. "We did not come here for infighting." He took a good-sized gulp of his drink, draining a third of it. "We need a strategy to keep our clans relevant."

"They can't really be thinking of only allowing smaller merchants at the new ones," Master Boresso said.

"I don't mind that." Master Callesi waved a hand. "It separates them from us." He smiled. "In a good way. You don't really want to mingle our higher end products with theirs on the same platforms?"

"That is why I have a problem with it." Master Boresso glanced over at Master Loengir. "We should get first rights at the new docks. The lower merchants could take over the West ones."

"It would give them practice at an already established hub," Master Loengir added.

"So," Master Strana snorted. "You merely want the shiny new thing."

"We've earned that much," Master Dakien retorted.

Master Strana kept his ire at bay. It wasn't just greed. Their level of entitlement boggled him. His clan once felt the same. And look where that got us. He had one of his spies in the palace send the official report for the docks. His mind had not been made up yet on whose side he wanted to be on. Emperor Tavelo or Manel.

The meeting ended with mixed feelings and stroked egos. Master Endaga waited for Master Strana to exit the building. Master Jaubro lingered inside with Master Bryhel.

"Come walk with me," Master Endaga pleaded.

"Well, this is a first. You usually avoid me like a disease."

"For good reason."

"True." Master Strana shoved his hands in his

pants pockets. "I know what you're thinking."

Master Endaga let out a laugh. He eyed the tall blond beside him, standing a couple of inches above.

"Yes. I guess you do. A pact then?"

"Are you afraid Tavelo will get a taste of true power and go astray?"

Master Endaga paused his stroll and looked down at the cobblestoned street.

"Perhaps." He didn't like feeling that way. He adored his nephew and praised him for taking his place as the East Emperor. Something started to change in the past few years. "I hope not."

"I'm worried too."

The two resumed walking down the deserted street. Evening meal would begin in an hour. Most people were home getting ready. The setting sun cast a bright grey light, making shadows around everything. Their boots echoed as they struck the stone.

"To think, we would be the only voices of reason," Master Endaga tsked.

"It's because we understand each other. There's no pretense between us."

"Our first priority should be to heal the wounds with our young traders and their offspring."

"I agree." Master Strana's expression became sorrowful. "More than you know."

They stopped at the end of the street and turned around. Their transports had followed them a few yards behind.

"Let's meet again." Master Endaga bowed his head. "Master Strana."

Master Strana returned the gesture.

"Master Endaga. I bid you a good evening."

The two parted ways to their transports and climbed in, not glancing back at each other. The deal had been made.

For weeks on end, Maxellia purposely tried to avoid Omaris whenever she encountered him in the palace halls. He would catch her eye and give a playful grin. It infuriated her. The more she thought about it, her chest tightened in fear.

After wearing those ridiculous coven garbs, and calling himself Chancellor Rayne, he finally dressed in normal royal attire with his hair down.

She didn't want to admit how ravishing he appeared. It made sense why Chalayl went after Omeron so heated and desperate. Maxellia felt her loins clench every time.

But the way he looked at me!

That time when Manel suggested they mate. His horrified expression hurt. Even though he said that wasn't the case.

And now he winks and gazes at her in the halls as if none of that happened. She ended up following him from a meeting. Not sure why she did it. He rounded the corner into the chamber wings. Probably another meeting with Dania.

More coven business.

Jealousy crept in.

Dania could easily monopolize his time. Deep in thought, she didn't notice he had stopped. She went right past him into the first room. The silence startled her, and she looked up. No longer in the halls with strolling royal members, Maxellia sputtered to speak as she turned to face him.

Omaris stood a good distance from her. His chamber! She looked down awkwardly.

"Maxellia. I'm certain I expressed my terms in regards to a mate. I don't mind engaging with you on occasion. Just know the duration and sincerity is up to you."

She clenched her fists at her sides, not sure what to make of the mush inside her head. He hadn't moved.

Could I? Should I?

"Fine. I'll let you have me for now." She heard a slight crack in her voice.

Omaris took hold of the door's edge and shut it. "Are you certain, your grace?"

Maxellia took a deep breath and marched towards him, removing her outer robes and tossing them to the floor. By the time she got to him, her clothes were no more. She grabbed his face with both hands and kissed him like a ferocious animal.

She tasted his saliva and liked it.

Omaris got his hands under and pulled her away.

"Patience. There's no need to rush." Omaris coaxed her to the bed and laid her down. He straddled her, removing his own clothes. "This isn't something to get over with quickly."

Maxellia gasped. That was her intention. She had heard from servants that the first mating session was painful and the faster it got done, the less to worry about. Her father made sure no man touched her.

"Breath." Omaris stretched over her, locking his stare with hers. She fought back tears. "I won't hurt you unless that's what you desire." Maxellia shook her head. "Look at me." She reluctantly obeyed. His member pierced her womb in one thrust, making her cry out in pain. Her body arched, severing their gaze. He brought her back. "Stay with me. Don't turn away."

"Hurt. It hurts!" Maxellia slammed her fists in his chest.

"Shh." Omaris' amber eyes glowed a golden hue as his cock went deeper. "I know."

She couldn't tear her gaze from him as he rode her relentlessly. The pain became something else she couldn't describe. Tears blurred her vision.

Why? Why did I have to want him?

It went on for eternity in her mind until late in the afternoon, with the sun setting, she felt an explosion in her body. Her talons partially extended and dug into Omaris' flesh.

She cried out, shrieking like a wounded Kataling. In that moment. She wanted no other. Only him.

Manel watched his sister duck in and out of palace hallways, marveling at her lack of stealth. Especially in her current condition. He noticed her opting out of meetings in the mornings. Her robes had more layers, looking heavy as they dragged across the floor. Gallic walked beside him down the main corridor with four imperial guards following.

"What is she doing?" Gallic asked, glancing over at Maxellia's form disappearing around the corner on his right. "There's no reason for her to sneak around."

"Oh, she thinks so." Manel giggled. "She doesn't want anyone to know how far she's fallen."

"Fallen?" Gallic squinted.

How silly. Anyone with decent sight could tell his sister had gotten herself impregnated. And by the route she took, he guessed by who. Not really a surprise. He suggested their engagement for a reason.

Maxellia needed to be sorted out.

"That conniving virgin got what she deserved." Manel rubbed a finger across his bottom lip. "Actually, she got more than that. He's too good for her."

Gallic suddenly stopped. He turned to look at where Maxellia went, then back to Manel.

"No!" His shocked expression turned comical. "I truly thought you were joking when you said she had never been taken. She's acting like," he tilted his head.

"A clueless maiden barely of adulthood," Manel responded.

"Pfft!" Gallic covered his mouth with one hand, stifling the guffaw ready to explode from him.

Manel glanced back at the imperial guards, who

also tried to stop their snorts. He wondered when his sister would announce her situation. Omaris only kept quiet out of respect for her wishes.

Again. Too good for her.

The next meeting took place at the dual throne room. Already underway, Maxellia entered with her guards in tow and slid into her seat.

Tavelo did a double take as he spoke, his eyes wide before narrowing back.

Maxellia's pregnancy was the worst kept secret in the palace.

Sunrays beamed through the wall windows of the palace's main corridor. People strolled in the gardens on the other side. Maxellia gritted her teeth as pain exploded within her entire body. She stumbled forward, her foot caught in the hems of her multiple robes. Her talons pierced her palms as she clenched her fists.

Biting her lower lip, she dropped to her knees and fell face down, turning her head in time to the side. She had ditched her guards yet again to go see Omaris. That was a mistake this time. She twitched, clawing at the floor as the pain intensified. Wetness oozed from her womb. From her angled view, she could see the blood pooling beneath her.

A strangled cry escaped her lips.

Her eyes burned red. Omaris appeared at her side, his hands moving her.

"Hurry! We need to get her to the royal physician!"

She knew he was yelling, yet it sounded muffled. He lifted her off the floor. She screamed.

"I got you. It's okay." Omaris' muted voice tried to soothe her.

Escorted by her guards, the group ran to the medical wing. Omaris' big body handled hers with ease. She felt like she floated in midair.

Her vision glazed over as the guards flung open the bay doors. The royal physicians turned around to see who arrived and their stares became horrified.

"Get her on the table!" The first physician dropped the items in his hand and rushed over.

"We have to remove these robes to locate the bleeding." Another went to the task. "How many is she wearing?" He got to the third layer.

Omaris helped them. Maxellia thrashed about, trying to get away. Fear gripped her, and she felt out of place. Like in a dream sequence.

"Hold still!" The first physician yelled. "We're trying to help you."

"Your child is in danger," the other shouted. "Please stop!"

Through her haze, Maxellia saw Manel and the rest of her siblings come into the bay. No! She started screaming, scrambling up, using her legs. Technicians came and grabbed them, holding them down by her feet.

"Stay away!" She cried. "Don't let him kill my child!" The tears made everything look underwater. "Please, don't," she whispered weakly, stretching a hand out to Manel.

Manel stood mortified at her words. Omaris glanced at him in pity. Even Megen was struck by her expectation of him.

"I would never do such a thing." Manel answered angrily. He stepped further in. "Why would you think that?" The moment he said it, he knew exactly the reason. "You need to let them assist you."

"She's bleeding out." The second physician glared at Manel, though his anger was not towards him. "The procedure done on her long ago is causing complications."

Everyone else in the room froze.

Omaris snapped out of his rage at those words and focused on Maxellia going in and out of consciousness.

Manel didn't hide his disgust.

Did father spare no one? Was this some extra measure in lieu of keeping her chaste?

Maxellia's screams resumed. The physician at the edge of the table leaned forward and reached between her legs to help clear the head coming out. More blood leaked around it as it emerged. Her eyes rolled up in their sockets. Omaris held her down by the shoulders as he watched the birth of his spawn.

The physician freed the child and immediately went to remove the membrane trails from its nose and mouth. Meaxellia's body slumped, not hearing the high-pitched keening of her newborn.

"Let's start repairing the damage while we stop the bleeding," the other physician ordered his technicians. He gestured to Omaris. "I'm sorry, you have to clear the way."

"Of course." Omaris went over to the technicians cleaning off his son.

The holoscreen above Maxellia showed her internal organs, veins, and muscles. Everyone could see the physician's hands inside with tools repairing her womb.

"What say you?" Manel asked the other physician.

"She will be bedridden for some time. Possibly a full moon cycle." He frowned. "This was bad."

Megen turned and left the room. The way his shoulders tensed signaled his rage. Manel glanced over at Omaris. The man gave him a sorrowful stare.

"Congratulations on the birth of your spawn."

"Thank you, your grace." Omaris bowed his head.

"Stop that!" The volume of his tone made everyone flinch. "You are not some sniffling subject!"

"I. Yes, I'm sorry. It's a habit."

"Royal blood runs through your veins. Have I not told you to take advantage? Dear cousin?"

Omaris snorted, then his expression fell.

He averted his gaze to Maxellia.

"I only want to show her some semblance of contentment. What it means to be wanted."

"Oh. No need to worry about that." Manel smiled crookedly. "She'll relish this."

Royal Collective

The feeling of talons tearing out his insides brought Omeron to his knees as he argued for the third time in the season with Chalayl's children. He refused to tell them her location, as promised. This time, he couldn't keep it. The psychic pain that knocked him down came from her.

Chiron, Caden, Olette, and Olivier stared at him, horrified. Seeing someone as strong as him fall shook them. Omeron frowned while he struggled to his feet, then winced as the pain spread. I'm not as strong as you think. He rose and met their gaze.

"We must go. Now."

He hurried out of the Kataling compound with them close behind. Outside, he turned around.

"Where's your transport?"

"There!"

Olette pointed one parked a few yards away.

They ran over and crammed inside. Omeron locked eyes with the pilot in the mirror.

"Take us to the Mount Sennu terrain."

"What?" Olette cried out. "Why would be go to that desolate place?" Then she got it. "No!"

"Go!" Omeron ordered the pilot.

The transport lifted off and sped towards the mountains littered with caves. Omeron had it stop at the bottom of a bluff. They would have to scale forty feet to get to the cave above.

He extended his talons and climbed up with ease. The others did the same, though not as fast except for Caden who arrived seconds after him.

Inside, a small portable lantern glowed, shining muted yellow light that barely covered a two-foot diameter. The bed sat unmade against the side wall. Omeron looked down. Chalayl lay unconscious, covered in blood. More spread wide beneath her from her thighs. A newborn struggled on the floor, flailing in the pool.

"Oh my god!" Olette screamed the Earth term as she came up.

Chiron clenched his fists and moved to the inside wall, out of the way. Omeron knelt and pushed on the newborn's sides and back until it finally spewed out afterbirth. It wailed weakly, coughing more blood. Caden came over and snatched the baby from him, wrapping it in the bed sheet.

"You take care of my mother," he snapped. "I have him."

Omeron didn't move. Stunned by Caden's swift action, he felt inept. He leaned over and placed a hand on Chalayl's chest. She still breathed.

"Hurry!" Olette cried. "We have to get her down."

Then they all stared at the cave entrance. Scaling down forty feet with another being in tow would be difficult.

Caden set the child down and waddled him in the sheet so that the excess fabric could be tied around his waist. He brought the ends around twice, then made a knot across his chest. The baby lay secure on his back, fully covered, allowing its nose to peek out.

"Let's go."

Caden began the climb down backwards instead of how Katalings usually would. "Be careful."

As he went down, pieces of the bluff crumbled off. Omeron lifted Chalayl. He stepped to the edge of the cave entrance and looked down.

"No! You can't do that," Chiron finally blurted. "It's too high. Her weight along with yours…"

"If both your legs don't snap, the impact would definitely worsen her condition," Olivier finished for him.

"There's no other way. Carrying her on my back would cause more damage."

Omeron's grip on her legs kept her from bleeding out. Uncertainty and fear gripped him.

"How could you impregnate her, then leave her in this place?" Chiron yelled. "How irresponsible are you? She's on the brink of death because you indulged her. Not letting anyone know."

Omeron understood his anger. Olivier glared at him, not saying a word. Then he turned to him.

"We'll have to catch you."

"Huh!" Chiron exclaimed, one eye squinting as his mouth gaped open.

"You can't handle that load?" Olivier mocked him. "What kind of Dakien are you? Is all that muscle for show?"

Chiron's expression changed to haute. He leaped down. A thud drifted up, letting them know he had landed. Olivier turned to Omeron.

"Just hold her tight and let us do the work."

Olivier clambered down, meeting Chiron at the bottom.

Omeron stared at Chalayl's face, etched in pain.

"I'm sorry. I should have told you no. Taken you from this place."

He gathered her close to him, feeling the warmth ebbing from her. Taking a deep breath, he stepped off the edge, straight down. As he neared the transport, Olivier, Olette, and Chiron formed a triangle directly under his feet.

With only a few yards left, Omeron tilted his body back at an angle. His butt landed right in the center of the triangle. The children's arms locked in, stopping his fall.

"Get in!" Caden ordered hotly.

He had the baby cradled in his arms. The others lowered Omeron so he could stand. He got into the transport with Chalayl's children behind him. The pilot pulled off.

"Where to?"

"Bryhel stronghold," Olivier replied. Omeron frowned. "You don't get a say right now."

They reached their destination in record time, Olette egging the pilot to engage the overdrive. Holnar met them at the entrance, ready to joyfully greet the twins.

His expression fell as Omeron carried out Chalayl.

"What is this?" He yelled. "Why is she covered in blood?" Holnar's furious gaze turned on Omeron. "What have you done?"

"There's no time for that," Olivier chastised him. "We need to get her to the physician."

Caden ducked to clear the top of the transport and stepped to the ground. Holnar eyed the bundle.

"This way." Holnar led them to the medical wing of his compound.

The physician nearly whelped when he saw Chalayl's condition. He regained his composure and guided Omeron to an empty slab. Omeron gently laid her down, hesitant to release her legs. The scan was already in progress.

"It's okay," the medical technician behind him said. "The bleeding has stopped. We will take it from here."

Caden handed the newborn to another medical technician.

"Now, out!" The head physician ordered.

The group left the medical wing.

Holnar led them to a small sitting room and gestured to a servant. They simply nodded and left. They all knew what he wanted. In minutes, they returned with a cart of spirits and multiple glasses.

He grabbed the darkest liquor and poured half a glass. Tossing the contents down his throat.

"All that vitriol and hatred over the decades and it was just folly? A mere performance?" Holnar glared at him. "I should pound you into the ground."

Omeron tilted his head back in amusement mixed with ire.

"Try it."

"Stop!" Olette held out her hands in front of her, palms out. "Not on my watch." She turned to her father. "I know you have a soft spot for our mother. We get that. This is not the time."

"Let me guess," Chiron interrupted. "It's complicated."

"Yes." Omeron lowered his head. "I would have gladly mated with her." A sorrowful expression fell on his face. "If only she'd asked."

Caden's lips went thin. Holnar puffed out his chest, inhaling slowly before letting it out.

"I know." Holnar shook his head and went for another round of liquor. "She probably realized that too late and didn't know how to fix it."

"It's not something that can be fixed!" Caden shouted. Tears rimmed his eyes. "She deprived me of everything! Yet…" Caden couldn't wipe the tears away fast enough. They kept coming.

"You still love her as your mother," Holnar said.

Omeron wrapped his arms around Caden, who tried to get out of his grip. After a moment, he gave in, crying into his father's chest.

"This is a real mess." Holnar went to take a sip and saw Olivier, Olette, and Chiron tossing back glasses of the lighter liquor. "I concur," he whispered to them.

Master Boresso flung open the transport doors before it made a full stop. She had pushed the exit override for emergencies. In a shiny, rust red slimline robe that resembled a wraparound trench coat, she stepped onto the Marchand sector of the Bryhel homestead.

The servants scurried away while members of the compound stared at her in awe. One of them rushed into the building.

Holnar came out to greet her.

She would have none of it.

"Take me to her!" She demanded.

Holnar's eyes went red.

"Why should I? What reason do you have for wanting to see her?"

"Don't make me ask again," she seethed.

"You'll take on the whole clan?" Holnar stood with his legs shoulder width apart in a defense stance. "Then shall we?"

"That's not happening." Master Bryhel came up behind Holnar. He addressed Master Boresso. "Just as you would not allow such behavior on your land, I will not either."

"I need to see her!" Master Boresso tried in vain to contain her anguish. "I beg you."

Holnar's eyes widened. Master Bryhel nodded.

"Yes, you do. It's a long time coming." He glanced at Holnar. "I know the feeling well." He motioned to a servant. "Escort Master Boresso to the medical wing."

Master Boresso felt her hands shaking. She clasped them tight.

"I am grateful for your hospitality." She kept her head down, not willing to show the shame on her face.

Master Bryhel waved an arm out towards the entrance. She followed the servant into the homestead. The interior surprised her. Not many leaders invited the others to their homes.

They held almost every event involving the top merchants at either Jaubro, Strana, or Callesi compounds.

Unlike the other strongholds, Bryhel had wide corridors with parlor entries of equal berth. Is it to accommodate their own size? She wondered. The strong arms of the clans, Bryhel, Dakien, and Boresso had bigger bodies than the others. Their females with combat talent sent to battle maiden training.

The scenery changed when she and the servant reached the end of the corridor and turned left. White walls and muted pastels greeted her. At the end of the hall, glass sliding doors opened to a state-of-the art medical wing.

Master Boresso clenched her jaw in envy.

"Lady Chalayl is resting in the far right away from the others. Please limit your visit so she can recover properly." The servant left.

Lady Chalayl.

It dawned on Master Boresso that the younger generation had respect for her. On Earth, she was considered a queen, ruling over a coven. And did so for nearly two centuries. The same truth applied to the others. She slunk towards the bed and stood over Chalayl's sleeping form.

"Hello my precious niece." She caressed her forehead. "I've come to plead for your forgiveness." She gave a small smile, followed by tears. "I know you probably shouldn't. But I want to ask, regardless."

Master Boresso found a chair and pulled it close to the bed. There she sat, holding Chalayl's hand and caressing her face. No one disturbed her. A stream of tears coursed out the corner of Chalayl's eyes, soaking strands of her hair.

The basinet on the other side of the bed caught her eye. She zeroed in on the dark hair and bandaged fingers hiding the tiny black talons. The little thing coughed, spraying pink spittle on the edges of the white swaddle cloth.

Master Boresso sprung from her chair, towering over mother and child. The baby's face scrunched up in pain and he mewed. Short intakes of breath with hiccups accompanied it.

She lifted the newborn out, careful to cradle him in the crook of her arm. Chalayl's eyes flew open. She reached out in terror, clamping her hand on her aunt's bicep.

"Please," she whispered in a raspy voice. "Don't.. hurt…him." Her eyes pleaded as her grip fluctuated between weak and deadly. "Please."

Master Boresso's eyes narrowed in fury. She wrenched her hand from her and sat down.

"Stop being foolish! How could you think I'd harm your child?" Chalayl stared at her, confused. "I would never do that." She looked down at the baby, settling back into sleep. "I never wanted to hurt you," she said to Chalayl. She watched her hand fall onto the bed. "You need to rest." Chalayl closed her eyes. Master Boresso bit her lower lip, stifling the sound of the cry that threatened to escape.

Ways of atonement eluded her.

I have to make this right!

Pravin waited in the sitting room adjacent to his private dining room. He paced nervously, then stepped out into the corridor. Coming towards him, Omeron and Omaris walked side by side behind Pridric in disguise with Dania. Only two imperial guards followed in the rear.

They came. He felt the knots in his stomach ease.

"Welcome home." He gave a slight bow of his head, then raised it. The corner of Omaris' eyes crinkled. Pridric's brow visibly furrowed. Dania and Omeron remained unmoved by the greeting. "I know you never considered it so, but this will always be your home."

"You're right." Omaris tilted his head. "To us, this was a den of horrors."

"Come. We can talk about that later." He glanced back as he walked into the sitting room. "Or not."

Pridric went over to Roren. The man seemed to shrink from her, standing awkwardly by the dining hall entrance.

"I finally get to meet your sons and talk with you."

"Uh, yes. Welcome back."

He walked into the dining hall.

Everyone followed him.

A deep red tablecloth with a black runner covered it. Gold-rimmed glasses and black plates sat at each seat. Bottles of spirits along with carafes of non-alcoholic beverages lined the center.

Three young men, the oldest no more than a hundred, the youngest sixty or seventy, sat at one end of the long table. They stood together when Pridric came in.

"Empress Pridric." They bowed their heads.

"Don't." Pridric raised a hand. "When I am here, I am only a Strana, not the Empress."

"But you are nevertheless," the oldest retorted.

His harsh tone took Pridric aback. Omaris bristled at his response.

The oldest son gave them a disinterested glance, setting his foot on the edge of his chair. Pravin glared at him. On his right, the youngest smiled apologetically and nodded. The middle son on the left stared at Omaris and Omeron.

"They're Stranas?" He asked loudly.

"Yes." Roren answered. "Stop being rude." He addressed his oldest. "That goes for you as well."

"He seems confident." Omaris quipped. "Have you had your coming of age rites then?" He asked the oldest. "Only then could you muster the courage to disrespect me."

"It's been postponed for the moment." Roren hung his head. "He turns one hundred in three months, but the delayed shipment of herds from our harvest planet means they won't get here until the next moon cycle."

"And they need at least two cycles to roam before the hunt." Dania gave him a look of pity. "That puts the rites about two weeks behind schedule."

"How many in the same situation?" Omaris asked.

"At least eight," the assistant replied.

"That's unfortunate." Omaris shrugged. "That simply means you have to wait a bit to be named an adult. Patience."

The oldest opened his mouth to protest. Roren went over and knocked his foot off the chair.

"Behave!"

"That one doesn't say much, huh?" the middle son nodded at Omeron.

"I do speak," Omeron answered, shocking them. "I had nothing to say at the moment."

His voice, much deeper than Omaris', sent chills through the sons. The way he carried himself exuded intimidation.

A royal Kataling.

"How is it we have one of those in the Strana clan?" The youngest one asked.

"We can discuss that later." Pravin's anxiety had returned. "Let's enjoy a meal first."

Pridric placed a hand on his shoulder as he went to sit at the front of the table. He paused midway and looked over at her. The assistant seemed to tense at the sight. Pravin smirked. There was no reason for that reaction. He no longer pined for Pridric.

"We should take our time." Pridric sat across from the sons. "I'll keep these monsters company."

"The only monsters at this table are …" He felt his parent's gaze lock on him.

"You don't have a filter," Omaris stated.

Dania covered her mouth and snickered.

Servants came through the side door pushing carts of food. They set the dishes on the table and did the first servings. They filled the glasses with a nonalcoholic drink to start.

Once the servants finished, the family looked around at each other.

Pravin stood, raising his glass. He waited for the others to do the same, his eldest son reluctantly last.

"To reconnecting bonds. May our family thrive and be kind to each other henceforth."

"That's a lovely sentiment," Omaris' said, as he toasted the air.

"I can get behind that." Pridric did the same.

They took a sip and Pravin sat down. He marveled at the food on his plate. The cook would be rewarded. He didn't ask for anything fancy.

Roasted vegetables, various starches, and a pheasant steamed, sending their combined aroma into their faces. A side plate of sliced fruits fresh from the hydroponic garden gleamed with their juices.

"I didn't know this was such an important affair," Omaris said.

"It is," Pravin replied. "Though not at this level."

His sons were ecstatic to enjoy the rare meal. The oldest let out a grunt.

"Guess we had to bring out the good stuff for the Empress. We wouldn't have something like this otherwise." He picked up his fork.

"Stop insinuating that we don't feed you decent meals," Roren snapped.

"How ungrateful." Pridric met the oldest son's gaze when he looked up after shoving a piece of meat in his mouth. "You poor mother."

"I agree," the middle son added. "Why are you being so mean today?"

"He's always mean," the youngest blurted. "To me anyway." He pouted sadly.

"That's not true!" The oldest hit his hand on the table. He glanced around, embarrassed. "It's not."

Pridric burst into laughter, her hands flat on the table as her head bent over her plate.

Strands of hair grazed the edges as her shoulders shook. Within seconds, the others joined in, leaving the oldest to shrink in his chair.

The meal went smoothly after that.

The sons left after the meal, citing better things to do than hang around elders. Pravin restrained himself from chastising them in front of everyone and let it go. All for the best. He didn't want them in the sitting room while they discussed the reason he invited his guests.

Lounging in a plush chair set in the corner near the door, he swirled the amber spirit in his goblet. He met Omeron's gaze.

"I offer you a position as a Strana guardian. You are the only Kataling in our bloodline. We need a keeper of the grounds."

"Why should I work to protect your clan?" Omeron asked briskly.

"Because it is also your clan."

"After the abuse we went through in this place?" Dania said in a heated tone. "Especially him!"

"I know that," Pravin yelled, leaning forward. His drink sloshed. He settled back. "I wish with my entire being that I had been strong enough to defend you. Just as you all protected Pridric and Omeron, I too wanted to do the same."

"Then you should have," Omaris responded.

"He couldn't." Roren cried. "And you know why."

"You father would have beaten you to near death," Omeron said.

"And then made you watch as he punished us for no reason," Pridric continued for him.

"All of us were too afraid to stop him." Pravin gripped the goblet and downed half of it.

"We should have ran." Dania took a gulp of her drink. "I don't know where, but." She slumped.

The mood turned sour as a heavy silence fell.

The west dock reconfiguration got underway, with the Callesi merchant bays being gutted first. Their workers moved into the temporary hub built on the other end of the boardwalk.

It meant a longer travel from the ports, but they could manage for a year. What usually took years would be streamlined with new construction tools created by the Marchand and Grieger covens.

Master Callesi waited outside the hub's entrance for Darean to arrive. He had invited his cousin to come assist with deliveries since his company's bays were also in the process of rebuild. There was also the conversation he needed to have with him.

Too much strife among their families bode ill for business. After letting the truth of Darean's status on Earth sink in, he realized his mistake treating him like a child. All the clan leaders had. Master Callesi spotted Darean coming up the boardwalk from the loading zones.

What is he wearing?

That change in Darean confused him. Some days, he dressed impeccably. Others times, like now, were questionable. He looked around and found many of the dock workers staring at his cousin in awe.

Wearing a dark waistcoat, opened at the top, Darean sported a shiny multicolored shirt of satin like fabric that assaulted the eyes. His burgundy pants had the same shiny fabric going down the sides. Polished short boots peeked from the hem.

Darean smiled, waving as he approached. The floppy hat looked out of place and the blue-tinted glasses made his eyes glow a strange grey.

"Cousin." Darean stepped close to him. "Morning greetings."

Master Callesi pursed his lips, not wanting to acknowledge him in front of people. Too late for that. He let out a sigh.

"I have to ask, Darean." He waved a hand up and down in front of him. "What is going on here?"

"What do you mean?" Darean opened his waist coat further. "I'm casually dressed. No need to have a suit on when we're going to be working, right?"

Master Callesi squeezed his eyes shut.

"True. If that's the case, you could have worn a dock uniform."

Darean's eyes went wide.

"Absolutely not! I'm a businessman!"

A clan member came from the back of the hub and reared back, flinching as he caught sight of Darean's attire.

"What in the Cellaxan skies!" He softly cried out. Master Callesi gave him a warning stare, shaking his head. "Ahem!" The man straightened himself. "Darean. I heard you were coming to assist. Will you be changing for the dock?"

"No. This will suffice."

Darean moved to take off his coat. Master Callesi stopped him by grabbing his arm. He led him into the hub. The other merchant clan members followed with their gazes.

"First, we need to go through the manifests. If you can get them all set and in order, we can send our runners to retrieve the cargo."

"Oh. That hasn't been done yet?"

"No. We only got here an hour or so ago."

"Then I shall gladly do it."

The members close by exhaled with relief.

A visual of Darean going down to the port sent shivers through them. After certifying the documents on the first manifest, he handed it over to the runner. Master Callesi stood by and watched him go through the second.

"I wanted to talk to you, Darean."

"Hmm?" Darean didn't waver from looking at the documents on the tablet. "What about?"

"How the clan and I have treated you and your brood since your homecoming."

Darean paused. His head raised up a bit.

"Is that so?" Master Callesi heard the sadness in his voice. "It did hurt."

"It shouldn't have been that way. I was more glad than anyone seeing you back home." He struggled with his words. "Seeing how much you had grown. Having your own trading company. It made me angry that we didn't get to experience those milestones with you."

Darean turned to him.

"There was no choice in the matter."

"Even so. I want you to know that we are proud of you. Envious even."

"Well," Darean gave a mischievous smile. "I did surpass you in a third of the time."

"Don't be cheeky! I'm serious."

"So am I." Darean went back to the manifest. "Now, I have to finish these." He waved him away.

Master Callesi grinned. Despite the outrageous outfit, he knew Darean had strong convictions. He walked out of the hub into the morning gloom, getting brighter. Across the way, he heard Master Bryhel talking with one of her merchant workers.

"What in all of Cellaxa was that brat wearing?"

"I'm not sure." The worker frowned. "Maybe an obscure Earth style?"

Master Callesi covered his face with one hand and let it slide down to his neck. Then it dawned on him. Darean wore it on purpose.

There are better ways to draw attention, cousin.

Tension permeated the dual throne room.

Manel noticed how quiet Tavelo had become. Pridric seemed apprehensive, her eyes squinting as if deep in thought. This made his siblings uneasy. The royal council fidgeted amongst themselves.

Reports on the renovated docks and the first shipments going through the new ones displayed on a holoscreen hovering midair.

Manel stood near his throne, gazing out through the opened curtains to his left. He shifted his gaze to Tavelo.

"What's on your mind, Emperor Tavelo?"

Tavelo snapped out of his reverie and sat straight.

"Trade is flowing much better now, and the docks are complete. Lower-class merchants are getting more business."

Manel knew where the conversation headed. He glanced at Maxellia. He wouldn't! They both thought. Lendor frowned.

"Cellaxa is thriving under our rule. Your family has overseen the empire for centuries on its own." Tavelo met Manel's stare. "I propose the West royal house take a step back. Let the East take the reins for a while."

"Step back?" Lendor cried out. "And what does that entail in your eyes?" He spat.

Pridric turned to him.

"This is not out of disrespect. None of this could happen without your input." She smiled. "Think of it as a reward for your hard work. A break."

Manel clenched his fists. He had a feeling it would come to this in some form or fashion. Tavelo began omitting information, attending different meetings without the west family, and treating Manel like an inferior.

"So what is it you want us to do then?" Manel's eyes glinted red. "Emperor."

That angered Tavelo. He glared over at him. A hint of defiance glimmered.

"The West ruled the empire without duality of the East. This time, the East shall reign…"

"While the West reigns in silence," Manel finished.

"You want the throne to sit empty," Megen said.

"Is that not how the East has been all this time?" Tavelo replied sweetly.

Pridric looked forlorn. "We're not saying you'll be cut from royal duties. Reports pertaining to the wellbeing of Cellaxa will be sent to you."

"You simply won't be obligated to address them. We will appoint new proxies for you."

The royal council whispered to each other.

"And this is your move to take credit for everything?" Maxellia said with disdain.

"That's not what I'm doing," Tavelo snapped. He took a breath, calming himself. "This is only a temporary adjustment."

One of the councilmen stepped forward.

"We too are concerned. How long is this proposal to last? The masses may not agree after accepting the reinstated dual rulership."

Tavelo finally smiled. "Not too long. Maybe five, ten years? Enough for me to get my bearings."

Manel squirmed in his skin.

The way Tavelo relished in gaining control fueled his rage.

"Then a rule must be established," a second councilman said. "Neither royal house will attempt to implement new laws that move to take the reign of the other during this time period."

"Of course," Tavelo answered. He glanced back at Manel.

"Agreed." Manel's eyes narrowed. "And when do you wish to throw us from our home?"

"No one is doing that!" Pridric heatedly replied. "We only ask that you don't engage in royal duties."

"Neither seen nor heard, then," Lendor said.

"As I said," Pridric came back frustrated. "That's not…"

Tavelo laid a hand on her thigh.

"This is your throne room. I have no power to stop you from using it."

Manel smirked.

Is this how you want to play this game, Tavelo?

"It would be in the best interest of the empire if this was done by the end of the next moon cycle."

"That's only fifteen days from now." Lenri's face showed her disgust for him.

"Again," Tavelo said. "For the good of the empire."

Tavelo and Pridric rose from their thrones. He addressed the royal council.

"I leave the details for this transition to you."

The two left to what Manel knew was another clandestine meeting with a different faction of the royal council. This proposal didn't come out of thin air and needed backing from inside.

Manel remained rooted in place, angry, disappointed, and unsure how to handle it.

Megen stood and came to his side.

"Let's discuss this later." He turned to the royal council. "We have demands of our own."

"As I would assume, Lord Megen." The first councilman bowed. "We look forward to your instructions."

"He thinks he can run the empire?" Lenri turned up her nose. "Hmph!"

❀ ❀ ❀

No announcements regarding the change of hands came. Tavelo didn't want to disrupt the palace. Instead, the people saw more of him and Empress Pridric. His own cabinet members flooded the meetings and courtyards. Manel and his royal family were nowhere to be found.

Per the agreement, Manel took sole responsibility for the Northern docks. In Tavelo's view, its smaller size, and fewer bays deemed insignificant to revenue as a whole. Manel gladly accepted, knowing how wrong Tavelo would be in the end.

Manel and his siblings entered the west throne room in silence. They evaded their thrones and sat in the chairs on the floor level. Lendor sat closest to the door with Lenri next to him. He plopped in the center, followed by Maxellia. Megen pulled one of the plush chairs to sit across from him.

"Tavelo wants to try his hand as sole emperor." Manel shrugged. "He'll find out soon enough."

"But he's doing it off your accomplishments," Lenri said hotly. "Does he really think he can sustain it all on his own?"

"Let him try." Manel slumped in his chair. Gallic stayed far away near the thrones. "I'm not surprised."

Lendor turned to him. "I should have let Maxellia kill you." The others stared at him in horror. "None of this would have happened. With the royal line rid of you, I could have taken the throne and stopped all of this."

"Is that so?" Manel gave a devious smile. "Then go ahead. Take it from me."

Lendor glared at him.

"Not once did I ever think of you as a brother. You were just a pitiful creature that shouldn't have lived in the first place. All those experiments done on you." He met Manels eyes. "Why didn't you kill yourself? Why struggle to live after all that?"

"That's enough!" Maxellia seethed, leaning forward with red eyes.

Lendor sighed and rested back in his chair.

"I don't want the throne. There's no point now."

Megen's demeanor shifted. Lendor shrunk away.

"Whether you like it or not, we are siblings. And our power has been usurped by a greedy child who ran a group of vampires for less than two centuries on another planet."

"There really isn't much to fear," Manel said. "Two merchant clans will make sure things run smoothly. They will not stand by if Tavelo proves troublesome."

"Endaga and Strana," Megen added.

He took stock of everyone.

The siblings fell silent. Maxellia scratched her head with partially extended talons. She had gone through a difficult birth only a few months ago. She expressed feeling tired a lot, skipping meetings to care for her newborn son with Omaris.

Lenri spent most of her off time with the Valkyrie, Anastasia, indulging in new flowy gowns to frolick in the gardens. Lendor still acted like a man whore, worse than Innego ever could be. He had yet found a mate to settle with, having multiple women spawn his seed.

He focused on Manel. No longer a pawn in their father's bloodline scheme, he found his true mate. Gallic's loyalty and love for him bordered on frightening.

Megen straightened his posture.

"We should do what we wants for now. Whatever happens going forward has nothing to do with us."

"What do you mean?" Lenri asked.

"This room will sit empty." Megen extended an arm behind him towards the dais. "I have requested everything be covered after the first year. By then, Tavelo and his cabinet will notice."

He lowered his hands, resting both on his thighs.

"So we are abandoning our roles," Lendor tsked.

"For now. Let Tavelo feel the pressure of being a lone emperor."

Lendor rose from his seat and walked out in anger. Megen knew his destination would involve hunting down one of the women he frequented. Lenri followed, not looking back. Maxellia jumped from her seat and headed out as well, leaving Megen with Manel and Gallic.

"Take him away from here," Megen ordered Gallic. The soldier raised his head in surprise. "I don't care where. As long as it's not in this palace. The farther away, the better."

"What are you saying?" Manel half rose, his hands gripping the armrests. "I can't just leave!"

"You have small offspring who need you. Strengthen your bond with Gallic and them. I will take care of our own."

"Am I supposed to not see them again for the next five or ten years?" Manel cried.

Megen sighed. "I'm not saying that. Go be happy for a while. Don't worry about the palace. Come see them when you feel the need."

"And you? What about your happiness? What do you want to do?" Manel's sad tone made Megen stiffen.

"I'm the general of our military. What would you have me do? I am the only one who cannot leave to do as I please."

"That's true." Manel hung his head. He looked at Megen with tears in his eyes. "I don't know what to do. I don't know what happiness is."

His voice choked.

"Then go find out." Megen stood and went to Gallic. "I'm putting my trust in you."

He slapped him on the shoulder, then left through the back entrance. He stopped at the doorframe and looked back once more.

Gallic went over to Manel and embraced him.

Good.

Children bustled around the commons of Gallic's home, laughing and screaming while chasing each other. His mother, Grasilda, swatted the ones who got close to her at the table, where she prepped for a long trip. She stopped and gasped as an entourage of people flowed into the area.

Gallic, Manel, her children, nieces, nephews, and a handful of imperial guards blocked the hallway.

"What is the meaning of this?" She wiped her hands on a towel and set it on the counter.

Gallic stepped forward and clasped her hands.

"Another secret, I'm afraid." He squeezed. "We wish to accompany you on the excursion jaunt."

Grasilda's eyes went wide. She looked at Manel. "Are you certain?"

"I know. Manel has never done something like this. It's only three months, but I'm certain it will be beneficial." Gallic gave her a nervous smile. She eyed the imperial guards. "Since we don't want too much scrutiny, we've assigned our family members to us, along with those four."

"That way, the emperor still has a unit of guards," Grasilda concluded. "Makes sense. They were being released from duty for this trip to begin with." She held out her arms. "Well? Where are they?"

The two guards directly behind Gallic and Manel opened their cloaks to reveal the sleeping twins. They walked over and Grasilda grabbed both, cradling them in each arm.

Despite being big for their age at almost five, she easily handled their weight. Both stirred but didn't wake up. She sat at the table and hugged them tight.

"She doesn't even greet her own children," Gallic's younger sister huffed.

"We're not small and cute anymore," their eldest cousin said.

Manel stood confused, not moving as the rest of the group went their separate ways. The four guards looked awkward by the entrance. Grasilda frowned, exasperated.

"Come sit down," she told Manel. Gallic already grabbed a seat at the table and fiddled with some of the meal sets already made. "Don't touch!" She slapped Gallic's hand. "And you," she addressed the guards. "Go to the back room and find better clothes. Those won't do."

The guards wore casual uniforms, yet they still looked regal. They nodded and walked off, following the flow of traffic in the halls.

Grasilda stared at Manel.

"The same goes for you. This excursion entails getting dirty, bloody, and requires lots of manual labor. Are you up for that?"

Manel raised her head.

A new resolve showed on her face.

"I want to know what it's like to have a family that helps each other. I will do whatever you ask."

Shocked by her revelation, Grasilda nodded.

Yes. Time for Manel to be normal.

New Beginnings

Trade and commerce thrived on Cellaxa.

Merchant clans played nice with each other, even making sure the coven companies were profitable. Behind the scenes, things weren't so well oiled. The monkey wrench that got thrown in occasionally stemmed from Emperor Tavelo's slight changes that didn't benefit trade.

Those implementations didn't last long, reversed within a year. His royal cabinet's handling of social affairs left a poor impression on the masses. As ruler, he and them were held to a higher standard. He tried to rule with an iron fist, not as horrid compared to Emperor Manel.

That only made the difference starker.

Five years passed with the West royal family nowhere to be found. General Megen went on his rounds when required. Every moment off duty found him spending time with his offspring.

Windsor halted near the children's room doorway and saw Megen lift the youngest in his arms and raise him above his head. The child giggled uncontrollably while the others sat at Megen's feet, observing.

A totally different demeanor than his menacing aura he wore in the palace halls. Windsor continued down the corridor, watching the royal members stroll along the windows to view the gardens.

He crossed over to see as well.

Off in the distance, deep in the garden, he caught sight of Lenri and Anastasia in the royal gazebo.

The two women wore billowy robes of multi-colored sheer fabrics. They had their hair styled in elaborate designs. Sitting side by side, they laughed with their heads against each other. He nodded in approval at their seemingly happy time.

He looked down at his tablet screen come to life, notifying him of a document coming through. A proof of acknowledgement from Maxellia that she received and read a proposal glared at him. While running an errand one day, near the empty throne room, a royal councilman asked her about it.

"Why do you not address the issues or attend the meetings?" the councilman asked.

Maxellia gave him a crooked smile.

"What for?"

"Our proposal didn't mean for you to abandon your royal duties."

"But Eterenia handles all of that in my steed as Emperor Tavelo's royal cabinet. As long as I make sure to go over the documents and send them back with my insignia stating I received and read them, I see no issue."

"That is true." The royal councilman backed off.

Maxellia smiled wide and turned away to resume her journey. Windsor knew she made haste to return to Omaris and their child. Ever since that day, no one had seen her again. Only he and the councilman saw her then.

He understood why the royal family did it.

Emperor Tavelo may have run an Earth coven for over a century and a half. That did not translate to being emperor over an entire planet. The previous emperor knew how to rule. Emperor Mallen's bloodline had never fallen out of rulership.

Even Manel's reign entailong horrors beyond imagination still kept trade flowing.

Windsor made it to the trade office reserved for Commissioner Polp. He had his own small desk and chair sat off to the side. The commissioner headed out earlier to handle yet another contract issue caused by Emperor Tavelo's meddling.

"You need to ask before you do those things," he sighed, plopping in his seat.

Master Endaga knocked on the doorframe as he leaned against it. Windsor looked over at him with a dejected expression.

"I know how you feel." Master Endaga walked in and stood near the window. "I'm almost to the point of giving up and letting him fail."

"You can't do that either!" Windsor slumped. "There are whispers among the people." He looked at him. "About his inexperience showing."

"I know. Master Strana and I are keeping any signs of rebellion at bay."

"I'm not worried about that. Tavelo can handle himself fine." Windsor sat up. "It's him putting his fingers in commerce."

"We're curbing that too." Master Endaga turned to lean against the window ledge. "We won't let him, or his cabinet go so far as to disrupt trade."

"And the commissioner and I thank you for it."

"The centennial ceremony is coming up."

"What is that?" Windsor felt a sense of foreboding.

"According to the historian, the two emperors celebrate one hundred years of prosperity. Since there has not been one in over a thousand years, it's due. Seeing how well trade is flowing the last ten, fifteen years."

"Does that mean?"

Windsor gasped at the implication.

"Yes. Manel and his family must be brought back to show a united front."

"Your nephew won't like that. He wants the West house out of sight, out of mind for the same duration as Manel's reign."

"I figured as much when he proposed the swap." Master Endaga smirked. "He never thought they would take it so literally and leave the throne room absolutely empty."

That jarred everyone in the palace.

All the royal siblings disappearing at once. And no one took notice until almost a year later. Tavelo fumed for days. He had suggested it yet apparently only as a joke.

"He doesn't have a choice in the matter. The key is how he approaches it."

"Badly," Windsor blurted. Startled by his own heated reply, he glanced up at Master Endaga. "I…"

Master Endaga raised a hand to stop him. "No need. I agree. Tavelo is," he paused, "stubborn. To say the least."

"I'd love to be a fly on the wall, as they say."

Windsor leaned forward to turn on his holoscreen.

"Yes." Master Endaga rubbed his chin. "So would I."

※ ※ ※

Tavelo glared at the historian standing below at the base of the throne's dais. Pridric sat beside him, looking agitated. Her usual expression the past two years. He adjusted his blue and silver robes, letting the wide sleeves flow over the armrests.

The historian kept his head bowed. The sandy brown and white robes weighed him down.

"What you're saying is that there needs to be a show of dual acceptance. To present ourselves as a united front for the masses."

The historian's head rose abruptly, his eyes wide.

"Are you not, your grace?"

Tavelo pursed his lips. That won't do.

"Of course we are." He saw the royal council glance at each other, their expression dubious. "I have no ill will towards the West royal family."

"That's an outright lie," Pridric stated. Tavelo turned angrily at her. She met his gaze. "By Manel's decree, your parents were murdered. You have not resolved that."

"That has nothing to do with this," Tavelo seethed. Pridric's face saddened. He reared back. "Don't."

"We must first find the royal family," the first councilman said.

Tavelo frowned, turning away from Pridric. He balled his fists in frustration.

"Yes. I don't know why they abandoned the throne room or the palace. I never suggested they do that. Manel spoke that option."

"Manel can be fickle." A councilman nodded to him. "He has kept contact with the Northern docks, as agreed, taking personal accounts of revenue."

Tavelo tried to hide his anger. The Northern docks thrived better than the others. Its revenue equaled that of the West docks, despite its size. He'd made a mistake letting Manel have it. At the same time, he came to understand it would not be that way if he ran it.

"Yet, no one outside of that has seen or heard from him." Tavelo leaned to the side, raising his arm to rest his head in his palm. "It's like he's blatantly hostile towards me because if my decree."

"I'm sure that's not the case," the first councilman admonished.

Tavelo's eyes turned red. That's exactly what it is. He focused back on the historian.

"When does this ceremony take place?"

"In three moon cycles. I have already informed Lady Dania of the details."

"Hmm." Tavelo gave a devious grin that made everyone flinch. "Even though the five-year decree is past, it is still in effect. Since I am the ruling emperor at the moment, I want to make a request that the West royal family does not appear in imperial attire."

The tension in the room turned thick.

The historian tried to hide his dismay.

They all stared at Tavelo in surprise. Even Pridric turned and frowned in disappointment. To deny a royal emperor to wear the colors of their lineage showed malice. Tavelo seemed to not understand.

"Make sure it's enforced."

"Of course, Emperor Tavelo."

The historian hastily retreated from the room.

Pridric let out a heavy sigh.

"This will go badly."

"How so?" Tavelo hmphed. "The people will see me as sole ruler. What else could be interpreted?"

The royal council fled the room as well. There was no convincing Tavelo how wrong he was.

Coded messages from the royal council reached each member of Manel's family. One by one, they entered the palace in secret, not allowed to use any of the main entrances. Which suited them fine. They converged inside the vacant throne room. white drop cloths covered all its furnishings.

Upon seeing Maxellia, they froze. Her long thick hair now sported a short, shaggy cut above her ears. The array of cowlicks grew haphazardly. She wore a cargo transport jumpsuit with dirty grey boots.

What made them cringe the most? The genuine smile that radiated from her.

Lenri gathered each hem of her frilly robes in one hand before sitting on a cloth covered chair. Her exposed left shoulder, now void of the scar Manel gave her, showed smooth creamy skin.

Lendor arrived looking peeved. Still not settled down with a mate, he ceased his excessive activities. Megen dragged the biggest chair in the room to the circle they formed in the center.

Gallic remained standing as Manel sat across from Megen. His siblings stared at him in awe.

The change was prominent, with him exuding a sense of calm. His hair resembled Maxellia's former length, touching the small of his back. The top lay shorter down to above his shoulders. Amber eyes glinted with joy.

"How good to see you all again," Manel laughed. Not a hint of condescension in his tone.

"I'm glad there's happiness in your eyes," Megen said, addressing all of them. He turned to Lendor. "Are you content yet?"

Lendo glanced sideways at the ceiling, then back at him.

"As well as I can be. My spawns mothers rebelled against me."

"Which is fitting, considering your behavior."

Lenri shook her head at him.

"And you?" Megen asked Maxellia. "I heard a rumor from my spies."

"Oh?" Maxellia clapped her hands together, then pulled out her smart device. She tapped it a few times, then turned it around for them to see. "My cute new little one! He's turned two last cycle." She beamed with pride.

They stared at an image of the oldest trying to keep hold of the little one as Omaris grimaced in the background. Their dark hair and amber eyes marked them as part of the royal brood.

"I think maybe one more in ten years." Maxellia turned it back around to close the device.

"Oh no." Lendor ran a hand down his face. "She now has a penchant for breeding." Maxellia frowned at him. "I will send a prayer to Omaris."

Manel settled back into his lush seat, forcing the cloth to pull at the tucks. His expression changed and his old rage flickered for a bit.

"We have been summoned for the centennial ceremony." His siblings gave him their undivided attention. "Emperor Tavelo has demanded we do not wear our royal garbs for its duration."

"What madness is he spewing?" Lendor raised his head from the back of his chair. "There is to be no divide in a dual empire."

"He's sowing his last oats," Megen answered.

Manel pondered the situation. He glanced over at Gallic, zeroing in on his blade. A sinister grin spread across his face. Gallic stared at him, intrigued.

"We will oblige him."

"What?" Lendor, Lenri, and Maxellia yelled. Megen tilted his head, waiting for the explanation.

"We will go out dressed as we are now. And with us, I will carry the royal sword of Pantola, passed down in our family for thousands of years." Manel tilted his head down while still looking out at them. "The symbol of our royal bloodline and dominance."

His siblings gasped.

No one had seen the blade in a thousand years. To bring it out would indeed send a statement to the masses. And Tavelo. Only the royal family and its historian knew of its location. It had not been spoken of in so long, many presumably forgot its existence.

Soft footsteps came from the side doors. Two royal council members and the historian entered. They stopped a few feet from the siblings.

"A grand idea, Emperor Manel," the historian praised him. "I will have the royal treasure prepared."

"I condone such action," the first councilman said with the other nodding.

"I commend Tavelo for getting this far without assassination attempts at his back." Maxellia crossed one leg over the other and leaned into the chair. "That we know of."

"Will we at least have our banner behind us?" Lendor asked.

The second councilman frowned.

"Only the vertical ones to bookend the separate entrance."

"Separate entrance?" Lendor's voice trailed off as his amber eyes glowed cinnamon red.

"Hmph!" Manel smiled. "Tavelo is in for a rude awakening. This will be his lesson. If he wants the Eastern royal palace to gain the respect and backing of the masses, he'll have to do better."

"If he wanted to know how to rule," Megen interjected, "all he had to do was ask."

"Yes." Maxellia snorted. "Who doesn't tap the resources of a ruler who's been in power for two centuries?"

"Or at the very least, the royal family and its cabinet?" Lenri added.

"So you side with my plan?" Manel asked them.

"Of course." Lenri gave a gleeful grin. "I can't wait to see the Sword of Pantola!"

Manel hid the anguish that gripped him, remembering the last time it had been removed from its chest. The last person who held it used it to murder the previous emperor. He saw the historian meet his stare.

It took days to clean the blood from its blade and hilt. The cleaners tackled every tiny detail until it was pristine once more.

He exiled the cleaners to keep their mouths shut. At first, he suggested killing them and the historian spoke against such a move. Manel nodded to him. They would have to be brought back to inspect the sword.

"With that settled." Manel looked around the throne room. "I think it's time our entire royal family assembled for a chat about our rule going forward."

"A banquet?" The first councilman inquired.

"That would have to be done in the lower sector of the West palace." Megen rose from his seat. "We don't want Emperor Tavelo to get wind that we're actually a close-knit family."

"True." Manel stood, along with the others. "In all this time, he never bothered to ask about the rest of us. The relatives of our mothers, our uncles, aunts, cousins."

"I could eat." Lenri said, arranging the fabrics of her robes so they flowed straight. "It's been a long time since we gathered together."

"I will contact the royal chef and have one of the old banquet halls ready." The second councilman bowed and left the room.

"I must send the invites via our internal royal channels." The first councilman did the same.

The historian bowed his head.

"The sword shall be ready before the procession. If you no longer have a need for me, I will be on my way." He rose, his clasped hands above his head.

"Go. I look forward to seeing it again." Manel waved a hand, dismissing him.

The historian raised his head, dropping his arms, and exited the room.

Manel turned to Gallic.

"You are no longer some guardian on the imperial payroll. You understand that don't you?"

Gallic's head nodded to the side as he tried to decipher his words. Megen stepped to him.

"You are part of the royal family. While you may protect Manel with your life, you have assigned guards to protect you as well."

Gallic's eyes widened. Manel saw he didn't think of it. Always so hell bent on defending his honor, he forgot to take into account the fact that he was the father of royal spawns.

"Let's adjourn." Manel walked towards the side door. "We must get prepared for our family evening meal."

They left into the empty halls outside. The only witness to their presence in the palace.

A group of forty royal family members gathered at the doors opened to the newly decorated banquet hall that hadn't been used in over two centuries. Before that, it toted many family soirees.

It ended with Emperor Mallen's reign. He had no desire to socialize with them, focused on experiments of horror.

Per Manel's instructions, the royal family did not dress extravagantly. That would draw attention to the palace, knowing Eastern spies roamed the halls looking for a hint of the siblings' whereabouts.

Only ten imperial guards scattered outside the doors and inside along the walls, out of the way of the tables. They were a handful from twenty-five loyal to the family who would never betray them. Even when one turns sour, like Mallen and Manel.

The spread of food and drinks, though half the size of a normal banquet, were impressive in quality and design. It all looked too good to consume. Lenri had no problem with that. She and Anastasia were one of the first ones headed to the tables, platters in hand. They laughed and giggled like schoolgirls gossiping.

Manel sat at the main table near the back wall with the rest of his siblings. Lendor stared at Lenri's blatant gluttony with disdain. For a tiny creature, she ate like a Kataling.

Omaris kept quiet next to Maxellia, taking in the sheer atmosphere of the room. Omeron did the same, scanning the room to see every face.

"This is our immediate family," Megen said to them. "We try to maintain contact."

"Everyone has their own agendas." Manel tapped the table with his forefinger. "It's difficult to gather like this lately."

"Come." Maxellia held out a hand to Omaris. "Let's get some food before those two wipe out an entire spread."

She grabbed his hand to pulled him up.

They headed for the other end of the tables to cut Lenri and Anastasia off.

Gallic gave Manel a bow and went to get food for them both. No servants were present to minimize the number of people who knew about the event.

Maxellia chatted with a few family members, stopping to pull out her smart device and show off her offspring. A doting mother. Manel felt his skin crawl. He shivered.

When everyone found their seats and had enough food and drink before them, Manel stood. He tapped his cutlery on the glass goblet, causing the liquor to ripple.

"My family, it's a pleasure to see you all well."

"Enough of that!" A woman spat. "Where have you been? Letting that brat run the empire!"

Manel paused mid breath, taken aback by the rude interruption of his prepared speech. Canvasing the room he saw the same expression as hers on the others' faces.

Fine.

"To answer your question," Manel tossed the cutlery on the table in ire. "We decided to let him flounder for a while. Let him get a taste of what it means to run an empire."

"That lesson could have been taught under yours or any of our tutelage." One of their uncles tsked. "No need to go this far."

"The only thing keeping his madness at bay is his own family clan and the Stranas," a cousin cried out.

"I see you are all angry." Manel smirked. "Good. I want you all to show your status at the centennial ceremony."

"Of course!" the first woman, an aunt, replied heatedly. "We'll be in our regal colors to represent the West Palace."

"We are forever grateful." Maxellia bowed her head. She met her aunt's glare. "Tavelo needs to see."

Manel wouldn't tell them about Tavelo's decree or bringing out the family sword. He wanted it to be a surprise. At Tavelo's audacity, and the pride of their bloodline. Megen gave him a knowing stare. There would be no mistake which house ruled at the end of the ceremony.

"You must never leave like that again." Another uncle rose. "No matter what the situation, we are here to protect you. Guide you."

"The plan wouldn't have succeeded if we had," Megen replied. "Disrupting Tavelo's agenda was our main goal."

"Oh, it did. When he found the throne room void of life, covered in cloth, he became livid." Their uncle sniffed, rubbing the tip of his nose. "It was comical."

"The fact that it took him so long to find out." Their cousin's lips thinned. "It showed his lack of observation."

"That will all end soon." Manel met their gazes. "Please put your trust in me. I know I have not earned it this past century."

Their uncle waved a dismissive hand.

"Your father is to blame for that. We understood long ago."

Manel clenched his fists behind the table's edge, hidden from view. Family. He should have asked for their help long before his own demise.

Blue and silver banners fluttered in the wind along the platform above the impatient crowd. Two thrones placed on the right of the entrance awaited Tavelo and Pridirc. Imperial guards stood in position behind them.

Displayed on the other side two twenty-foot tall red vertical banners with the black and gold symbols of the Western royal house billowed by the second entryway.

The faces in the crowd showed confusion and a sense of anger. Pridric tried to hide her anxiety. Seeing the actual omission of the West palace in plain sight made it clearer.

"This looks bad." She hid her hands in the folds of her robe sleeves.

Tavelo looked out at the platform and felt the crowd's tension as well. His brow furrowed. It wasn't what he expected. He figured five years would be enough to lay the groundwork for a transition.

Why? He narrowed his eyes at them. Why did the masses continue to put their trust in Manel?

The royal magistrate walked onto the platform to address the population. Holoscreens across the planet streamed the event. Two hovered above the crowd at the palace. While he placated them with the history of Cellaxa and its ruling powers, Tavelo checked the other entrance down the main corridor.

Manel and his siblings had not arrived to be staged before entering.

"They may not show up," Pridric told him. "Can't really blame them."

"They have to!" Tavelo turned a furious stare her way. "That would," he struggled to find the words.

"Be disastrous," Innego finished for him. "It would make you look like a tyrant."

"That's not what I want." Tavelo knew his actions seemed rash. But a tyrant? Not ever. "Do we need to search for them? It's almost time."

"Let's just see what happens." Innego saw the imperial guard by the entrance give the signal. He nodded. "Ready, Emperor Tavelo, Empress Pridric?"

They walked out accompanied by more imperial guards to the Eastern side of the platform. Their over-the-top full regalia made an impression. Many in the crowd gasped. A few distasteful stares from the royal members of the West Palace made Tavelo grimace.

The magistrate raised both arms out wide.

"I present to you the Eastern royal house. Emperor

Tavelo and Empress Pridric. May your reign continue to bring prosperity to Cellaxa."

Though thunderous applause erupted, it seemed lukewarm. It lacked passion. He looked over to the other side and winced at the bare embellishments. The crowd focused their attention on it.

They were not happy.

"And now, I present to you, the royal house of the West. Emperor Manel and the royal siblings."

Everyone gazed at the entryway, waiting for someone to come out. The seconds ticked away. Tavelo became nervous. Pridric gripped his hand. Footsteps echoed from inside. A marching of boots striking the marble floors. It resonated through the crowd. Tavelo forced his eyes to narrow as they tried to widen.

Manel stepped down the stairs to the platform first. His jet-black hair flowed down the middle of his back, swaying in the wind. He wore the sleeveless black kaftan with red and gold design. The slits at the sides near his thighs showed knee-high black boots.

A sinister smile spread. Slung over his shoulder, he held a giant sword by its massive hilt. It stayed in place with each step.

Behind him on his left, Maxellia kept in stride. Her short hair and cargo jumpsuit made her appear to be a dock worker instead of royalty. Lenri walked on his right wearing a simple palace dress seen on any young maiden in service. Lendor wore a white tunic, brown leggings, and black boots. His cloak hung over one shoulder. Megen came up at the rear with Gallic, both menacing in full battle gear.

The crowd hushed at the sight.

Tavelo felt his insides churn.

This is extremely bad!

Manel stopped at the marked point. With an evil grin and glowing red eyes, he swung the sword from his shoulders and slammed the blade into the platform.

He stood behind it.

"May the Western house of Cellaxa continue to reign victorious!"

Loud gasps and cries of astonishment rippled through the crowd.

Tavelo made out some of the words.

"Is that the Sword of Pantola?"

"What has happened to the royal family?"

"Is that truly Maxellia?"

Manel opted to add fuel to the fire.

"We are humbled to have received an invite to participate by the current ruler of Cellaxa. It's only fair he suggested we not come in full regalia and usurp his authority."

Manel and his siblings bowed to Tavelo.

Suddenly, hostile eyes fell on Tavelo.

The royal family gave him murderous stares. He looked over and met Manel's glowing eyes. He and his siblings didn't raise their heads for what seemed like an eternity, when only a few seconds had passed. When they did, the crowd cheered. Manel faced the masses.

The magistrate breathed a sigh of relief.

"The dual houses have previously worked in harmony for the sake of our home. Let us rejoice and enjoy the festivities. Vendors and marketplaces will have specialty items. And a limited-edition cube of the enemy will be available at the local pubs."

That sent the masses into a frenzy. They would get a taste of the ones who dared to attack their home.

Manel drew the Sword of Pantola from the floor and raised the tip to the sky, so the hilt sat at his waist. The four-inch-wide blade obscured most of his face, but you could still see his red eyes.

"Glory to Cellaxa." He didn't yell.

There was no need.

The thunderous roar surpassed the first, causing the platform to shake as people stomped with excitement. All eyes were on Manel.

Tavelo clenched his fist while Pridric kept hold of the other, preventing it from balling up. He turned to his uncle and saw the man pale at the sight of the sword.

"Pantola?" Master Endaga whispered.

The ceremony ended. Pridric tugged Tavelo's hand. He followed the procession out through the middle doorway that sat open for both royal houses to converge. Manel stepped to his side.

"Long time, Tavelo."

"Where have you been?" Tavelo seethed under his breath so no one else could hear.

"Hmm? Didn't you say to steer clear of your house? To let you reign alone?"

"I never said that. Not once did I tell you all to disappear!"

"Oh? I guess there was a misunderstanding." Manel shrugged. "Too late now."

Tavelo finally realized he'd done it on purpose. Well played. His plan backfired. Yet, he didn't want to admit that he had no clue how to rule an empire, let alone an entire planet. Asking for help at this stage would prove him weak.

The guards led the two houses to a large banquet hall filled with top merchant heads, dignitaries, and department leaders. Commissioner Polp waved at them as he stood in line at a table, waiting to graze the food and drink.

Master Jaubro, Loengir, and Bryhel opted to have servants attend to them. They glanced at the tables as if they were battlefields.

A long table, stretching across a raised platform nearly the width of the room, had been decorated so that each royal house's colors mingled. The pieces alternated down it. Carafes of liquor were equally spaced. Manel and Tavelo sat in the center.

Pridric, innego, Dania, and Eterenia were on Tavelo's side. Gallic, Maxellia, Lenri, Lendor, and Megen sat on Manels.

The Sword of Pantola rested on a display stand behind his siblings. People stared and whispered. The historian stepped onto the platform and raised a hand towards the sword.

"Behold! The Sword of Pantola. The first weapon forged in Kataling blood for the second emperor of Cellaxa. At the dawn of the dual rulership. The hilt is made of carved Kataling horns adorned in gold."

Tavelo's eyes went wide. That would make the sword thousands of years old. Then it hit him. To confirm his thought, the historian continued.

"This is the embodiment of the first emperor who died in battle. His essence now wields as a weapon against all who oppress us. Long may the bloodline of Emperor Xanen Pantola continue its reign."

The historian bowed and went back to his seat.

Tavelo then realized he knew nothing. That he didn't bother to go deep into Cellaxa's history or the ruling houses. He had some knowledge of the Kataling bloodlines purity. So much inbreeding and manipulation.

Did the East have the same history? Was there a sword with the true name of their royal line?

Tavelo saw the horror-stricken looks on his uncle and Master Strana's face. Master Jaubro sipped his drink, wearing a deep scowl.

What is going on?

Manel leaned close to him and whispered, "Not a sword, Tavelo. But a shield for the Pantola family."

It hit him. Pantola.

That's why his uncle went pale. It is the name of the royal bloodline. Kataling and Volshin. Two monsters born of the same lineage. Of course, there would be dual rulership. That also meant the thinned bloodline of the Volshin had consequences.

The Kataling side had done the right thing in keeping its line contained. He wondered who inside the Volshin camp decided to venture out and dilute theirs.

What purpose did they have?

Eterenia seemed to understand the implications of it too. The Jaubro and Endaga clans kept it all a secret. The Stranas were content until the war.

Tavelo found his hands balled into fists on the table. He glanced up to see some of Manel's family staring at them. He undid his hands and rested them on his lap.

"All you had to do, Tavelo, was ask." Manel shoved a piece of cured meat in his mouth. "I would never want to see you fail. That doesn't serve Cellaxa."

The room turned into a scene of jubilee as a six-foot cube of blood got carried in by four imperial guards. On the edge marked the manufacture date and name of the batch.

Malice Blend. The combination of both enemies.

Innego held on to Lendor' shoulder to stop from stumbling too much. Both had drank more liquor than they should have. They practically held each other up at that point.

Megen glanced at their sloppiness in disgust.

"Do you really think I should just pick one?" Lendor asked, slurring.

"That's the best solution." Innego slapped him on the chest. "Just make sure the others are on board with it. No need to incite jealousy."

"Huh." Lendor raised his head a bit to see him. "And what about you?"

"Oh, I chose my mate long ago."

"Heh? When? You were still lying with Tamar when you arrived."

"That stopped. The two I had on Earth arrived. Since one of them despised me, I went for the other. It worked out somehow."

"Lucky you."

Megen stopped at a vacant royal chamber.

He pushed the two in, watching them fumble over each other in an attempt to break their falls. Within seconds, they lay still, fast asleep. He shut the door and addressed the guards who followed him. Pointing to the two in the rear, he gestured to the door.

"Make sure they don't leave until morning."

"Of course, Lord Megen," they replied in unison.

He grimaced at the title.

The two posted themselves at the entrance. Megen continued with the remaining four guards. They rounded the last corner and circled back towards the dual throne room. The doors sat open and there were already people in attendance.

Tavelo sat barely upright, his face flushed from alcohol. Manel didn't fare any better. Gallic kept a hand on his back. Megen had seen him vomit before leaving the banquet hall. Pridric, slightly drunk, held onto Tavelo's robe sleeve, tugging it every now and then to stop him from leaning too far over.

Such a disgrace!

"Can any of you really conduct royal business in this state?" He yelled at them.

To his surprise, the two emperors perked up as if their drunkenness disappeared.

"This must be resolved now." Manel glared over at Tavelo. "Your little stint caused more issues than remedies. Were you going to suggest another five years? Get your ten years of practice in?"

The royal council nodded in agreement. From the closest end, the first councilman stepped forward.

"I propose that Emperor Tavelo's decree not be renewed. For the sake of Cellaxa."

"I wasn't trying to harm our world!" Tavelo snapped. "Did you not rule alone?"

"All the same," Megen interrupted. "Your actions did just that. And Manel didn't rule alone. He had advisors, albeit bad ones, and the royal family."

Tavelo's eyes glowed.

Clearly frustrated by his own mistakes. Megen felt a bit of pity for him. Manel looked away into the air, not wanting to discuss it further. He suddenly clamped a hand over his mouth to stop the spew of vomit. Some of it seeped between his fingers, dripping onto this lap.

The enemy blend apparently didn't mix well with liquir.

❀ ❀ ❀

Fireworks displays boomed in Cellaxa's night sky. Across the planet, the masses celebrated the last day of the Centennial ceremony that lasted a full year. The palace housed the top merchant clans, the coven leaders, and their offspring for a safe place to lay their heads afterwards.

They filled the outer terrace of the stone balcony overlooking the land. A sense of pride in their home-world and overcoming hardship permeated the air.

"We should do these more often," Master Dakien said, yelling over the fireworks.

Pink and yellow lit the side of his face as he stared out. His light grey suit turned technicolor. Beside him, Yutel watched with disinterest. He focused more on the workers manning the explosives.

Chiron nudged him.

"Seriously, father. They know what they're doing. Enjoy the show."

"Yes, and loosen up your jacket," Master Dakien added. He happened to get a good look at it. "Why is it not fitted correctly? What's the meaning of this, Endaga?" He addressed the clan leader.

"How is this my fault?" Master Endaga asked angrily. He looked over at Yutel. "Why indeed?"

"See what your petty aesthetic has caused?" Eterenia came up behind him. "Enough already."

"It worked fine on Earth."

Yutel seemed to almost pout.

"How childish," Master Boresso sighed.

Not long after the ceremony, the merchant clans met with the younger generation to reconcile. The strife between them suddenly looked unnecessary and petty. There were a lot of long talks in family strongholds with yelling, crying, and accusations thrown.

A messy turn of events.

The same was true for Manel. When it was all over and done, he and Tavelo focused on the planet.

Manel leaned over the stone ledge, folding his arms. Tavelo stood sideways against it, using his forearm for stability. They both stared at the horizon. Ignoring the fireworks.

"What do you think, Emperor Tavelo?"

"I think you should clue me in on navigating this whole rulership thing. Being the more experienced emperor."

"Hmph. Gladly. The point is to divide the duties. Not have one take over for the other." Manel turned his head towards him. "You should have realized that from the start."

"I wanted to prove to you and Cellaxa that I was capable of doing it."

"Which no one asked you to do. Despite my bouts of insanity, I still knew what my role entailed."

"Now what?" Tavelo glanced down at him.

Manel rose, placing his hands flat on the ledge.

"We shall make Cellaxa a trading powerhouse. Dominating the three systems was fine before. Now, we must spread out to the other two.

"Five systems plus Earth." Tavelo smirked. "That has a nice ring to it."

"Power always does."

Tavelo walked over to the other side of the terrace, where the rest of the coven leaders assembled. They didn't speak for a long time. Reflecting on the series of events that led them to the present.

Being chased off their home by Emperor Manel

and the imperial fleet after witnessing the murder of their family members. Crash landing on Earth and infiltrating the vampire covens.

Holnar finally took a breath and spoke.

"We've come full circle, haven't we?"

"In a sense," Darean replied.

"Establishing our own companies on a new planet." Yutel said. "And going too far. Deeming ourselves rulers over the humans."

"We shouldn't have advanced their technology and trade the way we did," Darean added.

A few looked away with shame while the rest hung their heads.

"Spawning children who are now related by blood," Eterenia continued.

They all heard the anger in her tone, collectively wincing at the breeding lottery they created. Only Chalayl agreed to it as one of only two females in their group. Eterenia rightfully refused.

Chalayl turned to Pridric, in male form wearing an Eastern imperial suit. The blue and silver suited him better than the red and black of the Ambrook slash Strana coven.

"I never wanted to be your enemy," she said softly.

"I know." Pridric smiled at her. "We were rotten children."

Chalayl snorted, her body bending over slightly as she laughed.

"Yes, we were." Darean let out a small one of his own. "And here we are now. Standing proudly as adults with children of our own."

"And bad at it." Tavelo met his eyes. "None of us are getting the parent of the century award."

They grew silent, for he spoke the truth.

"But we can start over." Eterenia spread her arms wide. "We are home. A new era has begun." She glanced back at Tavelo. "And we have one of us elevated beyond our imaginations."

Cellaxa. Their home.

Tavelo crossed his arms, inserting his hands into the sleeves of his robe. This time, he would be a part of its future.

"May Cellaxa reign in power for millenniums to come."

END?

ACKNOWLEDGEMENTS

And that's a wrap! Or is it?

Thank you for continuing to read the Blood Saga series. I hope you are enjoying it as much as I did writing it. Alien blood suckers are fun, sexy, and not talked about much. This is my due diligence to spread the word. The last installment of the series, Blood Devotion, is coming soon.

Big thanks to:

NIWA: (The Northwest Independent Writers Association)

for letting wrters be part of a great community.

NaNoWriMo: (Narional Novel Writing Month.

For supplying an awesome platform that drives writers foward.

PNWA: (Pacific Northwest Writers Association)

Craig Martelle and 20BooksTo50K

For all the tragic souls who volunteered to beta read my first vampire novel and gave me uncensored feedback:

My gratitude is infinite.

I cherish you all.

ALSO BY MAQUEL A. JACOB

THE CORE SERIES

CORE OF CONFLICTION, SEEDS OF CONVICION

BONDS OF CONTRITION, WRATH OF ACQUISITION

ACTS OF TRANSGRESSION

CURVE OF HUMANITY

ORIGINS, SHADOWMEN OBJECTIVE

PURGE SEQUENCE, CRIPPLED EARTH

AFTERMATH, HOMECOMING

WELCOME DESPAIR

A COLLECTION OF SHORT STORIES

THE BLOOD SAGA

BLOOD DOCTRINE

BLOOD DOMINION

BLOOD INCEPTION

(A BLOOD NOVELLA)

ABOUT THE AUTHOR

Hi there!

I'm Maquel A. Jacob. I've had a passion for the written word since the age of seven, reading everything I could get my grubby little hands on, which included encyclopedias and the thesaurus. At twelve, I had my first encounter with a Stephen King novel and got hooked. They inspired me to write my own brand of fiction, combining multiple genres to keep things interesting.

I am a HUGE Anime fan, love a great bottle of wine and rock out to heavy metal music. Green and lush Oregon is where I currently reside, spinning imaginary worlds in my head and daydreaming.

For updates, FREE short stories, Newsletters

...and more

Visit: www.maquelajacob.com

Like Maquel A. Jacob on Facebook

Follow on Twitter @MaquelAJ1

Also find me on Goodreads

www.ingramcontent.com/pod-product-compliance
Lightning Source LLC
Chambersburg PA
CBHW072007190726
48293CB00001B/190